CASTLE OF DOVES

BOOKS BY
CONSTANCE HEAVEN

The House of Kuragin
The Astrov Inheritance
Castle of Eagles
The Place of Stones
The Fires of Glenlochy
The Queen and the Gypsy
Lord of Ravensley
Heir to Kuragin
The Wildcliffe Bird
The Ravensley Touch
Daughter of Marignac
Castle of Doves

Constance Heaven

★   ★   ★

CASTLE OF DOVES

HEINEMANN : LONDON

William Heinemann Ltd
10 Upper Grosvenor Street, London W1X 9PA

LONDON   MELBOURNE   TORONTO
JOHANNESBURG   AUCKLAND

First published 1984
© Constance Heaven 1984
SBN 434 32614 3

Printed and bound in England by
Richard Clay (The Chaucer Press) Ltd,
Bungay, Suffolk

FOR
SIDNEY CHARLES
who also loves Spain

Oh, lovely Spain! renown'd, romantic land!

Childe Harold's Pilgrimage
Byron

Part One

THE FABLED LAND

1

The first time Charlotte saw the Spanish portrait was on a bleak windy morning in November with no knowledge of who it was or why it should have been hidden away in a secret drawer of her father's desk. Major Harry Starr had been dead for three months but it still seemed like yesterday. She had woken early that morning as she had so often done before waiting for his knock on her door. To lie sleepless hour after hour brooding on an uncertain future was more than she could endure so she got up, plunged her face into ice-cold water and pulled on her riding habit. She stole out of the room as quietly as possible taking great care not to wake her mother. She could hear Peg muttering to herself in the kitchen as she stoked up the fire and put the kettle on. Peg had been with them for as long as she could remember and would certainly pursue her with instructions to "wrap up warm, dearie, and not go out catching yer death like yer poor dear Pa," so she tiptoed along the passage, opened the front door carefully and let herself out.

The wind met her, cold and raw with a hint of sleet, but she was glad of it. Sometimes lately the house stifled her.

She fetched Whitefoot from the regimental stables where she was allowed to keep him. Lieutenant Jack Hardy was already there saddling up and annoyed her by immediately offering to accompany her. For a long time she and her father had always taken these early morning rides together. She had valued the time she spent with him and now he was gone wished for no one else, but Jack had been a loyal friend so she shrugged her shoulders saying nothing. She knew he followed her when she took the long bridle path that led up to the ridge above Shorncliffe.

She had forgotten him by the time she reached the summit and halted Whitefoot, suddenly besieged with memories that tightened her throat. From this spot she could see over the entire camp, the army barracks, the married quarters, the wide

3

parade ground, empty now except for a few leaves blown by the restless wind. She was remembering the last time she had stood there. Was it only three months ago? What a magnificent spectacle it had been, the long rows of men in their distinctive green and black uniforms, the Rifle Brigade, "the bloody fighting Ninety-Fifth, first in the field and last out of it," of which her father had been so justly proud. He had stood that day beside the hawk-nosed Duke of Wellington under whose command they had fought, laughed, loved and died across the Peninsula and at Waterloo had helped bring Napoleon to his knees. And now her father was dead, so suddenly, so heart-rendingly, that she still found it hard to believe in spite of the black band on her sleeve and the emptiness inside her.

It was not until he spoke that she remembered Jack Hardy. He had come up beside her, persistent as a puppy dog that never knows when it is not wanted. She dragged her mind back to the present and turned to look at his frank honest face.

"I'm sorry. Did you say something?"

Poor Jack. She knew she was being cruel to him but she couldn't help it. He blushed and shifted his gaze.

"I've seen so little of you lately, Charlie. I've had no opportunity – will you – don't be angry with me – but will you promise to think seriously – about marrying me, I mean?"

"Oh Jack, please, not again. I've said no once and I meant it, really I did."

Impatiently she moved away and he followed after her putting his hand on her bridle, his voice urgent.

"But it's different now. You must see that, Charlotte. With your father gone, it changes everything. I can't bear to think that you may go from here and I shall never see you again. It's driving me crazy. Your mother would be pleased about it – she told me so."

That touched her on the raw, unreasonably perhaps. "I'd rather you did not discuss me with my mother," she said icily and jerked away from him urging Whitefoot forward. He needed no spur and they went down the slope at a fast trot.

"Charlotte – please wait – I didn't mean –"

But she had outdistanced him by then and didn't stop until she reined in outside the small house set rather apart from the others that belonged to her father as acting Brigade Major. She was out of the saddle before he could dismount and help

4

her down, taking her in his arms as he liked to do and which she endured so unwillingly.

He leaned towards her. "Will you be riding tomorrow?"

"No, I'm afraid not. There is far too much to be done."

"You are not leaving yet surely."

"It's nearly three months now. The house will be wanted for Father's successor. Will you take Whitefoot back to the stables for me?"

"Yes, of course." He took the bridle. "Charlotte, when can I see you?"

"I don't know. Sometime soon perhaps. I must go in now. I'm late and Mamma will be waiting for me."

She turned her back and ran up the steps not waiting to see him ride disconsolately away. In the dining-room the fire was burning sulkily because of the contrary wind and her mother, still in her dressing-gown, was sitting as close to it as she could, a cup of tea on the little table beside her.

"Shut the door, for pity's sake," she said peevishly as Charlotte came in. "It's cold as charity in here with that wretched wind. Why you want to go riding at this hour in November I can't imagine."

The girl pulled off her hat and put it down with her gloves. "Papa always did," she said briefly.

"Well, that life is over now and the sooner you grow accustomed to the idea, the better. We shall certainly not be able to keep horses the way things are with us just now." She sipped her tea. "Who was that with you out there?"

"Jack Hardy."

"Was it indeed? He's persistent, I'll say that for him." She looked up at her daughter. "When are you going to marry him?"

"Never, and I'd be very glad, Mamma, if you wouldn't encourage him to think I will change my mind."

"You'll be very foolish if you don't, Charlotte. Jack Hardy has excellent prospects. His father has money and he is the only son. He would sell his commission tomorrow if you asked him. You'd not be condemned to an army life as I've been. You're twenty-two, my dear. Most girls of your age are married and settled already." She pushed away her cup distastefully. "You'd better ring for Peg and ask for fresh tea."

"This will do." Charlotte poured a cup from the cooling pot

5

and began to butter a slice of bread, her appetite vanishing as the familiar wrangle started up again. "Are you hoping to get rid of me, Mamma? Is that it?"

Her mother leaned forward to poke the fire and then got to her feet.

"What a thing to say! Of course I don't want to be rid of you. You choose not to believe me but I'm only thinking of your good. With your father gone – and of all the crazy things to do, leading his recruits in their manoeuvres himself in the drenching rain with his poor health – little wonder he developed pneumonia – no thought spared for me or for you for that matter – the regiment was the only thing he cared about first and last . . ." she stopped for breath and Charlotte said nothing because in a sense she was right. After a moment she went on again. "It was hard enough to manage on his salary but now with him dead at forty-five and not even in action, the pension will be tiny. The most we can look forward to is the cottage at Breakstone Park which your Uncle Nicholas has grudgingly offered us – living on charity – my God, how is it to be endured! We might as well be buried alive."

Charlotte looked up at her mother. Two years younger than her husband, Caroline Starr was still a very pretty woman. The velvet dressing-gown with its wide satin sash did not hide her slender figure and her hair, thick and glossy, was still the rich autumnal red that her daughter had inherited. She'll marry again, she thought with a sudden panic, and then what will become of me? For a moment the bread choked in her throat. Then she swallowed hard and lifted her head proudly.

"I'm not helpless, Mamma. I could obtain a post somewhere. I could keep myself."

"What kind of post, for goodness sake? Be your age, Charlotte. What could *you* do? Governess, companion to some rich old woman? There are too many nowadays seeking employment of that kind. Is that what you want from life? It's no more than slavery. Any kind of marriage is better than that, believe me, my dear." She sighed. "I must go and dress. There are a hundred things still to be done." She crossed to the door and then turned back. "There is just one task I'd be glad if you would do for me, Charlotte. Your father's study, his books, all the things he hoarded in that little room of his. They must be gone through before we leave here. Could you do that for me?"

6

There was a faint note of appeal in her voice and for the first time Charlotte wondered if there was still some slight feeling of grief for the man she had married at eighteen – handsome Harry Starr, the gallant soldier who after two years of married bliss had been swept into a war that had taken him away for six long years and brought him home at last, limping and sick, to eat his heart out in a staff job while his comrades went on to win promotion in campaigns he was no longer considered fit enough to command.

"Very well, Mamma," she said quietly, "I'll do it this morning as soon as I've changed."

"That's a good girl." Her mother went out closing the door behind her.

The tea was cold by now and the toasted bread tough as leather. Charlotte pushed her plate aside, rang the bell for Peg to clear and went upstairs to her own room.

She took off her riding habit and changed into the new dress of thick black bombazine which she hated. Her mother with her filmy widow's veil contrived to look alluring even in her heavy mourning but it had a deadening effect on Charlotte and she rebelled against it. Her father had loved colour and gaiety. Why mourn for him in such dreary funereal black? But she could see only too well the shocked faces of their army acquaintances if she had dared to ignore the rules of convention. They were already inclined to look askance at her which was not surprising since nothing in her upbringing had been exactly according to pattern.

Her hair had been so blown by the wind that she pulled out the pins, brushed it and tied it back with a ribbon. It was thick and curled naturally. Her mother was fond of saying that it was her only real claim to beauty and grumbled because she did not make enough of it. She had insisted on dressing it high with flowers and ribbons when they went to the regimental ball last winter and before the evening was over it was tumbling down around her shoulders. She did not often think about her looks but that morning she stared into the mirror. Perhaps now with the future so uncertain it was time to take stock of herself. Her complexion was good enough, she thought dispassionately, her eyes were large and green with long dark lashes, the nose short and straight, the chin too determined and the mouth far too wide, not the inviting rosebud lips of the other girls. Jack must

7

have thought her attractive, she supposed. It was a year now since he had proposed and she had laughed over it with her father, and then there was Clive, her cousin at Breakstone Park, but her mind shied quickly away from that. She did not want to think about it. It was too painful. Impatiently she turned away. It was obvious her looks were not going to get her anywhere. Better to forget such unprofitable speculations and start work on what her mother had asked her to do.

Her father's study was a tiny room which she had avoided these last weeks. It was too filled with happy memories. There was a small desk, a number of bookshelves, a large leather armchair and the footstool she used to pull up close beside him. She was eight years old before she really got to know him. He had sailed with the regiment before she was born and came home a stranger, a stern hero with a scarred face and a painful limp, of whom she was half afraid. It was not until her mother's bad miscarriage when he knew he would never have the son he hoped for that she became his close companion. She took the place of the boy he had wanted to follow him into the regiment and, much to her mother's disapproval, he fell into the habit of taking her with him everywhere he could so that she grew up with the Rifle Brigade, the pet of the officers and the men, and the companion of the boy recruits. He taught her to ride and had her habit made in the green and black of his own uniform. She knew the history of the Brigade by heart, how it began, its insistence on discipline and individualism, its gallantry, its madcap exploits, its long string of victories and its disasters. She never had any regular schooling but she picked up a little Latin from him, spoke some French, learned a great deal of history and above all he taught her Spanish.

He had come home with a love of the Peninsula and a passionate interest that he continued to pursue and in some magical way conveyed to her so that it became a fabled land in which she lived her imaginary childish dreams.

She remembered vividly the day it began. Her mother had sent her in to him with a tray of coffee and she'd put it down and climbed on to his knee to look at the book he was reading. There were pictures of a long thin man on a bony scarecrow horse who tilted at windmills and engaged in adventures that made her laugh. She asked what the words meant and he began to translate a few lines of *Don Quixote* which captured her interest. She had a quick ear and picked up Spanish remarkably quickly. It became their secret language with which they would sometimes infuriate her mother, giggling over some joke she could not understand.

"You'd be far better encouraging the child to cook and sew, and dress herself properly, instead of spending all her time chattering in that barbarous tongue," her mother had said irritably more than once. "She is not one of your boy recruits."

"Good God, woman," he would answer. "Charlie is not a ninny. She's got a brain. For heaven's sake, let her use it."

Her mother had shrugged her shoulders. "That's all very well but it's not the way to win a good husband," she'd remarked tartly.

Maybe it wasn't but Charlotte had never regretted the hours she had spent with him.

She found that battered copy of *Don Quixote* still on the shelf among the books and put it aside to keep for herself before she turned to the desk. Harry Starr had been a methodical man and his papers had been left in good order, regimental records neatly docketed, bills paid and receipted and clipped together. She went painstakingly through every drawer except one that to her surprise was locked. She found his keys and then hesitated. Even though he had been dead for several weeks there was a certain reluctance to open a locked drawer. It was like reading a private letter. She would be probing into something he had wished to keep hidden from her mother, from her, perhaps even from himself.

But it had to be done. She braced herself and turned the key. Inside there was something wrapped in a handkerchief, yellowed now and with brownish stains. She wondered if they were blood. She unfolded it slowly to reveal a portrait about four inches square set in a thin gold frame and possibly painted on ivory. It was a dark day and her hands shook a little as she carried it to the window to look more closely. She had half expected a woman, a secret love affair perhaps, but she was wrong. It was a man's face that stared up at her, young, dark-haired, with a thin line of moustache, a striking face and Spanish, she was sure of that though there was nothing else, no letter, no explanation of why it should be there wrapped in a blood-stained handkerchief and locked away so secretly. Was he someone her father had known well? She had understood

9

that the Spanish were mostly bands of guerilla fighters and did not march with the British. Had they been friends? Had he died? She was fascinated by the face, gripped by the eyes that seemed to look directly into hers. Her father had shared most things with her but not this. Why? Had it been too painful?

She heard her mother calling her to luncheon and hurriedly wrapped it up again and locked it back into the drawer. For some reason she did not want to show it to her. Later she would fetch it and put it with the few mementoes of her father she was keeping for herself.

Over luncheon her mother said, "I meant to tell you this morning. I've had a letter from Breakstone Park."

"From Uncle Nicholas do you mean? Is it about the cottage?"

"No, not from Nicholas, from Clive."

It annoyed her that she still could not hear his name mentioned without a quick stir of the heart. She swallowed a piece of cold beef before she said casually, "What does Clive want with us?"

"It seems he is to be in this neighbourhood next week and he would like to give himself the pleasure of calling on us."

"Whatever for?"

They had not seen him for some months and he had not even come to her father's funeral.

"He doesn't say." Her mother looked across at her frowningly. "I always thought you played your cards very badly there, Charlotte. That summer we spent at Breakstone, Clive was more than half in love with you."

"Don't be silly, Mamma. Of course he wasn't. It was just that he was very bored. He had to amuse himself somehow and I happened to be there." Try as she would she could not keep a touch of bitterness out of her voice.

It still made her heart burn when she thought of that last day in the summer house overlooking the lake. His arm had been around her shoulders. He had held her close against him and carelessly broken her heart.

She could still hear the light charming voice. "I haven't a penny of my own, Charlie, so what the devil am I to do? The army, the church, have never had any appeal for me. All I can do is paint after a fashion and I doubt if that will bring me a fortune so what is left to a poor younger son but to marry

10

money." He is joking, she had thought, in her foolishness, he can't mean it, but he did. He had been deadly serious.

"He has certainly done extremely well for himself," went on her mother musingly. "Lucy Weaver is an heiress and a splendid catch for any man even if her father was in trade."

"Is Clive bringing his wife with him?" she asked in a stifled voice.

"He doesn't mention her."

"Thank goodness for that."

She had never met Lucy and had no wish to be obliged to make her welcome in their shabby little house.

She thought she had got over Clive but found herself on tenterhooks during the week before he actually arrived. She tried to occupy every minute she could with the myriad tasks necessary when packing up years of living in the same small house, deciding what was to go with them and what must be sold or given away. They had constant visitors, some genuinely sympathetic, others falsely courteous, with sharp eyes summing up their possessions and wondering what bargains might come their way. And in between when she went walking or lay wakeful at night, she could not keep Clive out of her thoughts.

They had always spent a few weeks at Breakstone every year. Sir Nicholas Starr was her father's elder brother and felt in duty bound to issue an annual invitation. At these times Clive, four years older, took little notice of his young cousin. He treated her with a lofty disdain but was not above pulling her hair or giving her a sly pinch when no one was looking until his father told him "to stop those damned tricks, sir, and behave decently to your little coz."

Then there came the summer when she was eighteen and he was twenty-two. He was home from university recovering from a riding accident which had severely damaged his knee, keeping him from his usual pleasures. That year there had been an outbreak of cholera at the camp. Her father had insisted on his wife and daughter spending some months at Breakstone and for the first time in her life Charlotte forgot that her greatest desire had always been to be a boy and fell stupidly and painfully in love with handsome, charming, careless Cousin Clive.

How was she, who had grown up among the young soldiers like a sister among a family of brothers, who had had so little

11

experience of love, to know that it meant absolutely nothing to him until that last dreadful day? All those long hours she spent sitting with him when he was laid up, the slow walks they took together, the leisurely rides when he could sit a horse again, the fun at the summer fête, the picnics, laughing as he fed her stolen strawberries in the kitchen garden, dancing together in the long warm summer evenings – enchanted hours which vanished like a dream leaving her hurt and bewildered. That winter they had heard of his engagement and were prevented by heavy snow from attending the wedding. She thought her father had guessed at what had happened but he was wise enough to say nothing and Jack's bumbling proposal, though she refused him, did do something to restore her shattered self-confidence.

She told herself it was long over and she was no longer a silly impressionable girl yet when she saw the carriage draw up and heard his voice as Peg showed him into the parlour, she had to nerve herself to go down. She had spent an hour in preparation, something she very rarely did. Her hair was brushed till it shone, she had tucked a little cream lace frill into the neck of the hateful black gown and thrown the gold chain and locket that had been her father's last birthday gift over her head. Then she summoned her courage and went downstairs. It was extraordinary but when she opened the door and saw him standing with his back to the fire and the light of the candles falling on his face, the scales at last fell from her eyes and she began to see him for what he really was.

Gone was the boy who during that long summer had captured her heart so easily, the young man she had watched standing by his easel in paint-stained shirt and breeches, who had run races with her and raided the early plums in the orchard and nearly drowned her when the punt capsized in the lake, kissing her lingeringly when he dragged her from the weed-infested water. She would have given herself to him without a second thought if he had asked it of her. Now she was only grateful to have been spared that final humiliation.

Oh he was handsome still, no doubt about that, his fair hair rich and glossy, his fashionable blue coat and fawn pantaloons of impeccable cut. His wife's wealth had transformed him into a man about town but it had also made him smug, self-confident, detestably pleased with himself and doubtless selfish to the very

12

bone, or perhaps all these things had already been there only she had been too besotted to notice them.

He held out both hands. "Charlotte, my dear dear cousin, what ages it's been and how very pretty you have grown."

He drew her to him kissing her on both cheeks and for an instant the old magic stirred her as it had once done but not for long. She drew away sensing a falseness, an insincerity that had not been there before.

"I'm delighted to see you, Clive," she said easily. "Marriage appears to suit you. I declare you have grown fatter. You've lost the lean and hungry look. Why didn't you bring your wife with you? Mamma and I have heard so much about her."

She thought he resented the note of irony. He said shortly, "Lucy has not been well. In fact that is one of the reasons that has brought me to visit you this afternoon."

"Really. Is there any way in which we can help?"

Before she could say any more her mother intervened. She said hurriedly, "Well, I'm sure there is no need for us all to stand about like figures in a waxworks. We're not strangers, we're family. Do sit down, Clive, make yourself at home. Charlotte, my dear, will you ask Peg to bring in the tea?"

When she returned with the best silver teapot and the finest china with the thin sandwiches, the congress tarts and Peg's delicious Madeira cake, Clive and her mother were sitting each side of the fire and so she busied herself with pouring the tea and left Peg to hand the cups round.

They drank the tea, sampled the cakes and talked of trivial matters, about how much he had enjoyed the season in London, about his father's increasing attacks of gout and the birth of a new daughter to his elder brother. It was not until the last cup had been drained and the table moved away that he came to the real purpose of his visit and it took her breath away.

He leaned back in his chair, long legs stretched out, looking across at her with that secret smile that had once held a special meaning for her.

"Have you kept up with your Spanish studies, Charlie? I've never forgotten how you used to go searching through Father's library hunting up books on the subject."

"Yes, I have whenever it has been possible." She was surprised at the question. He had laughed at her then. "Why bother your head about a language you'll never use in a month

13

of Sundays?" he had said teasingly. "As a matter of fact," she went on, "some time ago Father brought a man here who spoke with fluency and we spent several evenings polishing up on conversation."

"Marvellous," he said. "When you get interested in something, you always worried at it like a dog at a bone. As for me," he shrugged his shoulders smiling, "a dozen words and I'm already at a standstill. Pity the whole world doesn't speak English instead of these tongue-twisting lingos. Don't you agree, Aunt Caroline?" and he included her mother in his look of amusement. "However the upshot of all this is very simple. I am the bearer of an invitation, Charlotte, from Lucy as well as myself. Would you care to accompany us to Spain in the New Year, no expense to you of course. You would be our guest."

"What!" She stared at him open-mouthed unable to believe her ears. How could he be so without understanding, so insensitive, or was it that what had once passed between them had meant so little to him that he had already forgotten about it?

Her mother gave her a quick glance and then said calmly, "I'm afraid you've taken us by surprise, my dear Clive. This is very unexpected. May I ask you why you are going to Spain and for how long?"

He smiled. "It's just like me. Father always complains that I rush my fences. It's like this. Lucy has not been at all well since the summer. She caught a cold at the races. Filthy weather as usual, and she developed a tiresome cough which refuses to leave her. The doctor has diagnosed a certain weakness and advises a warmer climate and as soon as possible."

"Surely Italy would have suited your purpose better than Spain," said her mother doubtfully.

"It so happens that we spent our honeymoon in Rome and Florence and very disappointing we found it. Too many ex-patriates and too many visiting English. If I must spend a great deal of time abroad, then I would prefer a wilder, more unexplored country. I'm taking my painting very seriously these days and Spain would seem to offer excellent opportunities for interesting subjects."

"How does your wife feel about it?" asked Charlotte.

"Lucy does not mind where she goes so long as there is warmth and sunshine. We were fortunate enough to meet the

14

Spanish Ambassador in London and he was most helpful. He has already recommended to us a villa in Seville in one of the best districts of the city. It was in fact Lucy herself who suggested that I should come to you. She says she will be delighted to have a companion when I go off on what she calls my painting sprees and of course your knowledge of Spanish would be invaluable to both of us. We will be taking her maid and my valet with us and intend to stay a year or possibly longer." His eyes sparkled across at her. "Well, what do you say, Charlie?"

"It's kind of you," she said carefully, "but I am afraid I must refuse. I couldn't possibly contemplate leaving Mamma alone so soon after losing Father. You must understand that."

"My dear girl," said her mother so quickly that it worried her. Had she already some plan in mind that she had not spoken of? "You need not worry about me if you would like to go and indeed it would be a wonderful opportunity for you to see something of the world."

They argued about it for a while, Clive very eager and her mother obviously on his side. Charlotte tried hard to stand out against them full of doubt at the prospect and yet at the same time not a little tempted by the thought of seeing at last something of the country which had filled her father's dreams.

At length Clive said, "I refuse to take no for an answer. I'm aware that I've surprised you with it and naturally you want time to consider. I'm staying with friends only a few miles from here. Think it over and I'll call again if I may in a few days' time."

"I'm sure that it is very kind of you, Clive, and I know that when Charlotte really thinks about it, she will appreciate what you are suggesting to her," said her mother.

"I hope very much she will come with us and I am speaking for Lucy as well as myself, Aunt Caroline," he said easily, taking her hand and pleasing her by kissing her cheek affectionately, thanking her for tea with a quite irresistible charm.

Charlotte went with him to the door and before he left he took both her hands in his, whispering in the narrow hallway, "Do come, Charlie. I've never known you hold back from anything before. Remember what you used to say at Breakstone – let's have an adventure. Well, this could be the very best adventure of all."

15

It was true enough but he was still a boy then, now he was a married man with the responsibility of an ailing wife and the time for adventures was past. How would she feel living in such close proximity, how would he react? It was too fraught with danger. She withdrew her hands and shook her head.

"There are far too many problems. Lucy may take an instant dislike to me."

"No, she won't. She'll love you. Lucy thinks and acts as I do and she is very lonely. She needs a friend." For a moment he sounded sincere and it surprised her.

"I promise I'll think about it. I can't do more than that."

"That's all I ask. Goodbye, my dear, or should I say, *Adios, mi amor.*"

His abominable pronunciation made her laugh. "Where did you learn that?"

"Never you mind but you see how much you will be needed," he said laughing with her as they parted.

"Has he gone?" asked her mother as she came back into the sitting room.

"Yes and in a very handsome carriage. Is it his do you think?"

"Why not? I understand his wife is rich enough to buy him half a dozen carriages. This could be a splendid thing for you, Charlotte."

She stared at her. "But I'm not going. You heard what I said to Clive."

"Yes, of course, but you didn't mean it."

"Believe me, I did. I meant every word."

"Now don't play the fool over this," said her mother with some exasperation. "To refuse at first is very proper. God knows we don't want to look like beggars jumping at every chance that is offered, but in a day or two – when he comes again – you can accept. Make him feel you're doing him a favour. I never thought that all that time Harry spent in teaching you Spanish would prove so useful. It just goes to show, doesn't it, how extraordinary life can turn out to be."

"You really want me to go with him, don't you?" said Charlotte slowly.

"If it is for your good, of course I do," went on her mother emphatically. "Only a few days ago you were talking about looking for employment. This would be a hundred times better

16

than any post you could obtain for yourself and far more suitable. Travelling with your cousins in the utmost luxury . . ."

"And constantly at Lucy's beck and call, obeying every one of her whims and fancies. Have you thought of that? She has the money, she will call the tune. I shall be expected to pay for my luxury, you can be sure of that."

"And what is wrong with it? Don't you think any employer will demand his pound of flesh from you? At least Clive is your cousin and on your side. He likes you. I could see that."

"Supposing he likes me too much?"

Her mother gave her a sharp glance. "What do you mean by that?"

"Oh I don't know." She did not want to explain. Her mother had never really known exactly what had gone on between them that summer.

"In any case," she went on, "you're not a child, Charlotte. You can surely deal with that situation if it does arise and I'm quite sure it won't. When all's said and done you're hardly a *femme fatale*, my dear, and Clive is a gentleman and your cousin."

"I know – I know – it's just that – that it frightens me a little."

"Oh for heaven's sake, don't turn missish and pretend to be nervous. Such airs and graces don't suit you, Charlotte. God knows I've no wish to force you into it but I do urge you to think about it very seriously. What was it your father used to say – something about a tide in the affairs of men which taken at the flood leads on to fortune. Well, the tide seems to be flowing our way for once so we had better take advantage of it."

To hear her mother quoting Shakespeare was strange enough to make her smile but Charlotte was to pass two days and nights of the utmost indecision before by mere chance she learned the real reason for her mother's urging.

She had been out all the morning taking a bundle of clothes to the mission for distribution to the needy poor and returned to see an unfamiliar horse tethered at the gate. Surely it couldn't be Clive! They were not expecting him until the end of the week. She opened the parlour door quickly and saw her mother looking flushed and oddly guilty standing with a tall heavily built man who contrived to appear both belligerent and self-

17

conscious. She knew him slightly. He was Colonel Alfred Armstrong, retired, who now held some post or other in the City of London. He had been an occasional visitor for the past year or so and had been regarded by her father with the faint contempt he felt for all civilians.

"I beg your pardon," she said, "I didn't know we had a visitor."

"Colonel Armstrong is just leaving, my dear. You remember my daughter, Alfred, don't you?"

"Indeed I do. Your servant, Miss Starr."

He bowed to her politely before he and her mother left the room. When she came back Charlotte said abruptly, "Well, when are you going to marry him?"

"Charlie really! What a thing to say!"

"I suppose it is with Papa hardly cold in his grave but don't let us pretend. We might as well be honest with one another. Has he asked you? Is that why he was here?"

"If you must know, he has," said her mother defensively, "and what is so wrong about that? It can't be for a year at the very least. It wouldn't be decent and he doesn't expect it."

"So that's why you were so pleased when Clive offered to take me with him to Spain," she said wearily, "getting rid of me would clear the decks so to speak."

"That's not true. It is simply that since the invitation had come so opportunely, it seemed exactly the right thing for you."

"And Colonel Armstrong with his mind set on marrying a pretty widow doesn't want to be hampered by a grown-up stepdaughter. I quite understand."

"No, you don't. You think I'm being unfair to your father's memory. That is what is upsetting you, isn't it? But it is not true. I was loyal to him while he lived but now he's gone and I'm left with very little. I have to look out for myself. I'm not a woman to live alone. I can't fill out my life with good works like Nicholas's wife, playing Lady Bountiful in the village of Breakstone. The chance is there and may never come again so why shouldn't I take it?"

"Why not indeed?"

From her point of view she was perfectly right, only the very thought of the heavy lumpish Colonel Armstrong in her father's place filled Charlotte with a burning resentment. It was something that she knew she would never be able to force herself to accept. She had to escape and there was a *way* if she could stifle her scruples.

"Very well," she said, "when Clive comes, I'll tell him I've changed my mind."

"Oh my dear, you won't regret it, I am sure. It will be a wonderful experience and in a year's time anything may happen."

"Yes, anything," she agreed. "We shall have to change some of our plans, won't we? Will you go to the cottage at Breakstone now?"

"For a while," said her mother happily, "but not for long, please God, not for long."

Charlotte had a strange dream that night. Before she went to bed she had taken the portrait from the drawer in her chest where she had hidden it. The candlelight flickered across it giving the features life and warmth. Whoever he was, this unknown Spaniard would be her father's age by now or perhaps even older. She stared at it for a long time, then wrapped it up again and put it carefully away. She thought her mother was right. Some invisible tide seemed to be pushing her into going to Spain and now she was committed and could not draw back, she was aware of a rising excitement.

Surprisingly she fell asleep quickly and in the confused way of dreams found herself in a place that was partly Breakstone Park and partly some wild haunted region of bare stony heights and distant mountains. She was running and running and Clive was behind her. He caught her up, his hands were on her shoulders, they were laughing and happy. He turned her round and it was not Clive's face at all but the man in the portrait, alive and so real that she could feel his heart beat, see the long dark lashes and the faint sheen of sweat on his face. She was trembling and at the same time longing for his kiss with a passionate urging that she had never experienced in her life before. He bent his head but before his lips touched hers, she woke up.

It had been so intensely real that she had the queerest feeling that he was still there in the room with her. Then as familiar objects slowly began to take shape in the darkness, she pulled herself together. Of course it was nothing. She had looked at

19

the painting just before sleeping and it had somehow imprinted itself on her unconscious mind. So she reasoned to herself and yet she was shaken. It was a long time before she could sleep again.

2

To her great surprise Charlotte discovered that she *liked* Lucy. She had never expected it. She had indeed made up her mind that she would find her abominable but would have to make the best of it. How could it be otherwise, she had thought? Lucy was the daughter of self-made parents, rich, spoiled, more than possibly a little vulgar. Then, when they met, she was completely disarmed. Lucy was not at all as she had imagined. To start with she was only twenty and very slight and small with a mass of golden hair, deep blue eyes, and possessed a beguiling childish charm that was irresistible. She reminded Charlotte of a kitten her father had once brought to her, a tender frightened creature which he had rescued from being mauled by a couple of savage dogs. It had aroused her strong protective instinct and she had loved it passionately during its short life. It was decidedly disconcerting to find that same desire to protect provoked by Lucy's look of extreme fragility.

Uncle Nicholas had invited Charlotte and her mother to spend the Christmas holiday at Breakstone Park where Clive and his wife would be staying until they left for Spain.

"Wonderful opportunity for you two girls to get to know one another," her cousin had said jovially when he had ridden over at the beginning of December, bringing his father's invitation and looking so smugly pleased with himself because he had got his own way, that Charlotte had a great desire to slap him.

It needed an heroic effort on her part to get everything settled in time for their removal, so much to be disposed of, so much to be sent by carrier to the cottage where her mother would be living. She hated leaving Whitefoot to be sold and there was a heart-rending parting from Jack Hardy.

"A year is not so very long," she'd said consolingly, "it will soon pass and then I shall be home again."

"A year can last for ever," he'd said gloomily, "and you'll

never come back here. You'll probably marry some rich Spanish grandee and I'll never see you again."

"I don't think that's very likely," she'd said smiling at him. "Papa used to say that they were all poor as church mice and proud as peacocks with ancestors going back to El Cid. We've had some good times together, Jack, don't spoil it all now."

She'd allowed him to take her in his arms and kiss her good-bye and had wondered why it was that good-natured and generous to a fault as he was, his embrace aroused nothing in her except a slight impatience for it to be over as soon as possible.

For many years the hunt had met at Breakstone Park on Boxing Day and though gout prevented Uncle Nicholas from playing host, Clive and his elder brother took his place. Strictly speaking Charlotte should not have gone out with them as she was still in mourning but it was her mother who urged her to do so.

"It's never appealed to me, I'm afraid, rising at dawn in freezing weather and feeling frightened to death in case I was pitched on my head jumping those abominable fences, but you're like Harry, bold as a lion, so you ride with them, my dear, and good luck to you."

It was not chasing the fox that specially appealed to her, actually if she thought about it, she would just as soon it got away. It was the sparkle of the cold frosty morning, the pleasure of riding one of Uncle Nicholas's blood horses, the lively company, the baying of the hounds, the thrill of it all with Clive beside her, tall and handsome in his 'pink' coat.

"Doesn't Lucy ride?" she asked him that morning as they trotted down the drive.

He shook his head. "Lord no, too damned scared. I tried to persuade her once but horses make her cough, she says. Queer fancy that."

Was it fancy? Charlotte wasn't so sure. One of her father's recruits only had to enter a stable to go into choking suffocating paroxysms of coughing – something the doctor had called asthma. It seemed to her a pity that Lucy could not join her husband in what was one of his greatest pleasures. Then she forgot about it in the sheer ecstasy of the morning, the rush of the wind as they galloped across the fields, the smell of the turned earth, the slow jog back talking over the day's events with the red

22

sun sinking behind black spectral trees and a marvellous feeling of well-being.

When she came into the house, tea was being served in the drawing room and Lucy, already dressed for the evening in a gown of sapphire blue velvet, was sitting close beside the fire. She smiled up at her.

"Did you have a good day?"

"Absolutely wonderful."

"Did Clive enjoy it?"

"Very much, I think."

"I do so envy you, Charlotte. I'd love to have been out with him today."

She was looking wistfully across at her husband drinking brandy and water with the other men and Charlotte was aware of a stirring of anger. Why couldn't he have come and greeted his wife, made her feel she mattered to him? It was so callously insensitive when he knew she had been ill. She accepted a cup of tea and sat down beside Lucy.

"What a lovely dress you're wearing. It's exactly the colour of your eyes."

"Do you like it? It's new. Clive hasn't seen it yet."

"He'll love it when he does. I can't tell you how thankful I shall be to get out of wearing black."

"Perhaps you can when we are in Spain. Clive says it will be very hot so we shall need lighter clothes." She began to tell Charlotte of what she had already purchased. It was an hour later and time to dress for the evening before Clive strolled across to them.

"Hallo, Lucy old girl, how's the cough?"

"Better, thank you."

"Must go and change. What about you, m'dear?"

"I'm dressed already, Clive."

His eyes ran over her indifferently. "Oh Lord, so you are. I'll be off then. Won't be long."

Charlotte saw the disappointment on her face. She rose to her feet feeling uncomfortable. It was only a few days since they had met and yet already she had begun to realize that Lucy adored her husband while Clive was showing all too plainly that love had played little part in his marriage. It made the prospect of the coming months together distinctly unattractive and yet she could not withdraw now. In fact she no

23

longer wished it. More and more as the days passed she found herself looking forward to the new life which could open up for her in Spain.

They were to leave England at the beginning of February which gave Charlotte time to see her mother comfortably installed in the cottage with Peg in attendance, to make a few useful additions to her wardrobe and to endure a visit from Colonel Armstrong who took it upon himself to become heavily paternal, warning her against the dangers to be encountered in such an uncivilized country ranging from contracting malaria and typhoid to being ravished at the hands of wandering bandits.

When he left them, her mother said awkwardly, "He means well, you know, Charlie."

"I suppose he does but seeing that he sat out the war in a comfortable staff job in England while Papa fought from Lisbon to the Pyrenees, it does seem a little ridiculous."

"Oh dear, I suppose it does." Then they both laughed and for once were on good terms with one another.

"There is one thing, Charlotte. Harry left little enough, God knows, but I'd not have you dependent on Clive and his wife for every triviality so I have a little money for you. It's only fifty pounds, I'm afraid, but it may help."

She took the purse doubtfully. "Colonel Armstrong had nothing to do with this, had he?"

"Certainly not. Do you think I'd accept money from him even if we are unofficially engaged?"

Maybe she would. Charlotte wasn't sure but she said, "Thank you, Mamma. I'm grateful, really I am, especially when I know it won't be easy for you during the coming year."

Then surprisingly Uncle Nicholas who, according to Clive, was as close-fisted as any rascally moneylender, was moved to present his niece with twenty guineas and in a mad moment she bought a length of exquisite silk organza in a delicate shade of green and there was just time to have it made up into an evening gown before they must pack their trunks.

The Peninsular and Oriental Navigation Company sailed from Southampton three times a month and the voyage to Cadiz, weather permitting, usually took no more than six days. It was a bitingly cold, blusteringly wet day when they went on board and were relieved to find that the *Iberia* was a well found ship manned by an English crew. Clive and Lucy had a large comfortable cabin while Charlotte had a tiny one to herself and Clive's manservant Matthew bedded down with one of the crew.

Lucy, exhausted by the journey from Breakstone Park, went to bed early that night and Charlotte supped alone with her cousin in the saloon. She looked around her with interest. There were not a great many passengers at this time of the year and what there were seemed to be mostly middle-aged businessmen since the ship would touch at Corunna and Lisbon before going on to Cadiz. They bowed and smiled at her when she entered with Clive as if glad to see a pretty young face among the few rather dowdy ladies accompanying their husbands. All except two she noted, who sat at a table apart. A tall, lean, dark-haired man with a hawk-like profile and his companion, shorter and thick-set with sandy hair, the ruddy complexion that usually goes with it and a pleasantly good-natured expression as he half rose and smiled up at her when she and Clive went out after the meal was over.

"Do you think they are Spanish?" she whispered to her cousin as they sat together in the lounge for a few minutes before retiring to bed.

"The dark man is – one of those top lofty hidalgos who believe themselves made of finer clay than the rest of us. I ran into him on deck just before supper, passed the time of day and got a stare down that long nose of his as if I were the dust under his feet."

Charlotte smiled. Clive had always had a very good conceit of himself.

"'Every man a king,' that was what Papa used to say about the Spanish. He rather admired their pride. Even the poorest peasant grubbing a living out of the bare mountains is an individual and considers himself as good as the next man, be he lord or commoner."

Clive grinned. "Then it will be up to us to teach them a thing or two, won't it, Charlie?"

She was not so sure about that but to someone who had never travelled further than Breakstone and one never-to-be-forgotten trip to London, each day was an adventure and she was prepared to enjoy every minute of it. She did not even mind the tasks she was obliged to undertake for Lucy. The maid who should have accompanied them had inconveniently fallen sick at the last moment so there was no time to replace her.

Clive had shrugged his shoulders, ignoring his wife's dismay. "For the lord's sake, don't fuss, my dear. We can engage servants out there easily enough," he had said impatiently.

"But they won't be like my Deb," she wailed, "and I can't speak Spanish."

"Oh you'll soon pick up some of the lingo and until you do, Charlotte will interpret for you."

So without anything being actually said, Charlotte found herself taking over much of the packing, anticipating Lucy's wants and generally taking care of her rather as she might have done for a delicate younger sister. But there was still time during those first few days to walk the deck well wrapped up against the biting wind and even once or twice to settle in a sheltered spot with a book for an hour or two. It was when she was sitting there one morning enjoying for the third time the adventures of Miss Austen's Emma, a heroine with whose rebellious temperament she felt very much in sympathy, that she suddenly raised her eyes and saw the dark man whom for her own amusement she had dubbed 'Don Juan' standing with his back against the rail. The broad-brimmed Spanish hat he wore was pulled down so that she could not see his eyes but she was uncomfortably aware that he must have been watching her for some time. She stared back defiantly and after a moment he gave her a polite bow, murmured something inaudible and walked away.

She was intrigued but there was no time to pursue the acquaintance further. That night the storms hit them when they sailed into the infamous Bay of Biscay. After the first shock it came as an immense relief to find she could stand up to its buffetings and contrive to remain on her feet except for a slight feeling of giddiness. It was Lucy who suffered most and Charlotte, overcome with pity, did what she could to help her. Clive proved utterly useless. He detested any form of sickness and had little patience with it, his own splendid health making him scornful of weakness in others. In the end Charlotte ordered him out of the cabin, told him curtly to take over hers and moved in with Lucy in his place. With the assistance of a kindly member of the crew she contrived to make her as com-

26

fortable as possible in the circumstances and after three days and nights of extreme misery, the ship steadied a little and she was at last able to persuade her to take a few mouthfuls of hot thin soup with a cracker biscuit.

She left her sleeping and thankfully escaped to the deck. Rain had fallen heavily during the day and though the wind had abated, everything was awash with water and dangerously slippery. She was standing by the rail breathing in great gulps of clean salty air when Clive came up beside her. She had seen little of him for the last few days and guessed that he had spent most of his time playing cards with those male passengers who had managed to remain on their feet.

"How is Lucy?" he asked.

"A little better. I have persuaded her to take some soup. I hope she will sleep for a while."

"Thank God for that."

"You might have come to sit with her, Clive. She felt it deeply."

"You know me," he said somewhat ashamed. "I'm no good at things like this. She was far better in your hands. I'm very grateful to you, Charlie, very grateful indeed. We'd have been in a sorry state without you."

"I only did what anyone would do."

"No, not anyone, not in the circumstances."

"What on earth do you mean by that?"

He leaned on the rail staring across the grey sea. "I've been a fool, haven't I, Charlotte? I threw away the best thing that ever happened to me because I hadn't the courage to stand up to Father and try to make something of my life."

She was far too tired to argue with him. "I haven't the faintest idea what you are talking about."

"Oh yes you have. Don't pretend to be indifferent." He turned towards her putting his hands on her shoulders and turning her to face him. "Did you hate me for what I did, Charlie, did you? Tell me, I really want to know."

Anger flooded up in her. How dare he talk about what had happened when it was in the past, when she had determined to put it behind her once and for all? She shook herself free.

"You seem to forget that Lucy is your wife, Clive. She is a good sweet girl and she happens to love you. Surely that is enough."

"Love me?" he repeated discontentedly. "I don't think she knows what love means."

"I don't understand."

"No, perhaps you don't but you will one day."

Charlotte was not as ignorant of the physical demands of love as he imagined. She had grown up in the society of hot-blooded young men and her mother had been more outspoken than some. She said quietly, "She is young and delicate. You should be gentle with her."

"Don't preach at me. You know nothing about it."

"I'm not a child, Clive."

"The worst thing I ever did was to marry her."

"How can you say that when she has brought you what you wanted more than anything in the world – wealth to do as you please, freedom to go your own way, and an undemanding love. You ought to go down on your knees and thank heaven for it and not complain about the fate you have chosen for yourself."

He swung round to look at her. She saw the glitter in his eyes, heard the laughter in his voice. "You look splendid when you are angry, Charlie, you always did. Remember? Don't be a spoilsport. We can still have fun together, can't we?"

He thought he could do as he pleased with her, take her up and drop her at will, and it so enraged her she could hardly speak.

"Is that why you asked me to come with you? When we reach Cadiz I've a good mind to stay on the ship and go straight back to England."

"Oh no, you wouldn't." He slipped an arm around her waist. "You wouldn't desert Lucy, would you?"

"It might be a great deal better for both of us if I did."

She wrenched herself away and turned her back on him, running across the deck towards the hatchway that led down to the sleeping cabins. But she forgot the effect of the heavy rain and the swing of the ship still heaving under the wind. She missed her footing, the brass handrail slipped from her groping fingers, she pitched down the stairs and hit her head against the corner post at the bottom so hard that she fell away into blackness.

She came groggily out of darkness with no memory of what had happened and a face swam out of the shadows, the eyes

28

of the man in the Spanish portrait were looking into hers and she was aware of pain and wonder and terror. She closed her eyes against it, swimming in a grey mist, and when she opened them again the face had gone and she thought she must have dreamed it.

"Where am I?" she muttered still dazed.

"Do not be alarmed," said a voice in a slightly accented English. "You had a fall and hurt your head. You will be better soon."

Something cool and wet was pressed against her aching head. She tried to sit up and was gently pushed back again.

"Do not move. Better to lie still for a little."

Weakly she did as she was told while recollection began to creep back. She had been talking to Clive. She had run away from him, slipped and fallen. Someone must have picked her up, removed her wet cloak, loosened the high neck of her gown, carried her into a cabin – but who?

She sat up with a jerk looking wildly around her. There was a candle burning on the dressing-table. By its flickering light she saw the two men and frowned, trying to bring them into focus. They were 'Don Juan' and his companion.

"I mustn't stay here," she said. "I must go back to – to Lucy."

"Not yet." The dark man came to the side of the bunk. "You have given yourself a shock, Señorita. And you are badly bruised. There is no surgeon on board but I do not think it serious. You can rest here till you feel better."

"No, no, I can't – it is impossible."

"Not impossible at all." Firm hands tucked the blanket closely around her. "You must keep warm and lie quietly. This is my cabin but I will not be using it." He turned to his companion and said something in Spanish so rapidly that in her dazed condition she could not follow the words. The sandy-haired man nodded. He came across to her.

"Don't worry, Miss Starr. You'd be far better resting for a while. I'll make sure that your friend is cared for."

He smiled reassuringly and she smiled faintly back. "Thank you."

She looked from one to the other of the two men. Weariness combined with the shock of the fall had made her feel remarkably weak and dizzy. It seemed easier to acquiesce than to argue.

29

"Where will you sleep?" she murmured.

"Do not be concerned about me, Señorita. Stay here as long as you wish."

He gave her a slight smile and both men went out together. She lay back, the pain ebbing a little, wondering at the chance that had brought such an unlikely acquaintance but still very shaken, until the effect of the broken nights took its toll and she fell into a light sleep.

It was very early when she woke. The pain in her head had turned into a dull ache. She felt the place cautiously. There was a lump as big as an egg, very tender to the touch, but the skin was apparently unbroken. She put back the blanket and only then noticed that it was woven in rich sombre colours, the kind of travelling rug that a Spaniard might carry with him strapped to the saddlebow of his horse.

She put it back, slid her legs over the edge and stood up. Her head swam but after a moment the giddiness passed and she looked around her. The cabin had a look of austerity as if its owner was a man who travelled lightly, not like Clive whose wealth had led him into extravagances of toiletry and lavish clothes. She looked curiously at the books by the bed, a text-book in French on vine culture, a book of Spanish poetry unfamiliar to her. She picked it up and opened it at random. Her eye fell on a marked passage and she translated it with difficulty:

> "I live without inhabiting
> Myself – in such a fashion that
> I am dying though I do not die –"

She put it down quickly. It was like prying into someone else's most inward thoughts.

She crossed the cabin unsteadily and grimaced at her appearance in the small mirror, pale, heavy-eyed, hair in a sorry tangle. What a fright he must have thought her, and she remembered with gratitude the gentle hands that had bathed her bruises and tucked the blanket around her. A small silver locket such as a woman might wear attracted her attention on the dressing-table. She took it up and then guiltily giving in to curiosity she opened it. Within was the picture of a girl, very young, a pure and lovely face, guileless and innocent, his wife – sister – fiancée? She closed it and dropped it back on the table with a strong feeling that she should not have touched it. Then she

30

picked up her heavy cloak, pulled it around her and stole out of the cabin.

The sea quietened considerably during the morning and the sun came out with some warmth reminding them that they were leaving the northern winter behind them and moving south. Lucy was better but still felt too weak to get up so after Charlotte had bathed and changed she went up on to the deck alone. The sailor who had taken her under his wing greeted her cheerfully.

"Glad to see you lookin' so bobbish, Miss, and the other lady too. She'll be right as rain in no time. Nothin' like a bit o' sun to put heart into you."

He fetched her a chair and put it carefully in the lee of the wind where she could feel the warmth of the sunshine and she had just settled herself comfortably when she saw her two companions of the night before strolling along the deck. The dark man bowed and walked on but the other, hatless, his sandy hair blowing wildly in the wind, came across to her.

"Good morning, Miss Starr. How are you feeling? No more trouble with the head, I hope."

"No, not at all. It hurts when I touch it but that's all. I'm extremely grateful to you and feel very guilty at depriving your friend of his bed for the night."

"Oh you needn't worry. He's not a man to concern himself about comfort. He shared my cabin." He looked around him, found another chair and brought it up beside her. "May I sit with you for a little?"

"Please do. You know my name but I don't know yours or that of your friend," she said shyly.

"No, by Jove, you don't of course. Terribly remiss of us but last night was a bit of an emergency, wasn't it? I'd better introduce myself – Guy Macalister at your service."

"Scottish?"

"Half. Scottish father, French mother."

"And your friend?"

"The Marqués Lorenzo de Merenda y Almedana – to give him his full title. He prefers to be called simply Don Lorenzo."

"He was so kind last night that I feel I ought to thank him personally but he does seem rather unapproachable, doesn't he?"

31

Guy Macalister smiled. "He gives that impression but he is not really like that, you know. Reserved perhaps, not a chatterbox like me, but he does notice things. It was he who insisted on carrying you into his cabin when we found you lying at the foot of the stairs and he who made sure that your friend was receiving proper attention while you were recovering."

His concern for her came as a surprise. "Have you known him long?"

"On and off for quite a time but not intimately till now. I hope to be working with him for the next few years."

"Working?"

"Perhaps I'd better explain. My father is a partner in one of the sherry firms in Jerez. I was born in Spain. I've grown up with vines as it were. I've been in England and France for the last couple of years studying the latest developments in vine culture and how to combat the hundred and one diseases that attack the vines. I came back from Paris and joined Don Lorenzo in London. He was there on some government business with the embassy and we decided to travel back together."

"Is Don Lorenzo also in the wine trade?"

He laughed. "Good God, no. He's a grandee, you understand, and most of them are far too proud to soil their hands with such matters. They'd rather starve on their scanty acres though I must admit that Lorenzo is not quite like the others I have met. As far as I can gather he is doing his level best to restore the family fortunes. The Merenda vineyards were devastated years ago during the war with Napoleon and have never been properly renewed. He has engaged me to do it for him."

"Are you an expert?"

"So they say," he grimaced. "It's certainly the biggest challenge I've had so far and I'm hoping I shall be able to rise to it."

She realized then that despite his boyish looks he was older than she had thought, nearer thirty than twenty.

"Don Lorenzo may be an aristocrat," he went on musingly, "but he is also a man of great intelligence and determination. I think I shall enjoy working with him."

And that was how it began, this rather unlikely friendship, which developed rapidly in the close confinement of a small ship with little other company. Charlotte was a good listener and Guy Macalister was eloquent on his own subject. She heard how the quality of wine depends on the grape and the soil,

32

how vines have to be cultivated with the utmost care and need unceasing attention and at the time of the vintage in September, the hearts, souls and bodies of all those concerned are completely absorbed in producing the best possible product from the year's labour, but apart from hearing that his home lay somewhere north of Seville in the foothills of the Sierra she did not learn much about Don Lorenzo. She begged Guy to talk to her in the Spanish he spoke fluently, and good-humouredly he did so, correcting her pronunciation painstakingly, so that in a short time she found it astonishingly easy to understand and reply.

She had confided part of what had happened that night to Lucy so that when she came to join her on the deck and the two gentlemen passed to bow and exchange a few words, the younger girl was vastly intrigued by Don Lorenzo's dark good looks.

"Do you know who it is he reminds me of?" she said very seriously.

"One of those romantic gypsy heroes in those dreadful romances from the lending library," said Charlotte teasingly. Lucy had brought a supply with her hidden in her trunk.

"Not at all," she replied loftily. "He is the Corsair."

"He's what?"

"Oh Charlotte, don't pretend. You must remember:

'That man of loneliness and mystery
Scarce seen to smile, and seldom heard to sigh –'"

"Really, Lucy, wherever did you read Byron?"

"At Miss Pinkney's Academy for Young Ladies of course." She giggled. "It was strictly forbidden and I'd have been expelled if it had been found out. We only had one volume and we used to pass it from one to the other and read it under the blankets. We nearly burned the house down one night when a silly girl dropped the candle in the bed."

She had recovered her spirits in the warmth and sunshine and bubbled over with laughter. "Don't you think it fits him exactly?"

Charlotte saw Don Lorenzo glance towards them and only hoped he had not overheard what they had been saying about him.

"You've made a conquest," went on Lucy irrepressibly.

33

"Don't be stupid. I've only exchanged a couple of words with him and it was like addressing God. I felt I ought to curtsey."

"Oh I didn't mean the Corsair. It's his friend, Mr Macalister. Can't you see him glowering at me because I'm preventing him from having his usual little tête-à-tête with you?"

"Lucy, if you don't stop this minute, I shall get up and walk away."

"Very well, I'll not say another word but I have eyes in my head and so has Clive. He's quite jealous."

"Clive is?"

"Haven't you noticed how annoyed he is every time they come near or smile at you?"

"That's absolute nonsense and you know it."

"Do I?"

Lucy pursed her lips and looked mysterious so that for the first time Charlotte wondered if she had guessed how close she and Clive had once been and resented it. She hoped not. Once she might have been pleased but not now. She was not blinded any longer. She saw him clearly for what he was, charming, irresponsible, utterly selfish. And yet occasionally even now the turn of his head, the touch of his hand, brought back memories she would rather have forgotten. She had made up her mind to forget the conversation between them on the night she had fallen. She had grown too fond of Lucy to abandon her and in any case to explain a sudden return to England would be far too painful. She felt pretty sure that Clive's volatile temperament would soon find other attractions more to his liking.

The heavy storms had delayed them and the ship unexpectedly stayed a day outside Lisbon before continuing to Cadiz, but Charlotte did not mind. She was enjoying it all too much, the sea and the sunshine, even the cold nights when she would come up on to the deck wearing a warm cloak, enchanted by the ripple of moonlight on the dark satin of the water. Sometimes she would see Don Lorenzo slowly pacing up and down and was careful to avoid him. By now she was on easy terms with Guy Macalister but his employer still held aloof until the very last morning.

Warned by her sailor acquaintance that they would be docking the next day, Charlotte woke very early, dressed quickly and went up on to the deck anxious not to miss the first sight of Spain which had been to her for so long a fabled land.

The sun was only just beginning to disperse the heavy sea mist and the city on its long isthmus rose white and dream-like out of the sea that surrounded it on three sides.

She thought she was the first on deck and the deep, slightly foreign voice startled her.

"You are up very early, Señorita. Does the first glimpse of my country meet with your approval?"

She turned to see Don Lorenzo at her side. He leaned over the rail, his eyes ranging over the view before them.

"When the mists clear, you may even be able to see the snow on the Sierra."

"It is beautiful," she murmured and thought this is how her father must once have seen it in far different circumstances, in the threat of war and death.

"The Phoenicians came here three thousand years ago and to them it was the end of the known world to which came tin and amber out of the sea mists of the mysterious foggy north. The Greeks were here and after that came the Romans. They called it Gades and it exported wine, gold, silver, wheat and dancing girls."

"Dancing girls?" she exclaimed. "Are you joking?"

"Indeed I'm not. The *puellae Gaditanae* were a star attraction at Roman feasts, with *testarum crepitus* or so says Juvenal. Do you know what that means?"

She frowned. "I'm not sure – clicking or clapping, isn't it?"

"So you know a little Latin. I congratulate you, Señorita."

"Why shouldn't I? Do you think all women are stupid?"

"Did I say that? If so, then I apologise."

She was so angry at the mockery in his voice that for a moment she could not speak. Then she said coolly, "Are there still dancing girls?"

"Oh yes, and with the castanets. Most of our foreign visitors find them fascinating."

There was an edge to his voice that she had noticed before when he spoke to her or Clive and it irritated her.

"We are not exactly visitors, Don Lorenzo. My cousin is an artist and he intends to spend a year here at least, possibly longer if his wife's health should require it."

35

"I am not altogether sure that such a stay would be wise."

"What do you mean by that?"

"There has been a certain amount of disturbance in the country since the King died leaving an infant daughter as Queen and her mother as Regent. I think that foreigners and the English in particular may not be too popular."

"Why ever not? We are not concerned with Spanish politics."

"It is not always easy to keep out of such matters and the British have a reputation for interfering unwisely."

"Do you dislike us so much? After all it was the British who rescued your country from Napoleon," she said indignantly.

"Not entirely single-handedly," he replied dryly. "My father died in that war."

"I'm sorry –"

"And if I remember rightly it was the British who at one time destroyed our Armada and razed Cadiz to the ground."

"But that was hundreds of years ago."

"So it was."

"You're making fun of me," she said accusingly.

"No indeed. You mistake me."

He straightened up and turned to face her and she felt for the first time she was seeing him clearly as a person. The sun brought a burnish to the lustrous dark hair stirred by the wind. To her surprise his eyes were a deep dark blue going back to some distant northern ancestor perhaps. He had discarded his English tweeds for Spanish riding dress, a short jacket over a white shirt, black breeches and boots, a wide scarlet sash bound tightly around a narrow waist. He was Lucy's Corsair to the life but his smile had a warmth and charm she had not noticed before.

He said, "I heard you talking to Guy. You speak remarkable Spanish for an Englishwoman. May I ask where you learned it?"

"From my father."

"Indeed. Did he perhaps travel in this country?"

"No, not exactly. He was a soldier, a Captain in the Rifle Brigade. He fought some years in Spain and he grew to love it."

Momentarily she saw him stiffen, then he relaxed and smiled. "And you have inherited this love?"

"Yes, I suppose I have. He died last year and when my cousin decided to bring his wife here and asked me to accompany them, I could not resist the opportunity to see for myself the country he had loved so much."

"And is his wife's health the only reason that has brought your cousin here?"

"Certainly," she replied, surprised at the question. "That and a desire to see something of the world."

"I see. I hope with all my heart that neither you nor your friends will be disappointed. And now if you will excuse me, there are final preparations to be made. I think we shall be docking soon. *Adios, Señorita*." He took her hand and held it for a moment. "*Vaya usted con Dios*." Then he bent his head and kissed her fingers before he walked quickly away.

"Go with God," an expression she found surprising from the man she had believed so stiff and unapproachable. She wondered why he had questioned the reason for Clive coming to Spain and then dismissed it. Her cousin was not given to concerning himself with anything but his own pleasures. She turned to look again towards the shore where houses, towers and spires were slowly emerging out of the mist, white and magical in the thin sunlight. A warm glow of excitement ran through her as the scented breeze tossed her hair and with a great leap of the heart she went below to the cabin to make sure everything was packed and ready for their disembarkation.

3

They arrived at Seville late that evening after a long day sailing up the river from Cadiz. When they landed from the ship into the crowd and bustle of the busy port Charlotte saw that men with horses had come to meet Don Lorenzo and Guy Macalister. They forced their way quickly through the passengers and goods piled on the dockside, mounted and rode away, only Guy turning and waving a friendly hand. He had promised to call upon them whenever he came to Seville on business and she looked forward to meeting him again.

They transferred to the steamer at the mouth of the river and went chugging through a wide marshy land of rushes and sand dunes stretching into an illimitable distance, empty except for an occasional gliding bird or a stately egret stalking its prey on the edge of a swampy pool. Once she caught sight of flamingos stepping daintily on their stick-like legs, faintly pink through the thinning mist. Then miraculously by the time they were breakfasting on freshly baked bread, fruit and coffee, the sun broke through warm and golden and they realized with delight that they had left the fog and frost of an English February behind them at last.

Lucy lay on a long chair under an awning, dozing for a good part of the day while Clive brought out his drawing pad and amused himself making quick sketches of the colourful characters who, staring curiously at them, occasionally wandered on to the part of the deck reserved for the first-class passengers. But Charlotte could not sit still. She wanted to see everything. She crossed from one side of the boat to the other watching the peasants who crowded on and off at the various stops, carrying crates of chickens and enormous baskets, with children leading goats and even a donkey. The Guadalquivir was a wide river penetrating deep into the heart of Spain and up it must once have sailed Greeks, Romans, Vandals and Arabs. She stared across the flat grasslands towards the distant blue ridge of the

38

Sierra still capped with snow where the enigmatic Don Lorenzo had his home. What a strange young man he was, so kind when she had been hurt and at the same time so withdrawn. She admitted to an intense curiosity about him that did not seem likely to be satisfied.

It was dark by the time they reached Seville and the carriage wound a tortuous way through narrow streets. The Casa de Fuente loomed up before them, blank white walls with tiny barred windows and a black nail-studded door, but tired as they were, there was little time that night to gather any impression what with baggage being unloaded and the servants engaged on their behalf gabbling so fast in an unfamiliar Spanish that she found it desperately hard to translate.

Lucy was too tired to do much and Clive only seemed to get irritatingly in the way so that much of the settling in fell on Charlotte's shoulders. She saw Lucy into bed with a tray of the tea they had brought with them and after eating a hasty meal with Clive by the side of a quickly lit fire of crackling aromatic wood, she was only too thankful to retreat to her own small bedroom with its white painted walls, dark furniture and narrow bed above which hung a black crucifix.

She undressed quickly and shivered for the night was cold after the heat of the day. The tiled floor was icy to her bare feet and she was glad to slip between sheets smelling sweetly of thyme and lavender.

She woke early to a revelation of light. The sun streaming through the uncurtained window was so inviting that with a tingle of excitement she could not stay in bed a moment longer. She washed in cold water, pushed aside the hated black travelling dress and selected an old gown of striped cotton which had always been a favourite. It was not yet seven when she ran down the stairs. Juanita, the maid, was already at work in the kitchen, brown-skinned as a gypsy with a scarlet handkerchief tied around her head. She called a merry *Buenos días, Señorita*. A warm smell of baking bread came from the stove where Rosa, the cook, was preparing flat wheat cakes on an iron griddle. She was large and plump and nodded to Charlotte as she went past her through the garden door and found herself in a small patio.

The house had been built in Moorish style with all doors and windows opening on to the garden. The fountain that gave the house its name bubbled up from a round stone pool. Large pots held a lemon tree, a myrtle and other shrubs already in rich leaf. Hibiscus, Bougainvillaea and strange exotic plants unfamiliar to her clambered up the walls and hung over the windows, soon to be in bloom. There could not have been a greater contrast to the sour black patch outside their small house in England and overcome with sheer joy she stretched out her arms to the sunshine and danced round and round the pool until she collided breathlessly with Clive who had just emerged from the kitchen door. He caught her in his arms, spun her round and gave her a boisterous kiss.

"Glad you came after all?"

"Oh yes, yes. I never dreamed it would be like this."

"Better than the old country in a pea-soup fog, eh?" He broke off a twig of myrtle, crushed it in his fingers and held it under her nose. "Smells dashed good too."

She sneezed and laughed up at him.

"You two seem to be having fun," said a voice from above and Charlotte looked up guiltily to see Lucy still in her wrapper peering down at them from the upper window.

"Thought you were still sleeping," said Clive easily. "Come down, my dear, and we'll breakfast out here."

By the time she had joined them they were already seated by the table loaded with hot delicious bread, fresh oranges, boiled eggs and pots of foaming chocolate.

Charlotte enjoyed those first few weeks of settling in. At the start she deferred decisions to Clive or Lucy but her cousin, who had never in his life exerted himself domestically, was soon out and about making friends with the English residents to whom he had been given letters of introduction, and Lucy, very shy of the servants whom she could not understand, was only too happy to lie reading and dozing in the sunshine leaving everything in Charlotte's hands. She decided which room should be Clive's studio and which their sitting room. She set out the books and possessions they had brought with them and found pleasure in making the little house homely and comfortable. In addition to Juanita and Rosa, there was Jaime, a little gnome-like man who performed a number of mysterious odd jobs, cared for the garden and established a sort of guarded truce with Clive's valet. Matthew had been employed at Breakstone all his life. He was older than Clive, sensible, down-to-earth and reliable. On the ship he had been decidedly wary of Charlotte but she with experience of regimental sergeant majors treated him with a pretty deference that soon had him eating out of her hand.

She discovered very soon that the Spanish dishes prepared by Rosa which she and Clive enjoyed did not suit Lucy's capricious appetite and after a few days decided to do some of the marketing herself. The servants, especially Rosa, were inclined to be touchy and resentful of criticism. She had to employ all her tact until, impressed by an *Inglesa* who could actually speak their own language and regarding Lucy with a kind of scornful pity, they excelled themselves in preparing dainty meals solely for her benefit.

"The Señora Lucia is a poor pretty thing, no wife for such a fine strong husband," confided Juanita to her cronies in the market. She had a great admiration for Clive's athletic figure and fair colouring. "He should have wed the Señorita Carlotta. She has the spirit of a lion."

One morning when they had been in Seville for about a fortnight Clive came back at noon bringing with him a certain Geoffrey Robinson, the English Vice-Consul in the city. He was a plain, sensible, little man with a pleasant manner.

Juanita brought wine and biscuits and Clive said cheerfully, "Mr Robinson is putting me on to someone who can supply us with a carriage and horses. In that way we can start taking some drives around the countryside. You'll enjoy that, won't you, Lucy?"

"My wife can help you there. She is an excellent organizer when it comes to picnics," said Mr Robinson. "She thought to give you a little time to settle in before she called on you but if you would care for her advice, she would be only too pleased."

"Oh we would above all things," exclaimed Lucy. "We're so anxious to see everything. My husband is an artist, Mr Robinson, so naturally he is very interested."

"So I gathered." Mr Robinson paused for a moment. "I would advise you however to make a few enquiries before you venture far into the Sierra. There have been incidents."

"What kind of incidents?" asked Charlotte with a vivid memory of what Don Lorenzo had said to her that morning on the ship.

41

"Perhaps I had better explain a little. You must understan that when King Ferdinand died, the succession naturally enough went to his infant daughter Isobel, with her mother, Maria Cristina, acting as Regent. But the King had a younger brother, Don Carlos, and there are certain elements in the country who would prefer the throne to go to him rather than to a child Queen."

"Surely these internal quarrels cannot affect us in any way," said Clive a little impatiently.

"Not directly of course, but it goes deeper than perhaps you realize. Ferdinand, while he lived, kept an iron hand over his country and certain of the leading ministers who were liberal in outlook attempted to interfere with disastrous results. A party led by an Englishman recklessly landed not far from here in support of their cause. The Spanish may grumble about their rulers but that does not prevent them greatly disliking foreign interference. The whole party were taken prisoner and I regret to say summarily executed."

There was a shocked silence before Lucy whispered, "All of them? But that is terrible."

"We protested of course but there was nothing we could do. To gain as much support for her baby daughter as possible Maria Cristina has opened the doors to a more liberal government while those who support Don Carlos are fiercely Catholic and conservative. They would wish to revive the old despotism and even reintroduce the Inquisition. Some of these so-called Carlists have allied themselves with the most unsavoury elements of society and there have been one or two cases of foreigners being kidnapped by bandits and held up for ransom."

"You will make us believe we are living in the midst of a melodrama," said Clive dryly.

"Everything in Spain is apt to be larger than life," went on Mr Robinson and then smiled at Charlotte and Lucy. "Don't be alarmed, ladies, down here in Andalusia there is little chance of any danger but it is worth bearing in mind perhaps when planning more distant expeditions."

Although he spoke lightly, Charlotte wondered if he meant his advice to be taken seriously. "Are you by any chance acquainted with the Marqués Lorenzo de Merenda?" she asked.

Mr Robinson looked surprised. "Why should you ask that, Miss Starr?"

"He was a fellow we happened to meet on the ship coming over here," said Clive.

"I have met him certainly but I wouldn't say I know him well. He is not often in Seville and takes little part in the social life of the city. He lives at the Castillo de Palomas which is about ten miles north of here on the edge of the Sierra."

Castle of Doves, thought Charlotte, what a lovely name and somehow unexpected when she remembered the dark hawk-like face of its owner.

"Is he married?" enquired Lucy with a quick grin at Charlotte.

"No. From what I've heard he has had a pretty hard time of it. His father died in the Napoleonic war leaving him head of his house at fourteen with a younger brother and sister as well as a grandmother to support from largely ruined estates. It can't have been easy." He rose to his feet putting down his glass. "Now I really must be going."

"Won't you take luncheon with us?" asked Lucy.

"Thank you, no. My wife will be expecting me but we will meet again very soon, I hope. My daughter will be coming to join us during the summer. She will be delighted to meet such charming additions to our little group out here."

Clive went with him to the door and Lucy turned a mischievous face to Charlotte. "Well, so much for our noble Corsair. Do you think Mr Robinson could contrive an invitation for us to the Castillo de Palomas?"

"Lucy, what *are* you talking about?"

"I think he sounds very intriguing and it would give you a splendid opportunity to meet that nice Mr Macalister again, wouldn't it?"

Then Clive came back very much inclined to disregard Mr Robinson's solemn warnings. "He probably thinks it is his consular duty to scare us off," he said easily. "I don't think we need worry ourselves unduly. I know my way about. I had plenty of contacts before we left England."

"What kind of contacts?" asked Charlotte.

"Men I met, Spaniards at the embassy in London and elsewhere. As a matter of interest some of them were strongly in favour of this Don Carlos. It seems this Queen Regent can be a bit of a tartar."

"You seem to know a lot about it."

He shrugged his shoulders. "Only what I picked up here and there. It's not really our concern, is it?"

"No, I suppose not."

She thought about it for a day or two and then in all the interests of this new life completely forgot it until something happened that lent substance to Mr Robinson's warnings.

Margaret Robinson, middle-aged and eminently respectable, duly came to take tea with them and expressed shocked disapproval of Charlotte taking such pleasure in walking alone through the streets of Seville.

"The Spanish are often good-hearted enough but *most* unreliable," she said. "Believe me, I've had experience. You don't know what you might meet. You should take Juanita with you or your manservant."

Charlotte smiled, agreed, and took absolutely no notice. She loved the colour and life of the market, the stalls piled high with fruit and vegetables, the squawking chickens, the bleating lambs brought in by the hill farmers, the donkeys with their packs, their bridles hung with multi-coloured tassels. She enjoyed seeing the surprise on their faces when she spoke to them in Spanish and was captivated by their friendliness and good humour. They were poor and they drove a hard bargain but they were sturdy and self-reliant and it made her feel that in this way she was getting to know the real Spain.

One morning, her shopping done and her basket full, she thought she might go into the Cathedral for a few minutes. She could see in front of her the enormous tower of the Giralda, pink in the sun with its fretted stonework and bell chamber which had once been a minaret. History had been made here, linking Spain and England. King Pedro's daughter, Constance, had married John of Gaunt, Shakespeare's time-honoured Lancaster. The Black Prince's ruby in the English crown had come originally from the infidel King Abu Said of Granada.

She loved the cool twilight of the huge Gothic Cathedral. Candles flickered in the side chapels gleaming on the gold of crowned Virgins and the embroidered robes of innumerable saints, the Aztec gold brought back by Cortés from the conquest of Mexico. The air was heavy with incense from the early morning masses. She stood still for a moment. Here and there black veiled women knelt, rosary beads slipping through their

44

fingers. She said a quick prayer for Lucy, for Clive and even spared a thought for the dark man who had linked himself in such a queer way with the portrait that lay at the bottom of her trunk.

When she came out of the great doors, the brilliant sunshine dazzled her so that she shut her eyes for a moment. When she opened them, she saw that a young man was running down the street towards the Cathedral followed by a rabble of screaming hooligans. She recognized him as he came nearer. It was Tomás, the big shambling nephew of Jaime who sometimes came to help his uncle in the garden and whom she had thought more than once was not quite right in the head.

He stumbled as he reached the steps and fell almost at her feet, gasping for breath, his chest heaving. Screams and curses were being hurled at him and someone threw a stone that struck him on the cheek. He cried out, one hand flying to the blood that trickled into his mouth. Furious with anger at such wanton cruelty Charlotte stepped in front of him.

"Stop!" she shouted at them in Spanish. "Stop! What are you doing? He is hurt."

They answered with a roar in which she distinguished the word *pérfido* – surely this poor idiot could never be a traitor. She stooped over the boy whispering urgently.

"Run – quickly – into the Cathedral. You'll be safe in there," but he only crouched lower, too terrified to move.

She looked around her desperately. In a moment she could be thrust aside and then what might happen? Murder could be done. The boldest among them had begun to surge forward when there was a clatter of horses' hooves. Two men came galloping down the street. They thrust ruthlessly through the mob and dismounted. Strong hands clamped around her waist and lifted her to one side and the Marqués de Merenda was standing in her place, tall and formidable, scorching the rabble with blistering words that left no doubt of his anger and contempt. They obviously stood in some awe of him and after a little began to slink away muttering and grumbling among themselves.

He watched them disperse before he turned to the boy who still huddled, white-faced and shivering, on the Cathedral steps. He pulled him to his feet.

"Are you hurt?" The boy shook his head dumbly. "Then get

45

back to your mother and don't go running about the city causing trouble."

"But it is true what I told them," he said, stumbling over the words. "It is true, Señor, every word of it. It is being spoken of everywhere."

The hand on his shoulder tightened. "What is being spoken of and by whom?"

"Men, many men, in the *posada* and in the cafés – they say the Carlists are coming soon and when they take Seville, we must join with them and then everything will be different for us – we shall be rich."

Don Lorenzo frowned. "Listen to me. It is not true. It is wicked lies. If the Carlists come, then it will be war, do you understand? The streets of Seville will run with blood. So keep your mouth shut and take no heed of men who boast of what they do not know. Now go and give this to your mother." He felt in his pocket and tossed a coin to the boy. "Go, go now and quickly."

"*Gracias, Señor, gracias.*"

He ran off clutching the coin, the vacant face lighting up with a smile, his terror forgotten.

Lorenzo looked after him before he turned to Charlotte.

"They did not touch you."

She shook her head. "No, but I don't know what might have happened if you had not come when you did."

"Didn't I warn you that there could be trouble? The fact that you happen to be British won't always protect you."

"I had to do something," she said indignantly. "They were stoning him. It could have been serious."

"Perhaps, but it is not your quarrel and we don't care for foreigners interfering in our affairs. Do you always do your marketing alone? Don't you take one of your servants with you?"

"Jaime is busy with the garden and Juanita has her duties. In any case I like to walk alone, then I can please myself." She raised her chin defiantly. "I am not afraid."

"I can see that," he replied ironically. "But a little prudence is only good sense."

It had shocked her that the good-hearted laughing people she saw daily in the market could behave so savagely. "Why? Why did they turn on that poor boy so brutally?"

46

"Fear," he said. "Men who are afraid must have a scapegoat, so they turn on the helpless who can't fight back."

"But it is not true, is it, that the Carlists are coming here?"

"Let us hope not."

"If they did, what would you do?" she asked curiously.

"That is a question I prefer not to answer. Let us say that I do not approve of war for any cause. I have other and more important things to concern me."

He beckoned to his companion who had handed the reins of the horses to one of the ragged urchins who haunted the gutters and was picking up the fruit that had rolled from her basket when she had hurriedly dropped it on the steps.

"May I present my brother? Roberto, you will escort the Señorita Carlotta to the Casa de Fuente."

"You know where we live?"

"Certainly. Most things are reported to me. I'll take the horses with me. I must see the *Alcalde* about this stupid affair. You can meet me there, Roberto. Take more care in future, Señorita. You may not always escape so easily."

He bowed, vaulted into the saddle, took the bridle of the second horse and trotted down the street.

She was irritated by his calm air of command and turned an icy look on the young man waiting for her. He was considerably younger than his brother. In his early twenties, she judged, not so forbiddingly handsome but with an open friendly look, laughing eyes and a disarming grin.

"I am perfectly capable of seeing myself home," she said coldly. "Please do not trouble yourself."

"I am sure you are," he said, "but when Lorenzo says jump, then we all jump."

"I don't."

"You will, Señorita, you will."

Then unexpectedly they both laughed. "Let me carry your basket," he said and took it from her.

They arrived back at the house on quite friendly terms with one another to find Clive and Lucy sitting in the garden. She introduced him giving him a warning glance as she slid lightly over the incident outside the Cathedral. He took her meaning as he bowed over Lucy's hand while Clive eyed him doubtfully. His English was not so fluent as his brother's but he had an

47

engaging manner and with Charlotte's help they were soon getting on famously.

Even Clive unbent after a while and mentioned that he was looking for good riding horses. Roberto responded at once.

"In that case you must come and visit us at the Castillo. We have a number of horses, real Andalusians and they are among the best to be found in Spain. Lorenzo will advise you. He is an excellent judge of horses."

"We are told that the Marqués does not care for company," said Lucy looking up at him demurely under her long lashes.

It was amusing, thought Charlotte, to see how Lucy's artless charm was beguiling the young man. In her gown of white muslin with blue ribbons in her hair she looked enchantingly pretty and he could not take his eyes from her.

"Don't let that disturb you," he said earnestly. "Lorenzo is not always there and I will ask my grandmother to send you an invitation. My sister Teresa will enjoy meeting you and your cousin."

His eagerness was so apparent, the suggestion so pressing, that Charlotte wondered if his brother's stern rule was not appreciated by the brother and sister and they sought every opportunity to rebel against it.

Very soon Roberto excused himself. "I must go. Lorenzo will be expecting me."

"And he doesn't care to be kept waiting," murmured Charlotte, "isn't that so?"

"I am afraid it is," said the young man with a rueful grin. "But you will come, won't you?" he went on as she went with him to the door.

"If my cousin agrees, then we will come," she assured him.

"You and the Señora Lucia."

"Yes, of course, both of us."

She smiled at him as he pressed her hand and hurried away down the street.

"I reckon that's the last we shall see of that young man," Clive was saying when she rejoined them in the garden. "Robinson tells me that the Marqués de Merenda keeps a tight hold over his family and has a particular dislike of the British. In any case I have no wish to go cap-in-hand to one of these Spanish grandees with their fine manners and touchy pride. I would not be beholden to any man."

"Mr Robinson doesn't know everything," said Lucy with unusual spirit. "I liked Don Roberto. I thought him quite charming and if we are invited, then Charlotte and I will certainly go, without you if necessary."

"Hoity-toity – you've a great deal to say for yourself for once, my dear."

"And why shouldn't I? Surely I can please myself occasionally."

And that is the very first time I've ever heard her speak up for herself, thought Charlotte. The obvious admiration of that young man has done her a world of good and Clive doesn't know what to make of it.

That evening she took the Spanish portrait from the bottom of her trunk where it had been hidden ever since they arrived in Spain. Looking at it again she wondered why she had ever thought it bore any resemblance to Don Lorenzo and yet as she turned it this way and that in the candlelight, there *was* something indefinable, something that was there for an instant and then vanished so that she was unsure whether it was real or imaginary.

She spread out the stained handkerchief to wrap it up again and noticed that something had been embroidered in the corner. Tiny stitches by some loving hand had outlined a capital L with what was perhaps a crest. She studied it under the light and saw it was a bird in flight, a dove, emblem of peace, the bird that had brought the olive branch to Noah after the flood. *Paloma* – a dove – she took a deep breath. Was it possible? Her father and Don Lorenzo? No, he could only have been a boy at that time. Then who? His father? And he hated the British. Suddenly for some inexplicable reason she was afraid as if she had touched on something dangerous, as if somehow the past could destroy the present. She wrapped the portrait up again and hid it in her trunk under the black dresses she had refused to wear any longer. She did not want to know whose blood had stained the white linen or why. Better that it should lie there forgotten.

4

It was several weeks later and the middle of March before a lean, brown-faced man rode up to the door of the Casa de Fuente and delivered a letter for the Señora Lucia Starr giving Juanita to understand that he would await a reply.

With some excitement Lucy and Charlotte pored over it together. On thick white crested paper and in stiff formal English, the Marquésa de Merenda requested the pleasure of their company for luncheon at the Castillo de Palomas.

Lucy looked up, her eyes dancing. "Clive has kept on saying that nothing would come of it but I knew Roberto would not forget. This must be from his grandmother. I shall write at once and accept for all three of us."

"Supposing Clive refuses to go?"

"Then you and I will go togesher and make excuses for him. Matthew can drive the carriage."

So the letter was written and handed over to the messenger and Clive was informed of their decision when he returned that evening. Not altogether surprisingly he immediately flew into a rage. He did not care for his womenfolk to decide anything without consulting him first.

"Go if you must," he stormed at the two girls, "but I'm hanged if I'm going to run hither and thither at the beck and call of some jumped-up Marquésa."

"Don't go into a tantrum, Clive, just because for once we did not wait to ask you," said Charlotte soothingly, as if he were no more than a fractious child. "And as for jumped-up, as far as I can gather from your Mr Robinson, the Merendas were grandees when our ancestors were still shop-keepers."

"Oh hell, Charlie, what a thing to say!" he grumbled.

"It's true and I'm not ashamed of it even if you are," she went on sturdily and exchanged a smile with Lucy.

He went on protesting that he had no intention of crawling to any high and mighty Spaniard and then when the day came,

50

descended the stairs impeccably dressed, took the reins from Matthew and off they drove to Lucy's great relief and Charlotte's secret amusement.

Spring had come in all its glory to Andalusia and the warm air was fragrant with the scent of thyme and juniper as the carriage jogged slowly up the rough mountain track. The cistus was in bloom, great purple-pink flowers blowing in the breeze. On either side there were green pastures where sheep grazed. They climbed through a grove of olive trees with their grey-green leaves and queer tortured branches, then they could see beyond to the mountains of the Sierra with their snow peaks providing a magnificently theatrical backdrop to the Castillo de Palomas.

"How very pretty it is!" exclaimed Lucy but Charlotte shook her head.

It was not pretty at all, it was breathtakingly beautiful with something wild and elemental about it that all the attempts at civilisation had still not been able to subdue. Part Moorish castle, part long low white house, it seemed to stretch in all directions. On the carefully tended grass in front of the great pillared doorway, doves circled and fluttered in dizzying arcs.

Servants sprang to take the horses as Clive brought the carriage to a standstill and jumped down. An elderly man came down the steps, greeted them with dignity and ushered them into a cool dark hall. A staircase with a gilded iron balustrade led to upper floors and a great bowl of orange blossom scented the air. They followed him across the tiled floor through a door at the back and into a large room flooded with sunshine, the walls white, the antique furniture sombrely splendid.

An elderly lady rose to greet them dressed in rustling black silk, a mantilla of fine lace on the white hair. Doña Gracia, Marquésa de Merenda, was in her late sixties, still slim and upright, her fine-boned face showing the remnants of beauty.

"Welcome to the Castillo," she said in slow careful English.

Clive, prepared to be offhand, was impressed in spite of himself. He bowed over the thin hand extended to him and presented his wife and cousin.

The Marquésa's dark eyes roved from one to the other, resting on Charlotte so that she had a fleeting impression of a powerful interest penetrating deep into her very soul. Then it vanished and she thought she must have imagined it. Doña Gracia was

51

smiling. She beckoned to the girl who stood just behind her chair.

"My granddaughter Teresa."

At first glance she was quite unlike her brothers. Bright brown hair framed a small proud head. In her simple white muslin dress she looked no more than eighteen. She stared at them, her face pale, a little mutinous. Charlotte wondered if there had been argument over something that morning and thought she would not have cared to tangle with that formidable old lady.

Then they moved through the long windows out on to the patio where tables and chairs had been set out. Flowers climbed up pillars, framed arches and spilled out of gigantic tubs, and everywhere there was the cool sound of water trickling into stone pools. Servants brought wine, pale golden sherry in fine thin glasses, the sweet Manzanilla and the iced fruit drink called *agraz* made of pounded unripe grapes, sugar and water which Lucy had recently discovered and loved. With the servants came Roberto taking their hands in welcome and immediately seating himself beside Lucy, much to Clive's annoyance.

The Marquésa had exchanged a glance with him as he came in. She said apologetically, "Forgive the absence of my elder grandson. Lorenzo, I hope, will join us later."

There was a gracious charm about the old house, about the Marquésa herself, the peaceful flower-laden garden, the doves that came floating down when Teresa crumbled a wine biscuit for them, and yet Charlotte was aware of a tension, a stillness when conversation lapsed, a sense of expectancy which she would have found hard to explain.

The butler came and whispered to the Marquésa and she rose to her feet.

"Very well, Marco, since luncheon is ready, we will not wait for Don Lorenzo."

The men had risen with her and she stretched out a hand to Clive. "Shall we lead the way, Señor Starr?"

Roberto offered his arm to Lucy and Teresa fell into step beside Charlotte.

"Bravo for Grandmother," she whispered. "Lorenzo will be so angry."

"Do you always have to wait for your brother?" asked Charlotte.

"Always when he is at home," said Teresa, "but not this time," and she gave a little skip.

When Lorenzo says jump, we all jump, Roberto had said, thought Charlotte. Mr Robinson was apparently right and the Castle of Doves was ruled by an iron hand. It seemed so absurd in these days that she had a regrettable desire to giggle. By the time they reached the cool dining room carefully shaded against the glare of the sun, her curiosity to see this domestic tyrant lording it in his own home had risen to fever pitch.

Lorenzo had come late to luncheon for a variety of reasons. To start with he had strongly opposed his grandmother when, in response to Roberto's prompting, she had suggested inviting the English party to the Castillo.

"You are opening the door to what could turn out to be a most undesirable friendship," he had said. "They are not our kind of people."

"What *are* our kind of people?" retorted Roberto ironically.

"For one thing, they are English . . ."

"Oh you and your prejudices! Must we live with them for ever? Because I happen to like them, you have made up your mind they are not suitable friends for us. I'm not a boy any longer, Lorenzo, and it is about time you realized it," and the young man had flung out of the room.

"For once your brother is right," said his grandmother when the door had slammed behind him. "If you wish to live like a hermit that is your own affair, Lorenzo, but you cannot expect Roberto and Teresa to do the same. They are young, they want to meet people, enjoy themselves. I know you grieved for Manuela but that is some years ago now. You must put it behind you. And as for the rest – what happened in the past is over and done with. How many times must I say this to you? If I can forget it, then so can you."

"And supposing I can't? Every time I look at Teresa, I am reminded of it."

"And so you are deliberately unjust to her and she rebels against it. If trouble comes, then you will only have yourself to blame, Lorenzo."

"Very well," he said at last. "Do what you please. I only hope we won't regret it."

So the invitation was sent and he was thinking about it as

53

he stripped off the sheepskin jacket he wore in the fields, washed his hands, changed his shirt and ran a comb through the thick dark hair. He would far rather have been eating bread, cheese and olives with his shepherds than spending a couple of hours in trivial small talk and afterwards showing off his finely bred horses to an overdressed young man whose behaviour had not impressed him on the ship from England.

The *gazpacho*, a delicious soup of onions, cucumbers and tomatoes fragrant with herbs, was already being served when he came into the dining room bringing with him a breath of the mountains outside, a sense of drama, so that everyone, it seemed to Charlotte, was immediately aware of him. He kissed his grandmother's hand, apologised for being late, bowed courteously to his guests and took his place at the head of the table with Charlotte on his right and Clive on his left.

The contrast between the two men was so strong that it came as a shock. Clive whom she had admired for so long, dressed in the very height of elegance, seemed somehow to have shrunk, to have become insignificant beside Don Lorenzo still in breeches and boots, with the scarlet silk scarf knotted in the neck of the dazzlingly white shirt, his only concession to convention the finely embroidered short black jacket. She did not know what she had expected after their last meeting, a grim-faced ogre perhaps, and found instead an exceedingly attractive man who spoke with charm and an exquisite courtesy.

"Forgive me for coming to the table in my working clothes," he said, "but I have been out with the shepherds since dawn. They are beginning to lead the flocks to the upper pastures."

"Do they always do that in the spring?" asked Charlotte.

"Usually in March as soon as lambing is over, so as to avoid the heat of the summer. It is a lengthy business since the opportunity is taken to count and brand them."

"But isn't it dangerous? Mr Robinson told us that there are wolves on the upper slopes of the Sierra and lynx and wild boars."

He smiled. "They have the dogs to guard them and the wolves retreat during the great heat. It is only in the winter when they are hungry that they come down the mountains."

"Is it possible to ride up into the Sierra?" asked Charlotte eagerly. "I should so much like to see something of the country up there."

"Yes, it is possible if you have the right horses, but it is very rough going, not at all suitable for a young lady such as yourself."

"Why not? Roberto told me that your sister sometimes goes up with him on such expeditions."

"That is different. Teresa was born to it." She sensed a withdrawal in his tone which she took for contempt and was furiously indignant but he had already turned to Clive. "I understand that you have had some difficulty in obtaining horses to suit you."

"Yes, those offered to me were beasts I wouldn't touch with a barge pole."

Lorenzo raised his eyebrows. "This is an expression I have not met before."

"It means I have no intention of wasting good money on them. At home in England my father bred only blood horses."

"You do not need a racehorse to climb mountains," said Lorenzo dryly. "I don't usually sell my horses but I may be able to oblige you. I have had some of the most suitable brought down from the paddocks into the stables. We will go later and look them over."

"May I come?" asked Charlotte.

"I thought ladies usually took a siesta after luncheon."

"I don't and I like horses. I used to ride with my father."

"The father who taught you Spanish?"

"Yes."

His eyes dwelled on her for an instant with a curious questioning look, then he shrugged his shoulders.

"Come if you wish, Señorita. It is not far from the house."

After luncheon was over and coffee had been served to them on the patio, Lorenzo rose to his feet. Conversation had been necessarily rather slow and stilted since he was the only one of the family who spoke English with real fluency and Charlotte sensed an impatience in his manner as if he would be glad to have the whole affair over and done with.

"Shall we go and take a look at the horses?" he said to Clive.

"Certainly." The young man rose with his lazy grace and glanced towards Lucy. "Will you come with us, my dear?"

"No, Clive, thank you. You know how horses terrify me. I shall be much happier here. Charlotte will go, won't you?"

"Yes, I'd like to."

"In that case I shall remain with Doña Lucia," said Roberto gaily. "I can show her the Nun's garden while Grandmother has her afternoon siesta."

Clive frowned but made no comment and Teresa who had sat for the most part in a sullen silence jumped up with alacrity and slipped an arm through that of Charlotte.

"I think I shall come too. You don't mind, do you, Lorenzo?"

"Why should I?" he said curtly.

They started off together, the two men going ahead and Charlotte following with Teresa.

"What did Roberto mean by the Nun's garden?" she asked as they crossed the patio.

"It's the oldest part of the house with a walled garden. Roberto will enjoy showing it to her and relating the legend. I think he has a 'crush' on your cousin's wife," she said mischievously.

"Where did you learn your English?" said Charlotte considerably surprised since during luncheon and afterwards Teresa had seemed to take no interest at all in their conversation.

"At the Convent. There were some English girls. That was two years ago and sometimes I think I had more fun there than I have now." She sighed. "I thought it was going to be so wonderful when I came home. Grandmother had promised that I would have a season in Madrid. She was going to present me at Court and there would have been balls and parties, all kinds of marvellous things. Then the King died and everybody went into mourning for a whole year so we came here. I can't tell you how boring it is. Lorenzo is so strict. He is more interested in his sheep and his horses and his vineyards than entertaining. We hardly see anyone."

"But now the mourning is over, it will be different. You will go back to Madrid."

"No, we won't," she went on gloomily. "The house is shut up. Everyone is terribly afraid of a war now that Don Carlos has come back from exile and is claiming the throne for himself. No one really knows what is going to happen and Lorenzo says it is better for all of us if we stay here." She kicked irritably at a stone on their path and sent it spinning away.

Walking through the peaceful garden so full of the scents of spring, Charlotte could not imagine how anyone could possibly wish to disrupt such a beautiful country with the horrors of

56

civil war, not yet realizing that Spain was a land of proud, passionate people who would fight to the death for an idea or a principle they believed in, a country where the Inquisition had once killed men and women hideously in a passionate desire to save their souls from eternal damnation.

They had reached the stableyard by now which, unlike some of the places she had already seen in Seville and elsewhere, was clean and tidy and extremely well maintained. Don Lorenzo obviously kept tight hold of his stable staff. The grooms had led out several horses. They were exceptionally beautiful, sturdier than the English bloodstock, with proudly arched necks and long flowing manes and tails. While the men stood looking them over and discussing various points, Teresa took Charlotte along one side of the stalls where inquisitive heads peered at them over the half doors. Charlotte, remembering her beloved Whitefoot with regret, was enchanted with them. One in particular, the colour of a ripe chestnut, tossed a proud narrow head and permitted her to fondle the soft nose with the air of a princess bestowing a favour on a lowly admirer.

"That is Zelda," said Teresa casually. "Lorenzo rode her at the *Fiesta de Toros* in Madrid four years ago."

"*Fiesta de Toros* – is that the bull fight?" asked Charlotte incredulously. "Your brother took part in a bull fight?"

"Oh *Dios*, not the *corrida*, not that kind of bull fight. He despises it. Entertainment fit only for the vulgar, he calls it. The *Fiesta de Toros* is something quite different. It is fighting the bull on horseback as it was performed hundreds and hundreds of years ago. There's a society that still keeps the sport alive and he is one of the most influential members. It is only performed now on very important occasions indeed and this was a great festivity in Madrid when King Ferdinand's daughter was born and he summoned all the noble families to swear allegiance to her. We were allowed out of the Convent to watch. All the girls were crazy about Lorenzo. He does ride rather well," she said grudgingly, "I'll allow him that."

"Don't you like your brother?"

"Sometimes," Teresa looked away. "Only I don't think he likes me."

"What a strange thing to say."

"It's true though. If you're interested in the bull fight, Roberto will tell you all about it. They practise up here some-

57

times. It's all rather slow and stately, not at all like the *corrida*. That's really thrilling. Roberto took me once – Lorenzo would have been furious if he'd known – it was in Madrid last year and Don Vicente was fighting. He is a famous matador. I saw him kill the bull." Her eyes were shining with hero worship and Charlotte smiled. Teresa might be eighteen but she was still very much of a schoolgirl. She was reminded of herself in the year she had fallen so desperately in love with Clive and she felt an instant sympathy.

"Everyone was throwing down flowers and favours. I tossed him my scarf," went on Teresa dreamily, "and he wore it bound round his arm. I met him afterwards. Roberto took me to a party and he was there. He is marvellously handsome and so brave. We danced together just once but it was absolute heaven and all the girls envied me."

"Have you seen him since?"

"Once or twice." Teresa glanced at her suspiciously as if she realized suddenly she had been talking far too freely to a complete stranger. "He has come to Seville occasionally and we do have some friends in the city whom I am allowed to visit. As a matter of fact he is here now. In a few weeks it will be Easter and after the Holy Week processions there will be the *Feria* and the bull fight."

"Will you be attending the festivities?"

"I don't suppose so. Lorenzo does not think it suitable for a properly brought up Spanish girl."

"What does your Grandmother feel about it?"

"She always agrees with him. He has been head of the house ever since my father died and I wasn't even born then."

"And your mother?"

"I never knew her. She died when I was a baby."

It couldn't have been easy for this young girl growing up with only her grandmother as a buffer against two elder brothers. Charlotte would have said something sympathetic but now the grooms were saddling two of the horses and Lorenzo came towards them.

"We are going for a short ride. Señor Starr would like to try out their paces. Perhaps you would take the Señorita back to the house, Teresa."

"Yes, Lorenzo, of course," she said demurely. "Enjoy your ride."

58

The girls watched as the two men swung themselves into the saddle and trotted out of the courtyard.

"He doesn't ride badly, your cousin," said Teresa critically.

"He is considered an excellent horseman," said Charlotte defensively. "We rode and hunted together a great deal at his father's house in England."

"Is he in love with you?"

Charlotte gasped. "No, of course not. Whatever made you say such a thing?"

Teresa shrugged. "I don't know. He does not seem to care very much for his wife though she is so very pretty."

It gave Charlotte a jolt that this young girl should have perceived so much so quickly but before she could say anything further, Teresa proved even more surprising.

"Shall we be like them? Shall *we* take a little ride and try out their paces?" she said mimicking her brother's phrase with a mischievous glint in her eyes.

Charlotte looked down at her flowered cotton skirts. "How can we – in these clothes?"

Teresa brushed that aside carelessly. "Why not? I've done it before. We won't go far. Just for the fun of the thing. Wouldn't you like to ride Zelda?"

"Yes, I would, very much."

"Well then, what's stopping us? Let's go."

It was curious to feel that this young girl had the same daredevil spirit as herself. She was sorely tempted even though she did try to protest.

"Do you really think we should? Won't your brother be angry?"

"He won't know till afterwards."

Teresa had already summoned one of the stable lads and commanded him imperiously to get the horses ready. He argued volubly that the Marqués would have the skin off his back for it if he were to find out but she swept his objections aside with a wave of her hand and at last reluctantly he did as he was told. The horses were led out and saddled. The ladies were given a hand to mount and under the admiring gaze of the whole stableyard, they were soon trotting out of the courtyard and down a path that led across the park. They passed through a grove of ilex with their rich foliage and then were out on a long grassy stretch. It was the first time Charlotte had ridden since leaving England and the springing step of the mare entranced her.

For a few minutes they rode side by side then Teresa pulled up. "You can ride around the field and then return," she said. "You can't go wrong, but I'm taking a different path. I'll join you later."

She cantered away down a side alley taking Charlotte by surprise so that she began to wonder if this was part of some deep laid plot on Teresa's part in which she was playing a secondary role. She had a sudden suspicion that the girl was hoping to meet someone forbidden entry to the Castillo and had seized her chance. For an instant she wondered if she ought to follow after her but it was not her responsibility and the sheer joy of being alone and free possessed her. Zelda was lengthening her stride and, filled with a sense of adventure, she did not stop her. Soon they were flying along at a great pace, the wind in her hair, her thin cotton skirts blowing wildly around her. On and on up the slope they went, her heart singing with sheer pleasure, and quite oblivious of the shout behind her and the sound of pounding hooves following after her.

Zelda soared over a gate and they flew on until at the crest of the hill Lorenzo reached her side. He leaned over taking hold of the reins. She was so angry that he should believe the horse was running away with her that she hit out at him wildly but he did not relax his grip and slowly brought both horses to a standstill. They faced one another panting.

"What the devil do you think you are doing?" he said furiously.

"And why the devil did you stop me?" she retorted with equal fury. "Zelda was not bolting. I had her under control. I could have stopped her any time I wished."

"*Madre de Dios*, but I believe you could," he said with reluctant admiration, "but it wasn't just that. Look!"

He pointed ahead and then she saw what he meant. She had jumped a gate into an enclosed paddock and on the opposite side stood a bull, black, formidable, like no bull she had ever seen in England. Even at a distance she could see the look of suspicion, the lowered head with the great horns, the angrily lashing tail.

"At any moment he is about to charge," said Lorenzo dryly. "Discretion is the better part of valour. Gently does it."

Slowly they turned the horses. He gave a quick look behind and said, "Now, ride like hell!"

Then they were over the gate and panting down the slope and heard rather than saw the bull career across the grass and charge against the strong fence with a crash that sent a shiver up her spine.

He glanced down at her. "Do you realize now how rash you've been? Have you ever seen a powerful bull in action?"

"No, never."

"It could have been you instead of the gatepost."

"I never thought . . ." she stammered.

"This crazy escapade was Teresa's idea, I presume."

"Don't be angry with her," said Charlotte quickly. "Believe me, I didn't need any persuasion."

He frowned. "All the same she had no right to suggest such a thing. Anything could have happened. You could have been killed. My sister always acts without thinking. One day it's going to cause real trouble. Where is she by the way?"

"I think she took a different path. I'm afraid I just let Zelda have her head – I didn't really notice." She glanced up at him. "Don't you think you're a little hard on her?"

"And don't you think you need to know us a little better before passing judgement?" he said dryly.

"I'm sorry. That was impertinent of me."

She had flushed at his rebuke and quite suddenly he wished he hadn't said it. This young Englishwoman with her sturdy independence, her bold manner, was everything he most disliked, he told himself. Women should be like Manuela had been, beautiful, gentle, loving and submissive, or should they? It struck him uncomfortably that in time he might have found that sweetness cloying and looked for something more tart, more unexpected. He pushed the disloyal thought away from him angrily. To remember her still gave him pain. Damnation, he thought irritably, what was wrong with him to be thinking of such a thing now?

Charlotte looked across at the unsmiling profile presented to her and said apologetically, "I hope you're not angry with me for taking Zelda. Teresa told me that you rode her at the *Fiesta de Toros*."

"Yes, I did. A horse has to be trained especially for these

events but that was some years ago, she is a little lightweight for me now."

"I never realized that you could fight a bull on horseback," she said wonderingly. "Isn't it dangerous?"

"No more than any other sport. It is the original art, the ancient form in which the bull was fought from earliest times when the Hapsburgs ruled Spain. It was the coming of the Bourbon Philip over a hundred years ago now that killed it. The Court was taken over by French courtiers who condemned it as barbarous preferring softer, easier accomplishments. In that way it was stripped of its noble origins and since no Spaniard will give up his bull fight, it has descended into vulgar butchery where the matador fights not for honour but for money."

"And you don't approve?"

"I neither approve nor disapprove. I simply think it is a tragedy that what was once a skill of very high quality should have turned into a sport appealing to the most bloodthirsty instincts of the mob."

"My father told me that every little Spanish boy dreams of becoming a bull fighter."

"Not all," he said. "I don't think I did." He suddenly turned to her with his attractive smile. "And so ends the first lecture. You must forgive me boring you with my own prejudices. I have been told in my turn that all Englishwomen who come to Spain long to see a *corrida* above everything."

"Then you've been told wrong. The English love all animals. I've no wish to see a bull slaughtered or horses tortured."

"Or a handsome matador gored by the great horns. It does happen you know," he said ironically, "and yet you hunt foxes, I believe, and watch them being torn to pieces by the hounds."

"That's different," she said flushing.

"Is it? A bull has at least a chance of fighting back and occasionally even winning. A pity you feel like that since I was about to suggest that you and your cousins might care to watch a combat on horseback. The *Rejoneadores* who are devoted to keeping the art alive will be meeting here shortly. There has been a suggestion that the Queen Regent would like to hold a Fiesta in honour of her daughter Isobel later in the year. Would you care to come if we promise not to kill the bull?"

She felt that in some obscure way he was laughing at her but she said, "I'm sure that Clive will be deeply interested."

62

"And you?"

"Naturally Lucy and I will be pleased to accompany him."

He could not think why he was handing out invitations to these British visitors whom only a few days before he had wished never to see again. It was just that there was a touch of gallantry about this young woman, the way she had faced up to him, the quite splendid way she had controlled a spirited horse in the most unsuitable clothes on an unfamiliar saddle and, against his will, it intrigued him.

By now they had reached the stableyard to find Clive waiting for them with a face black as thunder. He helped Charlotte from the saddle and looked with strong disapproval at her dishevelled hair and crumpled dress.

"What in heaven's name were you thinking of?" he said. "To take one of the horses and ride off like some madcap! Really, Charlotte, you might have thought of me and my position."

"I am sorry to have caused so much trouble . . ."

"No trouble at all," interrupted Lorenzo quickly, dismounting and tossing the reins to a waiting groom. "Since it is my horse and the Señorita rides quite magnificently," he went on crisply to Clive, "I scarcely think your reproaches are justified. I was only concerned for her safety in the bull paddock. Fortunately no harm has been done. Now to business, Señor. Did you find that the horse you were riding met with your approval?"

Annoyed at the implied rebuke, Clive said curtly, "It's good enough for my purpose. Perhaps you would send the horse with one of your grooms to the Casa de Fuente and let me know the price."

"And what about the mare for your cousin?" Lorenzo gave Charlotte a swift smile. "I believe you found her satisfactory, did you not?"

"Thank you, no," said Clive quickly. "I only require the one horse."

It was spite, Charlotte knew that at once. He was angry because she had broken away, because Lorenzo and she had returned together on apparently friendly terms. It was a petty silly spite. She longed passionately to be able to say she would buy the mare herself but knew it was impossible. She had never felt her utter dependence on Clive so keenly.

She saw the surprise on Lorenzo's face and it made her feel

63

ashamed for her cousin. Then into the tiny silence between them came Teresa, flushed, excited, a little breathless. She slid from the saddle and turned to Charlotte.

"Oh there you are. I missed you. I've been looking everywhere. I'm so glad you found your way back safely."

"No thanks to you it seems," said her brother dryly. "What have you been up to, Teresa? Were you meeting someone?"

"No, of course not," she replied all innocence. "Why should I?"

"Why indeed?" He gave her a keen look before he turned to the others. "We had better return to the house. Doña Gracia will be wondering what has become of us."

The two men walked ahead and Teresa put a hand on Charlotte's arm.

"Thank you for not telling Lorenzo," she whispered.

"I couldn't tell him what I didn't know. *Were* you meeting someone, Teresa?"

She turned a rosy pink. "Yes, I was. It's just that I knew he'd be there and I had told him that if I could get away for a few minutes, then I would."

"Do you think you should be meeting someone whom your grandmother does not approve of?"

"It's not my Grandmother so much, it is Lorenzo," she said hurriedly. "It's all right, really it is. I'm not doing anything wrong."

Maybe it was only some childish infatuation, some romantic desire for secrecy, but Charlotte was a little disturbed at being involved, however innocently, but on the other hand she did not feel that she, a stranger, could do anything to interfere.

Doña Gracia was waiting for them with delicious chocolate and little almond cakes. About an hour later they were driving home with Lucy chattering about the garden Roberto had shown her with the tall tower of fretted stone from which you could see right across the Sierra as far as the Merenda vineyards where that nice Mr Macalister was already at work.

"If we are interested," she went on happily, "Roberto is sure he will be delighted to show us over the bodega where the sherry is made."

"Oh for God's sake, Lucy, who on earth wants to go tramping around vineyards and listening to Macalister prosing on about the only topic he knows anything about – fermenting grape juice?" asked Clive irritably.

"Well, I'm sure Charlotte would enjoy it. Guy Macalister was charming to us on the ship and told us a great deal about it in the most fascinating way, didn't he, Charlie? Don't be such a bear, Clive. What is wrong with you?"

"Nothing. I have a headache, that's all."

He was still smarting from the noticeable coolness in Lorenzo's manner, still trying to justify his own action. Damn it, he wasn't obliged to supply his cousin with fine bloodhorses, was he? He lapsed into a sullen silence.

It was early next morning when the horses arrived. Jacopo and one of the stable boys rode up leading Zelda by the bridle with the stallion Clive had chosen for himself. All the servants had come out to watch with the lively interest they always showed in their employers' affairs. Juanita and Rosa were exclaiming loudly over the beautifully groomed manes and tails and were joined by Jaime and the big clumsy Tomás.

Clive said, "Why the devil has he brought two?"

"*Por la Señorita,*" said Jacopo and handed Zelda's bridle to Charlotte.

"*Por migo? Porque?*" she asked.

He answered in a stream of Spanish until Clive said testily, "What the devil is the fellow talking about?"

"He says that the Marqués de Merenda has taken the liberty of loaning me Zelda while we are in Seville since it would appear that she and I took a liking to one another and he hopes that I will accept the loan and not be offended by it."

"Damned impudence!" exclaimed Clive. "What the hell is he thinking of? Does he imagine I cannot afford to buy a horse for you if I wished? Loan indeed! As if we were beggarly paupers! I shall have it sent back at once."

"No," said Charlotte firmly. "You will do no such thing. It's not intended for you. It is a loan to me and I shall accept. I will write a note at once. It's no use arguing," she went on, seeing Clive frown, "my mind is made up. Tomás will care for her, won't you, Tomás?" and she smiled at the boy who had come shyly and stretched out a hand to stroke the shining neck.

"*Si, Señorita, si si,*" and he beamed back at her.

She went into the house at once to write a letter, not giving

65

herself time to wonder whether she ought to accept or not, only feeling it would be insulting to throw back into Lorenzo's face such a generous gesture. A horse of her own would give her the freedom and independence she longed for and somehow or other Lorenzo must have sensed it. She wrote quickly and brought the note back to Jacopo and then went with Tomás to the stables wanting to make sure that her lovely mare had everything of the best.

5

The first real hint that his wife's ill-health might not be the sole reason for Clive choosing to come to Spain occurred about a week later and even then Charlotte was inclined to dismiss it. Clive had never shown the slightest interest in politics or indeed in anything outside his own pleasures and comforts. She could not imagine him stirring himself to serve any cause, which only made it the more inexplicable. Even his painting was not an absorbing interest. He was an amateur with an eye for colour and a certain imaginative ability to transfer what he saw to a canvas, but he worked at it spasmodically as the fit took him and abandoned it the moment anything more interesting took his fancy. There must be some other explanation of what she saw that morning.

She had begun to ride every day, usually going out very early before either Lucy or Clive were up and about. The mornings she had discovered were delicious, cool and beautiful beyond belief. At that time she was alone and free to wander where she wished. She loved to watch the patient little donkeys come trotting into the market, their panniers piled high with produce, to stop by the well where the women were drawing water and gossiping in the time-old way. Through the open doors wafted the rich homely smell of baking bread and the children would wave to her as she trotted by.

On this particular day, aware that Lucy was entertaining the Robinsons, she decided to go further afield, cross the river by the bridge of boats and ride up into the hills where she had been told there were the remains of a Roman amphitheatre.

Mr Robinson had warned her on no account to go alone through the suburb on the opposite bank of the Guadalquivir. Triana was said to be the home of thieves and gypsies, the hiding place of anarchists, cut-throats and undesirables of every kind who would attack you as soon as look at you. She was inclined to discount almost everything Mr Robinson told her.

He was obstinately British with an insular distrust of everything foreign. It certainly looked poor enough, she thought, the houses crumbling, the children playing in the dust half naked, but the golden light of Andalusia somehow gave it a charm and it did not seem to her as degraded as parts of London she had glimpsed in her short visit to the capital. No one molested her or did more than stare curiously as she trotted through the narrow winding streets and climbed into the hills.

Her father, digging into the remnants of a classical education hammered into him at Eton, had told her a little of Roman history and here were the ruins of what had once been a fine city with a great theatre. She stared around her at the time-worn granite benches from which myriads of people had once gazed down at a vast arena where gladiators fought bloodily to the death and wild animals tore to pieces their wretched victims facing them helplessly, spear in hand.

Bushes had thrust their way through the stone. Fennel, thyme and sage filled the warm air with aromatic scents, flowers starred the turf and bloomed unexpectedly in crannies of grey rock. She tethered Zelda securely in the shade of a tree and walked up the crumbling steps till she could look across the enormous oval with its twin gateways. She sat down with her back against the sun-warmed granite and pulled from her pocket a crust of Rosa's delicious nutty bread and creamy cheese. She ate slowly while above her head birds sang and once she thought she saw an eagle sweeping down with its great spread of wings and then soaring up again and away towards the snow peaks of the Sierra.

She was drowsing in the growing heat when she heard the low sound of voices drifting to her on the soft breeze. She looked around her and after a moment glimpsed the two figures standing in the mouth of one of the dark cell-like caves which had served as dressing rooms for the actors in those ancient spectacles. Startled, she realized that one of them was Clive. The other was a tall man in rough mountain dress, his broad-brimmed hat pulled down to his eyes. What on earth could have tempted her indolent cousin so early from his bed and why was he talking so earnestly with a stranger who for all his gypsy appearance must be able to speak English?

She drew back a little not wishing to be noticed and a moment later saw Clive break away, leap up from one stone slab to another and disappear into the brushwood on the further side where no doubt he had left his horse. His companion remained where he was for some minutes. He had lighted a cigar and the blue smoke floated in the warm air, then suddenly and silently he plunged into the yawning entrance to the stone cave and vanished.

Impelled by strong curiosity she scrambled down the jagged stone steps and reached the edge of the arena but there was nothing to be seen, only the moss grown floor and a lizard which sat motionless, watching her with jewel bright eyes. She lifted a hand and it disappeared. She peered into the dark mouth of the cave and it seemed to stretch on and on into blackness so that she wondered if it was a passage linking the two sides of the arena. Inside the air smelled stale. A bat flew out suddenly, making her jump, and a faint hiss caused her to look down. A snake was slithering across the dusty floor towards her. It raised its flat ugly head and she stepped back with a stifled scream. Instantly two arms went around her waist lifting her out and into the sunshine. A voice said, "They look evil but they're harmless enough," and twisting quickly round she was looking up at Don Lorenzo.

Her surprise was so great that she could only stare at him. "Where on earth did you spring from?" she blurted out.

"Certainly not out of thin air," he said laughing down at her. "I saw Zelda tethered above so I knew you must be here somewhere. You should be more careful. These broken steps can be treacherous. You could easily sprain an ankle."

But her mind was still on what she had just seen. "There was a man here," she said slowly.

"So there was."

"You saw him too. Do you know who he is?"

"It so happens I do. His name is José Roméro. He is, I regret to say, quite a well known bandit."

"A bandit?"

"He is also an ardent supporter of Don Carlos."

"The brother of the late King who wants to take the throne for himself?"

"That's right."

She frowned. "What would this José Roméro be doing here?"

"That's what I have been asking myself. But these caves are deep and make a useful hiding place for a man who wishes to come and go quietly."

69

"As a spy – is that what you mean?"

"Possibly."

"But why?"

He shrugged his shoulders but his eyes never left her face. "As far as we know Don Carlos is at present somewhere in the north gathering an army and awaiting his chance. He may well be anxious to find out what support can be found for his cause in Andalusia." Then he smiled. "But all this is of no interest to you, Señorita, I'm sure. What are *you* doing here may I ask on this lovely morning?"

"Just exploring. Italica was once a great city and the birthplace of Trajan and Hadrian. I wanted to see it for myself. Isn't it strange that two Roman Emperors should be Spanish?"

"No stranger than Spanish Princesses who became Queens of England," he replied dryly.

"No, I suppose not."

But history was far from her mind just then. She was wondering what possible connection Clive could have with José Roméro, bandit and rebel, and if Don Lorenzo had seen them together as he almost certainly must have done, why had he said nothing about it?

"I might ask what has brought you to the ruins this morning," she said. "It is scarcely on your road to the Castillo."

"True, but then I often come here. It is a good place to be alone, far away from the problems of every day. Perhaps great age brings tranquillity. It makes you realize how small one's troubles are in the stretch of centuries." He smiled. "However, I don't suppose thoughts of that kind are likely to be troubling you. Shall we go? The horses will be growing restive."

He gave her his hand to help her up the steep steps. He had tethered his horse close to Zelda and rode back part of the way with her. She seized the opportunity to thank him again for the loan of his beautiful mare.

"It is nothing," he said. "I am happy that you can exercise her and if it gives you pleasure to do so, then so much the better."

He was different that morning, relaxed and easy, so that she ventured to ask him something that she and Lucy had already talked over together.

"Your sister told me how much she would like to see something of the *Feria* in Seville after Easter. If you do not care to

70

attend yourself, would you permit her to stay with us for a few days?"

He frowned. "Teresa should not have asked such a thing on such short acquaintance."

"Oh she did not ask. She just happened to mention it when we were talking."

"And she also told you what an ogre I am, I presume, denying her every simple pleasure."

"No indeed, you must not think that."

"I don't think it, I know it," he said with a grim smile. "I do have my reasons, you know."

She felt the rebuff. "I'm sorry, I should not have asked. It was foolish of me."

"No, not foolish. I think you have a natural kindness of heart and Teresa appealed to that in you. Isn't that so?"

She was staring straight in front of her. "Perhaps. I could see myself in her when I was her age."

"And now you are so very old and wise."

"You are laughing at me but I do understand how she feels," she said earnestly. "The more you forbid something, the more she will want it. Didn't that happen to you when you were young?"

He looked at the face turned to his. Not the haunting dark-eyed beauty of his long dead mother, or of Manuela, but with a charming freshness, an appealing candour in the clear green eyes that made his doubts about that cousin of hers seem unworthy.

"I was fourteen when my father died," he said, "and I have been forced to take his place ever since. Teresa has as many giddy turns as a weathercock whereas you, if you'll pardon my saying so, seem to see your way ahead very clearly. However, in this instance, it is not for me to say yes or no. You must ask Doña Gracia."

"Very well. Lucy will write at once."

"No need for that. I think I told you that the *Rejoneadores* will be coming over in a week or so to practise their skill with the bull. If you and your cousins care to spend the day at the Castillo, you can ask the Marquésa then."

"Thank you. That will be wonderful. We will do that."

They rode on together and parted at the bridge of boats. She saw him ride away up into the hills and thought about him as

71

she took her way slowly home. She had never yet been in the company of a man whose very presence stirred her so deeply. He had made no move towards her, in fact most of the time he seemed to be disapproving, and yet it was there, some subtle quality, some affinity, that made every nerve in her body tingle. She had never felt like that with Clive and it disturbed her greatly. She wondered if it would have been wiser to have returned Zelda with a polite refusal and discouraged Lucy from any further intimacy with the Castle of Doves, and yet she knew with certainty that she was not going to do any such thing.

The moment Charlotte set eyes on Sybilla she felt an instinctive dislike. She tried to argue herself out of it and failed utterly. Mr Robinson had told them that his daughter was due to arrive shortly and she was there when Charlotte arrived back at the Casa de Fuente, perched on the wide stone edge of the fountain, muslin skirts billowing around her, lustrous dark hair falling into curls on the white neck, one hand dabbling in the water while she looked up provocatively at Clive under long silky lashes. It was not so much that she was beautiful, it was the self-confidence, the bland assurance that she had the world at her feet, a sense of power bred into her by adoring parents and an indulged childhood. She knew exactly what she wanted and was prepared to walk over anyone to achieve it. She had spent the winter in Paris with an aunt and was now to pass the summer with her besotted parents in what she considered the dull provincial society of Seville. Some of this Charlotte guessed at even at that first meeting when she came in to the patio, hot and dusty from her long ride, and Clive turned towards her.

"Ah there you are at last. We've been wondering where on earth you had got to. May I present my cousin Charlotte, Miss Robinson?"

"Delighted." Sybilla held out a languid hand. "I've heard so much about you from Papa."

"As we have about you," said Charlotte smoothly. "Did you have a good journey?"

"Horribly tedious. I simply hated to leave Paris with the season in full swing but Papa insisted, so here I am for my sins." She pouted prettily and Clive responded at once.

"We'll do our best to make sure you pass the summer pleasantly," he said gallantly.

72

Lucy looked across at Charlotte. "You're very late back. Where did you go?"

"Up into the hills. I wanted to explore the Roman amphitheatre."

"My cousin has a passion for history," said Clive indulgently.

"How strange. I could never get beyond the ancient Britons," said Sybilla with a tinkling little laugh.

"I find it gives added interest to the place where you live and the people you meet," said Charlotte. "By the way, was it you I saw up there, Clive?"

"I? My dear girl I don't share your love for dusty ruins."

"I must have been mistaken. However, I did run into Don Lorenzo."

She saw at once the quick flicker of interest in Clive's eyes before he said casually, "Did you indeed? What was *he* doing there?"

"I've no idea unless he was meeting someone. He has invited us to the Castillo when the *Rejoneadores* are rehearsing for the *Fiesta de Toros.*"

Sybilla swung around, surprise tinged with jealousy. "You *are* being honoured. As far as I know even Papa has never set foot in the Castle of Doves."

"We owe it to Charlotte," said Clive. "Our Spanish grandee has taken quite a shine to my cousin."

"Clive, what a vulgar expression!" exclaimed Lucy.

"It's quite true, my dear. You weren't there to see. He risked his precious skin to rescue her from the bull and he has loaned her one of his best horses. What more evidence do you want? If you care to accompany us, Miss Robinson, I'm sure you will be made very welcome in Charlotte's company."

With a few casual spiteful words Clive had created an uneasy atmosphere. Sybilla was obviously annoyed that the family she had no doubt thought to patronise were already on visiting terms with the Castillo where she had always been totally ignored. It made Charlotte feel uncomfortable.

"You must not take too much notice of anything Clive says. He likes to tease me," she said lightly and stood up. "Excuse me but I must go and change." She was glad to escape.

In the next few weeks they saw a great deal of Sybilla Robinson. She flashed through the sober invalidish English group that circled around the Consolate rather like a spectacular comet and capriciously chose Clive as her constant escort. She was always very charming and considerate towards Lucy but Charlotte was not deceived. Her strong protective instinct was aroused. Sybilla was out to capture Clive and looked like succeeding. That most indolent of young men was rising at six to ride out with her. In the stables, saddling Zelda herself, Charlotte would hear him harassing Tomás because his horse was not as perfectly groomed as he would wish. Their quiet life was suddenly filled with invitations to picnics, to carriage drives and evening card parties and Lucy, who had sometimes excused herself from attending these affairs, was now determined to accompany her husband everywhere.

Charlotte saw the shadow on the pretty face when often enough he would be laughing and talking with Sybilla, leaving her to sit alone, but she was anxious not to make too much of it. It meant nothing, she told herself, Sybilla was amusing herself with little thought of who might be hurt in the process and if Clive burned his fingers then it would be his own fault. It never once occurred to her that it could lead to anything more serious.

It was nearly a fortnight before they went up to the Castillo de Palomas. Matthew drove Lucy in the carriage while Charlotte and Clive decided to ride. There had been a brief argument the evening before when he said casually over supper that he had invited Sybilla to accompany them.

"I don't think you should have done that," said Lucy with a little worried frown. "It's not as if the Merendas were old friends of ours."

"Oh hell," he said impatiently, "they are not royalty, are they? We'll say she is our guest and we couldn't leave her behind."

"I wouldn't have thought she would have wished to go where she was not invited," remarked Charlotte.

"What are you afraid of?" retorted Clive. "That she'll put your nose out of joint?"

Charlotte flushed and Lucy said indignantly, "That's a beastly thing to say."

"Oh Lord, why be so solemn about it? Can't I even make a joke?"

It was a glorious morning when they set out very early, warm

74

as an English summer, and it seemed as if the whole countryside had burst into flower. Sybilla in a close-fitting red and black riding habit looked extraordinarily handsome. She and Clive rode ahead while Charlotte was happy to be alone, trotting beside the carriage and now and again exchanging a word with Lucy.

By the time they arrived, there was already a number of guests gathered in the drawing room and outside on the patio, elderly gentlemen impeccably dressed with their wives in rustling black silk and lace mantillas, their daughters demure in white muslin, turning their dark eyes to look curiously at the good-looking Englishman with his three ladies.

Charlotte saw Doña Gracia's eyes flash for an instant as Clive presented Sybilla with an air of bravado, but her courtesy did not falter and it was Teresa at her grandmother's elbow who gave Charlotte a mischievous grin and an expressive little gesture. It was obvious that the Marquésa was not altogether pleased and she wondered why.

Coffee was being served with sherry, the deliciously fragrant Manzanilla and iced fruit drinks, then they were all moving up through the garden to the improvised bullring, a huge space carved out from the slopes, carefully levelled and securely fenced.

The young men were already there, Lorenzo and Roberto among them. The grooms were holding the horses, beautiful fiery creatures. Brilliantly coloured silk ribbons had been plaited into their manes and tails. They tossed their heads impatiently as if they were already scenting the bull and were eager for the coming contest. Charlotte was gazing at them with admiration when someone called her name and she turned to see Guy Macalister hurrying to greet her with outstretched hands.

"Miss Starr – Charlotte – may I call you that? How splendid to meet you here. How are you? Are you settled comfortably in Seville? Are you enjoying your stay?"

"Oh yes indeed." She took his hands with real pleasure. "And you? How is the work with the vines?"

"We've made a good start but it is going to be a long process. We've been so busy I've not been able to find time to visit you. This is almost the first day off since I arrived." He took her arm in friendly fashion and they walked towards the rows of chairs set out for the guests to watch.

"Does Don Lorenzo work you so hard?"

"It's not that. It's simply that the vineyards have been neglected and there is a great deal of leeway to be made up. I hope you realize you're highly honoured to be here today," he went on lightly. "I understand that as a rule Don Lorenzo only invites relatives and close friends of the performers to witness these practice fiestas."

"Have you seen it before?"

"Once – a few years ago in Madrid in honour of the baby Infanta who is now Queen Isobel. It was a very grand occasion indeed and all the riders were in sixteenth-century costume, silks and velvets with gold embroidered cloaks and feathered hats."

It crossed her mind that Lorenzo must have looked magnificent in such clothes. Today all the young men wore Andalusian dress, black breeches, white shirts, scarlet sashes and short jackets.

She looked around her as they took their seats. It made a splendid if sombre spectacle in black and white with touches of scarlet. She noticed that the Marquésa had an armchair in the centre and had drawn Lucy to sit beside her, a kindness which Charlotte appreciated. Teresa among the young girls gave her a cheery wave. Clive and Sybilla were sitting a little apart, talking and laughing, their heads close together, and for some reason a prickle of danger ran through her, a sudden shiver of ice, absurd on this warm sunny day. She told herself she was being fanciful.

The riders trotted into the ring and a little band of musicians, family retainers she thought, began to play a striking martial air. The eight young men on their finely trained horses moved across the ring in perfect formation performing a stately dance with exquisite skill and precision in all the figures of the manège, the piaffe, the courvette, the pirouette. She had never seen such horsemanship displaying such grace and brilliance and it thrilled her beyond measure.

"Every one of them with ancestry going back at least three hundred years," whispered Guy in her ear. "It's one of the rules. Only the bluest of blue blood is allowed to take part in the Fiestas de Toros. In a moment they'll bring in the bull, then you will really be seeing something. Do you know what they call him – Torbellino?"

76

"And that means –?"

"Whirlwind. And he is, by God. I wouldn't risk my skin against him for all the wealth of the Indies."

The gate in the upper part of the ring had been opened and the bull came in with a rush and then stopped, lowered head slowly moving from side to side. He looked enormous, immensely powerful shoulders sloping to sinewy hindquarters and angrily thrashing tail. It was the bull with whom she had herself nearly had an encounter and for a moment she held her breath.

Looking back afterwards she felt that she would never have been able to put into words what took place. It was like watching a fantastic ballet, a dance with death that gave it an unbearable tension that suspended the breath so that no one moved or spoke as they leaned forward, their eyes riveted on the scene before them. Again and again the bull charged and at the precise moment when you expected the savage horns to rip into the horse, it turned aside with unbelievable skill and the rider bent down to plant his spear into the thick hide.

Guy was whispering as she watched. "The spear they use is called a *rejon*. Today they don't want to kill, so they are only just pricking the tough skin. The more they plant the greater the honour. Watch Lorenzo. That horse of his has the most consummate skill – see how far he leans from the saddle and then is away on the instant. It seems extraordinary but accidents are very rare." Then he too fell silent, caught up like her in the sheer wonder of it.

It seemed to go on and on until the bull was as stuck with darts as a porcupine. There was no sound, only the thudding of the horses' hooves and the snorting of the infuriated Torbellino. Then suddenly it was over. Lorenzo called a halt. With a final flourish the riders streamed out of the ring with the bull charging after them and then standing quite still, baffled, angry, so that you expected him to be breathing fire and smoke like some dragon of legend.

Charlotte sat back, feeling utterly exhausted, conscious of sweat on her forehead and trickling down her back under her thin silk blouse.

"What will happen now?" she whispered.

"They will drive the bull back to his field, pull out the darts and doctor his back. He will live to fight another day. Have you enjoyed it?"

She wasn't sure. It was too elemental, too frightening, and yet there was something tremendous about it, man's skill and grace and intellect pitted against the brute power of the bull.

"It's magnificent but it's pagan," she said slowly.

"You're right there. I reckon it goes back to primitive man. It's like setting human knowledge against the elements, isn't it?" Then Guy suddenly sat up. "Good God, what the devil does that young woman think she is doing?"

Sybilla, annoyed at her cool reception and unaccustomed to being ignored by the company around her, was determined to draw attention to herself. She must have somehow persuaded one of the young men to lend her his horse. She had leaped the fence and was riding slowly across the ring as if defying the weary bull who had retreated to the other side of the field. She took off her hat and waved it to Clive and at that precise moment the bull charged. She screamed and pulled her horse aside. The spectators were on their feet, Clive begun to run towards the ring but Lorenzo flung him back. He leaped on to his horse and galloped into the ring. He drew the attention of the bull to himself and shouted to Sybilla to go quickly.

She raced for the fence and cleared it but in trying to deflect the bull, Lorenzo had not been able to employ his own practised skill. The bull plunged, one horn ripped into the horse, it stumbled and fell throwing Lorenzo from the saddle. In another moment those savage horns could have torn into him as they had done into the horse but he was on his feet and leaping aside so that the great beast went lumbering past him. Then others had flooded into the arena, grooms and servants were crowding up on the bull shouting, slowly beating him back towards the upper gate.

For an instant Lorenzo stood isolated staring down at the horse which was making pitiful attempts to scramble to its feet and Charlotte could not bear it. She had to reach him though she did not know what she could do. She raced across the grass with Guy at her heels and reached Lorenzo as he went down on his knees. He was stroking the horse's head, speaking to it soothingly, lovingly.

Without looking at her he said, "Ask them to bring me a gun."

"I'll go," said Guy.

"Must you?" she said in an agony of pity. "Can't it be saved?"

"The horn has smashed the bone of the leg."

She fell on her knees on the other side knowing how he felt but powerless to comfort. To lose an animal you have loved is like parting from a dear friend.

She put out a hand to stroke the horse's head and her fingers touched those of Lorenzo. He looked up, their eyes met and in a queer way something seemed to spark and fuse between them. His hand closed convulsively over hers for a moment, then Guy was back with Jacopo carrying his master's gun.

"Shall I do it, Señor?" he asked.

"No. Give me the gun and leave me alone – all of you."

Guy put his arm around Charlotte and led her away. She knew there were tears in her eyes and blinked them back fiercely. As they reached the gate, she heard a shot and a few minutes later Lorenzo walked quickly past them. Sybilla stopped him, putting a hand on his arm.

"I'm sorry," she said, "I never meant – it was stupid of me."

Charlotte thought he could not trust himself to speak. He gave her a look of withering contempt, removed her hand and walked on.

"Did he have to take it like that?" she exclaimed, baffled and angry. "I told him I was sorry."

"If you'll forgive my saying so, Miss Robinson," said Guy ironically, "you could hardly expect him to be happy about it. That was a valuable animal that had taken him years to train and I happen to know that Don Lorenzo cares deeply for his horses."

"Nobody asked your opinion, Macalister," retorted Clive.

"Maybe not but I'm giving it all the same. Next time perhaps the lady will think carefully before she makes a public show of herself and places others at risk."

He walked on with Charlotte and Sybilla looked after him, her face flushed with anger at the rebuff.

"How dare he speak to me like that!" she stormed. "How dare he! Who does he think he is?"

"He's one of those uncouth Scots who think it clever to speak their minds. Take no notice of him."

Clive put his arm consolingly around her shoulders but she pulled herself away.

"I'm not staying here to be insulted. I only came because you begged me to. I shall go now."

"I say, Sybilla, that's dashed unfair," said Clive following after her. "You can't leave now. What would they think of me?"

"They can think what they like, beastly snobs!" she muttered furiously, but she let herself be persuaded to stay.

Safely out of earshot Charlotte pressed Guy's arm. "I don't know whether you should have said that but I'm so very glad you did."

"It's my fatal habit of speaking first and thinking afterwards," confessed Guy ruefully. "However I'm not sorry I got it off my chest. An abominable young woman."

"Do you know Miss Robinson well?"

"I met her once or twice last year when I came back to Spain for a few weeks. She was causing quite a stir. I'm surprised to see her here this afternoon. Roberto made rather an ass of himself over her and the Marquésa does not care for any kind of scandal."

"What was the scandal or shouldn't I ask?"

"You'll probably hear about it sooner or later. Roberto had a violent quarrel with a young bullfighter who was also pressing his attentions on Sybilla. You can guess what happened – two fiery Spaniards threatening to blow one another's brains out until Lorenzo stepped in and it was hushed up."

"No wonder Doña Gracia looked displeased," said Charlotte thoughtfully.

She wished Clive had not insisted on bringing Sybilla. She would have liked to question Guy further but by now they had reached the long tables where servants had set out an alfresco luncheon and conversation became general. Delighted to find she spoke Spanish and had a knowledgeable interest in horses, she was soon drawn into the circle of young riders and presently Lorenzo himself came to join them.

She noticed that he was eating little but drained the wine in his glass and held it out to the servant to be refilled.

"Well, Doña Carlotta," he said banteringly, "what do you think of our bullfight now?"

"I don't know," she said seriously. "It was a fascinating spectacle of marvellous horsemanship but what happens when the bull is killed? I'm not sure how I should feel about it then."

"In the *Fiesta de Toros*, it is not usually killed publicly, only if one of the riders fails lamentably in placing his darts. Then he is required to face the bull alone, on foot, and kill him with one stroke."

"Good heavens, why?"

"To redeem his honour."

"And if it kills him?"

"So much the worse for him."

"I can't believe that. It's barbarous. You're teasing me."

"I'm doing no such thing. To a Spaniard his honour means a very great deal. For that he would give up everything – even life itself."

She was aware suddenly that he was not jesting but speaking absolutely seriously.

"Did it ever happen to you?" she asked curiously.

"Once – in my first fiesta when I was much younger. I've never been so terrified in my life."

"Did you succeed?"

"More by luck than judgement or I should not be here now. The King afterwards rewarded me and I felt a fraud." He paused for a moment and then said quietly, "Is this Sybilla Robinson a particular friend of yours?"

"No, not really," she said uncomfortably. "We have recently made her acquaintance and since she was to spend the day with us, we thought you would not object if she accompanied us."

"I see."

"I'm terribly sorry for what happened."

She saw the shadow cross his face. "It may be foolish but I find it hard to be forced to shoot a horse I have bred and trained myself."

"I know how you feel."

"Do you?" For an instant his eyes dwelled on her face then he shrugged his shoulders. "It happened and that is the end of it. It could have been worse." Unexpectedly he put out a hand and touched the silver froggings on her dark green riding habit. "Today you play the little soldier."

"You recognize it?" she said in surprise.

"Certainly. The Rifle Brigade, is it not?"

"Yes. My father had it made to match his own uniform."

"You were very fond of your father?"

"Very fond. I missed him a great deal when he died."

"I understand. My father too died far too soon."

She was tempted then to tell him about the portrait she had

81

found in her father's desk but something held her back. If there was some kind of tragic link she did not want to let it cast a shadow over their growing friendship. While she hesitated, someone came to speak to Lorenzo, he excused himself to her and the moment passed.

They left in the early evening and later that night when she was brushing Lucy's hair as she did sometimes before Clive came to bed, the younger girl looked up at her.

"Do you like Sybilla, Charlotte?"

"Not particularly," she admitted frankly.

"I think she is detestable and Clive is falling in love with her."

"Oh no, Lucy. She is the sort of flashy personality that always attracts attention but it doesn't last and I'm sure it doesn't mean anything."

"I wish I could believe that. I felt so ashamed today, especially as the Marquésa had just agreed that Teresa could stay with us for a few days during the *Feria*."

Charlotte drew back the silky blonde hair and tied it with a ribbon. "I'm sure *you* don't need to feel ashamed and Clive will get over his silly infatuation." She kissed the top of Lucy's head. "Goodnight, darling. Sleep well."

Alone in her own room she thought how strange it was that her anxiety lest the old feeling between her and Clive might cause trouble had completely vanished. Instead he had found a new distraction and despite what she had said to Lucy, it worried her. She sighed as she undressed and slipped between the cool sheets, only to find herself dreaming of horses and bulls and a man whose grief she had shared for one precious disturbing moment.

She stirred restlessly and woke up. The room was very warm and she felt stifled. She got up and opened the window wide. Outside moonlight drenched the quiet street. She stood at the window in her thin cotton nightgown breathing in the cool fragrant air and knew with a rather frightening certainty that this difficult enigmatic Spaniard possessed a magnetic attraction that she was finding it hard to cope with. She thought again of the look on Lorenzo's face when he watched the dying horse. He was not without feeling whatever they said about him, all the deeper perhaps because he did not reveal it easily. She shivered suddenly, hearing her mother's cool practical common sense condemning her for folly. You did not fall in love with men like him except in the pages of lending library novels. Byron's Corsair indeed! The very notion was ridiculous. Sweat prickled on her forehead. She pushed back the heavy hair, dipped her face in cool water, wiped it with the towel and went back to bed to sleep dreamlessly till morning.

6

The famous Holy Week processions began in April but Charlotte saw little of them. Lucy fell sick the Sunday before Easter soon after they had seen the children come running from the church with their hands filled with crosses of palm. By the evening Lucy was fighting for breath, her hair wet with sweat, her slight body racked with spasms that terrified Charlotte. She had been so well since they had come to Spain that it was totally unexpected.

"It will pass," said Clive impatiently, annoyed that his evening party had to be cancelled. "I've seen it all before. It looks far worse than it is."

Charlotte, bathing Lucy's forehead with cool water, said, "We ought to call a doctor."

"I doubt if these Spanish butchers will do much good except to draw a pint of blood from her. There's a French medico recently arrived, so Sybilla says, with a consumptive wife. I'll find out if he will oblige us."

Clive's callous indifference infuriated Charlotte but when the Frenchman arrived, a thin supercilious man, he only shrugged his shoulders and confirmed what Clive had said.

"*C'est l'asthme,*" he said, "unpleasant but rarely fatal. Keep her quiet, cool and make sure she has only the lightest of food. I'll provide a sedative that may help." He looked at Charlotte, frowning a little. "Has the lady been upset or worried? From experience I have found stress can often provoke one of these attacks."

Lucy had said little but Charlotte wondered how deeply she grieved over her husband's growing obsession with Sybilla.

The week passed slowly. Clive was out for most of the day with the other English visitors, all of them eager to watch the festivities. The servants, too, expected to be given time off. Juanita and Rosa got up at dawn to prepare food for the day and even Jaime and Tomás vanished so that Charlotte was worried as to whether the horses were being properly watered and fed. It was Matthew, the stolid Matthew unimpressed by these foreign goings-on, who reassured her.

She sat with Lucy in a shadowy room, the shutters drawn against the sun, while the processions surged by amid glittering banks of candles, carrying the statue of the Virgin, *Nuestra Señora de la Esperanza*, in her sumptuous jewelled robes and crown of pure gold.

"She is the patroness of bull fighters," said Mr Robinson calling to enquire after Lucy and staying to chat. "They dedicate themselves to her, pray at her shrine before every *corrida* and sometimes leave gifts on the altar."

One day she had a glimpse from an upper window of the *Penitentes*, in their purple and white hoods, carrying the great cross lifted high in their midst, the mounted guardsmen clearing the road before them. The women fell to their knees as the statue of the Virgin passed by, the men crossed themselves chanting *Ave Maria Purissima*, while every now and again from out of the crowds would arise a shrill voice crying out the *saeta*, piercing to the heart like an arrow, the song of love for the Mother of God. The first time Charlotte heard it she shivered. It was intensely, fervently Catholic of course, but it was also pagan, wild and primitive, akin in some queer way to the dance of death in the bullfight, part of a Spain stretching far back into some ancient time long forgotten in England.

By the end of the week Lucy had recovered. It had been a sharp attack but when it was over she was quickly up and about again and extremely apologetic because her illness had deprived Charlotte of enjoying one of the great events of the year. But now, the orgy of religious fervour over, Seville prepared to enjoy itself. Everywhere there were huge painted posters advertising the bullfight. In the middle of the week Roberto arrived with Teresa wild with excitement. He himself was staying with other friends in the city but he left his sister in their charge.

"Will your brother be joining us?" asked Lucy innocently.

"*Dios*, no! Lorenzo does not care for enjoying himself. He has gone to the vineyards. There has been trouble over there. He and Guy will be putting their heads together."

"What kind of trouble?" asked Charlotte.

"A riot among the workers. It seems that the Carlists have

been at work sowing the seed of revolt against our little Queen and there was something like a pitched battle with those who call themselves Cristinos. You needn't be alarmed. Lorenzo will soon have it settled."

There had been rumours of clashes between the opposing parties in the north but nobody in Andalusia had shown any anxiety up to now.

"Does that mean the civil war is coming closer?"

Roberto shrugged his shoulders. "It is possible. There may come a time when we are forced to take sides but until it happens, let's forget about it and enjoy ourselves."

Certainly in the next few days no one in Seville or its neighbourhood did any work or appeared at all worried about what the future might bring. The young men came riding into the city with their magnificent horses, their sweethearts perched behind them. They danced in the streets from dawn to dusk and then to dawn again. The day before the *corrida* the Matadors came riding down the street and Charlotte saw Don Vicente for the first time. He was excessively handsome with the dark flashing good looks calculated to appeal to any unsophisticated girl. He drew up beneath the window from which they were watching and with a charming impudence held out his hand to Teresa. Her eyes shining like stars, she took the proffered hand and before they could protest or prevent it, she had leaped lightly up behind him, her muslin skirts blowing out behind them as he cantered along the road, the crowd shouting and cheering while Vicente bowed and waved like some great actor receiving the acclamation of his audience.

That was the day when Clive, infected by the general gaiety, had his own horse saddled and to do him justice would have taken Lucy up behind him if Sybilla had not stepped in front of her.

"Do be careful, dearest," she said with sweet concern. "You know how heat and dust upset you. You don't want to bring on another attack, do you?"

So Lucy, always too conscious of her weakness, drew back and let the other girl's stronger personality assert itself.

"Why did you let her do that?" whispered Charlotte indignantly. "You should have gone with him."

"You know how horses affect me and if I start to cough again, Clive will be so angry."

"Why should he be angry? He ought to have stayed here with you."

"Let him go," said Lucy with a wisdom she was learning by bitter experience. "If I do not try to hold him, perhaps he will come back to me."

They worried about Teresa but she returned in the late afternoon with Roberto and Clive, flushed and ecstatically happy, drunk with dancing and excitement and love.

Charlotte could not remember afterwards who first mentioned the Café Diablo in the disreputable Triana district but suddenly it seemed that they must all go there that evening.

"You'll see the best dancing in all Andalusia," said Roberto enthusiastically. "La Gabriella is superb and she is here for this one night from Granada." He looked around at them a little doubtfully. "It is a small place and – how shall I say it? – perhaps not quite suitable for English ladies."

"Oh do let's go," exclaimed Teresa. "I've never been to anything like that before. Vicente mentioned it this afternoon." She glanced appealingly at Charlotte and Lucy. "If we are all together, surely there can be no harm in it."

"Lorenzo will be angry," murmured Roberto.

"Bother Lorenzo! He is not God. For once in a way let us do what we like and forget about him."

"Very well, on your head be it," said her brother laughingly.

"That's the spirit," said Clive. "We'll take Sybilla with us and make a party of it."

It was already late in the evening when they set out, the streets still crowded with happy singing people.

The Café Diablo was a strange place. They entered down a flight of stone steps into what was a kind of semi-basement, a great stone cavern lit by candles. On the smoke-darkened roughcast walls shadowy figures had been painted by some artist patron, an enormous bull surrounded by capering devils and a bullfighter with uplifted sword.

"We shouldn't have come," whispered Lucy looking around her with dismay.

Charlotte was inclined to agree with her but at the same time could not suppress a certain thrill. This was the real Spain, she thought, and we are foreigners, outsiders, not altogether welcome amongst them.

They sat at a table in the corner and Roberto with an air of bravado ordered Manzanilla. A little group of men, unshaven, dark as gypsies, sat below a small dais strumming guitars in a slow rhythm and presently a girl came through the red curtain draped across the back of the stage and began to dance, quietly at first, then more and more rapidly, castanets clicking. It was followed by what Roberto called an *alegrío*, a quick lively dance and then by a girl with a long scarlet scarf who mimicked the actions of a bullfighter, the *veronica*, the *afarolado*, when the matador swings his cape in a spectacular swirl over his head.

"This is nothing," whispered Roberto, "you must wait for Gabriella."

One of the men had begun to sing. It had a vibrant quality, melancholy but stirring, then the door was flung open and Vicente strutted in with a band of followers. He glanced around the room in a lordly manner before he crossed to their table. Charlotte thought Roberto was annoyed but he nodded unwillingly to the great man condescending to join them. Vicente sat down between Sybilla and Teresa and the young girl flushed with pleasure and pride as his hand touched her bare arm and ran down to clasp her fingers. Charlotte saw Sybilla's eye flash for a moment before she deliberately turned her back whispering something intimately into Clive's ear that set them both laughing.

The singing had died. There was a sense of expectancy. Everyone seemed to be holding their breath, then the curtain at the back was swept aside and a woman stood there, superbly slender, hair black as night with a single white rose and a dress the colour of flame clinging to the lovely curves of her body and falling into flounces around her feet.

The men lounging at the tables stiffened and sat up. She stood motionless for seconds in utter silence, then almost contemptuously began to dance, the guitars rushing to accompany her. It was like nothing Charlotte had ever seen and even Clive, inclined to scoff, sat spellbound. She had power, vitality, passion, perhaps even genius, at one moment slow and sensuous and then in a frenzy of movement, the castanets beating out a relentless rhythm as she flung up her arms and Charlotte thought that this was what Lorenzo had spoken of on the ship – the galleys with their long oars, the girls exported to the courts of Rome and the East. This was how they must have danced at Nero's feasts and in Herod's banqueting hall. When it came to an end the applause was tumultuous and it was then as Charlotte leaned back in her chair that she saw someone come in and stand just inside the door. To her astonishment it was Lorenzo.

The rhythm of the music, the power of the dancing had been disturbing, stirring depths in her she did not know she possessed and she stared at the dark profile that had become so familiar to her. He had obviously not noticed them and stood absolutely still, his eyes on Gabriella. She did not bow or acknowledge the applause but after a moment turned and disappeared through the curtain at her back. Almost at once Lorenzo followed after her thrusting his way through the tables and vanishing into some opening beside the dais.

For the first time in her life Charlotte experienced jealousy. It was absurd and she was deeply ashamed but she could not help it. Why was he there? Was the gypsy dancer his mistress? His dark good looks with the hint of hidden power and her vibrant vivid personality had something in common, she thought unhappily. No one else at their table appeared to have seen him so she said nothing about it.

"There won't be anything else worth watching after Gabriella," said Roberto although they did not leave immediately but sat drinking and talking.

It was about fifteen minutes later and they were just preparing to go when unexpectedly Lorenzo came back. This time he saw them and crossed at once to their table.

He did not raise his voice but one hand gripped his brother's shoulder painfully. "Roberto, you ought to know better than to bring your sister to such a place as this."

Clive reacted with a touch of anger. "Doña Teresa is in my charge and accompanied by my wife and my cousin. Surely that is sufficient protection."

"You can do as you wish with the members of your own family but I do not permit my sister to frequent the Café Diablo or associate with those of whom I could never approve."

"Are you referring to me?" Vicente had risen to his feet.

"If the cap fits, wear it," said Lorenzo contemptuously. "Teresa, you will come with me immediately."

They were speaking rapidly in Spanish but the meaning was plain.

"No, I will not," she retorted.

89

"Don't argue with me, Teresa. I would prefer you not to remain with those who have so little care for your reputation."

"Why must you spoil everything?" she exclaimed passionately. "I was happy and now you have ruined it. You insult my friends – you humiliate me in front of them."

"Don't talk so foolishly, child."

He grasped her wrist but she tore herself away. "I'm not a child. That's where you are wrong."

White-faced, she would have liked to defy him but did not dare. She gathered up her silk shawl with trembling hands, looking helplessly at Charlotte and Lucy. "I am sorry. Please forgive me."

"Come, Teresa," said Lorenzo more gently, "it is best, you know it is. Roberto will bring anything you may have left at the Casa de Fuente."

"You can't do this, Lorenzo," Roberto tried to intervene but his brother cut him short.

"I shall expect you back at the Castillo tomorrow." He ran his eye over them and bowed slightly to Charlotte and Lucy. "Good night."

He put his arm around Teresa and shepherded her out of the café without looking back.

"Oh dear," said Lucy. "I knew we shouldn't have come."

"Nonsense," said Clive. "Of all the high-handed behaviour! What possible harm could come to the girl, for heaven's sake?"

Roberto looked uncomfortable. "My brother forgets that Teresa is grown up now. He still thinks of her as a little girl."

It was the expression on Don Vicente's face that alarmed Charlotte. It was more than hurt vanity. It was something deeper and more venomous. She had a feeling that more lay beneath Lorenzo's behaviour than appeared on the surface and she wondered if it was Vicente who had been at the root of the scandal with Roberto and Sybilla. One thing seemed to her certain. Lorenzo had made a deadly enemy who would not scruple to avenge himself if the opportunity arose.

The incident had spoiled the pleasure of the evening and they were silent as they rode home. The next morning Roberto, still a little upset, came to collect Teresa's valise which Charlotte had packed ready for him.

"I am sorry," he said, "about last night. I should not have suggested it but I never dreamed that Lorenzo would be there."

"Don't blame yourself," said Lucy quickly. "It was a splendid evening. I wouldn't have missed the dancing for the whole world."

"Gabriella is superb, isn't she? She is really famous, you know. It was an honour for her to come to such a place. But she has always pleased herself. She dances for her people, she says, and not for the foreigner." He paused and then went on diffidently, "Don't blame Lorenzo too much. He worries about Teresa. She *is* rather wild. She ran away from the Convent once and he had to plead with the Reverend Mother to take her back. He has had many offers of marriage for her but she has refused them all."

"Has he ever tried to force her into marrying against her will?" asked Charlotte.

"Oh no," said Roberto shocked. "Lorenzo is not a tyrant."

"Isn't he? I'm not so sure. I think he is too strict with her. I understand how she feels. He is turning her into a rebel."

"Try telling him that," said Roberto ruefully. "It's not been easy for him. He has had to be father and elder brother ever since I can remember. Poor Teresa. I had promised to take her to the *corrida*. She'll have to miss seeing Vicente make one of his famous kills."

Charlotte was not at all sure that that wasn't a very good thing. If Teresa was falling in love with Vicente, then the sooner she got over it the better. That showy young man was not to be trusted an inch, she felt quite sure of that.

"I imagine that's the last we shall see of the Merendas and their Castillo," said Clive later that day when they were lunching on the patio. "And I for one can't say I'm sorry."

"Well, I am," said Lucy. "I like the Marquésa. I only hope she doesn't think too badly of us. After all she trusted Teresa to our care and then to have Lorenzo take it like he did, it was most upsetting."

"It's no use crying over spilt milk, my dear. It's over and done with," said Clive. "Are you quite sure it's not Roberto you are worrying about rather than his grandmother? A pity he won't be accompanying us to the *corrida* this afternoon."

Lucy gave him a quick look. "I'm sure I don't know what you are talking about and I don't think I want to go very much, not after seeing all those wonderful riders at the Castillo."

"Please yourself, but the *corrida* is the real Spain, you know,

91

not dressed-up aristocrats showing off their fine horses. Sybilla will think it very strange on your part when it was all arranged and we have excellent seats."

It was a challenge that Lucy could not ignore though neither of the girls had been particularly enthusiastic. It had been Clive who had made up the party and obtained expensive tickets in a box on the shaded side of the arena.

Charlotte had mixed feelings about it. One part of her was very eager to understand more about this fascinating country which so appealed to her imagination but on the other hand she shrank from what she thought might be a savage and bloody exhibition. However, despite their doubts, she and Lucy were dressed and waiting when Matthew brought the carriage to the door.

Sybilla met them there looking very striking in a flame-coloured gown, a cluster of amber roses at her breast, and Charlotte wondered if it was Clive who had sent them to her. She smiled sweetly at Lucy as they took their seats.

At first it was a thrilling sight, the huge sanded bull ring, the rows and rows of spectators all wearing their colourful best from the President's lady in deep rose pink and a white lace mantilla to the peasants, men, women and children, crammed into the cheaper places chattering and laughing while boys pushed up and down the aisles with trays of drinks and food.

The opening procession was gaudily magnificent, led by the *Alguacils*, the police officers in ancient costume, the picadors on their padded horses in bright silk coats and beribboned hats, the matadors with their attendants, led by Vicente, gold embroidered coats glittering, the magenta cloaks folded over their arms.

When they had passed to cheers from the crowd the President gave a sign and tossed down a key. The gate was unlocked and the bull came storming in, not so large as Torbellino, but with the same majesty, the same haughty defiance as he paused, glaring at them, and slowly turning the huge head with the powerful horns from side to side.

The first act began, the taunting of the bull by the picadors, his infuriated rushes. The horses, old and untrained, had none of the skill of the riders she had seen at the Castillo and she closed her eyes against the blood, unwilling to watch their terror and their pain as the bull charged against them.

It was not until the moment when Vicente was in the arena

92

alone that she noticed Sybilla. It was the moment for which everyone was waiting, silent, holding their breath, tense with excitement, the supreme moment when one man, sword in hand, with nothing but his knowledge and skill, faced alone the maddened tortured bull. Sybilla was leaning forward, lips apart, a look of avid expectancy in every line of her taut body. When the deadly duel was over, when the sword had driven in with a clean precision that had something magnificent about it and the bull crumpled to his knees and then slowly to the ground, the audience was on its feet shouting, cheering, yelling, and Sybilla had risen with them. She snatched the cluster of roses from her bosom and threw it to Vicente who caught and kissed it. Perhaps it was just a gesture, born of the moment and meant nothing, but Charlotte was disturbed by the look on Clive's face, a look of agony, of thwarted passion. He loves her, she thought, he really loves her and she is driving him crazy, and it frightened her. Lucy had seen it too. She had gone very pale.

"I can't stay here, Charlie," she whispered. "I can't – I can't –"

She was trembling and Charlotte put an arm around her.

"I don't think I want to stay any longer either. Shall we go?"

The dead bull was being dragged away as they pushed their way out of the box, past the crowded seats and into the passage. They went down the stairs into the street and Lucy leaned up against the wall, panting for breath, her handkerchief pressed to her mouth.

"I'll be all right in a minute," she gasped. "It was so hot in there. It made me feel faint. Will Clive be very angry?"

"It doesn't matter if he is. You stay here and I'll find Matthew and the carriage."

"We can walk if he wants to see the rest of the bull fight."

But Matthew, sturdily British, did not approve of any sport that included what he called "murderin' dumb beasts that had never done nobody any harm" and she found him leaning against the carriage and smoking a Spanish cigarillo which was one of the few foreign habits to take his fancy.

Back at the house Charlotte persuaded Lucy to lie down for an hour and neither of them spoke of what they had seen that afternoon. To put it into words would somehow make it too real. Ignored it might vanish, an infatuation which perhaps in time would die of its own accord.

*

It was a few weeks later when Guy called on them early one morning. They were taking their chocolate in the garden. He accepted a cup gratefully and with a glance at Charlotte asked them if they would be interested in driving over to the Merenda vineyards and seeing something of how sherry was produced.

"Of course we are not one of the great firms like Gonzalez or Domecq but we have our own bodega and produce a particularly delicate wine which, with Don Lorenzo's co-operation, I am hoping to improve within the next five years."

"Roberto told us you have had trouble at the vineyard."

"So you heard about that." Guy shrugged. "You must know by now what Spaniards are like. There was an argument over politics. It flared up suddenly with knives flashing and everyone shouting their heads off. After a great deal of noise and a few bloody noses it was all over. Lorenzo had them eating out of his hand with glasses of Manzanilla all round."

"Manzanilla, not sherry?" enquired Charlotte.

Guy smiled. "No, indeed. The Spanish peasant does not drink sherry. That is only for export to the foreigner."

It was arranged that they should go at the end of the week and then, when the time came, Lucy cried off saying that the long drive in the heat would be too much for her.

"Besides it is you he hopes to see, Charlie, not me."

"Lucy, that's rubbish."

"Is it? I'm not so sure."

Clive had never showed any interest so in the end Charlotte went alone riding Zelda and refusing flatly to take Tomás with her.

"It will end up with me looking after him instead of the other way round," she said firmly.

She had always preferred to be independent and she was not altogether sorry to escape from the Casa de Fuente for a day. Lucy never spoke of Clive's neglect but Charlotte knew she felt it deeply. Eyebrows were being raised and comments made about his pursuit of Sybilla and rumours reached their ears of a quarrel with Vicente which he dismissed with a shrug.

"The fellow was insolent. I had to teach him a much needed lesson."

The handsome bullfighter's rising fame had brought him invitations from other cities. He took an apartment in the Triana district and was being courted and flattered by the more raffish

94

society who frequented places like the Café Diablo. It was worrying but for the time being Charlotte made up her mind to put it behind her.

She enjoyed the ride through the foothills of the Sierra where the chestnuts provided welcome shade and here and there little streams came bouncing down rocky channels overgrown with moss and fern. Guy had given precise directions but she found the Merenda name a magic password when she enquired the way from passing peasants with their patient donkeys trudging beside them.

Presently she emerged into open land where she could see the vines stretching up green in long terraces. There were small stone huts built for the workers and then the large flat-roofed white house that belonged to Don Evaristo, the *Cápataz* or Foreman of the vineyard where Guy was staying until his own house could be made ready for him.

He came to meet her, taking her into the cool shaded room where she met Don Evaristo himself, a solid looking man with a merry eye, the dark hair curling on his forehead like one of the black bulls grazing on the mountainside. His plump middle-aged wife bustled around serving coffee with *alpisteras*, so delicious and so crisp that Charlotte could not resist asking how they were made. Flattered by her interest and delighted to find an *Inglesa* who spoke Spanish, Doña Catalina burst into a voluble explanation of how you must have the finest white flour and sugar, four eggs fresh from the nest, all beaten together into a soft dough, rolled out thin as paper, cut into narrow strips, then dropped into boiling lard so that they curled up like bunches of ribbon and were then dusted with sugar.

"You must take some back with you for your friends," she said, glowing with pride. "I will have them put into a box for you."

Afterwards, walking down the garden path towards the bodega, a little girl came running to meet them, her hands filled with flowers. She held them out to Charlotte with a shy smile. She must have been about eleven years old with long straight black hair falling to her waist and a thin brown face with astonishingly large dark blue eyes.

Charlotte accepted the flowers and asked her name. The child shook her head and suddenly bolted away up the path and into the house. Her frilled white muslin dress, the satin ribbon

95

that tied the black hair, were not what a peasant's child would have worn.

Charlotte said, "Is she Don Evaristo's daughter?"

"They have no children. Paquita is an adopted child, I believe."

There had been something oddly familiar about the girl's face and the unconscious grace of the small body that teased her for a moment, then she forgot it as she entered the bodega.

It was like a cathedral, she thought, so cool and airy and full of shadows, rising high with vast arches and everywhere like incense the pervading perfume of the wine. On each side were ranged the enormous casks, one mounted on top of the other in four tiers.

"When the wine is ready," explained Guy, "it is drawn from the bottom row which is then refilled from the one above and so on to the top row which is the new wine. This is what is called 'educating the wine' and the process can take as long as ten years."

"It is a university of wine," exclaimed Charlotte.

"An excellent name for it," said Guy laughing. "It is our intention to produce a wine which will have a special quality of its own and bear the Merenda trademark."

He went on talking with enthusiasm and she listened with interest until she saw that the child had followed them in and was standing at the end of the row, absolutely still, hands clasped, small face intent.

"What is she watching?" asked Charlotte intrigued.

Guy put a hand on her arm smiling. "Ssh, it is the mice. They are the special pets of the *Cápataz*. Stand quite still and you will see them come out."

Tucked away in a corner there was a full glass of sherry and leaning against it a miniature ladder. After a moment a mouse appeared, looked nervously around, then scurried up the ladder, dipped its nose into the wine, had a good drink and then staggered down again and away to its hole while another took its place. They watched fascinated until Paquita suddenly burst into delighted laughter and the mice immediately vanished.

Lorenzo had come in at the other end of the bodega and the child raced to meet him. He lifted her high, tossing her up in the air, and she squealed with pleasure, pressing her cheek against his. He put her down and she began to rummage in his pockets. He laughed, pulled out a packet and put it into her hands.

"There, little robber, now be off with you."

She giggled and scampered away.

It was at that moment that Charlotte realized what had been teasing her memory. The child's unusual blue eyes were those of Lorenzo. Was she then his daughter, a bastard child being brought up here away from the ancestral Castillo by the foreman of his vineyard? She had no time to think how she felt at such a startling revelation, if it were true, since he had reached them, was taking her hand, saying how delighted he was to see her there as if the last unpleasant encounter at the Café Diablo had never taken place.

Guy said, "We are waiting for Don Evaristo. He is going to draw some of our sherry for Miss Charlotte to taste."

"Excellent. How is the wine proving itself?"

Guy shrugged. "Some good, some not so good. You must understand," he went on, turning to Charlotte, "wine is a living thing and as capricious as a pretty woman. From the same pressing of grapes, one barrel can turn itself into a fino, another into an amontillado and the third out of sheer spite become sharp as vinegar."

Lorenzo laughed. "A very apt comparison. You will wonder why I concern myself with a product so volatile and uncertain. The truth is that I am obstinate and hate to admit defeat. Over thirty years ago my grandfather achieved a splendid wine, then came Napoleon and years of war. The vineyards were devastated. After my father was killed, my guardians said that I must sell. I refused. 'I will replant,' I said grandly, but money was short then and it was many years before I could fulfil my promise to myself. On my twenty-first birthday we began to replant. Now ten years later, with Guy's help, we are going to produce a vintage of which we can be proud. Isn't that so?"

"With the help of God," said Guy dryly. "There are wind and weather to be taken into consideration."

Then Don Evaristo was with them respectfully saluting Lorenzo. He had brought a *Venencia* with him, a long wooden handle with a metal cup attached to one end. He thrust it into the darkness of the barrel, withdrew it and then raising it high in his right hand poured a golden stream of wine into a glass with exquisite skill not spilling a single drop. Solemnly he

97

handed it to Charlotte. She took it and sipped. To her unpractised palate it tasted very rare and fine. Lorenzo took it from her and drank, then passed it to Guy. It was like a solemn wine tasting between the three of them with Don Evaristo beaming at them like some ancient Bacchus.

"It certainly has a bouquet," said Lorenzo. "I believe in time we will achieve what we are looking for."

They went back together to the house where Doña Catalina had a late luncheon waiting for them. Charlotte had learned already that mealtimes in Spanish households were elastic and did not follow rigid English rules. You could lunch at teatime and dine at midnight. Afterwards she sat in the garden under a gigantic walnut tree while Lorenzo talked business with Guy and Don Evaristo and presently Doña Catalina came to sit beside her, bringing the child with her. Paquita sat dutifully with them for a few minutes stitching at a grubby piece of embroidery. Then a gigantic dog came bounding down the path and it was too much for her. She dropped her needle and was off racing with him in the sunshine.

Doña Catalina sighed. "She is a wild one. I do not know what will happen when she goes to the Convent. It will be like shutting a bird in a cage."

"Must she be sent away to school?"

"In a year's time. It is Don Lorenzo's wish."

And that of course was final, thought Charlotte rebelliously. Didn't anyone ever dare to suggest to him that he might be wrong? She said, "Señor Macalister told me that Paquita was adopted. Have you had the care of her since she was a baby?"

"No, only since she was five years old."

"Is she an orphan?"

"Not exactly. But her own mother could not provide a suitable home for her. She visits her occasionally."

Charlotte would have liked to ask more but there was something in Doña Catalina's manner that made her realise that her questions would not be welcome. In any case it was growing late. She rose to her feet.

"It has been a wonderful day but I really think I ought to leave now."

The men had risen too and Lorenzo came quickly across the patio to join them.

"Guy tells me you rode over here alone. I am returning to the Castillo. If you are ready to go now, I shall be happy to accompany you."

"There is really no need," she said coolly. "I found my way here very easily and I'm not at all afraid of riding back alone."

"Then you ought to be," he said brusquely. "I'm surprised your cousin permitted it. You are a young woman, alone and unprotected, anything could happen to you."

"I don't think I am likely to be abducted by bandits or murdered between here and Seville," she said lightly.

"Such things have happened when they could easily have been avoided," he replied so coldly that she felt foolish.

In the manner of Spanish households everyone gathered to say goodbye, Guy pressing her to come again and bring Lucy with her next time, Don Evaristo smiling benignly as his wife shyly offered the box of sugared biscuits, the child Paquita, one small hand clutching the big dog's collar and gazing up at Lorenzo who patted her head whispering something that brought a gurgle of laughter. Then they were riding side by side through the cool of the evening.

They did not speak very much at first except about the vineyards, her interest and his hopes for the future. They had been silent for quite a while before she plucked up her courage and asked a question.

"How is Teresa?"

"Well enough, I hope. I am in her black books at the moment."

"I am not altogether surprised."

He gave her a quick glance. "You think I was too harsh."

"It *was* a party made up at the last moment to see Gabriella dance. We saw nothing improper in it."

"Nor was there. Gabriella is a supreme artist worth watching at any time. I meant no criticism of you and Doña Lucia but I could not tolerate seeing my sister on familiar terms with a man like Don Vicente."

"Because he is merely a bullfighter and not a grandee like yourself?"

"Do you think so poorly of me? There are other reasons and Roberto knew them well enough. He should not have invited him to sit with you."

"It would have been very awkward, very discourteous for him to refuse."

"Perhaps." He turned to her with his rare smile. "Maybe I did act hastily. The truth is it was just one more thing coming after a very disturbing day."

"The riots at the vineyard?"

"Yes, and more than that." He looked at her sharply. "How did you know about that?"

"Guy told me."

"You have greatly impressed my friend Macalister. Are you aware of that?"

"I haven't thought about it, but I like him."

"So do I. He is a man to be trusted."

She would have liked to ask him what else on that day had so deeply disturbed him but did not dare.

After a while he said, "There is one other thing. My grandmother tells me that I have been neglecting my social duties. It is Teresa's birthday in two weeks' time and Doña Gracia is planning a summer ball for her. I hope you and your cousins will honour us by attending."

"Are you sure you want us to come after our shocking behaviour?" she said with a glint of mischief.

"Touché," he replied. "I think we might call a truce now, can't we?"

"I would love to come," she said frankly, "and so would Lucy."

"Good. The invitation will be sent in due course."

Happy that the awkwardness between them was cleared away she enjoyed the ride home, the mountain peaks standing out gaunt and rugged against a sky beginning to turn pink and gold with the setting sun. This was the land he had known since boyhood and loved with passion so that in listening to him answering her questions, she longed to explore it with him and wondered whether an opportunity would ever arise. It did not seem very likely.

He accompanied her to the door of the Casa de Fuente despite her protests, but refused an invitation to come in. She watched him ride away before she took Zelda to the stable herself and unsaddled her. Tomás appeared and began to rub her down and she petted her for a moment watching the mare settle down to her feed. When she went into the house she found Lucy sitting alone. She looked up as Charlotte came in.

"So you're back at last. Did you have a good day?"

100

"Wonderfully interesting. You must come with me next time, Lucy. I didn't mean to be so late."

"Did Guy come back with you? I thought I heard voices outside."

"Not Guy. Don Lorenzo himself," she said gaily. "Think of that! All is forgiven and forgotten. In fact we are to be invited to Teresa's birthday party in two weeks' time."

"Heavens! It must be on your account, Charlie. I thought Clive and I were quite beyond the pale from now on."

"Apparently not. It was Don Vicente whom he objected to and I can't say I altogether blame him. That young man has much too good a conceit of himself."

She was interrupted by Juanita coming in with a lighted lamp and asking when the ladies would like supper to be served.

"In about half an hour," said Lucy. "We shall not be waiting for Señor Starr."

"*Bueno*," said Juanita and shot a pitying glance at Lucy before she bounced out of the room.

"Where is Clive?" asked Charlotte.

"I don't know. He didn't say." Lucy began to fold up the embroidery that lay idle in her lap.

By the light of the lamp Charlotte could see how pale she was. She said, "Is anything wrong?"

"No. Why should there be?" Lucy got up and put the needle-work in her sewing box before walking to the window.

"Have you quarrelled?"

"Not exactly." She stood staring out into the darkening garden. "I suppose in my secret heart I always knew that it was not I Clive wanted at all, it was just Papa's money, but at first it was so wonderful that it was easy to deceive myself. He was so handsome I couldn't help loving him – everyone envied me so much."

"What happened tonight?"

"We had an argument, stupidly I suppose. I told him how they were all talking about him and Sybilla, even the servants, that it was unfair to me as his wife, and then – and then he lost his temper. Oh Charlotte, he said horrible things to me, vile things – that I had never been a true wife to him, that no man could be expected to put up with a woman who was so often sick, and all I was good for was to provide him with the means to go his own way and do as he wished . . ."

She was shaking now, the tears running helplessly down her cheeks and Charlotte filled with pity put her arm around her waist and drew her to sit beside her on the sofa.

"He didn't mean the half of it. I know Clive – he says foolish things on the spur of the moment."

"He meant it, Charlie, he meant it. It was horrible. You see I've seen it grow between him and Sybilla ever since that day at the bullfight. Oh dear God, how could he be so brutal?"

Charlotte held her close until the spasm of bitter weeping was over and wondered whether something had gone terribly wrong between Sybilla and Clive and in his wretchedness he was hitting out at his innocent wife. She was beginning to know her cousin too well.

Lucy tried to pull herself together. She sat up and wiped her eyes resolutely.

"I'm sorry. I didn't mean to be so silly. Juanita will be back in a minute. I mustn't let her see me like this. Already the servants despise me. They think me a fool who cannot even manage her own husband."

"No, they don't. They're very fond of you."

"I don't want their pity." Lucy was twisting the sodden handkerchief between nervous fingers before she looked shyly at Charlotte. "You know I thought once that Clive might have been in love with you."

"Once, years ago, before he met you, I thought he was."

"Did he make you very unhappy?"

"For a while. It's long over now."

"He used to talk about you, his wonderful cousin who could do all the things I couldn't. I thought I was going to hate you."

"I felt the same about you," said Charlotte ruefully. "If Mamma had not decided to marry Colonel Armstrong, I'd never have decided to come to Spain."

They stared at one another for a moment and then began to laugh.

"How strange to find we were both wrong," went on Charlotte cheerfully.

"And how wonderful that you *did* decide to come and that we like each other in spite of it," agreed Lucy. Then her smile faded. "The worst part about quarrelling with Clive is that I think I may be going to have a baby."

It was totally unexpected and Charlotte said quickly, "Are you sure?"

"No, not yet, and I hope with all my heart that I'm wrong. It frightens me." She suddenly clutched at the other girl's hand. "You won't leave me, will you, Charlotte? I think I should die if I had to go through it out here alone."

"Of course I won't leave you. How could you ever think of such a thing! Now I'm going up to change," said Charlotte briskly, "and you are coming up with me to bathe your eyes. Then we'll have supper and forget about Clive. He'll be quite different tomorrow, I'm sure of it."

She was partly right. Clive, who had gone on his conquering way, believing himself invulnerable where women were concerned, had fallen victim to Sybilla's flaming beauty, to a maddening subtle attraction that was driving him crazy. Ever since the *corrida* he had been made to realize that he was only one among many. She would melt in his arms one day and snap her fingers at him the next, smiling at other men, taunting him with his ineffectiveness beside Vicente's virility until in frustration he had lashed out at his wife.

When he came in late that night Charlotte sat alone reading, the lamp close beside her. She asked if he wanted supper and he shook his head.

"Where is Lucy?"

"She has gone to bed." Charlotte put down her book. "You distressed her very greatly."

"What has she told you?"

"Enough. You should be ashamed to treat her so heartlessly."

"Now don't you start," but he had the grace to look ashamed. "You don't understand, Charlotte. This has nothing to do with you."

"I know that but I can't be blind to it. What has happened to you, Clive?"

"Oh for God's sake, leave me alone," he said violently.

"Very well. If that's what you want."

"I do. I suppose I'd better go up."

Inside the door of their bedroom he paused uncertainly, then crossed to the bed. Lucy was not asleep and she turned her head away from him.

"Sorry, old girl," he mumbled.

"Are you, Clive? Are you really sorry?"

"Oh hell, what do you want me to say?" He dropped on his knees beside the bed. "It was a devilish way to behave but you ought to know how things are sometimes."

"I do know," she said painfully, "only too well. Do you love her, Clive?"

"I don't know," he muttered thickly. "I don't know. Not as I love you."

"I wish I could believe that."

"It's true, Lucy."

She paused for a moment and then put out a hand and touched his cheek. He captured her fingers and kissed them. She knew it changed nothing, knew sadly it didn't mean he loved her, only that he was uncomfortable to have behaved so atrociously, but she let herself be deceived into believing him.

"It's late," she whispered. "You had better come to bed."

7

The ballroom at the Castillo was completely different in style from the rest of the house. It had been re-created by Lorenzo's grandfather who had spent many years in Paris and came home inspired by what he had seen at Versailles and Fontainebleau. The walls were papered in white and gold satin stripes, the furniture gilded and fragile, lit by lamps in ormolu and crystal. It presented a brilliant spectacle on the night of Teresa's ball and the girl herself standing between Doña Gracia and Lorenzo in her gown of mousseline de soie seemed the radiant heart of it, thought Charlotte, as she watched her greeting the guests.

Clive was on his best behaviour and she was glad to see that Lucy appeared happier. She was determined to enjoy herself and knew she was looking her best. The green organza sprinkled with gold stars which Uncle Nicholas's generosity had provided emphasized the tawny colour of her hair which was behaving itself for once. She had pinned up the silky curls with golden roses from the garden. The sun of Andalusia had warmed the pallor of her face to a peach-like glow and excitement had brought a sparkle to the green eyes with their long dark lashes.

"By Jove," said Guy Macalister to himself coming to claim her for the first dance, "that rather mouse-like little girl is blossoming into a beauty and is quite unaware of it." He felt his heart quicken as she took his hand.

The evening began like any other ball. She danced with Guy, with Clive, with Roberto, with the other young men she had met at the bullfighting, and last of all with Lorenzo. By that time the atmosphere had subtly begun to change, the guitars in the small orchestra beginning to take over as if these Spanish aristocrats had paid their formal tribute to the customs of polite European society and their own native exuberance was sweeping them away.

Lorenzo was different from the others. He did not indulge in the usual small talk and she gave herself up to the pleasure of the slow languorous waltz, their bodies seeming to fuse together effortlessly. At Breakstone Park, dancing in a man's arms had still been considered rather shocking but dreamily she wished it could go on for ever, thought wryly how absurd that was and then was jerked into awareness.

"There is something I would like to ask you," he said guiding her skilfully and gracefully through the dancers. "Have you seen or heard anything of José Roméro in Seville during the last few weeks?"

"Do you mean the man we saw at the Italica that morning? Why should I?"

"A rumour has reached me that he has been currying the favour of some of the British residents here and in Granada. I thought it possible your cousin might have mentioned it."

"Clive has absolutely no interest in politics." But was that entirely true? She felt a spasm of alarm.

"Are you sure of that?" he went on. "There is a suggestion that some of the British might favour Don Carlos since he took refuge in England when his brother exiled him and, if so, that could cause great trouble for all of us."

"It's a subject that is never discussed among the people I meet," she said slowly and then wondered about the many hours Clive spent away from the house. She had assumed he spent them with Sybilla, but did he? Surely he could not be concerning himself with anything so dangerous.

"And you would remind me that it is in any case hardly the subject for a ball," said Lorenzo with a wry smile. "I must apologize for bringing it up. Teresa looks happy tonight, don't you think?"

"Very happy. Has she forgiven you?"

"Temporarily at any rate. I'm not sure how long it will last."

His arm tightened around her waist and as the music quickened he swung her round until dizzily and ecstatically it came to an end and they were both laughing and breathless.

It was midnight and after they had supped that the surprise came. Servants had come in rearranging chairs and sofas. The guests had begun to seat themselves. Guy who had been dancing with Charlotte stood close beside her.

"What is happening?" she asked.

"It seems that we are going to be entertained."

There was a buzz of anticipation. Three men strolled in,

106

gypsies, she thought, in their gaudy splendour, the real *Gitanos* you read about. Almost casually they took up a position and one of them struck a run of chords on his guitar. There was a pause held almost to breaking point and then to her intense surprise Gabriella appeared in the doorway and walked slowly to the centre of the room. It was a repetition of the night at the Café Diablo but more compelling, more brilliant, in this princely setting, as if she contemptuously flaunted her genius and her pride before these aristocrats not one of whom could have touched her skill and whose favour she despised.

She ended as she had done before, suddenly and dramatically, to a storm of applause. But then there was something different. Charlotte was near enough to see the large dark eyes widen, the slow secret smile that curved the finely cut lips. She began to dance again with a sensuous enticing movement that took her across to where Lorenzo leaned against one of the slender pillars. She held out her hand to him. He shook his head smiling. Again she beckoned. All eyes were turned to him. There was a murmur running through the room urging him forward so that almost as if compelled against his will he took the outstretched hand.

The guitars burst into a throbbing rhythm, the violins in the orchestra taking it up. The two began to dance together. Whether they followed some set steps or whether it was improvised, Charlotte did not know, only that she could not drag her eyes away. It was a dance of courtship, pursuit, rejection, acceptance, Gabriella leading, Lorenzo following, so perfectly attuned to one another that she felt she could not endure it a moment longer and yet was rooted to the spot. It seemed to last for ever and was actually quite short and at the end there were shouts of *olé* from the young men as they clapped and stamped their feet. They surged forward laughing, Lorenzo protesting he had not done such a thing for years. Gabriella aloof still and yet at the heart of it. Even Doña Gracia was smiling and Teresa flung her arms around her brother's neck and kissed him.

On this warm May night the doors to the terrace were standing open and Charlotte, her cheeks burning, slipped through them and away from the heat and overcharged atmosphere of the ballroom.

She walked quickly, scarcely noticing where she was going, glad of the freshness of the scented night breeze blowing off the mountains. Here and there lights burned under coloured glass globes, gold and green and red. How ridiculous, she thought, to be so disturbed by a dance! What was happening to her? Whatever she did, she must not allow herself to become entangled with a man like Lorenzo and yet that dance had been so filled with passion, so fiercely compelling, that she felt choked by it. Was it a nostalgia for something past or did it stir within them now? She couldn't bear the thought, despised herself for such a fierce reaction and walked faster and faster to escape from it until she came to a gate, a lacework of finely wrought iron, and it pulled her up short.

Slowly the urgency that had carried her there began to ebb. She took a deep breath, pushed upon the gate and found herself in an enclosed garden. The moonlight blanched the roses and gave a ghostly radiance to fluted columns and slender arches hung with flowers, to a round stone pool and a fountain that glittered like silver. It reminded her of the gardens of the Alhambra that they had visited at Granada, only they had been sadly neglected, while here was a Moorish garden in miniature preserved in all its fragile loveliness. She let herself drop on the wide edge of the pool, felt the cool drops of the water touch her cheek and was calmed by the tranquillity and silence.

She was not sure how long she had sat there when she realized she was not alone. The faint fragrance of a cigar drifted to her, then the sound of a footstep. She would have escaped but there was no time. Lorenzo came through the arch and stopped, obviously surprised to see her.

"So you have discovered my hiding place?"

"Yours?"

"I like to think so. Not many people come here at this hour. It has a ghost."

"Are you serious?"

"Quite serious. I've never seen her but sometimes I have sensed her presence and once I believed I heard her laugh."

They had been speaking in hushed whispers and it was such an unusual admission from a man she had thought so entirely practical and self-sufficient that she was silent for a moment.

He said, "Do you mind my cigar?"

"No, I like it. My father smoked them occasionally. Is this what you call the Nun's garden?"

"Yes. Hasn't Roberto told you about it?"

108

"No, not yet."

"It's probably not true, but it makes a pretty legend."

"May I hear it?"

"If you wish."

He dropped the cigar into the pool and watched it float away and then sat beside her on the stone ledge.

"About four hundred years ago there was a King called Pedro, not a bad King as rulers go, but with an unfortunate passion for beautiful women. One young girl whose rare beauty had caught his fancy rejected him. Inflamed with rage at her resistance, he pursued her even to within the convent walls and in a desperate attempt to escape her fate she threw boiling oil over her face destroying the loveliness that had inspired his desire. Overcome with remorse, Pedro had her nursed back to health and had this garden built for her within what had once been a Moorish palace. Here, so they say, she lived and grew to love the man who would have destroyed her. She died bearing his child."

"A sad story," she murmured, "but perhaps she found happiness for a little while."

"That is all any of us can hope for. Maybe it was for the best. Pedro was notoriously unfaithful. I like to think there is peace here, a rare tranquillity."

"I have felt it already. How did it come to be yours?"

"Pedro was assassinated by his own half brother but by that time he had granted this estate to my ancestor who served him in one of his many wars and so we have kept it ever since."

"It is a most beautiful place."

"I find it so. Even in the worst of the summer heat there is shade and coolness in the garden."

She let her hand trail in the water before she said hesitantly, "I was surprised to see Gabriella here."

"I have known her for a very long time. She does not dance at private houses as a rule but my grandmother was once good to her and she repays a debt." He laughed suddenly. "I did not expect to be drawn into her act."

"You danced superbly."

"You flatter me. I am greatly out of practice. There was a time when like many young men I prided myself on my skill but that was a long while ago. Gabriella knew that. She has a wicked sense of humour. She took pleasure in shaming me."

Sitting alone with him in this exquisite garden was far too dangerous a pleasure. She said, "I must go back. Lucy will be wondering where I am."

She got up too quickly and stumbled. He caught her in his arms steadying her.

"Careful. You don't want to end up in the pool with the fishes."

Then stirred by some impulse that he could hardly have explained even to himself he drew her to him and kissed her. She stood quite still in his arms afraid of betraying herself and yet he was aware of a yielding, a softness in the lips that met his. He drew away and she saw the smile and the glitter of his eyes in the moonlight.

"I'm waiting," he said. "Aren't you going to slap my face?"

"Why should I do that?"

"Isn't it the usual act of outraged virtue?" he said teasingly.

"I don't feel in the least outraged, not here in this garden of delight."

"And if I should kiss you again?" His voice was suddenly rough and she trembled.

"I don't know . . ."

"You tempt me to try."

"No, please . . ."

He took her hand, pulling her into his arms so suddenly she had no time to resist. His kiss, hard and searching, like nothing else she had experienced, almost overwhelmed her when the sound of voices and a burst of laughter drove them apart. She stood dizzy and breathless as Lorenzo released her.

"Who was that?" he said and stiffened as the sound grew nearer. "That is Teresa's voice."

He moved quickly to the gate and opened it. Charlotte following him saw the two who stood so closely entwined. She saw the white blur of Teresa's gown and in the dark the figure that drew quickly away from her she recognized as Don Vicente.

Lorenzo said icily, "I do not believe this gentleman is among our guests this evening."

"He is here at *my* invitation," said Teresa quickly.

"Indeed. In that case you had better bring him to the house and not leave him skulking like a beggar in the gardens."

There was no mistaking the contempt in his voice and Teresa flushed angrily.

110

"It's what I intended to do. Come, Vicente."

But the bullfighter had no intention of risking his luck and his reputation in that distinguished company. There he would invariably lose the glamour and excitement of the secret meetings that so entranced the young girl.

"Better not, Teresa," he said. "I will go now."

"Are you afraid she won't like you so much in the light of day?" said Lorenzo. "I do not much care for my sister being tempted into assignations alone and at midnight. Do you know the way through the gardens or shall I order my servants to escort you?"

Vicente threw up his head. "You'll live to regret saying that, Don Lorenzo," he said insolently. "One day you may be glad to invite me into your Castillo." He turned to Teresa, "*Adios, cara mia*," kissed her hand and then walked jauntily away down the path.

"Oh how could you, Lorenzo, how could you be so hateful?" raged Teresa.

"What have I done? It was his choice. I invited him to join us."

"Knowing full well that he wouldn't."

His voice hardened. "Where else have you been meeting him, Teresa? What is this man to you?"

"I love him," she flung at him. "I love him and now you know."

"Nonsense. How can you love a man like that?"

"I know what you think. You despise him because he is one of the people, because he has fought his way up from poverty."

"No, not for that. Because he is a braggart and a liar who only runs after you because you are a Merenda and my sister. Because he is seeking his own advantage. Can't you see that, you little fool?"

"No, I can't. He loves me and I love him. Don't you know what love is, Lorenzo? You ought to. What about Gabriella?"

"Be silent, Teresa," he said dangerously.

"I won't be silent. You hate me. You don't want me to be happy, you spoil everything."

"That's not true. Listen to me, Teresa," he said more gently. He reached out to take her hand but she tore herself away from him.

"I'm not listening to you any longer. I know whom you want

111

me to marry but I won't do it, I won't, I won't! I'll kill myself first."

"You're talking like a child," he said in exasperation, but Teresa swept on heedlessly.

"You think yourself so much better than Roberto and me and yet you bring your – your whore into the house tonight. You dance with her in front of everyone . . ."

In ungovernable anger he struck her across the face and she stood aghast, her hand flown to her cheek, her eyes blazing.

"I'll never forgive you for that, never, never, never!" and she ran away from him up the garden path, stumbling in her haste, disappearing like a white moth into the trees leaving her brother staring after her, half ashamed of what he had done.

Charlotte wished passionately that she was not there. She would have liked to steal away unobserved but there was no way except past Lorenzo.

After a moment he stirred and turned to her.

"I apologise for my sister, for both of us. It was unpardonable in front of a guest."

"She is very distressed. Should I go after her?"

"No. Leave her. She'll come to her senses. We all have to at some time or another. Come, it is time we returned to the house."

It seemed strange after such a disturbing outburst of raw emotion to find the orchestra playing and the dancers still whirling merrily around the ballroom.

Lucy was sitting with Doña Gracia. She looked up as Charlotte joined them. "We wondered what had happened to you. You disappeared after Gabriella danced."

"It was so hot in here. I went for a little walk and found the Nun's garden. What a wonderfully beautiful place it is."

"It's our great pride that we have contrived to keep it intact through the centuries despite wars and weather," said Doña Gracia smiling.

"Roberto showed it to me the first day we came to the Castillo. It was so lovely I could have wished to live there for ever," said Lucy dreamily.

"You would soon become very bored, my dear, as that poor girl must have done hiding her ruined beauty from the world. By the way," went on Doña Gracia, "where has Teresa hidden herself? Some of our guests are leaving. She ought to be here to thank them for their gifts and say goodbye."

112

"I thought I saw her return to the house ahead of us," said Charlotte carefully.

"She has no doubt gone up to her room. I'll send one of the servants to fetch her."

But Teresa did not appear and it was Lorenzo who came to take his place beside his grandmother.

"What has upset our Corsair?" whispered Lucy wickedly. "He looks black as thunder."

"I've no idea."

"Oh Charlotte, don't pretend you don't know. I saw you come in with him. Is it Teresa again?"

"I tell you I don't know. I was only with him for a few minutes."

She did not want to talk about what had happened. It was too upsetting. Those few magical moments in the Nun's garden had been spoiled by Teresa's revelations which might have been inspired by anger but must have truth behind them. In any case why should she be concerned over Lorenzo's love affairs, she told herself, and found to her dismay that she was – very concerned.

She realized that Lucy was still talking.

"The Marquésa hopes soon to arrange a marriage for her with a young man who is very much in love with her. His name is Enrique de Tajo – did you see him? He was dancing with her."

So that had played a part in Teresa's defiance of her brother that night. "I'm afraid that young woman has a will of her own. If they try to force her, she might do something silly."

"I don't think the Marquésa would do that," said Lucy doubtfully.

"No, but Lorenzo might and live to regret it," murmured Charlotte.

It was four o'clock by the time they arrived back at the Casa de Fuente and were all three of them glad to fall into bed. It was only Charlotte who lay wakeful, the events of the evening going round and round in her head, still feeling Lorenzo's kisses that had awakened a response she had never yet known, not even in those far-off days when she had believed herself in love with Clive. This was different, this was something so powerful that it frightened her, unaware that within her there lay a well of deep feeling inherited from a father to whom it had brought an overwhelming passion and a searing anguish.

113

She slept at last and woke to an agitated knocking on the door. She struggled to consciousness through heavy sleep, aware of Juanita's voice, and dragged herself up in the bed.

"What is it?" she called. "What has happened?"

"It is Don Roberto, Señorita. He is asking to speak to you."

Juanita had opened the door and stood just inside, black eyes snapping with curiosity.

"What time is it?" asked Charlotte yawning.

"After eleven o'clock."

"Is Señor Starr up yet?"

"Both he and the Señora are still sleeping and it is you whom Don Roberto is asking for most particularly."

"Very well. Tell him I will come."

Juanita bustled away and Charlotte, stretching and yawning, struggled into a dressing-gown, splashed water on her face, ran a comb through her hair, pushed her bare feet into slippers and went down the stairs.

Roberto turned as she came into the sitting room. He was wearing breeches and boots and by the sweat on his face he must have ridden hard and fast.

"I apologize for disturbing you but I had to come. Teresa is not with you, is she?" he asked eagerly.

"No. Why should she be?"

"No reason, I just hoped." He paused, rubbing his hand distractedly across his face. "The fact is, she has disappeared."

"Disappeared? How do you mean?"

"She was not in her room this morning and her bed hadn't been slept in, but we didn't know until after ten o'clock, since her maid thought she was sleeping late when she did not ring. One of the horses had gone from the stables and we think she has packed a valise and taken it with her. It seems she and Lorenzo quarrelled last night. He thinks she may have ridden off to one of our friends out of temper. It's the kind of thing she might do. He has sent messages and is searching himself. I thought she might have come to you or told you something about what she intended to do. I know how much she admires you."

Oh no! thought Charlotte remembering every word of that painful scene in the garden. Pray God she has not run to Vicente!

"When did she leave the house, Roberto?" she asked.

114

"We don't know exactly. Lorenzo was angry because she did not come down when the guests were leaving. Afterwards he went up to her room. She would not let him in but spoke to him through the door and that is the last we know. The men and boys at the stables slept late and did not hear her lead out the mare and saddle her."

"She said nothing to me, Roberto, but the quarrel with Lorenzo was over a secret meeting with Don Vicente in the garden last night."

"*Madre de Dios*," breathed Roberto. "If Lorenzo thinks she has gone to him, he will kill them both."

"Surely you exaggerate."

"You don't know him, Charlotte. The honour of the family means everything to him. I must go. I must find her before he does. There are some people here in Seville, a girl she was friendly with in the Convent, I will call on them. If you hear anything, anything at all, you will send us word."

"Yes, of course. I wish I could do more."

He went out quickly and a moment later Juanita came in with a tray. She had learned to make English tea and was proud of her skill.

"You'll be needing this, Señorita." She put the tray down on the table. "That Doña Teresa is a wild one and no mistake. The Marqués should take a big stick to her. That's what my father would have done."

"No doubt, but Don Lorenzo is not her father but her brother," said Charlotte dryly, "and don't talk about this in the market, Juanita. It's probably some childish prank."

"Now would I do such a thing, Señorita? Not a word will they get out of me. I know when to keep my mouth shut."

Charlotte hoped she did but doubted it, knowing how Juanita loved to gossip. She carried the tray upstairs, drinking the tea while she hurriedly dressed.

Lucy and Clive were inclined to take it lightly when she told them what had happened.

"It's a silly trick but the girl probably wants to give her prig of a brother a damned good fright," said Clive. "She'll come back just at the right moment to find them falling on her neck in thankfulness that it's not something worse."

Charlotte wished she could believe him but her cousin had not heard the bitter words or seen the look of desperation on

115

Teresa's face. At eighteen you can believe yourself passionately in love and any opposition can seem sheer cruelty and become world-shaking. If she had gone to Don Vicente, what would he do? Hold the family up to ransom to protect her reputation? She did not think that Lorenzo would give in to any threat made against him.

The day wore on and no news of any kind reached them. The weather had turned very warm and Lucy, weary after the late night, took a siesta during the afternoon lying on her bed in a shaded room. Charlotte was too restless to follow her example. She picked up a book and after a moment threw it down again. Then impatiently she fetched a shady hat and went out into the sunshine. There was a hush over Seville. Even the stall-keepers in the market were nodding over their flowers and fruit. There was to be a *corrida* on the following day, the last of the season. Huge gaudily painted posters met her everywhere with a crude picture of Vicente's handsome face. She walked down to the river and sat on the tree-shaded bank worrying about Teresa and about her own conflicting feelings about Lorenzo, until at last heat and drowsiness overcame her. She woke up with a start from a brief doze as a parasol gently prodded her in the ribs and she looked up quickly to see Sybilla with Don Vicente beside her.

"You were smiling so sweetly, you must have been enjoying a beautiful dream," she said lightly.

"Not particularly."

Charlotte scrambled to her feet feeling awkward and yet aware of relief. If Vicente was strolling with Sybilla, then Teresa could not be with him. All the same there was something odd about the searching look he gave her.

"Forgive me, Señoritas," he said brusquely, quite unlike his usual smooth easy manner, "if I leave you. Tomorrow as you know I fight and there are still preparations to be made."

He bowed to her and Sybilla and hurried away as if he were glad to escape.

Sybilla linked her arm with Charlotte and they walked together along the path.

"There is a strong rumour that the little Merenda girl is throwing herself at Vicente. The poor man is at his wits' end to know what to do about it," she said.

Charlotte knew she had been extremely annoyed at not being invited to the ball and guessed that she was retaliating with the first spiteful gossip that occurred to her.

"Like most rumours I imagine there is little truth in it," she replied coolly. She wouldn't give Sybilla the satisfaction of hearing about Teresa's running away. "I can't imagine that a daughter of the Castillo de Palomas has any need to throw herself at anyone. It would be rather the other way about. Where did you hear it?"

Sybilla shrugged her shoulders. "Here and there. He mentioned it himself."

"Indeed. *Does* a gentleman talk about such things?"

"Oh Charlotte, isn't that rather old-fashioned?"

"I don't happen to think so." She glanced up at the other's flushed face. "Do *you* find him attractive?" she asked bluntly.

"Heavens, what a question!" She twirled her parasol airily. "I suppose I do – in a way. I like a man with a touch of the brute in him."

"And you think Vicente is like that?"

"Oh yes, definitely. Didn't you see it for yourself when we watched him fight the bull?"

"I'm afraid I shut my eyes to most of it."

Sybilla looked at her curiously. "I don't understand you, Charlotte. You like to be independent. Don't you long for things to happen?"

"What kind of things?"

"Oh, I don't know, something thrilling and dangerous in which you can play a part. It would be like lighting a fire and watching it burn not knowing what it might destroy."

"That sounds rather irresponsible."

"Oh I suppose I am sometimes, or so Papa says."

They had reached the Casa de Fuente by now and Charlotte said, praying Sybilla would not accept, "Will you come in and take tea with us?"

"Thank you, no. We have guests this evening and Mother likes me to be there. Such a bore."

Charlotte watched her walk away, slim, graceful, with a self-confidence she was inclined to envy. If that was how Sybilla thought about men, she wondered why she bothered with Clive, unless his fastidious elegance made a contrast to Vicente's more obvious charms. Perhaps Sybilla liked the best of both worlds, but it did strike her that she might be playing a very dangerous game. She sighed and went in to Lucy. There was still no news of Teresa and Clive had gone out.

"There's a card party," said Lucy. "He'll be gambling half the night, I expect. I think I'll go to bed early. I'm still tired from yesterday."

Was it Mr Robinson's card party or was it more serious, one of those political meetings Lorenzo had spoken of? Charlotte wished she could be sure.

In the end they both retired soon after ten o'clock but Charlotte did not sleep. She lay propped up in bed reading and it must have been well after midnight when she heard a strange noise. It sounded like someone weeping, the sobbing breaths of a child who has cried itself into utter exhaustion and for a heart-stopping moment she thought it might be Lucy before she realized that it came from outside her window. She got out of bed, opened the casement wider and peered out. Below her the wall went down sheer beside the entrance door and she thought she could see a figure leaning against it. Again there came that sobbing intake of breath and she leaned further out.

"Who is it?" she called softly. "What do you want?"

A white blur of a face turned up to her. "Charlotte," whispered a voice, "is it Charlotte?"

"Teresa! Wait," she whispered, "wait. I'm coming down."

She threw a shawl around her shoulders and hurried down the stairs. The bolts were heavy but she managed to pull them back noiselessly and opened the door. Teresa was standing just outside. Faint moonlight showed her hair hanging loose around her shoulders, her riding habit bedraggled and filthy.

"Oh my dear, what have you done to yourself?"

"May I come in?" said the girl pitifully and took a wavering step forward. She was very close to collapse and Charlotte put a steadying arm around her.

"Come this way. What have you done with your horse?"

"I left her in your stableyard. There was a light."

That would be Jaime. On some of these warm nights he bedded down over the stables. He would see to the horse. One good thing about Spanish servants, they were always ready to accept without question any strange behaviour on the part of their employers.

"Come inside." She drew Teresa into the hall, shut the door and then led her into the sitting room.

"Wait a moment. I'll get a light."

With the candle lit she saw that Teresa's riding skirt was soaked almost to the waist and thick with mud and green slime.

"What on earth happened to you?"

"I thought I would drown myself," she said in a hoarse whisper. "I walked into the river but then at the last moment I was a coward. I couldn't do it. It was so dark and smelled so horrible." She shuddered and seemed to draw into herself. "Besides I couldn't drown Bianca as well, could I? It wouldn't have been fair. She had done nothing."

"Oh Teresa!" Charlotte was appalled at what must have driven the girl to such desperate measures. "Come upstairs with me," she said bracingly. "You must take those wet clothes off."

"You're not angry with me for coming here? I didn't know where else to go."

"Of course I'm not angry. First things first. You can tell me what happened afterwards."

She persuaded Teresa to come up to her bedroom, helped her to undress and put her into one of her own nightgowns. She saw then that despite the warm night Teresa was shivering uncontrollably.

"Now slip into bed," she said. "Have you had anything to eat?"

"No, I don't think so. Not since I left the Castillo."

"I'm going to get you a hot drink."

She stole down to the kitchen, found some of the chocolate they had been drinking at supper, warmed it on the dying fire and brought it up with some biscuits.

"Now drink that."

"I don't want anything."

"Don't be silly. You decided not to drown yourself so there's no point in starving to death."

Teresa managed a wan smile. "No, I suppose not."

Charlotte was glad to see that after the first sip she finished the cup and began to nibble one of the biscuits.

"That's better. Now do you want to tell me about it or would you rather wait till morning? I must send Tomás to the Castillo as soon as it's light."

119

"No." Teresa dropped the biscuit and seized her arm. "No. I'm not going back. Lorenzo will kill me."

"Nonsense. He'll do nothing of the kind."

"He will when he knows the terrible thing I've done."

"We'll see about that. There's your grandmother too. We must think of her. She will be out of her mind with anxiety."

"Yes, I know," muttered Teresa unhappily.

Charlotte took one of her hands. "Tell me," she said gently, "what did you do that was so terrible?"

Teresa was silent for a little, one hand plucking nervously at the sheet. "I went to Vicente. You see, I believed he loved me as I loved him. I thought it would be marvellous – we would brave it out together – defy Lorenzo, defy the whole world."

Gallant, heroic, childish gesture! thought Charlotte, but life is not like that and certainly not for Vicente with his career still only in the making. The Marqués de Merenda was powerful enough to damn him for ever if the scandal broke just then and Lorenzo was quite capable of it.

"Go on," she urged. "What happened?"

"You know where he lodges. He has an apartment in the Triana not far from the Café Diablo. It was about seven o'clock in the morning when I got there – it was silly but I couldn't wait. If I had, perhaps I wouldn't have had the courage. He was still in bed. I sent in word by the servant and he came out to me." She stared in front of her, her eyes tragic. "He didn't want me, Charlotte, he was angry because I had come. He told me to go away. He was to fight in the *corrida* and – and I would only be a burden to him." She caught her breath in a sob. "But that wasn't the worst. Someone called out to him from the inner room – a woman's voice – and I knew then why he wanted to be rid of me. She must have been there with him – he must have gone straight from me to her last night. Lorenzo was right. He didn't love *me* at all – it was all a pretence . . ." She turned away, burying her head in the pillow and shaking with dry sobs.

Charlotte said nothing, letting the spasm pass, and after a moment, when Teresa had pulled herself together, she said quietly, "Who was she? Do you know?"

"No, but she was not Spanish."

Sybilla? Could it be? If so – poor Clive, but this was no time to think of that.

120

"Did anyone see you there? Did they recognize you?"

"I don't know. There were several men outside – hangers-on. One of them laughed when I came out. I felt so humiliated I wanted to die."

"Why didn't you go back to the Castillo?"

"I couldn't," she said fiercely, "I couldn't bear to hear Lorenzo say 'I told you so.' It was so hateful. I rode Bianca up into the hills. I don't remember where I went or what I did till I came down to the river. No one would care if I ended it all but I didn't have the courage even for that." She knotted her hands together. "What am I going to do, Charlotte, what am I going to do?"

"Rest now," she said soothingly. "We'll think about it in the morning. Try to sleep."

"You won't go away. Please don't leave me here alone."

"No, I won't go away."

Charlotte hesitated and then blew out the candle and slipped into the bed. She felt the girl's body tense and trembling beside her and after a while put an arm around her shoulders and drew her towards her as if she had been comforting a child. A long time later exhaustion took over and Teresa slept while Charlotte lay wakeful, wondering how she was going to face Lorenzo's anger and reconcile him to his sister's wilful folly.

She was not left very long in doubt. She got up early, leaving Teresa still sleeping, sent Tomás with a message to the Castillo and told Lucy and Clive over breakfast of their unwelcome guest in the room above.

"Jupiter!" exclaimed Clive. "What an idiot the girl must be to trust herself to a fellow like Vicente!"

"When you fall in love at Teresa's age, you don't always think sensibly," said Lucy. "You believe the man you love to be a paragon of all the virtues. It's cruel disillusion when you find out he has feet of clay."

Clive looked uncomfortable for a moment and then shrugged his shoulders.

"Lorenzo will be in a flaming temper, that's for sure," he said, "and I'm getting out of it. I'll leave you two girls to deal with him. It's his responsibility, thank God, not ours."

"He's perfectly right, you know," said Lucy when Clive had left the house. "Teresa must face up to her brother herself."

"Yes, I know," said Charlotte doubtfully. She could not rid

herself of a feeling of sympathy for Teresa. Juanita had sponged and dried the stained riding habit and she took it up to her with a tray of coffee, some freshly baked rolls and fruit.

Teresa was standing by the window in the plain cotton nightgown, looking pale but defiant.

"Is Lorenzo here yet?"

"No."

"You know what he will do if there's the least hint of scandal. He will send me back to the Convent, he will shut me up for the rest of my life. One of the girls at school eloped with a man and she was forced to become a nun by her family. I won't go, I tell you, I won't go whatever he does."

"Lorenzo would never be so cruel. Why are you so afraid of your brother, Teresa?"

"He hates me, he always has. He'll be glad to find a reason to be rid of me."

"I can't believe that. Why should he hate you?"

"I don't know," said Teresa moodily. "It's always been there. I think it's something that happened before I was born."

"Well, drink your coffee and try to eat something. When he comes, I'll speak to him first."

Teresa gave her a quick glance. "That's kind of you but it won't make any difference."

For all her brave words Charlotte felt her knees begin to shake when she heard the horse that came thundering down the narrow street, saw Jaime snatch at the bridle thrown to him and braced herself to face Lorenzo as he came striding into the sitting room.

"Where is she?" he demanded. "Where is Teresa?"

Charlotte forced herself to speak calmly. "She is upstairs."

"Fetch her down if you please."

The peremptory tone put her on her mettle. "In a moment. I'd like to speak to you first."

"No doubt you mean well but this has nothing to do with you, it is between my sister and myself," he said uncompromisingly.

"Perhaps an outsider can see things more clearly," said Charlotte steadily. "Teresa is very afraid of you. She thinks you hate her."

"That is utter rubbish. Why should I hate her? But if she runs away from home and throws herself into the arms of a

122

man like Vicente, how does she expect me to feel? Doña Gracia is sick with anxiety, the entire household is talking of it – *my* sister running after a bullfighter! It's the choicest piece of scandal that's broken for years," he went on savagely.

"Perhaps it's not quite as bad as you believe."

He turned on her angrily. "What do you mean by that? Are you trying to tell me that she did *not* go to Vicente?"

"No, but she certainly spent no time in his arms. I doubt if she was with him longer than half an hour."

"This is the tale she told you, I suppose, and you swallowed it whole," he said contemptuously.

"I had no reason to doubt it. It was midnight when she came here, utterly exhausted, desperately unhappy and soaked to the skin having tried to drown herself."

He looked startled. "Was he weary of her so soon? Did it only take him a day to use her and reject her?"

"She did not spend the day with him."

"Then why did she not return to the Castillo?"

"Chiefly because of you."

"I? What the devil do you mean by that?"

She took a deep breath. "If you would just be quiet for a few minutes and let me tell you what really happened, perhaps you might understand."

He stared at her for an instant and then said abruptly, "Very well. Go on. I am listening."

He walked away towards the window and stood with his back to her. Faltering a little she told him the sad little tale of disillusion and despair as Teresa had related it to her.

"And you are sure that this is what happened?" he said slowly, when she had come to an end.

"Yes, I am sure. Teresa was too heartbroken to lie. Also I myself had seen Vicente during the afternoon with another companion."

He turned round to face her. "It would give me the greatest pleasure to break that young man's neck."

"I hope you won't. That would cause even greater scandal."

"Perhaps, but it would prevent him causing more trouble to me or anyone else." He was looking at her curiously. "Why have you so much sympathy with my foolish little sister?"

"Have I? I thought I was just being ordinarily sensible about it."

"Oh no, it's much more than that. Is it because you have suffered in the same way?"

"Why should you say that?"

He went across to her, stretching out a hand and turning her face towards him.

"Was it your cousin Clive who won *your* love?"

"You have no right to ask me that!"

"No, perhaps not, but it doesn't prevent me from thinking him a great fool to throw away a pearl of such price."

She stared at him, feeling the colour flood up into her face and quite unable to think of a suitable reply.

For a moment his eyes held hers, then he went on brusquely, "Would you ask Teresa to come down to me now? She has trespassed on your hospitality long enough."

"You won't –?"

"For God's sake, I'm not an ogre," he said impatiently. "I won't beat her or shut her up on bread and water or send her back to the Convent she dislikes so much. I won't even force her to marry Enrique de Tajo – I've too much respect for him! Her grandmother and I will think of something else."

She wasn't sure but she thought she had won her battle. The anger had died out of his eyes and the stern face held the merest hint of a smile. She went out and up the stairs, meeting Teresa halfway.

"I felt guilty," she whispered, "at leaving you to face him alone. I can't hide for ever."

"He is waiting for you, Teresa."

They came down the stairs together and she saw the girl hesitate in the doorway. Then Lorenzo held out his hand.

"What's all this I've been hearing about you, little one," he said, but his tone was gentle.

"Lorenzo," she murmured in a strangled voice and then ran across the room and into his arms.

Thankfully Charlotte shut the door and retreated to the garden. Now it was all over she felt remarkably shaky.

"What happened?" asked Lucy. "Has he eaten her up?"

"Not quite," Charlotte laughed. "I think it is going to be all right."

A few minutes later they came to say goodbye. Teresa was tearstained but Lorenzo's arm was around her. Jaime brought the horses and Charlotte watched them ride away together.

"Well, that's the end of that," said Lucy thankfully.

But it was not quite the end though Charlotte did not hear about it till afterwards. Lorenzo took his sister back to the Castillo, left her with Doña Gracia and immediately rode back to Seville. It was still early and Vicente who was fighting that afternoon had not yet left for the bullring.

Lorenzo went to his apartment in the Triana, threw the reins of his horse to one of the urchins in the gutter and, riding crop in hand, strode through the little crowd hanging about outside, scattering them to right and left. He flung open the door of the inner room where Vicente was dressing and slammed it shut after him.

What he did or what he said no one knew for sure. He came out shortly afterwards, took his horse, threw down some money and rode away. Vicente led the usual procession into the ring that afternoon but for the first time since he had risen to fame, he failed to kill the bull cleanly with one stroke of the sword. The mob, who were as eager to condemn as to cheer, booed him relentlessly even when he was knocked down and narrowly escaped being gored.

A murderous anger burned inside him. His pride, his self-confidence, had been deeply wounded and that night as he sat in the café moodily drinking and brooding over his humiliation, a man came furtively through the door and crossed to him, slipping silently into the seat beside him.

José Roméro was a persuasive talker and Vicente listened sullenly. He cared nothing for Don Carlos or his cause and even less for his country's future, except where it concerned himself, but he longed passionately for an opportunity to punish the insolent and all powerful Marqués de Merenda who had effectively destroyed his ambitious plans, and now it was miraculously being offered to him. The two men went out of the café arm in arm.

8

June had come in with golden skies and a flaming heat but Charlotte revelled in it. She had never felt better or more tinglingly alive. The sun had given a bloom to her creamy skin and burnished her hair to a rich red gold. One morning she was sitting on the patio enjoying the sharp scent of the lemon tree and the sound of the cool water bubbling in the little fountain while she stitched at a new gown in thin white cotton patterned with green leaves. She held it up examining the fall of the flounces critically as Lucy came out of the house.

"How fresh and pretty that material is," she remarked. "It's going to suit you, Charlie."

"Do you really think so? I wondered perhaps if it was too *jeune fille*."

"What nonsense! You're not an old married matron like me," and Lucy subsided into one of the chairs with a long sigh.

Charlotte glanced at her anxiously. The Spanish sunshine she so much enjoyed did not agree with Lucy. She wilted under it. Her skin was sallow. There were dark shadows under her eyes and she had lately suffered several sick and dizzy spells.

"Are you feeling better this morning?"

"Well enough," said Lucy listlessly. "For the next few months I suppose I shall have to make the best of it."

"You don't mean –?"

"Yes. It's the second month I've missed. Whether I like it or not I'm going to have a baby."

"Oh dearest, don't look so wretched about it. It will be wonderful."

"Will it? I'd much rather have waited until we go back to England."

"Oh Lucy, why? You know how much you hate the damp and the cold in London. You won't have to suffer any of that here. The winter will be mild and warm and the baby will be born before the spring. Have you told Clive?"

126

"No, and I don't intend to – not yet. He is going away. Didn't he tell you?"

"Going away? Where?"

"Up into the mountains. They are making up a party, about six or seven of them, I think. They will take their guns, do a little shooting, visit all kinds of places. He says he hopes to do some sketching."

Charlotte frowned. "But is that wise? There's been a lot of trouble in the Sierras. Don't you remember? Mr Robinson told us about the mailcoach that was attacked, all the letters burned and one of the guards killed."

"Clive thinks he is safe enough. He has a pass signed by a man calling himself José Roméro."

Roméro – the man she had seen talking with Clive in the Roman amphitheatre, the man Lorenzo had spoken of with such contempt.

"But he is a bandit and a Carlist, everyone says so."

"Clive is not worried, nor, I gather, are any of the others." She leaned her head back wearily. "It seems that Sybilla is to be one of the party."

So that was what was tormenting Lucy. "You should tell him about the baby."

"No. Let him go," said Lucy with a flash of anger. "I'm not begging him to stay with me simply because I'm unlucky enough to be bearing his child."

It distressed Charlotte to hear her talk so bitterly and she was greatly tempted to tell Clive herself, but she would not go against Lucy's wishes and, in any case, she doubted if it would make him change his plans. He was behaving very strangely these days, out of the house a great deal of the time, and then quite accidentally going into his studio one day she saw him counting money into a leather bag.

"Isn't that rather a large sum to keep in the house?" she asked him. "It's far more than we need."

She thought he looked disconcerted but he calmly went on putting away the pesetas. "We may be on the road for a few weeks. We shall need plenty of cash for travelling expenses," was his glib explanation, but she still thought the sum was far greater than they could possibly want for such an expedition.

After a moment he looked up. "What are you staring at?" he said irritably.

"Nothing in particular."

"I suppose you are thinking that this is Lucy's money and I should be asking her permission first. Is that it?"

"Why should I think any such thing?"

"Oh, God, I don't know, but you look at me so disapprovingly sometimes, Charlie."

"I've never thought you cared very much whether I approved or disapproved."

"The fact is . . ." He seemed on the point of confiding in her, then abruptly changed his mind, tied the neck of the leather bag, opened a drawer and dropped it in.

"Clive," she said hesitantly, "Lucy said something about José Roméro giving you a pass. What did she mean?"

"Oh that. It was just a joke when we were talking one evening. You know how the Spanish think of their bandits – a kind of Robin Hood as far as I can gather. Someone said all we needed was a pass issued by Roméro. Lucy must have thought we were serious."

"Is that all?" She was not sure she believed him.

"Of course it is all."

He said nothing more and made light of the various rumours that were reaching them of the spread of the civil war. A party of Carlists had ravaged through the streets of Madrid and been expelled after a bloody battle. The royal family had prudently withdrawn to one of their summer palaces, keeping their exact whereabouts uncertain, and marauding bands calling themselves soldiers occasionally attacked travellers in the mountains. Only Andalusia still seemed to be living in its golden paradise.

All the same, Charlotte was still worried more on Lucy's account than her own and one afternoon, about a week before Clive was to leave, she rode up to the Castle of Doves ostensibly to ask after Teresa, but also with the intention of seeking advice from Lorenzo – or was she simply looking for an opportunity to see him again? It was something she refused to acknowledge even to herself.

The air grew fresher as she left the simmering heat of the plain behind her and the garden of the Castillo as she rode under the chestnuts seemed pleasantly cool. Doña Gracia received her kindly. She was brought a long drink of freshly squeezed lemons and drank it gratefully as she asked after Teresa.

"She is spending a few weeks with cousins of ours who live at Toledo. Lorenzo thought it best that she should be away from here for a time." The Marquésa leaned forward putting a thin hand on Charlotte's arm. "My dear, we are deeply grateful to you for all you did for that foolish child. I tremble to think what might have happened to her if you had not been there to give her refuge."

"I was only too glad to help. I hope she is not too unhappy."

"She will get over it and learn from it, I hope. Teresa has always been wilful but she is a good girl at heart."

They chatted pleasantly for a while and, sitting in that cool and lovely room opening on to the stone patio where the roses hung heavy with perfume and the white doves sleepily fluttered down in the afternoon heat, Charlotte found it hard to believe that in other parts of Spain men were being mustered, arms collected, rifles distributed and already lives had been uselessly sacrificed.

Presently, Roberto came in looking bronzed and cheerful, apologizing to his grandmother for entering her drawing room straight from the stables.

"Marco told me you were here," he said smiling at Charlotte. "Lorenzo is away today so I'm afraid you must make do with me."

"Take our guest into the garden, Roberto, it's cooler now. I'll order the servants to make some English tea. It will refresh Señorita Carlotta before her ride home."

Strolling beside Roberto in the scented quiet of the Nun's garden she asked him bluntly how much the threatened war was likely to touch them in the coming months and whether Clive should think again before undertaking his hunting trip.

"I don't really know any more than you do," he confessed, drawing her to sit beside him on the stone seat under the arcaded terrace. "I only know one thing for sure – Lorenzo will take no part in it."

"Is there any reason why he should?"

"There could be," he went on, leaning forward and staring down at his clasped hands. "Our family is an old and honourable one. He would be expected to use his influence, even to fight if necessary, for the Cortés and for the little Queen Isabel."

"And you think he is wrong not to do so?"

"Oh I understand him," said Roberto earnestly. "You see Lorenzo grew up in a war. When Napoleon was finally defeated, he was only fifteen but he saw all the ruin and devastation it had caused. He fought hard to rebuild the family estates and they were desperately cruel years, Charlotte. I was only a child but I remember the killings and how the battle still went on. There were many who did not want to see Ferdinand back on the throne, many who resented his harsh rule and were exiled, driven into poverty, their possessions confiscated, and then there was Manuela."

She looked up at that name. "Who was Manuela?"

"It was five years ago now. She and Lorenzo were betrothed."

"Was he very much in love with her?" The question slipped out before she could stop herself.

Roberto smiled. "I don't know about that. Lorenzo doesn't wear his heart on his sleeve. He was fond of her, of course, we all were, she was so sweet and beautiful. It was a suitable match – you know what I mean – in families such as ours marriages are often arranged in that way."

"What happened?"

"Manuela's father, the Conde de Tajo, was linked with the liberal party in the state. Ferdinand could play the tyrant at times. I don't know precisely how he had offended, but I do know it had something to do with the Englishmen who landed here in a crazy attempt to bring down the government. They were all executed and soldiers were sent to arrest him. His own servants, in an attempt to give him time to escape, tried to prevent their entry. There was a scuffle. The Conde was attacked and Manuela, who adored her father, threw herself between them. Some trigger-happy guardsman shot her dead."

"How terrible!"

"It was hushed up, of course. They called it an accident. Her father was allowed to leave the country unharmed but it sickened Lorenzo. He had been on his way to visit them. If he had arrived a few hours earlier he might have prevented the tragedy. He never forgave himself for that. He swore then that he would take no part in any politics. He was offered an appointment at Court and refused it. What the country needed and what he needed, he said, was to live in peace for a generation, to be given time to cultivate the land, care for the family

130

and make a better life for his dependants. Perhaps he is right."

"You don't agree with him, Roberto?"

"I'm not sure. For him maybe, it *is* right." He made a sweeping gesture. "All this is his responsibility, but it is not mine. They are crying out for volunteers. Enrique de Tajo – he is Manuela's brother – has gone already."

"Is he the young man who wants to marry Teresa?"

"Yes, he is very disappointed that she has refused him. I would like to join him in Madrid and fight with the Cristinos."

"Can Lorenzo prevent you from going?"

"No, not really, though he is my guardian until I am twenty-five and that is not until this winter, but I know he would be strongly against it and though we fight like dogs sometimes, I *am* fond of him, Charlotte."

"I think he is absolutely right," she said slowly. "I believe that civil war must be the very worst thing that can happen in any country."

"Perhaps," he said ruefully, "but I sometimes feel so useless here."

She thought she understood. Lorenzo was so dominating a personality that his brother felt he lived in his shadow and longed to strike out for himself, but not surely in a war. She had a vivid memory of her father, often sick, his health ruined, only able to enjoy half a life and could not wish such a fate for Roberto.

"We've come a long way from what you asked me," he said cheerfully, taking her arm and helping her to rise. "Let's go back and drink tea with Grandmother. I don't think your cousin will meet with any real difficulties or has anything to fear, provided he travels with a well armed party and takes care to hide his money. Most of these ruffians are arrant cowards."

She rode back to Seville slowly. The talk with Roberto had given her a great deal to think about. She had begun to understand Lorenzo better, to realize that the harshness, the authority he wielded at the Castillo, had sprung from the difficult circumstances of his life and perhaps also served as a protective shield against the problems he had been obliged to face. She remembered the lovely face in the locket she had seen in his cabin on the *Iberia* and guessed that it must have been a portrait of Manuela. Did he still grieve for her? The lines he had marked and she had laboriously translated still stayed in her mind –

> "I live without inhabiting
> Myself – in such a state that I
> Am dying though I do not die . . ."

And then there was Gabriella – what did she mean to him? Had she provided him with consolation? She tried to thrust these painful speculations out of her mind but they kept coming back. After all she had problems enough of her own, Lucy and the coming child, Clive whom she suspected of involving himself in some dark plot that he regretted.

Zelda, scenting home and her supper, quickened her pace and as Charlotte guided her across the bridge of boats, her spirits began to rise. Life in Spain might have its trials but how much more exciting it was than a dreary existence at Breakstone, running a hundred errands for her Aunt and Uncle at the great house or becoming the unwilling stepdaughter of the lumpish Colonel Armstrong. From guarded references in her mother's last letter she gathered he was now a frequent visitor at the cottage and far away from having to watch him in her father's place, she felt no resentment, only a hope that her mother might find in him the satisfaction she had never really known with Harry Starr.

A few days later they watched the hunting party ride away. In addition to Clive there were three other young men whom they had met frequently at card parties and social evenings. Sybilla, looking remarkably handsome in a new riding habit, was chaperoned by Mrs James, the dashing widow of an army officer who had lately come from Gibraltar bringing with her a certain barrack-room freedom of speech that shocked Lucy and amused Charlotte who had experienced it in her father's company.

When they turned back into the house together Lucy said a little shyly, "I thought at one time that Clive might have asked you to go with them."

"Good heavens, why?"

"You ride so well and he always admired you for that. Are you sorry that you are obliged to remain here with me?"

"I must admit that I'd like to explore the mountains," she

said honestly, "and I hope one day it may be possible but certainly not on this occasion."

"The going may be rough, I suppose," went on Lucy doubtfully.

"It's not that. I wouldn't mind that at all, but imagine having to share a room every night with Sybilla and Mrs James and be obliged to listen to those highly-coloured stories of her conquests!" Lucy giggled and Charlotte put an arm through hers. "It will be very pleasant to be on our own. We can do as we please and go wherever we like."

And in one way it was true. With Clive gone from the house, the feeling of friction, the occasional barbed remarks between him and Lucy, had all vanished and they were very comfortable together until something happened that swept everything else out of their minds.

Charlotte had taken to rising very early. It was the coolest part of the day and many little tasks could be done at that time, leaving long lazy hours to be spent in the garden or riding or driving when Lucy felt well enough. She came down one morning about a week after Clive had left to find Juanita with Rosa, Tomás and Jaime outside on the pavement agog with excitement and deep in agitated talk with some of the market people. They turned to her as she joined them, all speaking at once so that it took her several minutes to disentangle what they were saying. The news had come through the peasants walking down from the hills with their donkeys.

"It's the Carlists," said Juanita dramatically, black eyes on fire with righteous indignation. "Do you know what they have done, Señorita? They have burned the Merenda vineyards, destroyed everything . . ."

"Don Evaristo half dead and the woman and child too," went on Rosa, not to be outdone and holding up her hands in horror. "May the good Lord forgive them for what they have done!"

The story was so tangled, so full of horrific details, that Charlotte scarcely knew what to believe.

Considerably shocked and with Juanita and Rosa still lamenting loudly, she prepared some tea and carried it up to Lucy who was still troubled with morning sickness. She put the tray on the table and sat on the bed to tell her about it.

"What a dreadful thing to happen," said Lucy. "Poor Mr

Macalister – he was so proud of the work he was doing there."

"And Don Lorenzo," added Charlotte, remembering the happy day she had spent at the vineyard, how they had tasted the sherry together and spoken of the vintage they hoped to produce that autumn.

She stood up and walked to the window, the resolution beginning to harden within her. Impulsively she turned back to Lucy.

"Would you mind very much if I rode over there to find out what has really happened?"

"Should you go?" said Lucy with a little worried frown. "Mightn't it be dangerous?"

"Oh I don't think so. I could take Tomás with me. I can't help thinking of Doña Catalina and the little girl. They must be terribly distressed."

She was aware that it was foolish – who was she, after all, a comparative stranger and a foreigner? – and yet she knew she had to go. She must know for certain who had been hurt and why. She could not rid herself of an uneasy feeling that Clive had known something about it and had escaped out of Seville for that very reason and she could not rest until she had found out the truth.

"Do be careful," pleaded Lucy still doubtful. "Don't rush into anything. Those wretches might still be there."

"The farmer who brought the news said they rode through, setting fire to everything they could, and then escaped into the hills before anyone could stop them. But I'll take the greatest care, I promise you, so don't worry, and look after yourself while I'm gone."

She kissed Lucy and hurried to her room to change into her riding clothes. She went out to the stables and saddled Zelda herself. Without telling Lucy she decided to leave Tomás behind. She could ride a great deal faster without him.

She covered the distance quicker than she had thought possible and she smelled the smoke long before she reached the vineyard. It hung thick and dark, eddying in the hot still air. Then, as she drew nearer, she saw that part of the bodega still burned and teams of men were working frantically to put out the smouldering fires. What had happened, she thought, to those hundreds of barrels, to the university of wine of which

134

they had been so justly proud, to the little family of mice cherished by Don Evaristo?

The white house appeared undamaged but the garden was crushed and ruined where men had ridden ruthlessly through it, trampling and destroying all in their path. Everyone was too busy to take any notice of her so she dismounted, tethered Zelda in the shade of some trees and walked towards the bodega. Don Evaristo was directing the men, looking twenty years older, his shirt ripped from his back, his arm in an improvised sling. Then Guy came hurrying towards her, his face blackened, his clothes filthy and pulled on anyhow.

"Charlotte," he exclaimed, "what are you doing here?"

"I heard about it from men coming into the market. I had to come. How bad is it?"

"Bad enough," he said grimly. "Half the vintage is utterly destroyed. The rest – God knows. We may be able to save something. I don't know yet."

"Is anyone hurt?"

"Don Evaristo has a broken arm, one man is dead and some of the others have been badly knocked about."

"Is Don Lorenzo here?"

"I sent a message. He and Roberto came at once. He has gone after the child."

"Gone after the child? What do you mean?"

"That's the worst part of it. They've taken Paquita."

"But why, for God's sake?"

"She's a valuable hostage and then there is the ransom. It's money they're after and they know well enough Lorenzo would never let any harm come to that child." He put a dirty hand on Charlotte's sleeve. "Could you stay for a little? I ought not to ask you but I would be grateful. The servants have gone to pieces and I'm very worried about Doña Catalina."

"What happened?" She was only just beginning to realize the full horror of that night.

"It was after midnight when they came. We'd had no warning so we were totally unprepared. It was difficult to see in the darkness but there must have been more than thirty of them. The men rallied and did what they could but it was useless. Those damnable robbers rode through like madmen with flaming torches. The place was tinder dry from the weeks of heat and it was easy for them. In the darkness and the confusion no

135

one thought of the child. She must have woken up and run out of the house in terror. One of the men seized hold of her. Doña Catalina tried to stop him and he hit her – he must have used the butt end of his rifle. She is still unconscious. The doctor has been sent for. He should be here soon but the servants are still in a state of panic . . ." He looked at her helplessly.

"I'll go to her. I don't know what I can do but there must be something."

"I'm sure Evaristo would be eternally grateful if you would. He is deeply distressed about her."

"Who were they, Guy? Do you know? *Were* they Carlists? Is this part of the war? Has it come to us here?"

"They were shouting something but they were not soldiers, they were rabble, thieves, killers," he said contemptuously. "They had nothing to do with any political party. It was an organized attack to pay off some private grudge against Lorenzo. That's my opinion and I'm sticking to it. I'd take my oath that rogue José Roméro played a large part in it."

Roméro, the man who was said to have given Clive a pass ensuring his safety and that of his friends in the mountains. A chill feeling that the two events were somehow connected crept over her. It couldn't be true. She tried to shake it off.

Guy sent one of the lads to take Zelda to the stables while Charlotte went into the house and up to the big bedroom with its great bed of black oak, the crucifix hanging above it, the prie-dieu before the statue of Our Lady of Elcho. Catalina lay propped up against the pillows seeming somehow small and shrunken, the heavy bruises beginning to darken on her forehead and cheek. An elderly woman with greying hair sat by the bed, now and again wringing out a towel in cool water and laying it across her mistress's forehead. The doctor had not come yet, she told Charlotte with tears in her eyes. Despite a sharp tongue Doña Catalina had been well liked by her servants.

Charlotte stroked the large capable hand that lay lifeless on the brilliantly coloured counterpane, lovingly embroidered by Doña Catalina herself, but the unconscious woman did not stir. She had never felt so helpless. There was nothing they could do till the doctor came. After a little it occurred to her that Don Evaristo and Guy with the other workers would be badly in need of food. She could at least take upon herself the duties of

136

the household. She said a word to the woman beside the bed and went down to the kitchens.

Not surprisingly the shock had disrupted the usual working day. The servants were huddled together discussing over and over again the appalling events of the night while the cooking pots stood empty and the food lay neglected on the table. It took all her powers of persuasion to rally them but after staring at her resentfully, the stranger and foreigner, her crisp orders were obeyed. They began to work with a will so that presently she could go out to find Guy and tell him that food had been prepared and would be brought out to them where they could eat and rest in the shade of the trees. Only too glad of a respite, the men flung themselves to the ground. Don Evaristo went up to see his wife looking so weary and anxious that Charlotte's heart went out to him but there was no comfort she could offer.

Guy came to thank her for what she had done. "We're conquering the fires," he said, "but it's not possible yet to assess how much damage has been done, especially in the fields. They rode through the new plantings slashing to right and left." He pushed back the sandy sweat-soaked hair. "If you don't mind, I will stay out here and eat with the men. It will put heart into them until Lorenzo comes back."

"May I stay with you?"

"Of course, if you wish. We're not very inviting company, I'm afraid," he said ruefully.

"I don't mind."

She did not want to stay alone in the silent house with the sick woman upstairs. She sat on the grass beside Guy and while she shared the bread and meat, sipping the cool Manzanilla brought up from the cellars, she wondered about Lorenzo. Where was he? Had he found Paquita and, if so, what was the price they would be demanding from him?

The message from Guy had reached the Castillo soon after dawn that morning and Lorenzo had left at once with Roberto to find the bodega in flames, Catalina savagely struck down and the little girl, who held a larger part of his heart than he was willing to admit, carried off by the invaders. A pretty child of eleven in the hands of men who knew no scruples, men who would violate her without another thought – it was unbearable.

He thanked God for Guy who did not panic, who could safely be left in charge, and rode himself after the bandits. He thought he knew most of Roméro's hideouts, but it had been midday before he and Roberto tracked them to their lair in the mountains.

They approached cautiously but he knew by the way the men on watch parted silently to let them through that he was expected. He looked around him at the circle of dark faces, eyes glittering, guns at the ready, and to his fury he knew that he was helpless in their hands.

Roméro faced him with a cool insolence. "To what do we owe the pleasure of your company, Don Lorenzo?"

"You know why," he said curtly. "Give me back the child and name your price."

"All this fuss over a bastard brat – how admirable! Or is it perhaps the proud Merenda blood that runs in her veins? Surprisingly it is not money that is of first importance, Señor, but something else."

"What else is of value to a leader of cut-throats?" he asked with contempt.

There was an angry stir among those around Roméro but he held up his hand checking them.

"You are mistaken. We are Carlists, we fight for a cause. You yourself suffered under the late king's tyranny. Wasn't it his hand that struck down your betrothed? When his brother sits on the throne, it will be different for both of us. Join with us, Don Lorenzo, lend us your name, your influence, your prestige, and the child is yours."

The very notion was ridiculous and they knew it. "You sicken me with such lies. I do not give my support to a rabble of thieves and murderers."

Roméro's face darkened and his hand went to the knife in his belt. "There are others among your friends, your British friends, who hold different views."

"What the devil do you mean by that?"

"You will find out soon enough and in the meantime the price is high. You will pay and pay and leave your brother as proof of your good faith."

"Isn't my word sufficient pledge?"

Roméro shrugged his shoulders. "I have learned to trust no man's word."

138

"Do as he asks, Lorenzo," whispered Roberto. "I will stay."

It maddened him to be forced to leave his brother to their mercy and it would not be easy to find the money quickly. His wealth lay in lands and possessions. It would mean a loan that would have to be repaid and all for a child he was not even certain was his. He would have liked to defy them but the sight of the little girl held in a brutal grip, shivering in her cotton nightgown over which someone had thrown a dirty blanket, weakened him. He held out his hand and they pushed her towards him. She stumbled over the stony path and he caught her up in his arms.

"God damn you, Roméro, but you will have your price," he said through clenched teeth. "Come, *querida*," and he thrust his way through them to where they had tethered his horse.

It was late afternoon by the time he reached the vineyard. Charlotte had gone up to see Doña Catalina again and was disturbed at her appearance. She was breathing heavily and her face had a strange death-like pallor that so alarmed her she came running down the stairs with the intention of asking Guy to send off another urgent message to the doctor.

They both went to meet Lorenzo as he rode wearily into the courtyard, Paquita held in front of him. He had wrapped his black sheepskin jacket over her nightgown but she shivered though the day was warm. He let Guy take her from him before he dismounted, tossing the reins to one of the men. Immediately Paquita pulled away from Guy and ran back to him, her face buried against his shirt. He stroked her hair as if she were a sick puppy.

"She is still very shocked. She believed Catalina to have been killed. It must have been terrifying."

Guy frowned. "They have not harmed her?"

"No. Roméro is too clever for that. He knew while he held her I would do nothing. It's money he wants. Roberto has remained at the camp, a hostage till I can deliver it."

"How much?"

"Enough."

"It's a damnable outrage," exploded Guy. "How dare he after what he has done to you here?"

Lorenzo shrugged his shoulders. "True, but what else can I do? Would you leave a child in the hands of men like that?"

"No, by God, but there must be a way."

139

"There was no way," said Lorenzo wearily. "But I swear that one day he and Vicente shall pay for it."

"Vicente was with Roméro?" exclaimed Guy.

"Two rogues in league with one another. He dare not meet me face to face but I saw him skulking behind the others."

"It's because of Teresa. He can't forgive you for that," said Charlotte and then wished she had not spoken.

Lorenzo in his preoccupation seemed to see her for the first time and frowned. "Forgive me but may I ask what you are doing here?"

"Charlotte came to offer any help she could," said Guy warmly. "And we have been most grateful for all she has done."

Lorenzo's eyes went from Guy to Charlotte. "In that case you have my thanks also. How is Catalina?"

"Still unconscious. I'm very worried. Could another message be sent to the doctor?"

"God damn it, isn't he here yet? See to it, Guy, will you? I must go to Evaristo and the men."

"Won't you eat first? There is food prepared and you must be exhausted," said Charlotte.

"Later." He glanced across to where the servants were gathering up the remnants of the food. "Were you responsible for all this?"

"I did what I could. It was very little. It just needed someone to take charge."

He smiled faintly. "The capable English Miss. Since you are here, will you do something else for me? Will you take care of Paquita for a little while? I shall be carrying her with me to the Castillo when I leave."

"Yes, of course."

She held out her hand but Paquita only clung more fiercely to Lorenzo.

He bent down whispering to the little girl. "Listen to me, *querida*," he said gently. "You can't come with me in your nightgown, it would not be proper, would it? Go with Señorita Carlotta and I will come again in a little while."

"You promise?"

"I promise. Go now."

Reluctantly she let Charlotte take her hand and lead her into the house. In the hall she hung back looking up beseechingly, the dark blue eyes wide with remembered horror.

140

"Tía Catalina – is she dead?" she asked fearfully.

Charlotte realized then that the child must have passed long hours of numbed terror after seeing the woman who had been closer than her own mother brutally struck down and not knowing whether at any moment it might happen to her.

"No," she said quietly, "she is not dead but very sick. Shall we go to your room? When you are washed and dressed, you can see her for a moment."

In the small bedroom with its white curtained bed, the statue of the Christ Child with its blue lamp and vase of fresh flowers, the child was silent while Charlotte helped her to strip and wash, found a fresh cotton dress and combed the tangles from the black hair. Then she took her to the sick woman's room.

The elderly servant exclaimed at the sight of the child and Paquita hushed her with a finger on her lips.

"Don't, Amalia," she said, "you might disturb her."

She wanted to stay but Charlotte would not permit it. She said firmly, "You must come and eat or you will be sick too and then Don Lorenzo will be angry with me."

She thought afterwards that oddly enough it was the dog that helped the child back to normality. As they came down the staircase the door to the kitchen quarters flew open and he shot out barking madly, leaping up at Paquita and licking frantically at her face. She hugged him to her, laying her cheek against his rough furry head. Then the servants were there, all exclaiming at once, hugging her, asking questions and not waiting for answers, carrying her off to the kitchen to be petted, scolded and loved all in a breath. Charlotte left her there feeling she would be happier with them than in the strained atmosphere of the rest of the house.

She stood in the large pleasant room that opened onto the garden, wondering whether now it was time for her to go. She had come filled with an overpowering desire to help and comfort but she might have realized that Lorenzo in his pride and self-sufficiency needed no one. He would lick his wounds in private and show a bold uncaring face to anyone who offered either pity or sympathy. A desolate feeling of loneliness, of not being wanted by anyone, crept over her as she stared out at the ravaged flower beds, the overturned stone pots, the orange trees hacked to the ground, the roses smashed under the horses' hooves. Then resolutely she pulled herself together. She had

141

never been one to indulge in self-pity. She would go upstairs to see Doña Catalina once again, then fetch Zelda and ride home to Lucy who must be worrying herself sick at her long absence.

As she turned from the window, someone came galloping through the gateway. It was a woman, bareheaded, her long hair streaming out behind her as she pounded furiously up the path. She flung herself from the saddle and Charlotte to her surprise saw that it was Gabriella in a closefitting riding habit that moulded her slim figure to perfection, black eyes flashing, riding crop in hand.

A scared boy appeared and she said imperiously, "Is Don Lorenzo here?"

"Si, Señorita," he quavered.

"Then fetch him. Now – at once."

He ducked away from her anger and she strode up and down as she waited, flicking her boot impatiently with the whip, her eyes roving over the wrecked garden and still smouldering bodega.

Charlotte moved back a little out of sight. She knew she should not have stayed to watch the meeting between these two and yet she could not move away when after a moment she saw Lorenzo come walking up the path at a leisurely pace that seemed to infuriate Gabriella.

She rounded on him before he reached her. "Where is Paquita?"

"She is here," he replied calmly. "Where else should she be?"

"That is not what I have heard. I give my child into your care and this is what happens. You leave her with that old fool Evaristo, you allow her to be abducted by ruffians who are no doubt using her for their pleasure. It is disgusting. Where is she?" Her voice had risen stridently.

He said coolly, "Don't distress yourself, Gabriella. The child is unharmed. Roméro gave her back to me – at a price."

"Don't lie to me."

"Have I ever lied?" he replied with a growing anger. "And I seem to remember that five years ago when you begged me to take her from you, you were not so concerned for her future."

"How dare you say that to me? How dare you reproach me? You of all people!" And she raised the whip and slashed out at him. It struck him lightly across the face and he caught her wrist and held it in an iron grip.

142

"Don't ever do that to me again, Gabriella. I suffered it once but not any more. Paquita is quite safe. Surely you know me better. Did you imagine I would leave a child, any child, in the hands of men like that?"

For an instant she still glared at him, then he relaxed his hold and she let her hand drop.

"I'm sorry, Lorenzo, I should not have said that but when the news reached me, all I could think of was that I must come at once to find out the truth. You believe I do not care but it is not so. She is my daughter."

"Mine also or so you have told me often enough," he said dryly.

"Do you doubt me?"

"Enough of this," he said impatiently. "Now you are here you can see her for yourself. I will have her fetched."

"In a moment." She put a hand on his arm lowering her voice a trifle. "You know who is behind all this, don't you?"

"I think I'm beginning to find out."

"Vicente is part of it, of course, with his bully boys. You brought that on yourself. You stopped his game with your foolish little sister. He'll never forgive you for that." She laughed suddenly and unexpectedly. "What did you do to him that day? No, don't tell me, I can guess. You humiliated him so that he lost his nerve. For once he won the hisses of the crowd instead of their cheers. To a man like him that is worse than death on the horns of the bull." She made a contemptuous gesture. "But Vicente is of no importance. It is Roméro whom you should watch."

"What can Roméro do to me?"

"He can force you into taking sides in this war. This attack is only the beginning. It's going to come, Lorenzo, and you won't be able to turn a blind eye to it. He has ambitions. He sees himself as a great man when Don Carlos pushes the little queen off the throne and do you know who is helping him? The *Inglés*, with whom you have had dealings, the man you have welcomed to your house with his silly pretty wife and his cousin who is not so pretty but a good deal cleverer than she appears."

Charlotte froze where she stood. It was Clive of whom she spoke, it must be, but why, why should he have done anything so foolish?

Lorenzo said quietly, "Are you sure of this, Gabriella?"

"Yes, I am sure. I have my ear close to the ground. I hear these things. I believe the Englishman to be a great fool, one of those who like to make themselves important and show off before their friends. Roméro feeds his vanity and in the meantime pockets his money. Take care, Lorenzo, it could be dangerous for you. The Queen Regent can be vindictive and you offended her greatly when you refused the offer she made to you. You may have to make a choice."

"There is no choice. Let them tear one another to pieces if they wish. I will not fight in any war."

"Dear Lorenzo, always so arrogant, always so sure of yourself," she said and slid an arm around his neck whispering something Charlotte could not hear. He laughed indulgently.

"No, Gabriella, no, it is long finished. I'm not your plaything any longer."

"You never were, not entirely," she said ruefully, "but I warn you – don't fall in love with the Englishman's cousin."

"Why should I do any such thing?"

"People talk. You have never shown any liking for the English until she came, now you loan her your finest horse, the Marquésa makes much of her at the Castillo. My dear, you should really be more careful."

She touched his cheek caressingly. There was a familiarity about the way she took his arm that stabbed at Charlotte. She drew back as they moved towards the house. Then there was an interruption. Amalia came hurrying down the stairs crying out to Lorenzo as she came.

"What is it?" he said.

"Doña Catalina, Señor," she gasped, "she has opened her eyes, she knows me, she has spoken."

"Thank God. I'll come at once. Someone go quickly for Evaristo."

He went bounding up the stairs. Charlotte came out of the sitting room meeting Gabriella's cold stare before she went herself to find Evaristo.

When she came back, she followed him upstairs and into the bedroom. Catalina was still deathly pale but her eyes were open and she managed a faint smile as her husband appeared in the doorway. He went stumbling across the room to fall on his knees beside the bed and her hand reached out feebly to touch his face. Charlotte saw Lorenzo grip the older man's shoulder for a moment in a gesture of affection, then she went quickly out and down the stairs feeling she had no place amongst these people so closely united. One of the stable boys was crossing the courtyard as she came into the hall and she called out to him to bring her horse. He nodded and she was waiting just within the drawing room when Gabriella came down the stairs followed by Lorenzo. At the same moment the door to the kitchens opened and Paquita came out like a whirlwind with the dog at her heels.

Lorenzo caught her as she collided with him. "Careful! You'll hurt yourself."

"Amalia says she is not going to die," she said breathlessly. "Is it true? Is Tía Catalina really going to get better?"

"Yes, it is true."

"I'm so happy, happy, happy!" and she spun round like a top, stopping only to hug the big dog. "And so is Tonio, aren't you?" and she kissed the top of his head.

"Paquita," said Lorenzo reprovingly, "don't you see who is here? It's your Mamma. She has been worried about you. Go and greet her."

The child's exuberance vanished immediately. She took a step forward and bobbed a little curtsey. "Good evening, Mamma," she said with careful formality, "I hope you are well."

"*Madre de Dios*," exclaimed Gabriella, "what a little dressed-up doll you have made of my child." Impulsively she held out her hand. "Would you like to come away with me, Paquita? Come and live with your Mamma? You're a big girl now. I'll teach you to dance. We will visit beautiful places together."

"Is this wise, Gabriella?" said Lorenzo quietly.

"Wise or not," she retorted, "perhaps the time has come for Paquita to make her own choice. She is eleven years old. At her age I knew exactly what I wanted."

He shrugged his shoulders, leaning against the newel post at the bottom of the stairs, and she turned again to the little girl, coming close to her, her voice seductive.

"Well, Paquita, what do you say? Will you come?"

The child stared at her and then back at Lorenzo. He made no move. Her hand tightened on the dog's collar. "Could I bring Tonio?"

Gabriella nodded impatiently. "If you wish but he may not like it. It's not a life for a dog."

Paquita still hesitated. It was almost as if the magic of the mother she saw so seldom was pulling her away from the only real home she had ever known, then quite suddenly the invisible thread snapped. She turned and ran to Lorenzo. His arm went around her and he held her close.

"Damn you!" exclaimed Gabriella. "You win!" and she went out of the door shouting for her horse, and before he could say anything she was mounted and riding out of the gateway as tempestuously as she had entered it.

Paquita looked up at Lorenzo. "Should I have gone with her? Are you angry with me?"

"No, *querida*, no. Now go and find Amalia. It must be time for your supper." He ruffled the black hair and sent her off with a slap on her small bottom.

It was only then that he noticed Charlotte as she came out of the shadows and moved to the door.

"*Dios!* I had forgotten," he said. "Forgive me if I have seemed to neglect you. There have been so many distractions."

"Don't concern yourself. I'm only too glad that Doña Catalina is recovering."

"We shall find out when the doctor comes, if the damnable fellow ever turns up," he said. "In any case I must arrange to take Paquita back to the Castillo. This is no place for a child at present."

"I am surprised you have not taken her there before. After all, she is your daughter."

She regretted the words as soon as she had uttered them. Would he guess that she had overheard the scene between him and Gabriella?

He raised his eyebrows. "Is that what you think?"

"It is obvious," she said quickly. "She has your eyes, your looks, even your manner."

"Has she indeed? You are very observant." He paused for an instant. "Does it shock you?"

"Don Lorenzo," she replied, nettled by his tone, "I'm not an ignorant child. I grew up in a garrison town. I know something about people and about men."

"Is that so? I stand rebuked."

A faint mocking smile played about his mouth and it maddened her after all she had heard that day.

She said sharply, "Don't laugh at me. I am serious."

"Believe me, I was far from laughing. Quite the contrary." Then before she could utter another word he had crossed to her taking both her hands in his. "I haven't thanked you properly for coming here to us today. It was a most generous gesture on your part. I know Guy appreciated it greatly."

The warmth in his voice, the pressure of his hands as he drew her towards him, nearly overwhelmed her. She didn't know whether she wanted to burst into tears or fall into his arms, but awareness of what he must be thinking of Clive's treachery and of her part in it effectively prevented her from doing either. She snatched her hands away from him.

"I must go. Lucy will be anxious."

She ran down the steps and he followed after her. "You can't go back alone. I will send one of the men with you."

"Thank you but I don't need anyone. I prefer to ride alone."

She saw the boy leading Zelda and called to him. He came at once and she was in the saddle and away before Lorenzo could organize one of his grooms to accompany her. He was standing looking after her when Guy came up the path and joined him.

"A young woman in a thousand," he said warmly. "Some man is going to win a splendid wife one of these days."

"If independence, plain speaking and a most damnable determination to go her own way are what you are looking for," said Lorenzo tartly, "then go ahead, my dear fellow, the field is open." He strode towards the house, then paused to call back over his shoulder, "Better send one of the men after her. Make sure she comes to no harm."

Damn this young woman! She had a most uncomfortable way of getting under his skin. He had wanted to shake some sense into her and at the same time had a tremendous desire to kiss that obstinate mouth into submission, which was ridiculous. He wondered how much truth there was in what Gabriella had told him. It confirmed Roméro's taunt. Clive he had despised from the start, the worst kind of Englishman, self-opinionated, conceited, believing himself one of the lords of creation, and playing the fool with his money, but Charlotte was another matter. Did she know what her cousin was mixed up in – was she part of it too? He did not want to believe it but at the moment he was too tired and too hungry to think straight about anything.

Gabriella had surprised him. She had never sought before to take the child back from him. Was she jealous of the affection that had grown between them? While he waited for food to be brought he stood by the window drumming his fingers against the glass, unwillingly remembering that brief and passionate affair. Gabriella was the daughter of one of his father's shepherds who had unwisely married a gypsy. The girl had deserted him a year after her baby was born. He had grown up with the child Gabriella on his father's estates here in Andalusia, as a boy had run wild in the hills with her, and then when she was twelve she had vanished like her gypsy mother. The war with Napoleon was still raging and she disappeared into it. "Gone off with the soldiers," everyone said disapprovingly and her father and grand-father solemnly cursed the hour she was born and brought shame upon them.

It was to be seven years before he saw her again, traumatic years after his father's death, a boy of fifteen struggling with insuperable problems, ruined estates, a young brother and a baby sister with only his grandmother to give help and support.

He was twenty-two when he met her and she was dancing in a Madrid café with a band of gypsies, the darling of the people, her genius already apparent. She was like a living flame, he thought, and was utterly captivated. She came to his table recognizing the boy in the handsome young man and the passion that sprang between them was mutual and overwhelming.

He thought of the first time he made love to her in the tiny room she rented above the café, her beautiful body the colour of pale honey when he stripped the dress from her, her desire fierce and all consuming, leaping to meet his. Their love was too fiery to last. In those first weeks he was crazy enough to offer marriage and she had laughed at him. For six months it burned with a fury that consumed him and then one day she disappeared. He went as usual to the attic room and she had gone, vanished without trace, taking everything with her. Her gypsy companions were silent as only *gitanos* know how to be. For months he had hunted for her uselessly. Then five years later he received a message passed on to him casually in the market of Seville. He went to a hovel in the Triana district. There he found Gabriella sick almost to death and with her a child, a strange little creature who stared at him with the wary grace of a half wild kitten.

Gabriella would accept neither help nor money, only asking him to take the child.

"She is yours," she said. "I would not see her starve."

"Why didn't you tell me?" he had asked.

And she had looked up at him from fever-bright eyes in the thin, still lovely, face. "I have my pride. I would not beg from the Marquésa de Merenda, but now it is different. Who will care for her if I die?"

"Come home with me to the Castillo," he had said impulsively.

And she smiled. "Never. I would stifle there. It was good while it lasted but it has burned itself out."

She was right, of course. The flame between them had died. In a week they would have been fighting like cat and dog. Her wild spirit would never have fitted into the ordered calm of his home.

So he left money and took the child. But Gabriella did not die. She went on to achieve fame, leading her own solitary enigmatic life and later that year he had agreed to the marriage with Manuela de Tajo which Doña Gracia had been pressing on him.

But destiny, fate, call it what you will, had not yet done with him. It had snatched Manuela from him and now seemed likely to create a barrier between him and the only young woman who had aroused a spark of interest in him since her death.

He sighed and turned back into the room as the servants brought in lighted lamps and began to spread food on the table. The doubts about Charlotte and her cousin he pushed to the back of his mind. He had no intention of playing the informer. If the fool burned his fingers, it was his own affair. Then Evaristo and Guy came in together, reporting that the doctor had come at last and had pronounced guardedly that Catalina seemed likely to recover.

It was time to take up the burden again. There was a great deal to be discussed if the vineyards were to be saved, while the money for Paquita's ransom had still to be found. Personal problems must be put on one side.

149

9

The attack on the Merenda vineyards was talked about and discussed endlessly in the drawing rooms and in the market place. A half-hearted attempt was made by the police authorities to round up the gang with absolutely no result. Men and women were questioned but were far too afraid of José Roméro's swift reprisal if they dared to say too much. No one knew better than Lorenzo himself how easy it was for men to melt away into the caves and peaks of the Sierras where no search could ever find them. He was also very aware that nothing could prevent his brother being ruthlessly murdered if the slightest hint was dropped of their whereabouts, so the money was duly handed over, Roberto returned to the Castillo and for the time being José Roméro vanished until the disturbed state of the country should give him another opportunity to further his ambitions. Work began on repairing the bodega and replanting the vines. Life in Seville went on sunnily as usual except that Charlotte reluctantly realized that even this golden paradise could have a serpent at the heart of it.

When she came wearily back to the Casa de Fuente after that eventful day, her clothes and hair still reeking of the acrid smoke, she had said nothing to Lucy about Clive's part in the affair. It worried her that she did not know if it was true or not or even if Lorenzo had believed it, and there was no one she dared to discuss it with except Clive himself. Again and again she thought of the scene she had witnessed between Lorenzo and Gabriella. She realized painfully that she was wildly jealous of the passion that must have flamed between them, the love he bore the child for whom he was willing to risk so much. What possible place could she have in the stormy lives of these people and yet in these few short months he had so wound himself into her mind and heart that she could not tear him out without mortal wound. Every day she told herself it was humiliating to care so deeply and every day the feeling

150

grew stronger. She would wake early after a restless night, saddle Zelda and ride her furiously, returning exhausted in the blistering heat of midday and then spend hours reading and studying Spanish in an attempt to occupy her mind.

Guy called, reporting that the damage was extensive but Lorenzo had refused to be defeated. They were now seizing the opportunity to make changes for the better both in planting and rebuilding.

"How is Doña Catalina?" she asked.

"Improving but it is a slow business. There was shock and concussion, the doctor says. Lorenzo has taken Paquita to the Castillo and Amalia has gone with them as her nurse. He talks of engaging a governess for her till she goes to the Convent."

He stayed to sup with them and asked if he might come again. After he had gone Lucy said, "Guy is in love with you, Charlie."

"Oh no. I think he's lonely. That's why he enjoys coming here."

"You could do a great deal worse," said Lucy thoughtfully. "He may not be wildly handsome but he has all the right virtues."

"Lucy, really. When did you set up to be matchmaker? You talk as if it were a foregone conclusion."

"I think it may be," she said stubbornly, "so be prepared."

"That's just being silly," said Charlotte, "and anyway what about you and Roberto?"

"What about him? He only calls to bring the baskets of fruit and flowers the Marquésa is kind enough to send us."

"You don't imagine it's the oranges and peaches that bring him twice a week, do you?" said Charlotte teasingly. "He could send Jacopo with those."

"Now it's you who are being silly," but Lucy blushed. The young man's attentions had done a great deal to help her through the misery of Clive's neglect. Once he brought her a white kitten with eyes as blue as her own and it curled up on her lap as they sat together on the patio, sometimes talking, sometimes silent, but happy in one another's company.

A month after he had set out, Clive returned and it was obvious in the first few minutes that the expedition had not been the success he had expected. Two of the young men had found the going too hard and had abandoned the tour half way through.

Mrs James, the merry widow, looked decidedly disgruntled, and Sybilla had developed an unpleasant heat rash and was scarcely on speaking terms with anyone. They grumbled about everything. The food had been atrocious, the *posadas* where they slept filthy and infested with vermin, they had sweltered in the midday heat and shivered in the icy winds that could sweep across the great bare central plateau even in summer.

Charlotte wondered unkindly if Clive had dreamed of an idyllic love affair under the golden skies of Spain and found that, saddlesore and weary, it wasn't so easy to act the light-hearted cavalier and sweep Sybilla into his arms. Perhaps now, after Lucy had told him about the baby, he would learn to appreciate his wife and the devotion she had once been only too willing to give him.

He had been back for a few days when she decided she must tackle him on the subject that had begun to haunt her. He had made a number of sketches while he was away and was now working them up into full scale paintings.

She took a tray of chocolate into the studio one morning and stayed to watch him at work.

"Did you happen to see anything of Don Vicente while you were away?" she asked casually.

"The bullfighter? Any reason why we should?"

"I just wondered. He does seem to be a particular friend of Sybilla's."

He chose another brush with great care before he said, "He did join us for a few days. You don't like Sybilla, do you?"

"Not very much." She came to look over his shoulder. "Where is that?"

"Sunset behind one of Don Quixote's windmills."

"It's beautiful. I wish I could have seen it."

"You probably will one day. I'm sure that Guy or even Don Lorenzo would be only too glad to make the trip with you."

She ignored the taunt and perched herself on a stool. "Clive, what do you know about José Roméro?"

"What on earth do you mean? Why should I know anything? What has Roméro to do with me?"

"You do know he was responsible for a vicious attack on the Merenda vineyards."

"So I've been told." He did not look at her but went on working.

152

"Did you know about it before you went away?"

The brush in his hand slipped. "Damnation! Now look at what you've made me do!" He picked up a painting rag, bending to look more closely at the canvas. "What the devil are all these questions leading to, Charlotte?"

"I saw you with him once in the Roman amphitheatre. Are you working with him for Don Carlos, Clive? That money I saw you with before you went away – was it intended for him?"

He put down the rag very deliberately before he turned to face her. There was an odd pinched look about his mouth and his eyes did not quite meet hers.

"I never heard such a farrago of nonsense in my whole life. Are you telling me that I am some sort of spy – a secret agent? You must be mad or else you've been reading too many of Lucy's rubbishy romances."

"I wish it were as simple as that," she said steadily. "There are quite a number of people who believe you are supporting the Carlists."

"Who, for God's sake? Your friend Don Lorenzo, I suppose. I might have known. If he suffered an attack on his property, then it's his own arrogance he has to thank. You can't ride roughshod over people for ever. And you can tell him so with my compliments!" He was blustering in order to hide something. Was it fear perhaps? He turned away from her. "You ought to have more sense, Charlie."

"Yes, perhaps I had. Perhaps I should have guessed at something like this before," she said quietly. "Do please be careful what you do, Clive. This is not our country and there is Lucy to think of and the baby."

"I'm not likely to be allowed to forget it, am I?" he retorted. But she saw his hand shake as he picked up the paint brush. Then he said a queer thing. "You won't go off and leave her, will you, Charlotte, whatever happens?"

"Why should I want to leave her?"

"No reason." He laughed but it didn't ring quite true. "No reason at all except I'm told that chap, Guy Macalister, has taken to hanging around you."

"Oh Clive, for heaven's sake! He has visited us twice. Guy is a friend, that's all." She moved towards the door. "Better drink your chocolate before it gets cold."

He had taken up the palette and was beginning to work again.

He had denied any link with Roméro but she did not believe him. She knew Clive too well. Something was wrong and he was not happy about it, of that she was very sure, but she did not realize how deeply he was involved and how dangerous it was.

For a few weeks everything went on as usual and she began to think she must be wrong and all Clive had been guilty of was opening his mouth too wide about matters of which he knew little. They were all suffering from the sudden onslaught of a summer heatwave. During the middle part of the day the streets scorched under the burning sun. They had to keep the windows closely shuttered until the evening. An awning was spread across the patio to make welcome shade and Tomás seemed to spend most of his time pouring buckets of water on to pots and flower beds so that the garden remained a green oasis. Lucy visibly wilted, finding it almost impossible to eat anything, and Clive began to talk of moving up into the hills and not returning to the Casa de Fuente till the autumn. Then quite suddenly, without any warning, the blow fell.

Charlotte had gone to the market very early that day taking Juanita with her. At that hour it was still pleasant to wander through the stalls picking and choosing among the fruit and vegetables. Juanita turned up her pert nose at anything that was not in prime condition. There was nothing she enjoyed more than a heated argument with a stallkeeper and just when it seemed that it must come to blows between them, it ended in smiles all round and Juanita triumphant.

They were returning with laden baskets when she uttered a stifled scream and clutched her heart dramatically.

"Mercy of God, the *alguaciles*!" she exclaimed. "Do you see them, Doña Carlotta? Outside the house – is it a fire or a robbery?"

But it was neither of these things. As they came nearer the door opened and two more police officers appeared with Clive, pale and defiant, between them. The two outside fell in behind and they marched away down the street.

Juanita was staring, her eyes large as saucers. Some of their neighbours were already at doors and windows scenting drama.

"What is it? What is happening?" one of them called excitedly.

"None of your business," she snapped.

Charlotte, her heart gripped with fear, pushed Juanita into the house and gave her the basket she was carrying.

"Take it to the kitchen and don't say anything. Above all don't talk to anyone outside," she said and hurried into the sitting room.

Lucy still in her morning gown ran to meet her.

"Oh Charlotte, thank heaven you're back. They've arrested Clive. They've taken him away. What are we going to do? Oh God, what *are* we to do?"

Charlotte put an arm around her. "Now calm down. You'll only make yourself ill. It's probably just some stupid mistake. Sit down, dearest, and try to tell me exactly what happened. What did they say when they came?"

"I don't know. They spoke in Spanish. I couldn't understand," she said wildly. "One of them had a paper in his hand. He read from it. I heard some of the words – *pérfido*, he said over and over again. What does it mean?"

"Traitor," said Charlotte slowly.

"But Clive is not a traitor. How could he be? It's wicked to say such things about him. He has done nothing."

"No, of course he hasn't," said Charlotte soothingly while her mind tried to grasp at what was behind this arrest. Had someone betrayed him, admitted under severe questioning that it was the Englishman who was responsible for what had happened? Could they prove anything? Surely not.

"Listen, Lucy," she said, "I'll go and see Mr Robinson. He is bound to know about this and he will tell me what we should do. I'll warn the servants to stay in the house and speak to nobody. Now go and dress and try to keep calm. If anyone else should come while I'm out, be careful what you say. I'm sure it will be all right but we're in a foreign country so I must find out the right way to go about it."

"They won't do anything terrible to Clive, will they?" she said fearfully.

"No, of course they won't."

She kissed Lucy and went out to the kitchen, warning the servants to speak to no one about what had happened. They nodded solemnly, enjoying the drama but fiercely loyal to their own household. Then she took Matthew on one side.

"Keep Jaime and Tomás quiet. Those men may come back

and search the house before I return, so take care of Mrs Starr."
She was thankful at that moment for his steady reassurance.

He said quietly, "Is there any truth in this charge, Miss Charlotte?"

"I don't know, Matthew, I don't know. I'm only sure that Mr Clive is not guilty of anything but foolishness. We must do all we can to help him."

Matthew came from Breakstone and she could rely on his loyalty. She hurried upstairs, bathed her face, changed into a more suitable gown and went to call on Mr Robinson.

He was at home and received her at once. She realized immediately that he knew about the arrest already and she was very conscious of something withdrawn and guarded about his replies to her questions.

"It will be best if I go and see the *Corregidor*, that is the magistrate before whom Clive will be charged."

"But he has done nothing, Mr Robinson."

"My dear young lady, I only hope you are right. These are difficult times and the Cortés is sensitive of any attack being made on it. If they were to think for one moment that England was in any way supporting Don Carlos, it could bring a great deal of trouble on his head. Indeed upon all of us, to say nothing of the reaction of the Foreign Office at home. I will do what I can but I must warn you that these people move very slowly. He may have to resign himself to some weeks in prison before they make up their minds what to do or even bring him to trial."

"Surely it won't come to that," she said appalled.

"It could," replied Mr Robinson gravely, "and if they can prove anything, it could go hard with him."

In both their minds was the memory of that helpless little band of rebels who had been summarily executed before any move could be made to save them.

"Will we be able to visit him in the prison?" asked Charlotte.

"Oh yes, I think I can arrange that, also that he is given a decent room and a few luxuries, provided they are paid for. Like everything else here, a few judicious bribes can work wonders."

"Anything – we will gladly pay anything," said Charlotte earnestly.

"Very well. I will let you know immediately I have found

out more about the situation and tell that little wife of his not to worry too much."

He pressed her hand and she went away convinced that he knew more than he had told her, but there was nothing else she could do for the time being. She returned to Lucy and tried to sound as heartening as possible while they waited anxiously through that long day.

Mr Robinson called in the evening and one look at his face told Charlotte he did not bring good news. Lucy who had persuaded herself that he could have worked a miracle and brought Clive back with him sat with stricken face.

He glanced from her to Charlotte before he said heavily, "I am afraid that to say the very least, Clive has been guilty of grave indiscretion."

"What do you mean? What *can* he have done? It is ridiculous."

"I only wish it was, my dear Mrs Starr. It would appear there is a witness prepared to swear that he was present when the dastardly attack on Don Lorenzo's property was planned and not only that. They also hold a letter which he is alleged to have written to José Roméro promising whole-hearted support for the Carlist cause together with money to purchase arms for their future campaigns."

How could Clive have been so reckless? It didn't seem possible. "Did you actually see this letter?" asked Charlotte.

"No. They refused to show it to me and it could be false of course. It could be that someone is deliberately trying to incriminate him but I am afraid that for the time being there is no possibility of him being released. However, I have made sure that he is not too uncomfortable and I have also arranged that you may see him the day after tomorrow."

"Thank you," said Lucy. She was very pale but quite composed, showing a steadfast courage that surprised Charlotte. "We are greatly obliged to you."

"I promise you that I'll do all that lies in my power to get him freed but I must warn you that it may prove difficult. I will go now but we will keep in close touch." He moved towards the door and then paused, turning back and looking directly towards Charlotte. "I understand that you are on good terms with Don Lorenzo. The Marqués has a reputation for loyalty and integrity. Why not ask him to speak on behalf of your cousin?"

157

The very suggestion seemed to her so outrageous that it took Charlotte's breath away. Mr Robinson had bowed to them both and Juanita was there to show him out before she could find a reply.

Lucy turned to her as the door closed. "Could you, Charlotte, could you go to Don Lorenzo?"

"No," she said, "no, it is impossible. You must see that, Lucy. How could I ask him to help the very man partly responsible for his ruined vineyards, for all that happened on that terrible night? It's out of the question."

"But Clive was not guilty of that. He could never have agreed to such a thing. I don't believe it. It's some wicked lie."

"Perhaps." But Charlotte remembered only too well Clive's evasions when she had confronted him with it. She said slowly, "We must wait until we see him. We have not heard his side of it." She sat down by Lucy, taking her hand. "You've been so brave, dearest, don't lose your courage now."

Clive's arrest could not be hidden. She knew that when she walked through the market and people fell silent as she passed or gave her sly pitying glances.

It was Juanita who told her the gossip. "They're saying it was that Don Vicente who talked. Questioned him day and night, they did."

"How do you know this, Juanita?"

"Esteban who sells the fish had it from one of those policemen, drunk he was and bragging." Juanita had all the sturdy Spanish contempt for those in authority.

So it was Vicente who had implicated Clive to save his own skin but he was Spanish and a popular star of the *corrida* so he had gone scot free while the Englishman took the brunt of it.

Sybilla kept well away from them and then one morning Charlotte saw the carriage outside Mr Robinson's door and the luggage being packed into it. Her father was wasting no time in hurrying his daughter away from the dangerous connection. It seemed that they were close to being ostracized both by the English community as well as some of their Spanish acquaintances.

The room in which Clive was confined was bare and comfortless but not the appalling prison cell conjured up by their too vivid imaginations. He had a bed, a table and a chair. He could

158

order what food he liked and have it sent in to him, but it was stiflingly hot in the summer heat and to a man accustomed to air and exercise, a man who had always done exactly as he pleased, the confinement became unbearable. He lacked the inner resources, the patience that might have helped him to accept it with a shrug. He was frustrated, bitterly resentful, refusing to admit that his own folly had placed him where he was and he vented his ill temper on his wife and cousin when they came to visit him.

He was brusque with Lucy's tears and to Charlotte's questions he gave evasive answers but gradually a picture began to emerge. A weak man, a younger son who had always felt life had denied him what should have been his, it had fed his self-importance to be singled out by those Spanish supporters of Don Carlos living in exile. In London it had all seemed so easy and gave him a pleasant feeling of taking part in great affairs. They talked glibly of the cruel injustice suffered by the King's brother in being set aside by the baby daughter of Ferdinand's fourth wife when the law brought in by the Bourbons a hundred years before, provided that the Spanish throne should never again go to a woman. They had talked at length and, flattered, he had listened.

In Spain it had been very different. The squalid details disgusted him. There was a wide gulf between the drawing rooms of Mayfair and the dirt and smell of a disreputable café in the Triana. He did not relish his dealings with José Roméro. The Spaniard gave him lip service but did not trouble to conceal his contempt for the foreigner. Clive drew back from allying himself with the ruffianly crew of bandits and mercenaries that made up Roméro's ragged army but then Sybilla came into the picture, Sybilla who loved danger, who fascinated him by her looks, her bold manners, leading him on and then drawing back, all smiles and yielding one day and the next flaunting herself with Vicente, whom he despised. He had to do something, had to prove himself better than the others. He had boasted of being the bold revolutionary, a secret agent who had mysterious dealings with those at the very heart of affairs, and now he was caught in his own web of half-truths and there was no easy way out. And, worst of all, Sybilla was lost to him, had in fact never been his. He knew the bitter truth now and was gnawed by a feeling of failure.

All this Charlotte guessed at, piecing it together by degrees.

"Did you really help to plan the attack on Don Lorenzo?" she asked him one day when Lucy was unwell and she had gone alone to the prison, taking fruit and choice delicacies prepared by Rosa in their own kitchen.

"God, no! What do you think of me?" He moved away uncomfortably avoiding her eyes. "It was Vicente who told me about it. He had a grudge against Lorenzo. It was meant to be a little roughing up, nothing like what really happened. Roméro seized his opportunity and took full advantage of it."

She did not believe him. She thought he had been eager to escape out of Seville, afraid of what he had himself started.

"Oh Clive, didn't you know anything about the kind of people you were dealing with? How could you be so gullible?"

"What do you know of these things, Charlotte? Sybilla was driving me crazy."

And you had to show yourself the great man, thought Charlotte. How Roméro must have laughed at him. She could feel only pity mingled with contempt.

"What is going to happen to me, Charlotte?" He was pacing up and down the narrow room. "Shut up here they tell me nothing. I'm British. They can't keep me here indefinitely. What the devil is Robinson doing? Isn't it his duty to look after the English residents?"

"He is doing his best but the authorities here are frightened to make any move on their own account. They are waiting for word to come from Madrid."

"Is that to be my fate?" he said bitterly. "Put up against some filthy wall and shot down like a dog?" He stared through the dirty window, beating his hand futilely against the bars. Outside the street was empty in the intense heat of midday. Only a cat slept in the scant shade of a stone wall. Something pricked his selfishness and he sighed. "Poor Lucy, she doesn't deserve this. The child too. I ought never to have brought her here."

It was August, a torrid burning August, when day after day the city simmered in a breathless heat, that the edict came through at last. Clive was to be sent under escort to Madrid and tried for treason against the state. The Cortés had stuck their toes in, refusing pointblank to listen to any appeal. If a foreigner chose

160

to interfere in the affairs of Spain, then he must be prepared to face the consequences.

Lucy was stunned. "What will they do to him if they prove him guilty?"

"They won't."

"But if they do, he'll be executed." All Clive's faults, his neglect, his unkindness, were forgotten. Trembling, she pressed her hands against her pale cheeks, her eyes wide with horror. "Oh why did we ever come to this hateful country?"

It was only then as a last desperate resort that Charlotte made up her mind to go to Lorenzo. At first the very idea had seemed impossible but now it was different. She saw Lucy's distraught face and was aware from Mr Robinson's grave manner that a government dealing with a shattering civil war was only too likely to take the opportunity of making a scapegoat of Clive.

Saying nothing to Lucy, she went out early one morning riding Zelda up the mountain path through fields brown and golden under the blistering sun, the glory of the flowers already vanished.

The Castle of Doves seemed a haven of peace and coolness when she reached it. A breeze from the mountains tempered the heat. The gardens had been kept well watered, the lawns were green velvet, the flowers still blooming in the huge stone pots. She asked formally for the Marqués de Merenda and was left standing in the tiled hall. The house was very quiet. Once she thought she heard a child's laughter and wondered if it was Paquita. The day at the vineyards seemed a very long time ago though it was not much more than a month. Then the butler came back and led her to a room which she had not entered before, part study, part library, the walls hung with fine gilded leather and bookcases that rose from floor to ceiling.

Lorenzo rose from behind a massive desk and came to greet her, asking if she would take some refreshment after her dusty ride. She shook her head and he dismissed the butler with a wave of his hand.

When the door closed, he studied her for a moment and then smiled. "We are being very formal this morning, Doña Carlotta. Won't you sit down and tell me what I can do for you?"

For an instant she let her eyes dwell on him hungrily. Despite her anxiety about Clive, she had thought about him

161

so much in these last few weeks that to see him there in front of her in white shirt and breeches, his coat discarded because of the heat, his dark hair ruffled as if he had run his fingers through it as he worked, was almost too much for her. But she must not give way to her own feelings now.

She said bluntly, "I have come because I want your help."

"In what way? Anything within my power, of course." He was courteous but guarded. "What is it you are asking from me, Charlotte?"

"You know about my cousin?"

"I am aware that he has been arrested."

"Do you know that he is being sent to Madrid for trial?"

"Yes. I have been informed. I am afraid there is nothing I can do to prevent that."

She hesitated, realizing suddenly the enormity of what she was asking from him, but she must do it for Lucy's sake if not for Clive.

"You are well known here and in Madrid, a person of importance. Your loyalty to the throne is unquestioned. Could you speak for him in some way? We know no one who has the same influence, no one who would carry so much weight. They would listen to you."

He got up and walked away before he replied, turning back to face her across the desk.

"I am afraid you greatly exaggerate my power," he said levelly. "In any case I do not feel very much inclined to plead for a man who, in addition to betraying my countrymen, has also been responsible for an attack on my people and my property which has cost a great deal in lives and happiness for those under my charge."

"But he didn't, you are mistaken," she said earnestly. "Clive never meant it to be like that. He was himself deceived by Roméro. It was not deliberate wickedness, only foolishness which he now bitterly regrets. Would you condemn a man to die for folly and leave his wife a widow and her child fatherless?"

"You plead for him very passionately," he said coldly. "Is he perhaps your lover?"

"No, no, no! How can you say such a thing!" She stared at the dark implacable face. "I see now. I should not have come. It was madness. I should have known better than to beg from you." She turned away and went stumbling towards the door.

162

"Stop!" The command halted her and she paused, bewildered. He went on more quietly. "I apologize. I should not have said that."

"It doesn't matter," she said shakily.

"Yes, it does. It was unforgivable. Come back . . . please, Charlotte. I have not yet refused to give what help I can."

"It was foolish of me to expect such a thing from you. I realize that now."

"No, not foolish, but I think sometimes your heart rules your head. I was not aware that Doña Lucia was bearing a child. It must add greatly to her distress." He pushed a chair forward. "Now come, sit down and tell me everything that has happened. I have been away for some days. I do not know all the details."

She came back slowly, almost reluctantly, and while she told him, trying to show Clive in the best possible light, he watched her and wondered how much she really cared for this contemptible cousin of hers. Women were so strange in the men they chose to love. He knew that only too well. The sun caught her hair, turning it to a fiery red gold. It hung in damp curls on her forehead and the large green eyes were bright with unshed tears. He resisted an impulse to take her in his arms and promise all the help he could give. That would be a folly he would be bound to regret.

He got up from behind the desk and walked towards the long windows that looked out on to the patio. A flight of doves swooped down and then soared up again. Bird of peace, peace for his divided country. All his life he had been forced to face trouble of some kind. He was only too well aware that anything he might do for Clive, if it were known, would stamp him as a Carlist and, though he had determined he would hold himself aloof from both parties in this conflict, his loyalty was firmly to the hapless child who was Spain's Queen, and yet . . . He turned to Charlotte. She was sitting quite silent now, her eyes downcast, the long dark lashes on cheeks pale from stress and the enervating heat. He abruptly made up his mind. He had an idea that might succeed and might not. It was a risk but when had he not taken risks?

"Do you know when they leave for Madrid?" he asked.

She looked up. "Mr Robinson said it would be within two or three days."

"That doesn't leave us much time." He came towards her.

"I can't promise but there is something I might be able to do. Better that you know nothing about it yet and above all say nothing to your cousin. That is important. If it succeeds, then I promise you will be informed."

She was gazing up at him with her heart in her eyes. "I am grateful, deeply grateful."

"Don't thank me yet. Wait till we know the result," he said dryly. "Now let me order you something to refresh you – coffee, chocolate, a glass of wine?"

"Nothing, thank you. I must go back to Lucy. She doesn't know I have come here."

"Don't raise her hopes too high. I'm not all powerful, I'm afraid."

He went with her through the hall to the door. Outside, the boy still held Zelda's bridle. She did not know what he intended but he had given her hope. She gave him her hand and he held it for a moment, then leaned forward and kissed her cheek.

"I owe you something for what you did for Teresa," he said. "*Vaya usted con Dios.*"

10

Clive was to go to Madrid at the end of the week. During the next few days no word came from Lorenzo, and Charlotte said nothing about his promise or even that she had asked his help, fearing that Lucy might drop a hint when she saw her husband and it would in some way prejudice whatever was being planned.

The day before he was to leave they were permitted to see him. Charlotte went with Lucy to the prison, left her with him and walked up and down the street outside. It still seemed impossible that her charming elegant cousin should have placed himself in such a desperate situation. He had tried to persuade them to return to England but they had stubbornly refused. To leave Spain without knowing what was to happen to him would have been unbearable. When Charlotte went back to the prison, Lucy met her at the door.

"He wants to see you," she said in a choked voice. She had borne up stoically during their leavetaking but now her courage was beginning to falter. Charlotte pressed her hand and went in.

They had been allowed to pack a valise with necessities and bring him fresh clothes. Shaved and with clean linen for the first time for days he looked more like the Clive she had always known. Faced with the inevitable, he had recovered his courage. He turned to her as she came in with the smile that had once meant so much to her.

"Well, Charlie, so this is it," he said with a hint of the old jaunty manner. "A sorry state of affairs, isn't it? I never thought I would land you in a fix like this when I persuaded you to accompany us to Spain."

"It's going to be all right," she said bracingly, trying to match his cheerfulness. "In a few weeks you will be acquitted and we shall all be laughing about it. It will make an interesting page in our travel diaries, that's all."

"Perhaps and perhaps not. I always wanted to see Madrid

165

but maybe not quite like this. Still, I'm in good company. Didn't your favourite Cervantes write *Don Quixote* in prison? Perhaps I'll paint my masterpiece." He walked away from her to the window, his voice muffled. "It's Lucy I feel guilty about. I've asked you so many times, Charlotte, but you will stay with her?"

"Oh Clive, do you really have to say that?"

"No, I suppose not. You're a good girl, Charlotte." He paused and then went on with an effort. "There is something I would like to know. I couldn't speak of it to Lucy."

"If it's about Sybilla, I understand that her father has sent her back to her aunt in Paris. I saw her leave myself." She looked across at her cousin. "Clive, you do know that she was Vicente's mistress?"

"You can't be certain of that," he said too quickly.

"No, not absolutely certain," but she remembered what Teresa had told her.

"And it was Vicente who cleared himself by accusing me. That's what you are trying to tell me, isn't it?" he went on bitterly. "And he got all he wanted from her."

"Did Sybilla know about you and Roméro?"

"Oh yes, it excited her, made her feel important. I think I knew it all the time but I wouldn't accept it." He passed a hand wearily over his face. "What a God-damned fool I've been, Charlie. I wanted her too desperately to realize it was all a game to her, a thrilling, dangerous game, that she could step out of at any time she liked. And that's exactly what she has done."

Charlotte thought he was speaking as much to himself as to her and was filled with pity and a kind of exasperation.

"I suppose you despise me for that," he said wryly.

"Why should I? We all make fools of ourselves at some time. Don't wallow in self-pity, Clive."

"I deserved that."

He looked so wretched she couldn't bear it any longer. "I must go. Lucy will be waiting. Goodbye, Clive."

She reached up to kiss his cheek and his arms went around her, holding her close, his mouth against her hair. "Don't hate me for it, Charlie," he whispered.

"Oh Clive, you idiot, how could I ever hate you?"

She broke away from him and went quickly from the room,

not wanting him to see the unexpected tears that had sprung to her eyes.

The next day the small party that was to escort him to Madrid set off at dawn. There were six of them, well armed with knives in their belts and rifles slung across their shoulders, with Clive riding in their midst, leading reins attached to his horse. It was a long journey across the mountains and they did not much fear an escape. Where would he go if he attempted anything so rash? Many a reckless foreigner had met his death helplessly lost in these rocky heights. Nor did they anticipate an attempt at rescue from Roméro and his band. In the opinion of the *Alcalde* and the Chief of Police, both firm supporters of the monarchy, the bandit chief had cynically washed his hands of the Englishman who had served his purpose and could now be left to pay the price.

Even travelling fast the journey would take more than a week but it so happened that they never accomplished more than thirty miles of it. Towards dusk on that first day just as, hot and thirsty, they were looking forward to a halt for food and drink, disaster struck. Their attackers came unexpectedly out of the Sierra down a precipitous path they had not even noticed, trapping them in a rocky defile. Opinions differed afterwards as to their number, some saying a dozen, some saying more. Actually there were only six but they were very determined and very sure of themselves. The extraordinary part was that no actual blood was shed. They came like a thunderbolt out of the sky and before the astonished guards could unsling their rifles, they had crashed through them, unseating two completely, and in the subsequent confusion of falling horses and struggling men, someone cut the straps that held Clive's horse and with him between them they disappeared in a cloud of dust, taking a path through the rocks known only to themselves, "like bats out of hell," muttered one of the dazed guards later.

An attempt was made to follow them, shots were fired but fell wide of the mark. By the time the soldiers were back in the saddle, they had vanished. Weary and disheartened, the escort was forced to return to Seville and report their dismal failure much to the fury of the police who felt they would become a laughing stock in the eyes of the supercilious authorities in Madrid.

In the meantime the rescue party, after making very sure that their pursuers had been left far behind, pulled up, conferring together in a rapid colloquial Spanish, completely ignoring Clive. In the half light they looked a particularly ruffianly bunch and he had no idea whether they were part of Roméro's gang or some other group of desperadoes who had captured him for some purpose of their own. He was so bewildered by the suddenness of the action he did not know whether to be angry or grateful. Then their leader came to him, taking firm hold of his bridle.

"You – come with me, Señor," he said in fractured English.

"Who are you?" said Clive. "*Quien esta usted?*"

"*Mi – amico,*" he replied pointing to himself. He waved his hand towards the others. "*Todos – amicos.* Come."

There was nothing else Clive could do. He saw the rest of the party melt away into the shadows and then he was riding beside his rescuer through the darkening night. He had no idea where he was. He was bone-weary after the long day in the heat and he followed without question the man who chose their path unerringly, without a trace of hesitation. Presently, after what seemed a very long time, the moon rose and he looked around him. He could see a scrubland of bushes and broken boulders and realized that in some mysterious way they had reached the Roman amphitheatre at Italica where once in another life, it seemed, he had thought himself so important conferring with José Roméro.

His companion pulled up, looked cautiously around and then indicated that they should dismount. He unstrapped a rug and a large leather bag from his saddle, tethered the two horses and then took Clive's arm, leading him down the stone steps to the caves behind the centre of the arena. He put down the blanket, a leather bottle of wine and the saddle bag.

"You . . . wait," he said.

"*Porqué?*" said Clive, exasperated beyond measure because he felt so helplessly inadequate. "Wait for what?"

"*El Señor* – he come – *mañana.*"

"Tomorrow?" said Clive in dismay. "*Quando?*"

His rescuer shrugged. "*Mañana,*" he repeated. "*Buenos noches, Señor,*" and the man who looked like a brigand and was obviously nothing of the kind suddenly grinned broadly, clapped Clive on the shoulder and climbed back up the steps to the horses taking both of them with him, leaving Clive with the queer feeling that he had been rescued from one prison only to end up in another.

Well, at least it was not a stuffy evil-smelling room, he told himself philosophically. The air was fresh and thyme-scented, an enormous relief after the last few weeks of close confinement. He spread the blanket and opened the saddle bag to find bread, cheese, olives and a hunk of spiced sausage. He tried rather unsuccessfully to tip up the leather bottle and direct the long stream into his mouth as he had seen the peasants do time and time again in the *posadas*. A good deal of it went down his neck but he didn't much care. With his fair hair, English clothes, lack of money and only a few words of Spanish, he could not hope to make his escape across the Sierra on foot so he leaned back against the rock, pulled the blanket around him and prepared to wait. There was little else he could do.

Early the next morning Charlotte was accosted in the market by a slim boy with wild black hair who dangled a bunch of dead rabbits slung on a stick in front of her. She shook her head vigorously and under cover of a shrill description of their cheapness, freshness and succulence, he pushed a slip of paper into her hand and then moved off thrusting his wares impudently under the nose of every buyer. Surreptitiously she unfolded the note. There was only one word "Italica" and an initial "C". She stared at it uncertainly. What could it mean? The news of Clive's escape had not yet spread beyond the police. Could it possibly be that he had got away from his escort, was hiding up somewhere and needed help – food perhaps or clothes? She must go to him. It struck her as she made a few necessary purchases before hurrying home that if it was so, then police might be watching the Casa de Fuente so she must make sure to leave as secretly as possible telling no one, not even Lucy, where she was going.

She invented a story about Zelda needing to be reshod, took a roundabout route through the city and eventually crossed the river going through Triana at a fast trot and then circling up into the hills above the amphitheatre.

The first thing she saw as she came nearer was a horse. She drew back to watch and then with relief realized that the man who was standing just within the shade of the trees was Lorenzo. She tethered Zelda and went to join him.

He frowned when he saw her. "What are you doing here?"

"So it *was* you," she said joyously. "I might have known. *You* did it."

"Did what?"

"Clive is here, isn't he?"

"How do you know that?"

"I had a note this morning. A gypsy boy brought it."

"Mother of God," he exclaimed. "Is he out of his senses, this cousin of yours? All Seville ringing with his escape and he sends a gypsy with a note! The boy could have sold it to the police."

"But he didn't did he?"

"How can you be sure? It could have led them directly to you."

"I was not followed. I am certain of that."

"Let us hope you're right."

"What happened?" Her eyes were shining. "Do tell me – please."

He looked at her with exasperation. He was risking a great deal for her sake and by the look on her face it might be no more than an adventure in some trashy novel. Didn't she realize the gravity of the situation?

"Some of my men ambushed the escort and brought him away. There's nothing the Spanish peasant enjoys more than a fling at authority," he said dryly.

"Wasn't it dangerous?"

"It could have been but the *Guardia Civile* are not anxious to risk their lives, however good the cause, and my shepherds know every inch of the Sierra."

"I never dreamed you would contrive an escape," she said wonderingly.

"Neither did I intend it at first. The truth is I made some enquiries. It seemed quite certain to me that the journey to Madrid was something of a farce. At worst it could end in the firing squad, at best in a long term of imprisonment. This is a case where the Cortés cannot afford to be lenient if they are to keep their shaky authority intact."

"I see. So what do we do now?"

"I have certain friends who ply between the coast and

Tangier. For a price they will take him with them. From Tangier it should be easy to take ship for England."

"Do you mean they are smugglers?"

"They call themselves fishermen."

"The Marqués de Merenda hand in glove with *contrabandistas*," she said teasingly.

"At times. It has its uses," he replied austerely. "Come, there's no time to be lost. We had better find this cousin of yours."

She followed him down the broken stone steps. Within the cave, Clive was waiting, his back defensively against the wall, unsure of whom he was to meet. They were only dark figures against the dazzle of the sun. Then as they came into the cave opening he recognized Lorenzo.

"You!" he exclaimed. "So they were *your* men." Then he saw Charlotte. "The boy found you, I see."

"Of all the stupid tricks," said Lorenzo. "Didn't you realize that you could have put yourself and Charlotte into the utmost danger?"

"How was I to know? I might have jumped from the frying pan into the fire. Your man told me nothing. Was I to sit in this damned place and wait for recapture?" he said sullenly. "She is here, isn't she, and no harm done."

"No thanks to you," said Lorenzo shortly. "Now listen to me. There is nothing I can do to help you in Madrid but I know men who sail between here and North Africa. They will take you on board at my request and for a price."

"You mean I must run out of the country like some hunted criminal without a chance to clear myself? What about Charlotte and my wife?"

"They will be no worse off than if you were shot or imprisoned for a number of years," said Lorenzo dryly. "It's the best I can do. Take it or leave it."

Clive hesitated, his pride up in arms at the other's curt manner, hating to be obliged to a man whom he disliked.

"Why are you doing this?" he said at last. "Is it another trap? How do I know these friends of yours won't sell me back to the police here?"

"You don't know," said Lorenzo quietly. "You will have to trust me and them. If you still prefer to go your own way, I shall be happy to supply you with an escort to take you to Madrid."

"I suppose that is what you would really like to do."

Lorenzo shrugged his shoulders. "Why should I? It is a matter of indifference to me."

"Clive, how can you say that after Lorenzo has done so much for you?" said Charlotte indignantly. "You must go. Once you're back in England everything can be explained. It will be best for Lucy, best for all of us. Can't you see that?"

"I don't know . . ." He glanced from her to Lorenzo who leaned back against the wall, his dark face giving nothing away. "I suppose this is your doing, Charlie," he said awkwardly. "Very well, I'll go if I must. What do I have to do?"

Lorenzo rapidly outlined his plan. The smugglers sailed from Palos, a small harbour north of Cadiz. He himself would escort Clive by a circuitous mountain route setting out at dawn on the following day. He looked critically at the fair hair, the elegant coat and well cut breeches.

"You must go disguised in case we should meet any of the parties who will certainly be sent out in search of you. I will bring peasant's clothes. We must darken your hair and face and you must act the dumb servant. It should be safe enough but we cannot be sure and it would be folly to be unprepared."

"I shall come with you," said Charlotte suddenly.

Both men turned to look at her.

"No," said Lorenzo, "it is unthinkable."

"No, it isn't. The Marqués de Merenda travelling with two of his servants and a pack mule, nothing suspicious about that."

"And what makes you think you look like the wife of one of my shepherds?" enquired Lorenzo ironically.

"Not now, but I shall. I shall borrow Rosa's clothes. I know how the hill people dress. I see them in the market every day and I can speak for my poor dumb husband if necessary. You are doing a great deal for us and I want to play a part in it."

"By jeopardizing the whole plan, I suppose," said Lorenzo sardonically. "This is not a drama in the theatre. You are behaving like a child and I will not permit it."

"If Charlotte makes up her mind to something," said Clive with a faint grin, "you'll have the devil's own job to stop her. I know her of old."

"Indeed. It's a long exhausting ride, not at all suitable for a young lady," said Lorenzo freezingly.

172

"I'm prepared for that. I'm a great deal tougher than you think and I've always longed to meet smugglers."

"*Dios!*" he exclaimed. "Are all the English as crazy as you two?"

But she thought she might have won her point. They sat down together in the dark of the cave and began to plan the details.

"I shall need money," said Clive at one point, "a great deal of money if these smugglers of yours are to be bribed. Lucy must draw on our account and Charlotte can bring it to me here."

"No," said Lorenzo decisively. "Questions may be asked if a sudden demand for a large sum is made. I will settle all payments. Doña Lucia can return it to me later."

"It is very good of you," said Clive a little grudgingly.

"It is plain commonsense. So that is settled." Lorenzo rose to his feet. "I will be here at dawn with suitable clothes. In the meantime I'm afraid you must stay in hiding as far as possible. Not many come to Italica – this place has a reputation of being haunted by the victims of the Roman circuses, but it is impossible to be certain and you are too easily recognizable."

Charlotte had been sitting silent but now she raised her head. "I've been thinking," she said slowly. "When I come with you, I shall not try to disguise myself after all. You are quite right. I could not make it look authentic."

"You are not coming with us at all," said Lorenzo firmly. "I thought I had made that quite clear."

Her eyes flashed at the peremptory tone. "Oh yes I am, but I shall ride with you as myself. To anybody who questions us, I shall say that I have asked for your kind assistance in searching for my cousin because I have realized it would be far better that he should give himself up to Spanish justice. Who will then suspect the identity of the dumb servant riding beside Jacopo?"

For a moment Lorenzo was too taken aback to say anything. Was she so attached to her cousin that she was willing to risk her reputation by riding so openly with him? And yet the idea had an audacity that appealed to something in him and by its very boldness might well succeed if they were challenged. Then impatiently he shook it away from him.

"And who do you imagine is likely to believe such romantic nonsense?" he said dampeningly. "The idea is quite preposterous."

173

"You think I can't carry it off but I assure you that I can. And you cannot prevent me coming with you unless you lock me up."

"I'm beginning to think that's the best course I could take," he said threateningly.

Clive suddenly laughed aloud. "What did I tell you? My dear sir, you don't know Charlie as I do. She always had a passion for adventure. I remember Uncle Harry telling me once that she ought to have been a boy."

"Is that so?" said Lorenzo dryly and sighed. "I don't like it in the very least but I must admit that it just might work."

"I knew you would see it my way when you thought about it," said Charlotte. "Then it is agreed. I meet you here at dawn tomorrow and now I must go back to Lucy."

"Give her my love," said Clive huskily. "Tell her that as soon as I reach England I will make arrangements for you both to return."

"I'll tell her."

She kissed Clive's cheek and went quickly, afraid that if she lingered Lorenzo would find other and stronger arguments to prevent her accompanying them.

It was midday by the time she reached the Casa de Fuente to find Lucy nearly out of her mind with anxiety.

"Wherever have you been?" she burst out almost before Charlotte was inside the room. "Mr Robinson has been here. He says Clive has escaped and the police are furious at being tricked. Search parties are scouring the countryside for him and they are offering a reward to anyone who can give information. These people are so wretchedly poor, they will be only too eager to betray him."

Charlotte closed the door carefully and leaned back against it. "Never mind that for the moment. What else did he say?"

"Not very much except that he seemed to think we must know something about it," she went on breathlessly, "and he warned me that if we did and said nothing, it could be bad for us." Then she turned on Charlotte with sudden suspicion. "Did you know about it, Charlotte, *did* you? Are you hiding something from me? Is that where you've been this morning? Have you seen him?"

The questions tumbled out one after the other until Charlotte held up her hand. "Ssh! Keep your voice down. We don't want the servants to hear. I didn't tell you before because I didn't know whether anything would come of it but I went to see Lorenzo a few days ago."

"So you did ask him to help us after all."

"Yes, I did, and he agreed. They were *his* men who rescued Clive and he is in hiding and perfectly safe. I have just come from him."

"Oh my God, I can't believe it," exclaimed Lucy. "How does he look? Is he hurt? What will he do?"

"Tomorrow he will be taken to the coast and put aboard a ship for North Africa. From there he can reach England."

Lucy was staring at her. "But how can he do that without papers, without a passport?"

"He won't need any. Lorenzo has friends among the smugglers and it is they who will carry him on their boat to Tangier."

"Smugglers! But won't that be terribly dangerous? If he is recaptured, they will shoot him."

"He won't be taken. Lorenzo will make sure of that."

"Can we trust him? Why is he doing this?" said Lucy slowly. "He never liked Clive."

"That has nothing to do with it. It is you he is sorry for and he feels he owes us something for what we did for Teresa."

"For what *you* did," said Lucy. "He is—doing this for you, isn't he?"

In her concern for Clive, Charlotte had never thought of the personal angle. Now suddenly it struck her and a flood of colour ran up into her face.

"Oh heavens, what does it matter why he's doing it?" she said impatiently. "It's Clive who is important. Once he is safely out of Spain we can breathe again."

The day was spent quietly in making a few necessary preparations. Lucy was appalled at the thought of her travelling with them but all her arguments were overcome by Charlotte's determination. She had told herself she could not allow Lorenzo to take full responsibility. She had involved him in something which she knew he did not entirely approve of and she had to play her part in it. But there was something else, something that had always lived within her – a longing to break away from the dull monotony of everyday life, to be different from the other young women who accepted so easily the conventional round. It had been there since childhood and had blossomed since she had come to Spain and the spice of danger gave it an added zest. Of Lorenzo himself she tried not to think too much. But he would be there, they would be united in a common purpose and the thought lay warm in her heart.

It seemed strange that after making all these plans and trying to think of all kinds of possible setbacks, the journey was almost completely uneventful. The worst problems came from the rough road and precipitous climbs through rocky passes under the blistering sun of midday, for Lorenzo took solitary paths and gave no concessions to fatigue or thirst. Certainly they met very few travellers and those mainly peasants driving their laden donkeys. They called a cheery greeting as they passed and stared at Charlotte curiously. Once a flock of some hundreds of sheep streaming across their way held them up and they were forced to wait impatiently before they could ride on.

Only once did they meet any kind of challenge. A small company of soldiers blocked their road and circled around them when they were only a few miles from their destination.

The young lieutenant at their head, his handsome uniform powdered with dust, looked them up and down asking bluntly if they had seen or heard anything of the damned *Inglés* who was causing so much trouble and was by now almost certainly making for the coast.

"If the wolves have not already made short work of him," said Lorenzo jestingly. "I am afraid we cannot help you."

"May I ask, Señor, where you are travelling to?" asked the young man.

"Certainly. We visit the monastery of La Rábida. I am the Marqués de Merenda and I have some business there."

"Indeed. And the Señorita?"

"I do not discuss my private affairs with strangers," said Lorenzo austerely. "She travels to the monastery with me. That should be sufficient."

One of the soldiers muttered something under his breath and there was a burst of coarse laughter. He slapped Zelda's rump and the mare jerked forward almost unseating Charlotte. She recovered quickly and saw Lorenzo bite his lip but he said nothing.

The implication was obvious and Clive reacted angrily. He raised the whip in his hand. He would have slashed the insolent

176

soldier across the face if Jacopo quick as lightning had not struck down his arm with a bruising blow.

"*Pardone, amico*, the man is an idiot," he growled in apology.

For an instant everything seemed to hang in the balance and Charlotte held her breath. Then the lieutenant shrugged and ordered his men to stand aside.

"*Adios, Señor, Señorita* – good travelling."

Clive was rubbing his bruised arm as they rode on.

"I'm sorry about that," said Lorenzo quietly, "but one English word and you would have been done for."

"My cousin is not your slut," retorted Clive furiously. "I would have shut that scum's dirty mouth for him."

"And given yourself away hopelessly," said Lorenzo crisply. "I think she would rather suffer the insult than see you recaptured and led back to prison. That lieutenant was by no means a fool and I think he half suspected who she was, so the sooner we reach Palos the better. He might have second thoughts."

They went on in silence for a few minutes until Charlotte broke it. "Is there any special reason why we should be visiting the monastery of La Rábida?"

"It was the first thing that came into my head to put him off the scent. La Rábida is closely connected with Christopher Columbus. It was there he came, an obscure, starving foreigner, and it was there that the voyage that led to America was planned. Many visitors come to see the statue of the Virgin before whom he prayed before he sailed, so it did not seem so strange that we should be going together to make this trip."

Lorenzo had tried to protect her but she was well aware that no Spanish girl would be travelling alone and unchaperoned with a man who was neither her father nor her brother. It troubled her a little. Then she put it aside. The only thing that mattered was that Clive should reach safety.

Palos had once been a thriving port and was now only a small place but there were fishing barques in the harbour and boats drawn up on the beaches. As they approached through the rank grass a man stood up and hailed Lorenzo.

"*Hola, Felipe*," he replied. "*Como esta usted?*"

"*Bueno, Señor, muy bueno.*"

The smuggler was short and thickset with a sweeping black

177

moustache. He gave a shout and one or two other men came loping across the beach shaking Lorenzo by the hand. He replied cheerfully, asking after wives and children, obviously on the best of terms. Then they dismounted, the horses were led away and they were all crowding into the little drinking house. There were more than half a dozen of them by now, small dark men, greeting Lorenzo jovially but with a sort of gruff respect, and throwing curious glances at Charlotte. He introduced her as the cousin of the *Inglés* and they burst into a flood of voluble Spanish slapping Clive on the back and assuring her that they would make sure he was carried safely across the straits to Tangier.

They would be sailing with the tide, said Felipe, who seemed to be their leader, but first they must eat. Food was brought, *gazpacho* of course and roasted kid and some kind of potage which when Charlotte tasted it seemed to be filled with every kind of game bird. The wineskins were passed from one to the other, Clive's faltering efforts being received with boisterous laughter. The youngest there, a boy with thick black hair, was hoisted up on to a stool and ordered to sing. She could not understand the dialect but guessed it was bawdy by the guffaws of laughter and the occasional shamefaced looks in her direction. She was reminded of the day she had gone with her father to a celebration in the sergeants' mess. There was the same frank enjoyment and the same touching deference to her as the Major's daughter.

Lorenzo for the most part was silent, trying to make up his mind about this baffling young woman who intrigued and exasperated him at the same time. Gabriella would have joined in the bawdy song, Manuela would have sat silent and trembling if she had ever accompanied him on such a venture, but this girl was something between the two. Was that because she was an *Inglesa*? Once, long ago, when still a boy, he had knelt beside the dead body of his father and sworn a solemn oath that he would make the British pay for what one of them had done to him. Years had passed but the strong prejudice had remained and yet . . . oh hell, he sighed, and fixed his attention on what Felipe was whispering to him.

"There has been trouble – the men of Gibraltar – you know whom I mean – they are jealous of our trade. They say we are taking their profits from them but have no fear. Trust me,

178

Señor. We will deliver him safely." He pocketed the leather bag of pesetas that Lorenzo handed to him.

It was dusk when they went down to the beach. The men had brought lanterns. Charlotte could see the ship bobbing on the quiet water, a faint light showing at the masthead. It was time to say goodbye.

Clive gripped Lorenzo's hand. "I owe you my thanks." He hesitated, wanting to ask more, and Lorenzo answered the unspoken question.

"Have no fear. I will see that no harm comes to your wife or your cousin."

He walked away leaving Clive and Charlotte alone together.

"Well, this is it, Charlie," he said awkwardly, "wish me luck."

"Oh Clive, take care of yourself. Don't run any foolish risks." She put her arms around his neck, hugging him, and he kissed her full on the lips so that for a few seconds it was as if the years had rolled back and they were boy and girl again.

From a little distance Lorenzo watched them, saw them part lingeringly at last and Clive climb into the boat. It was pushed out and the lantern danced across the dark water. Charlotte was standing with clasped hands staring after it and he saw the tears glittering in her eyes as he came back to her.

He took her arm to guide her across the beach and she stumbled as they reached the rank grass that grew at the edge of the sand.

"Do you see these rings?" He stopped and parted the reeds. "These are the very rings to which Columbus moored his three ships, none of them much larger than that one out there. He and his crews heard mass in the little church and then sailed on the tide with the whole village crowded together to see him leave."

"It's like living the past," said Charlotte, grateful to him for easing the moment. Mingled with relief that Clive was now safe was a queer sensation of loss. She wondered if she would ever see him again. She and Lucy were alone in a country which, however much she loved it, was still not their own. It made her feel very lonely.

"It's rough accommodation but you must have a few hours of rest before we ride back," Lorenzo was saying.

He was right of course. It was dark by now and he took her to the door of the one guest room in the *posada*, small and whitewashed, with only a narrow bed and a stool, but scrupulously clean.

"Try to sleep and don't worry too much," he said. "He'll be quite safe, I'm sure of it."

"Thank you," she said, "thank you a thousand times for all you've done," then she went in quickly and shut the door.

The night was very warm. She took off her riding dress and lay on the bed. The rough linen sheets smelled of the salt sea wind where they had been hung out to dry.

It seemed that she had scarcely closed her eyes when she was roused by a loud knock on the door. The woman of the inn came in with a cup of strong black coffee and she realized that it was six o'clock already. Every bone in her body ached from the fatigues of the previous day's long ride but she knew it was important she should return as soon as possible in case questions should be asked. Lorenzo was waiting for her downstairs with a breakfast of eggs and bread.

"Eat," he commanded when she shook her head. "It will be a hard day and I don't want you fainting from hunger."

"I shall do nothing of the kind," she said indignantly.

"You will if you don't eat something. Come now," he pushed the plate towards her, "must I feed you as I do Paquita when she is obstinate?"

"Does she breakfast with you?" she asked, intrigued at the domestic picture conjured up. "I had never imagined you in the role of father."

"I am learning," he replied briefly, "since she has been with us at the Castillo."

To satisfy him she forced herself to eat some of the ham-flavoured omelette and a few mouthfuls of the coarse brown bread. Then they were outside in the freshness of the early morning. A thick mist had blown in from the sea. She felt the clinging dampness and could taste the salt on her lips as she settled herself in the saddle. The people of the *posada* called a cheery farewell after them as they turned their back on the sea and rode towards the hills of the Sierra.

They did not speak much during the journey, she was too weary and Lorenzo seemed occupied with his own thoughts. He did not push so hard as on the previous day, taking a longer rest in the midday heat, so that it was evening by the time they glimpsed the pink tower of the Giralda outlined against the

180

golden sky. The horses were as weary as they were and they were walking them slowly through the narrow cluttered streets of Triana when someone called to them. They looked up to see Gabriella framed in the window above the Café Diablo.

"So you're back from La Rábida," she said, her eyes running over the tired horses and coming to rest on Charlotte's face, smudged with dust and fatigue. "It was a very long journey for a very short visit, wasn't it?"

"I had business there and Doña Carlotta had long wished to make the trip. The study of history is an obsession of the British," said Lorenzo smoothly. "But you wouldn't understand that, Gabriella."

"Oh I'm not so illiterate," she said ironically, "but it seemed a strange time to choose when her cousin is still on the loose with a murder charge hanging over him."

Charlotte licked her dry lips. "Murder charge? I don't understand."

"So you don't know, but then of course you wouldn't. You have been out of the city. One of his guards has died. It seems his horse trampled on him. There is a great deal of anger. It won't help the *Inglés* when he is recaptured." Her eyes flickered from them to Jacopo who was leading the spare horse. "Surely there were four in your party. Have you lost one on the way?"

"It so happens he was left behind at La Rábida," said Lorenzo. "The poor fellow is deaf and dumb and the monks are accepting him as a lay brother. That was the reason for my business there." He frowned. "You seem to know a great deal about us, Gabriella."

"Lieutenant Alváro was here last night, greatly chagrined that his mission had been so unsuccessful. He is an ambitious young man with an eye to the future. He mentioned the Señorita Carlotta, seemed to think her your *novia*, Lorenzo. Am I to congratulate you?"

"It was his own assumption and I do not choose to explain myself to any young officer who has the impudence to question me."

"Still the same pride, Lorenzo," said Gabriella mockingly. "I did not imagine it could be true. 'The Marqués de Merenda engaged to an *Inglesa*! Never!' I told Alváro. Such an idea is laughable. You must have been mistaken."

"More than likely." Lorenzo shrugged it off carelessly.

"Forgive us, Gabriella, if we move on. It is growing late and we have had a long day."

"Be careful how you go," she called after them. "There has been trouble in the city."

"She knows," whispered Charlotte breathlessly as he came up beside her. "She knows about Clive. That lieutenant did not recognize me but she has made sure that he knows now."

"They can prove nothing and he is safely out of Spain."

"But she knows what you have done to help us. She could do you harm."

"Not Gabriella."

But he was not so confident as he sounded. Gabriella had always been unpredictable, and for the first time he wondered if she were jealous. She did not want him herself but resented his interest in any other woman, particularly a foreigner. She was passionately Spanish with a vast contempt for the rest of the world.

Immediately they entered Seville they guessed that something was wrong. Surprisingly, there were very few people about and those who were stood in little groups and stared at them as they rode past. Usually this was the time of the day when men and women gathered outside their houses to gossip, enjoying the coolness after the heat, but most doors were closed and there was a queer hush in the streets. They passed the Cathedral and as they came up to the Casa de Fuente they saw an excited crowd of youngsters, teenage boys for the most part, bunched together on the road outside. They were yelling abuse, egging each other on with screaming insults and as they came nearer, the leader waved his arm and a shower of heavy stones crashed against the closed shutters and fell to the ground.

"Oh no!" exclaimed Charlotte. "Oh no, how could they?"

"Wait!" Lorenzo spurred his horse forward and at the sight of him bearing down upon them, the boys broke and fled. He dismounted and hammered on the door. Breathlessly Charlotte slid from the saddle and joined him while Jacopo caught at the bridles of the horses.

"Who is it?" quavered a muffled voice from within.

"It is I, Doña Carlotta, and Don Lorenzo."

There was the sound of bolts being withdrawn, then the door was cautiously opened and they slipped through.

"Send someone to look after the horses, Jaime."

"Tomás will do that," he growled and shouted for him. The boy appeared from the kitchen looking scared and slid through the door.

"What the devil has been going on?" demanded Lorenzo.

"You may well ask, Señor. They've been at it all the day," muttered Jaime disgustedly. "Damned rascals! Who do they think they are, shouting and abusing honest folk?"

"Where is Doña Lucia?" exclaimed Charlotte, suddenly very frightened. "Is she hurt?"

"No, Señorita, it is Juanita who is hurt. Roughed her up, they did, when she went to the market. If I'd been a few years younger I'd have been after them with a stick."

Charlotte pushed past the old man and went into the sitting room. Juanita was lying on the sofa with Lucy kneeling beside her, bathing her bruised face and the bleeding cut on her forehead. She looked up, the towel still in her hand, and then scrambled to her feet. She was very pale.

"Thank God," she breathed, "thank God!" and clung to Charlotte who had run to put her arms around her.

"It's all right, dearest, it's all right. We are here now."

"It would seem we have arrived back just in time," said Lorenzo grimly. Juanita tried to sit up and he pushed her gently back. "Stay there, girl, and tell us, if you can, exactly what has been happening."

It seemed that it had begun in the morning when news of the guard's death had spread rapidly through the city and a wave of hostility against the foreigners had run like wildfire through the people.

"They seemed to believe that Clive was hiding here with us," said Lucy wearily. "All day they have been shouting outside the house. I told the servants not to go out but Juanita said we needed food. Some brute attacked her as she came back. Matthew managed to drag her in and bar the door against them. It was horrible. At any moment I thought they would break it down. One window was broken and we closed the shutters." She shivered and Charlotte put a hand on hers.

"Poor darling. I shouldn't have left you alone."

"You weren't to know."

"Where is Matthew now?"

"He went to Mr Robinson to ask if there wasn't some way

183

we could be protected. He hasn't come back yet." She looked appealingly at Charlotte. "Clive? Is he . . .?"

"Yes, he is safe now."

Lucy let out a long breath and smiled tremulously at Lorenzo. "I'm so deeply grateful to you."

He brushed it aside. "That is nothing. What we must think of now is your safety. I can speak to the *Alcalde* and the police but I doubt if they will be very helpful."

"Their sympathy will be with the mob out there rather than with us," said Lucy. "Isn't that true?"

"It is possible." He stood for a moment in thought, then he said, "I have not much influence here in the city but no one will dare to raise a hand against the Castillo. May I suggest that you take refuge with us till things settle down?"

"Oh but we couldn't," said Charlotte quickly, "we couldn't impose on you. It would be unfair when you have already done so much and then there is the Marquésa – how would she feel at strangers forcing her to share her home?"

"You are scarcely strangers and the house is a large one. You could have a wing to yourselves if you wish. Doña Gracia would agree with me that I should offer you the only protection I can."

Lucy was gazing up at him. "We would be deeply grateful but I don't know whether we should, whether Clive would wish us to be such a burden to you . . ."

Her voice died away and he came to take her hand in his. "My dear Doña Lucia, the last thing I said to your husband was to assure him I would see that no harm came to you or to your cousin. I am only fulfilling my promise."

"If you are sure . . ."

"I am very sure." He looked from her to Charlotte. "So it is agreed. In the morning I will come with a strong escort and take you both back to the Castillo. Anyone who then wishes to question will have me to deal with. Bring whatever you wish and your servants also if they want to accompany you. There is room for all."

He swept all before him not giving Charlotte time to protest. Matthew had returned from Mr Robinson with only vague promises of help and Lorenzo spoke to him outside, rightly assessing him to be the most reliable of the servants. He advised him to lock the house carefully and let no one enter under any pretext. Then he returned to make his farewells. He was very gentle with Lucy, taking both her hands and giving her comfort and reassurance.

When he had ridden away she leaned back against the sofa with a long sigh. "Oh dear, it is rather like dealing with a whirlwind, isn't it? But I must say I feel safe for the first time since Clive was arrested."

"It is generous of him to offer us his protection but I still think we shouldn't go," said Charlotte doubtfully. "We ought not to involve him in our troubles. How do we know what the consequences will be?"

"Oh Charlie, you don't know what it has been like today. I couldn't stay in this house, I couldn't – I'd live every hour in fear. As soon as we hear from Clive, then we can go home. I want that more than anything but until then – please, please don't make difficulties. I can't bear it – not any longer."

The strain of the day was beginning to take its toll and she dissolved into helpless tears.

It was against her better judgment but Charlotte could not stand out against her pleading. The responsibility was too overwhelming.

"Don't cry, Lucy. If you feel like that, then we will go and we'd better start packing up what we are taking with us and finding out what the servants want to do."

Lucy did her best to help but in the long run only hindered. After a while Charlotte told her to rest and leave it to her and Juanita. The girl asked if she could go with them, partly from a desire to see the inside of a great house which had been a long cherished ambition, and partly from genuine devotion to Lucy and admiration for Charlotte. Tomás looked so desolate at the thought of parting from Zelda that Charlotte took pity on him and consulted Matthew as to whether they might take him with them.

"He's got a screw loose somewhere," he said grinning, "but he's willing, Miss, and a wizard with the nags."

"We'll take him then. I don't think Don Lorenzo will have any objection."

Jaime and Rosa would stay to look after the house till decisions were made as to the future.

With so much to be done it was very late before Charlotte, quite dizzy with sheer fatigue, could at last go to her own room.

185

She looked at herself in the mirror. There were dark shadows under her eyes, her hair felt gritty with dust and she longed for a bath but to ask for water to be heated at such an hour and after such a day was unthinkable. She washed as best she could and when she was in her nightgown stood for a moment looking out of the window. Outside the road was quiet and empty but for how long? She shivered and regretfully pulled the shutter into position.

It had been a bewildering two days. Events had so rushed upon her there had been no time to sort out her reactions. At first the most pressing necessity had been to make sure of Clive's safety. Alarm at what Gabriella might do to Lorenzo had been swept away by finding the Casa de Fuente, as it were, under siege and now they would be going to the Castillo. She would be seeing Lorenzo perhaps daily. The thought was both thrilling and deeply disturbing. How long would it be before the summons came from Clive and she must travel back to England with Lucy? She knew with utter dismay that she did not want to go. She did not want to leave Spain and take up her life with her mother and her new husband. Everything in her rebelled against it and yet what was the alternative?

On impulse she opened her trunk and took out the Spanish portrait which she had placed with her books on the top. It was many weeks since she had looked at it or even given it any thought. It was strange but there had been a sort of compulsion about it from the very start. How strong had been its influence? What part had it played in her decision to accept Clive's offer? And now – what would happen now? It was a teasing question and she was not sure she wanted to know the answer. She sighed as she put it back carefully into the trunk and closed the lid.

Part Two

CASTLE OF DOVES

11

It was very quiet in the Nun's garden that afternoon. The fierce heat of the summer had abated and a yellow October sun lit Charlotte's hair to a rich autumnal red as she leaned back against the stone bench with closed eyes. Beside her Paquita was bent over a large picture book, one small hand laboriously following the words as she spelled them out in broken English. Tonio lay with head on paws twitching sleepily as a late bee buzzed around his nose waiting patiently for the moment of release.

Lorenzo coming quietly up the path paused in surprise. He stood for a moment watching them, partly hidden by the stone arch.

Paquita closed the book and looked up. "You've not been listening," she said reproachfully. "I have finished and it was good."

Charlotte opened her eyes and smiled. "I have been listening and it *was* good – very good but I think it's enough for today, don't you?"

"May I go now?"

She nodded and the child put down the book and was on her feet at once, a slim brown sprite in a pink cotton dress taut with restless energy. She raced down the path with Tonio at her heels and ran full tilt into Lorenzo.

"Gently now," he cautioned, steadying her.

She giggled up at him, bobbed a dutiful curtsey and was off again.

"What is this? An English lesson?" he said, moving towards Charlotte. "I didn't know you had taken to teaching Paquita."

She sat up a little guiltily. "Do you mind? She seemed so anxious to learn."

"No, I don't mind. Why should I? I am only surprised that you can keep her still for so long." He sat beside her on the bench. "In the New Year I shall send her to the Convent."

189

"Is that wise?"

"I think so. The child has run wild long enough. It is an excellent institution where Teresa was at school."

"And will you then acknowledge her as your daughter?"

She saw him stiffen and regretted her question instantly. Would she never learn to be tactful with him?

"Do you think I am in the habit of evading my responsibilities?" he said dryly. "She will of course go to the Convent as Paquita de Merenda."

"I'm sorry. I shouldn't have said that."

Unexpectedly he smiled. "Perhaps you are right to reproach me. I've not done as much for her as I should."

"She is sure of your love – that's the most important thing," she said earnestly. "It is what every child needs."

"You speak from the heart. Did your father love you so much?"

"He made me think so." She paused before she said daringly, "Does Paquita know who her father is?"

"No. Legally she is my ward and in my care. There's time enough. I have to feel my way. My grandmother is not too pleased with me for bringing her here."

"Does Doña Gracia know –?" she hesitated, a little embarrassed.

"That Gabriella is her mother? Oh yes, she knows but she would never speak of it, even to me. A Merenda may sin but not publicly." He leaned back in the seat looking at her quizzically. "You never cease to astonish me, Charlotte. No other young woman I know would dare to say to me what you do."

She flushed. "You think me too bold."

"No, it is refreshing. Many Spanish girls are brought up too strictly."

"And yet you have always been very stern with Teresa."

"That is different."

"Why?"

"There are reasons." He sat up, abruptly changing the subject. "I didn't come to talk about Teresa or Paquita. Roberto and I will be riding up to the high pastures tomorrow. Very soon now they will be bringing the sheep down the mountain and I like to be there at the start. You've often said how much you wish you could see something of the high Sierra, would you care to accompany us?"

190

"Oh yes, above all things. If you're sure I would not be any trouble to you."

"None at all but it will be an early start. We leave at six and will not be back until evening."

"I don't mind that."

"Good. I will tell Jacopo to have Zelda saddled for you. Dress warmly. It can be cold on the heights at this season. We will take food with us."

He got up to go and she put a hand on his arm. "Lorenzo, is there still no news of Clive? We have been here for nearly six weeks and we have had no word from him."

"It may have taken him longer to reach England than he anticipated. Felipe did promise he would let me know of his safe arrival in Tangier but I've heard nothing yet. A smuggler's life can be uncertain, you know, they can easily cool their heels in prison for a month or so. Are you so weary of your stay with us?"

"Oh no, no indeed, but Lucy worries. We are imposing on your hospitality by remaining so long."

"I think the Castillo can stand it. Teresa will be coming home in a few days. She would never forgive me if I were to let you go before she returns. Please give my regards to Doña Lucia. She has not joined us in the evening lately. She is well, I hope."

"Oh yes, quite well. She tires easily, that's all."

"Until tomorrow then."

She watched him walk away and thought how remarkable it was that they could sit and talk together almost like old friends and yet she still felt she knew so very little about him.

In some ways these weeks at the Castillo had been among the happiest she had ever known and the fact that soon they would have to leave only seemed to make them more precious. She and Lucy had been settled in the suite of rooms that looked out on the Nun's garden, part of them still decorated in the exquisite Moorish style created for Pedro's beloved. They were free to live as they wished with their own servants, to eat alone or join the family at luncheon and for the evening meal. Occasionally they took chocolate or English tea with the Marquésa in her own sitting room and Roberto came and went, sitting with Lucy, walking with her, taking her driving. Charlotte watched them with misgiving, wondering whether the friendship begun so lightly was deepening into something much stronger.

It was a relief to relax in Guy's company. He had taken to riding over from the vineyard at least once a week when he would stroll with her in the garden telling her of his problems, sure of her interest and sympathy. It was he who had told her that awkward questions had been asked about the Marqués de Merenda befriending the wife and cousin of the English spy, but Lorenzo had refused to let them disturb him. When questioned by the *Alcalde* and the Chief of Police he had replied icily, "Since when has it been the Spanish custom to take revenge upon the innocent? The Señora and her cousin were the victims of a man's folly and I would not see them persecuted unjustly."

She did not know that Guy had already mentioned to Lorenzo his firm intention of asking her to become his wife.

"I've been in love with her since we met on the *Iberia*, but never dreamed she would look twice at me," he had confessed ruefully one morning when he had been discussing business with his employer in the library.

Lorenzo had been standing at the window with his back to him. "If that's the case, then go ahead by all means, my dear fellow. Try your luck."

"You would not object?"

"Why should I? I am not her guardian. Charlotte strikes me as a very independent young woman who will make up her own mind."

"I thought once that – well, forgive me for saying it – but I was under the impression that you found her attractive."

"I? God forbid. What should I be doing marrying an Englishwoman who is not even a Catholic? Doña Gracia would not be at all pleased."

Guy was of the opinion that Lorenzo would go his own way, family approval or not, but he did not care to say so.

"I would have thought your greatest rival would be that abominable cousin of hers," went on Lorenzo, "but fortunately for you, he is now removed from the scene."

Guy frowned. "You don't mean that they were . . . ?"

"Lovers? That's not for me to say. I am no judge of English morals. But there was a strong attachment, no doubt at all about that."

Guy looked at him curiously. There was an edge to his voice

that gave a personal touch to what he had said but he knew him too well to make any further comment. He turned back to the affairs of the vineyard.

There were moments during that day in the mountains that Charlotte thought she would remember all her life. From the time they set out and the early morning mist vanished into the clear pearly light above the valley, it was pure enchantment. Roberto was in a merry teasing mood, sometimes riding ahead and sometimes coming back to trot soberly beside them. The air smelled rich and nutty. There had been a light rain recently and it brought out the spicy scent of the pines mingled with thyme, lavender and rosemary. As they climbed higher the wind struck colder and Charlotte involuntarily shivered.

"I warned you," said Lorenzo laughing down at her. "Our winds are famous, the levante from the east, the gales from the Atlantic in the south-west and the devil wind that scorches across the central *mesita* and can kill a man though it will not blow out a candle."

"That sounds terrifying."

"It is but don't worry we shall not be travelling as far as that today though we might see snow. Scurries come early and it can lie."

They met a herd of brown speckled pigs, lean and half wild, squealing shrilly as they rooted across their path. Kites soared in the sky above them and Lorenzo pointed out an eagle poised solitary on a crag before spreading enormous wings and swooping across their heads to his prey in the valley below. They saw a large owl perched high up on the branch of an umbrella pine watching them unblinkingly from round yellow eyes and Lorenzo told her of the ancient legend that an owl sat upon the beam of the Cross and ever since its descendants have been hooting *"Cruz! Cruz!"*

"Lorenzo once started to make a collection of Spanish legends, pagan as well as Christian," remarked Roberto with a sly glance at his brother. "Why don't you ask him to show them to you?"

"They are nothing," said Lorenzo, "only odd tales I have scribbled down from time to time."

"Don't you believe it," went on Roberto irrepressibly, "he has pages and pages hidden away in the library somewhere."

"Perhaps I could copy them out for you," said Charlotte. "I used to do work like that for my father."

"I wouldn't dream of putting you to so much trouble," said Lorenzo, giving his brother a crushing look.

She stored the knowledge away with a determination to do something about it when they returned to the Castillo. In that way she might be able to make some slight repayment for his generosity.

Mid-morning they stopped to eat and rest the horses. The view was magnificent, peak after snow-capped peak glittering in the sparkling air. They sat on a sun-warmed rock eating bread, meat and huge juicy tomatoes.

"We never see anything like this in England," mumbled Charlotte laughing as the juice ran down her chin and she reached for a handkerchief. From somewhere far away there came a long piercing howl that was taken up by another in a weird chorus and she looked up startled. "Are those wolves?"

"Probably. They hunt in packs and unless starving in the winter months rarely venture near the villages. There are wild boar too. They can be dangerous if cornered. Roberto can show you a scar he had once from a fierce tusker. There are even bears but nowadays only in the most remote parts."

It added to the strangeness, the sense of wonder. She was exhilarated by the keen mountain air into a happiness all the more precious because she knew it could not last. They found the sheep in grassy plateaux between the high peaks, hundreds of them it seemed, lean creatures nothing at all like the sleek fat flocks feeding on the downs of Sussex and the marches of Kent. The shepherds were as gaunt and brown as their fierce shaggy dogs. The bells hanging round the necks of the leaders had a sweet silvery chime. The men waved, calling a greeting and Lorenzo went to speak with them while Roberto remained with Charlotte.

"He doesn't have to do this, you know, but he likes to feel he knows personally all the people who work for him no matter how humble."

"Isn't that the right way to run a big estate like this?"

"Many of our friends don't. They appoint a steward to do it for them and are cheated, of course. They think Lorenzo should spend more time following the court and currying favour with the Queen Regent but that has never been his way. He says

194

that absentee landlords have been the curse of Spain and the country will never achieve prosperity until they remember it and change their attitude."

"Don't you agree with him?"

"Sometimes but he's not right about everything."

"Such as?"

But he only shrugged and smiled. Then Lorenzo had come back to them frowning so that Charlotte asked if anything was wrong.

"Nothing more than usual. A number of this year's lambs are missing, that's all."

"Stolen?" asked Roberto.

"It looks like it." He turned to Charlotte. "Now we are here, there is someone I'd like you to meet."

"You're not thinking of taking her to see old Pepe, are you?" exclaimed Roberto. "If so, I'm off. I know all his tales by heart. I'll meet you later," and he went trotting up the slope.

Lorenzo smiled. "Roberto has no patience with me sometimes. Pepe was my father's huntsman and very close to him. He taught me all I know about the mountains. I killed my first wolf with him when I was still a boy and he would be hurt if he knew I was here and did not trouble to look in on him. God knows how old he is – must be past eighty – but he is hard as a nut and lives quite alone since his wife died. I'd willingly house him nearer the Castillo but he won't hear of it. He has a great scorn of those who live the fat easy life of the valleys. Don't come if you don't wish to but it would please him greatly."

"Of course I will come, I'd love to. Must we leave the horses?"

"Yes."

He took the bridles as she dismounted and looped them around one of the posts. They took a narrow path and almost at once came upon a thatched hut looking more like a haystack than a house with sturdy grey stone walls. An old man sat on a stool outside, his head tilted up to the sun and he rose to his feet as they approached. He was very tall and thin with a thatch of white hair contrasting vividly with a face the colour of mahogany. Here, thought Charlotte, is Don Quixote to the very life with long melancholy features and dark eyes full of dreams.

He greeted Lorenzo with immense dignity before he turned to Charlotte. He took her hand in a strong warm clasp before

195

courteously inviting them to enter the hut. The men bowed their heads under the low doorway and she looked around her with interest as they talked together. The rough white walls were blackened with smoke from the open fire, his guns and hunting knives hung on one side and a row of kitchen utensils were stacked on the other. The furniture was home-made but had a sturdy strength of its own and the palliasse bed in one corner was piled with brightly coloured handwoven blankets neatly folded.

"You will eat with me," said the old man turning to her politely.

"Only a mouthful for we have lunched already," said Lorenzo and threw her an appealing glance.

She knew that to refuse the proffered hospitality would be to offend deeply, so she nodded and he poured some of the stew from the iron pot on the fire into three bowls and handed them round with spoons of horn and a slice of coarse brown bread. What meat had gone into it she was not sure but it was hot, well flavoured with herbs and surprisingly appetizing. She ate it and pronounced it delicious to the dignified pleasure of the old huntsman.

"Trouble is coming very near," he said taking the emptied bowls and offering the wineskin. Charlotte shook her head but Lorenzo tipped it expertly and took a draught before he handed it back.

"What makes you say that, Pepe?"

"I have seen the armies on the move already and soon they will reach us here and pass on to Andalusia. What will you do then, Señor?"

"Defend my house against them as we have done for centuries," said Lorenzo.

"Against which side?" said the old man gravely.

"I have sworn I will take no part in this civil war but if I have to make a choice then I am the Queen's man. I pray it will not come to that."

"This is a conflict that strikes at our very heart and it will come sooner than you think. Gaspar, the shepherd, tells me that Roméro's men have taken more than a dozen already of his young lambs. Armies are perpetually hungry."

"Roméro," repeated Lorenzo thoughtfully, "is he in these parts?"

196

"Travelling south, I'm told, and gathering men as he rides, so be warned and guard your house and your flocks against them." The old man sighed. "They carry the banners of Don Carlos but I think they look first for easy pickings. It is not right. When the French were driven out of our land I thought to live out my days in peace."

"That is something we all hope for, old man, and seldom find. We must go now, Roberto will be waiting and we have a long way to ride if we are to reach home by sundown."

"It is good of you to remember and bring the Señorita to see me. She may be an *Inglesa*," said Pepe gravely, "but she has a pure and honest face and that is good."

Walking back along the path Lorenzo said, "It was generous of you to come with me. It gave old Pepe the greatest pleasure to feel he is not forgotten."

"I think he is a wonderful old man and to be called pure and honest is a marvellous compliment."

Lorenzo smiled. "You don't know how honoured you are. Pepe fought alongside my father in the war and had a strong prejudice against the British though they were our allies." He stopped for a moment and turned to look at her. "Pure and honest and lovely." He stretched out a hand, turning her face to his. "Thank you, Charlotte, for being so understanding," and he kissed her lightly on the lips.

For a moment time stood still. She was too shaken to move, then Roberto was calling to them and they moved on together.

It was absurd to read anything into such a casual gesture of affection. It was simply Lorenzo's charming way of saying thank you and yet when they returned to the Castillo that evening Charlotte was quite absurdly happy. It was Lucy who brought her abruptly down to earth.

"You've missed Mr Robinson," she said. "He came up to see us today. He wanted to know if we had heard anything from Clive. It seems the police are still not sure whether he has got away or been eaten by wolves."

"What did you tell him?"

"Well, of course, I couldn't say anything about the smugglers or Lorenzo's part in his escape but I could see that he thought it very extraordinary that we should stay here for so long."

197

"What is it to do with him?" said Charlotte edgily. "He gave us no help at all when we needed it most."

"I know. I don't like him very much either but I couldn't shut the door in his face, could I?" went on Lucy.

She was standing at the window, silhouetted against the golden light of the evening sun, and Charlotte thought how little her pregnancy showed. She was more rounded, that was all. She had lost the look of extreme fragility, the delicate bones were not so apparent and she had a bloom she had not had before. The prettiness had become beauty.

"He told me that he is resigning his post and returning to England," she went on. "His wife is nervous of the war and very afraid that it may move south. He asked if we would care to travel with them when they leave."

So it had come, the inevitable which she had been schooling herself to expect, not that it made it any easier to bear.

"I don't see that we have to do what he suggests," she argued. "Shouldn't we wait until we hear from Clive?"

"Are we ever going to hear from him?"

Charlotte was startled. "What do you mean? Of course we will."

"I don't know. Sometimes it all seems like an unbelievable dream. It would be best for us to leave, Charlie, really it would. We don't fit in here. Oh I don't mean they have not been kind – the Marquésa particularly – but sometimes I have felt we are outstaying our welcome."

"Lorenzo has said nothing and it is his house."

Lucy shot her a glance. "Ah, but then he likes *you*."

"No more than he likes any guest. It is the Spanish way to show courtesy." Charlotte paused before she went on. "That isn't the only reason you want to leave, is it, Lucy?"

"Yes, it is. Of course it is."

"No. Let's be honest about it. It's Roberto, isn't it?"

For a moment Lucy did not answer, then she made a helpless little gesture. "I may as well admit it. I know it's crazy but I love him. I tell myself over and over again that it is impossible. I'm married to another man and I'm bearing his child and all that means absolutely nothing. I realize now that I never really loved Clive, only the idea I had of him, and when that crashed, when he killed it so completely, I felt I must cling to the shadow, so I went on telling lies to myself. It's different now

198

with Roberto. Something happened between us from the very beginning but I refused to recognize it and so, you see, Charlie, that is why I can't stay, I daren't stay, I mustn't. I can't trust myself any longer."

"What about Roberto? Has he ever told you how he feels?"

"Not in so many words, but it is the same for him. I know it is. I feel it in my very bones. He takes my hand and it is all I can do not to throw myself into his arms and if I did, we should be lost and I can't let that happen, it wouldn't be fair to him. Oh, Charlie, I've been so miserable and so wildly happy at the same time – can you understand that?"

"Oh yes, I understand." Indeed she did, only too well. "When does Mr Robinson think of leaving Spain?"

"Soon. Perhaps in another month – at least before the end of the year."

One month, two months – so short a time – is that how desperate a condemned prisoner feels? How ridiculous it was – what magic did the Castillo possess to have captured them like this, both hopelessly in love and the situation utterly impossible for totally different reasons. She had known it from the very start but here in his house it had been fatally easy to yield to Lorenzo's charm, to believe in a friendship deepening into love. She had let herself be deceived but now suddenly her eyes were wide open to the grim reality and it was Teresa's return at the end of the week that in some curious way helped to harden her resolution.

She and Lucy watched the carriage draw up escorted by Roberto and Enrique de Tajo, who had contrived to get a few days' leave from his regiment and looked a fine dashing figure in a resplendent uniform. They felt it tactful not to join the family for dinner on this first night of her arrival so that it was the following morning before Teresa came into their apartment looking very soignée and sophisticated in a rich gown of dark green silk, her hair fashionably dressed with a high comb, no longer the *jeune fille* in white muslin but a grown-up young lady.

"My aunt bought it for me in Madrid," she said offhandedly when Lucy complimented her on her appearance. "She told me I looked utterly provincial and something had to be done about it and so here I am with a dozen new gowns," and she spun round showing off the flounces and rather spoiling the new elegant poise.

"What marvellous adventures you have had since I've been away," she went on making herself comfortable on the sofa. "I wormed it all out of Roberto. To think I missed it all!"

"It was certainly not all fun," said Charlotte dampeningly.

"No, I don't suppose it was," she said more soberly. "To have someone you love thrown into prison must have been dreadful. But to think of Lorenzo playing the hero – I never thought he had it in him, particularly as he didn't care for your cousin at all." Then she stopped abruptly, "Oh dear, I shouldn't have said that, should I? Do forgive me."

"Think nothing of it," said Lucy calmly. "We are quite aware of your brother's opinion."

"Actually we had an adventure of our own, a most unpleasant one," went on Teresa irrepressibly. "The Carlists made an assault on Madrid on the very day we were at the dressmakers and there we were caught up in the thick of it. My aunt was in a dreadful panic. The Guards drove them back but there was a real battle going on underneath the windows. Afterwards the carriage could not reach us and there were dead in the streets and blood everywhere when we picked our way through them. My aunt was angry and terrified at the same time. It was Enrique who got us out of the city in the end with two of his men as escort. We did not dare to go to Madrid again which was maddeningly disappointing."

It brought the threat of the distant war suddenly very close and Lucy shivered. "Were you very frightened?"

"Yes, I was, but it was exciting too."

"Did you happen to see anything of Vicente?" asked Charlotte.

Teresa was very still for a moment. "Haven't you heard? He was gored by the bull at the *corrida* in Toledo. Oh not killed but bad enough to put him out of the ring for quite a while. I didn't see it. My aunt would not let me go, not that I wanted to, especially when I heard what he had done to Lorenzo at the vineyard. I made a fool of myself over him, didn't I? I shall never do that again, not for any man."

"Not even for Enrique?" said Lucy teasingly.

"Least of all for him," said Teresa scornfully. "I've known Enrique since I was six years old. Of course he is very brave but he would never do anything really thrilling."

Charlotte smiled. The old hero-worshipping Teresa was still

200

there beneath the new sophistication. She hoped it would not lead her into some fresh folly.

A few days later, the Marquésa invited a few friends to welcome Teresa on her return home. They drove up in their carriages, handsomely dressed men with their wives and daughters, jewels glittering on their fingers and in their silken black hair, moving with subtle languorous grace, laughing up at Lorenzo from behind gilded lace fans. Watching them Charlotte knew she had been living in a dream. What place had she amongst these wealthy aristocrats with their idle luxurious lives? Oh they were courteous enough, complimenting her on her Spanish until she felt like the governess or the poor relation who had somehow wandered into the ballroom. Some of them seemed to eye her curiously, wondering what on earth Lorenzo was thinking of to have become involved with such dubious people. Perhaps she only imagined it but it was painful all the same.

Later in the evening Teresa, who had been dancing, flopped into a chair beside her exhausted but very happy.

"Glad to be home again?" asked Charlotte.

"Oh yes. You know it is strange. I thought I hated it here and yet when I was away all I wanted was to come back." She sat up. "I tell you one thing. Lorenzo is so much nicer than he used to be. What have you done to him?"

"I? Nothing. I'm quite sure your brother would never be influenced by anything I could say."

"There must be something," she said thoughtfully. "He is so sweet to me. Do you think he is in love?" Her eyes swept around the room. "I don't think there is anyone here. It couldn't possibly be Gabriella again, could it? Oh no, not even Lorenzo would dare to do that to Grandmother. She would never forgive him but he has brought Paquita here. Of course Roberto and I knew all about her ages ago but no one ever *said* anything. Now she is one of the household and it's so much more sensible but I never thought he would do it."

"It doesn't shock you?"

"Of course not," said Teresa scornfully. "Oh I know we're all supposed to be very innocent and know nothing about what is really important but there were some hair-raising tales told even in the Convent." She giggled, "Only don't ever tell Grandmother I said so."

Listening to her cheerfully rattling on Charlotte guessed that there was very little about women, or about men either come to that, which Doña Gracia did not know and understand even though she disliked gossip and always discouraged it.

That same night when she and Lucy were drinking a cup of hot chocolate before going to bed, she said, "Let's give ourselves another month here. Then after that we will accept Mr Robinson's offer and go back to England with him."

Lucy shot her a quick look. "If you think that's wise. It will take at least that time to make the necessary arrangements."

And so it was left until the afternoon when she was in the library looking for a book. She had Lorenzo's permission to take anything she wished from the shelves and, turning from one to another, she came across a portfolio tied with a ribbon. Was this the collection of Lorenzo's writings about which Roberto had spoken? Greatly daring, she untied the string, saw the gathered notes in the now familiar handwriting and began to read.

Lorenzo, coming in an hour or so later, checked at sight of her. There was something endearingly childish about the way she sat curled up on the sofa intent on what she was reading, her chin in her hand, strands of bright hair escaping from their pins falling on the slender neck. He wondered fleetingly what her reaction would be if he were to kiss it and then resisted the foolish impulse.

He said, "What is it that you find so absorbing?"

She looked up guiltily. "I hope you don't mind. They are your stories and they are fascinating. I'd like to copy some of them out. May I?"

"Do what you like with them, but not just now." He shut the portfolio and took it from her. "Charlotte, I was looking for you. I have news. Felipe has been here."

"News of Clive? Is that what you mean?" She sat up eagerly. "Then it is all right? He has reached home at last?"

"No, it is not all right." He paused not knowing how to soften the blow. He saw her eyes widen in alarm.

"Is he sick or hurt?"

"It is worse than that. I'm afraid he is dead."

She stared at him with horror, unable to take it in. "Dead? But he can't be. How? When? Why haven't we heard before?"

He sat beside her. "Their ship was attacked when they were

202

approaching Tangier. There are rival gangs operating in the straits. Felipe says it was not all that serious. It has happened before and they were well prepared but Clive – perhaps fearing recapture – threw himself overboard with the intention of swimming to the shore."

"He was always a strong swimmer," she said slowly.

"No doubt, but the currents there can be dangerous. He never reached it."

"But couldn't they have rescued him if he were in difficulties?"

"It seems they tried to do so but by the time they could attend to what had happened it was too late. His body was never found."

"But that was weeks ago. Why haven't we heard before?"

"It appears there was some trouble with the customs officers. Felipe himself spent a month in gaol. When he was freed, he made enquiries but could find out nothing. He has only just returned to Spain and he came to me at once."

Clive was dead – it did not seem possible – and all because of her. She had urged him to escape in this way and it had ended not in freedom but in death.

"Oh God," she said, "if he had gone to Madrid, he might still be alive."

"You must not think that. We acted for the best. You must not blame yourself."

"I can't help it. I can't bear to think of it. How am I to tell Lucy?"

"Would you like me to tell her?"

"No, no, it is better that I do."

He put a hand on hers but she pushed him away from her. It seemed in that terrible moment that she and Lorenzo had killed Clive between them.

"I can't forgive myself for what I did."

"Charlotte," he said with a touch of sternness, "you are talking wildly. I am sorry for what has happened, deeply sorry, but at the time it seemed the best solution to his problem. We could not foresee what would happen and if he had not acted so foolishly, if he had only waited, if he had trusted Felipe, he would not have drowned."

"How can you say that, how can you be so callous?" she said passionately. "You never liked him and now you don't care

203

that he is dead. If you knew this could happen, why didn't you warn us that it was dangerous? He must have believed he was being betrayed. Between us we have sent him to a terrible agonizing death."

"What are you accusing me of? Murder? I never expected this to happen. Felipe has made a hundred crossings in perfect safety."

"I'm sorry," she said chokingly, "I'm sorry," and suddenly could not bear it a moment longer. She ran away from him out of the library, out of the house and into the garden, running away distractedly until she had mastered herself sufficiently to speak to Lucy.

He saw the door close behind her. The wave of anger at her unjust accusation vanished as quickly as it had arisen. He had never imagined for one moment that the plan would not succeed. He had tried to help but it seemed that this damned Englishman in his arrogance and folly rose up between them at every turn. Why had he been crazy enough to let her persuade him into acting as he had? He paced up and down the library, angry with himself. God knows he had enough to worry about without concerning himself with a young woman weeping over a man who had never been worthy of her or of the pretty child he had married. Wasn't it bad enough that Roberto should be losing his head over Lucy, who was pregnant with another man's child, and threatening every day to go and fight in this damnable war, and Teresa was still flatly refusing to marry Enrique? The vintage had been ruined and would take years to recover, there were long-standing accounts to be settled, a dozen new orders to be given. He had a steward to manage his affairs but obstinately liked to oversee everything himself.

He sat down resolutely at his desk and saw the portfolio which she had been reading. He pushed it aside but could not so easily thrust out of his mind the picture she had made, the tenderness it had provoked. With an unpleasant jolt he realized that half his present anger arose from jealousy. He, Lorenzo de Merenda, was jealous of the callow young Englishman who had seemingly captured the girl's love and then thrown it away. It ought to have been laughable and most damnably was nothing of the kind.

He settled down to study Guy's detailed report. Paquita,

putting her head timidly around the door, was told with unusual sharpness to take herself off and not come back. Doña Gracia, noting his silence during the evening meal and the damping effect it had on Roberto and Teresa, began to think that it was high time that the two Englishwomen removed their disrupting influence from the Castle of Doves.

12

Lucy received the news of Clive's death in a stunned silence. Charlotte had expected grief, wild weeping, easy tears, the kind of distress which she could have comforted, not this frozen stillness, not the haunted look in the blue eyes that stared in front of her as if she were watching the helpless struggle as the cruel waters closed over her husband's head. It frightened her.

"Lucy, you do understand, don't you? It was no one's fault. It was just a tragic accident."

"Yes, I understand." She still did not move but the colour slowly drained from her face. "The dreadful, horrible thing is that in these last weeks there have been times when I hoped for it, even wished for it, and now it has come," she whispered. "Dear God, what kind of a monster does that make me?"

She suddenly clapped her hand to her mouth and ran from the room. Charlotte followed after her but she had shut herself in her bedroom and locked the door.

"Leave me alone," a muffled voice told her when she knocked. "Leave me alone, please."

Much later that day she came down to the sitting room looking very pale but quite calm and resolved.

"I shall write at once to Mr Robinson and take him up on his offer," she said quietly. "It is best that we go home – best for both of us, don't you agree, Charlotte?"

"I'm not sure," she said uncertainly.

"If you're thinking of Roberto," said Lucy quickly, "do you imagine for a single moment that I would burden him with Clive's child? It wouldn't be right or fair."

"But if he should come to you?"

"No, no, no!" she said emphatically. "I know what he will say and I'm not taking advantage of it. Nothing will make me do so."

It was astonishing how she had grown up, achieving maturity

206

in a single night, and she clung to her resolution, taking refuge in illness when he came to offer them his sympathy.

"I can't face him," she said to Charlotte. "I mustn't – I daren't – I shall give way. When it is all settled, then it will be different. I shall be braver."

It was to Charlotte he turned. "Why won't she see me?" he demanded. "You know how I feel about her – you must know. I fell in love with her on that very first day you took me to the Casa de Fuente."

"She was married, Roberto."

"What difference does that make?" he said impatiently. "I know she will be feeling distress just now but that will pass. I want to marry her, Charlotte. I know we must wait but I want to take care of her, make her happy. I have known all along how wretched Clive made her."

"Roberto, it is far too soon. We have had no real confirmation of his death yet and in any case I am sure Lorenzo will not approve."

"Damn Lorenzo! It is my life, isn't it, and I shall do as I please."

"She has quite made up her mind and I cannot shake her. As soon as we hear from Mr Robinson, we shall make our arrangements to return home."

"Then I shall follow after her. I swear I shall not take no for an answer."

He was so young, so impetuous, with an obstinate mutinous look that she hoped did not mean trouble. Sometimes she wondered how much was real love for Lucy and how much a desire to defy his brother.

Doña Gracia came to offer her condolences. She nodded quietly when told of their imminent departure and Charlotte thought that she looked relieved.

Mr Robinson called and they discussed the arrangements to be made. Quite a number of foreigners were leaving Spain and they might have to wait to obtain passage on the ship.

"I will make enquiries and let you know," he said. "There are some alarming reports that the Carlists have won some success in the north and are driving south. God forbid that they should occupy Seville. Anything could happen and we might be trapped in the city for months. It is also important that we get out of the country before the rainy season."

"Rain?" said Charlotte in surprise. "Surely that could not delay our departure."

"Indeed it could. You've not yet experienced the winter storms. They have held off this year but usually they come by the end of October. They vary, of course, but you can be completely cut off. I know that from experience, bridges down, rivers flooding, roads utterly impassable. They can last a week or even longer before they subside and if we miss our passage, we could be held up for months."

Mr Robinson was always so full of gloomy predictions of some sort or another that Charlotte paid little heed to his warning.

They had been keeping to their own rooms these days and not joining the family for meals so she saw very little of Lorenzo. She knew she had been unjust to him when he had told her of Clive's unhappy death but could not bring herself to speak of it.

"He doesn't care," she told herself wretchedly, "the fact that I shall soon be gone doesn't matter to him in the very least. Why should it?" He had befriended them and all she had shown was ingratitude.

Then Guy came hotfoot one afternoon not even waiting for Juanita to announce him but bursting into the sitting room where she had been giving Paquita one of her last English lessons.

"I've just run into Geoffrey Robinson," he said, "he tells me that you are leaving Spain very soon."

"Yes, we are." She kissed the little girl. "Run off, Paquita. I'll see you again tomorrow."

The child grimaced. "Mamma is here. I may not be able to come."

"Well, we shall see, won't we? Off with you now."

When Paquita had gone, Tonio as usual bounding after her, Guy impatiently threw down hat and gloves and came to take both her hands.

"I can't let you go without speaking, Charlotte. I would have come before but Lorenzo told me of your cousin and I felt I must wait a little, but not now. It's been in my mind for some time, only I had to make sure of my position here. Now Lorenzo has given me his blessing so we shall have everything we could want, though we may have to wait for a while before a house can be prepared fitting for you."

"Guy, what on earth are you talking about and what has Lorenzo to do with it?"

"I'm sorry, you must think I'm out of my mind but I never thought that you would be going so soon," he went on and then paused, taking a deep breath. "Charlotte, will you do me the honour of becoming my wife?"

She was so taken by surprise that she just stared at him. "Oh Guy, I don't know – I had not thought –"

"But you must have guessed. We have had so many long talks, we have always got on so very well together. I've thought of little else for the last few months. I think – I know – we could be very happy. Dear Charlotte, will you marry me?"

"I – I don't know what to say or how to say it," she said slowly. "I like you so very much but marriage – that's another thing – I never dreamed of it."

"Does that mean – you don't care for me?"

"Not in that way. Oh that sounds so stupid. I'm sorry, terribly sorry –"

"Is there someone else?"

"No, no, how could there be?" she said hurriedly.

"Someone in England perhaps?"

"No, no one. But there is one thing. I have promised to stay with Lucy until her baby is born. I couldn't desert her, especially now, and let her travel home alone."

"Won't you think again – please, Charlotte? If you feel you must go back to England with Lucy, I shall understand. Then in a few months when she is settled, I will come and fetch you back to Spain."

"No, no, I couldn't, Guy. I couldn't make any promise. It wouldn't be fair to you."

"Is it because of what is happening here in Spain? Is it because of the war?"

"No, that has nothing to do with it. If – if I loved someone that would not matter to me at all."

"And you don't love me – is that it?"

She saw the bitter disappointment on his face and went on quickly, "Oh I wish this had never happened. I've never wanted to hurt you and now I have. I've valued our friendship so much."

"And will continue to value it, I trust," he said bravely. "But I shall not give up all hope. I shall ask you again."

"Oh no, don't, please don't."

She was so distressed for him that she went with him to where the boy still held his horse in front of the Castillo.

"It's not goodbye, not just yet, I shall see you again before you go," he said, taking her hands in his.

"Dear Guy, I'm so grateful to you for wanting to marry me and so desperately sorry that I cannot accept."

Impulsively she leaned forward and kissed his cheek. He drew her into his arms and held her close for a moment.

"I must go," he said huskily, "but I'll be back."

She waved to him as he rode down the drive before she turned back through the garden.

Lorenzo saw them from the window. So Guy had asked her at last, he thought, and it seems she has accepted him. Well, perhaps that was how it should be. Then he paused suddenly, aware that she would not be leaving Spain after all. She would be living only a few miles away from him, the wife of a man with whom he would be closely linked, and in all fairness could not dismiss. It was so disturbing a thought that suddenly he had to know the truth of it. He could not live with the uncertainty.

He turned to Gabriella who was in the room with him. "Forgive me, there is something I must do. I shall be back instantly."

Gabriella watched him walk swiftly down the path taken by Charlotte. Lorenzo, outwardly so master of himself, could occasionally act as recklessly as he had as a boy. Was he going to make a fool of himself over the *Inglesa*? Once he had begged her, Gabriella, to marry him and she had laughed at him, but that was a long time ago. All the same a flicker of jealousy ran through her because she had lost him so completely. Even her child now looked at her with the eyes of a stranger and she resented it.

She had come to give him a warning. Moving from town to town and with informants in all of them, she was in a much better position to hear rumours than he was. Both sides in this civil war, the Cristinos and the Carlists, would soon be struggling for the possession of Andalusia and the Castle of Doves lay directly in their path.

Charlotte had reached the gate to the Nun's garden before Lorenzo overtook her.

He said breathlessly, "May I speak to you for a moment?"

She turned to look at him. "Yes. What is it?"

Abruptly he found himself at a loss for words. "I saw Guy with you just now," he said lamely.

"Yes. He was here and now he has gone. Did you want to see him?"

He plunged in rashly. "Has he – did he ask you to marry him?"

She frowned. "I don't know that you really have any right to ask me that, but as a matter of fact he did, and with your approval it would seem," she said ironically.

"There was no question of approval, he simply asked my opinion."

"And the Marqués de Merenda graciously gave his consent."

"It was not like that at all."

"Wasn't it?"

"He does after all work for me," he went on blunderingly.

"And so you own him body and soul, is that it? Well, you don't own me."

She turned to go and he put a hand on her arm.

"Don't be angry with me. I simply wanted to know –"

"If I had accepted him," she said icily. "What we have agreed is between ourselves and does not concern you or anyone else. I understand from Paquita that her mother is here. I am sure you will have a great deal to discuss with Gabriella. Please excuse me. Lucy and I are very busy just now."

She walked quickly away leaving him standing there angry with her, with himself and with the whole damned world before he turned back and returned to the house.

A variety of reasons drove Charlotte to take Zelda and ride up into the Sierra on the following day. It began with a foolish quarrel with Lucy when they drank their morning tea together. Though Charlotte had said nothing the younger girl had guessed at the reason for Guy's visit.

"You should have accepted him," she said lying back against her pillows and sipping the tea. "Then you would not have had to worry any more about having to live with your Mamma and that horrid Colonel Armstrong you dislike so much."

"I couldn't. I don't love him," said Charlotte briefly.

"But you like him very much and that's a lot better and more

211

satisfactory than being in love," argued Lucy with an air of mature wisdom that was very irritating. "He may be a little dull but you would be very safe with him."

"Who wants to be safe?"

"I do, for one," sighed Lucy. "Oh well, if you won't, you won't. You and I will go home to England and live together, snapping our fingers at men and husbands. Would you mind very much being my companion?" she went on wistfully.

"I'm not accepting your charity," said Charlotte obstinately. "I shall earn my own living."

"You really are very perverse, Charlie. Oh Lord, what a pair of great fools we are, aren't we? I longing for Roberto and turning my back on him and you sighing hopelessly for Lorenzo."

"I'm doing no such thing," snapped Charlotte, picking up the tray. "It's getting late. Time you were up and dressed."

"Oh don't pretend, Charlie. Admit it for once. It's Lorenzo you want and poor Guy is very much second best beside the Marqués de Merenda."

"You're quite wrong. Lorenzo can – can go to hell for all I care!" said Charlotte violently and stormed out of the room.

It maddened her to know that Lucy was right and had known all along though she had said nothing. She gave the tray to Juanita and went out into the garden. It was cool for Spain and the sky was heavy with cloud but she scarcely noticed it. She felt out of sorts and on edge. Her mother had written saying she and the Colonel were to be married in the New Year and after the wedding trip would be settling in London. Perhaps in the city she would be able to find some sort of post and avoid the necessity of sharing their home with them. It was a gloomy prospect.

On impulse she took her way across the Nun's garden to the Castillo chapel where occasionally she liked to spend a few minutes. It was very simple and austere with white painted walls, the crucifix suspended above the altar and a statue of the Virgin, very unlike the rich over-decorated churches she had seen in Seville and Granada, dazzling the eyes with gold and jewel-encrusted robes. She was not religious in any way, attending church in England had been more of a convention than anything else, but though she knew little of Catholics, she felt the chapel was a holy place that could bring calm to a disturbed

212

spirit. Once or twice she had seen Doña Gracia there in her black lace mantilla or Teresa dropping in to light a candle and say a hasty prayer. On Sundays the whole household attended mass said by the priest who came up from the Cathedral.

She was still rebellious at Lorenzo's high-handedness. Did he want to run everyone's life for them, even hers? He baffled her sometimes: so charming, so close to her at one moment and then at other times so withdrawn and brusque. She pushed open the door and went in quietly. Light slanted through the stained glass and candles shimmered. To her surprise she saw Gabriella kneeling near the altar, rosary beads slipping through her fingers. Her face in profile had a stern beauty and as she stood there, partly hidden by the stand of candles, she saw the door open and Lorenzo come in. He crossed himself hurriedly and moved to Gabriella. He bent down whispering something and she rose at once and they went out together.

It probably meant nothing but it was sufficient to bring her restlessness and unhappiness to a climax. She went quickly back to the house, changed into her riding dress and crossed the garden to the stables. Tomás saddled Zelda for her looking worried. He tried to tell her she must take care pointing to the heavy sky but she took no heed of him. She longed to get as far away from the Castillo as she could. Only then she felt would she be able to breathe again, regain balance and sanity, instead of being tossed from one conflicting mood to another.

She took the road that was already familiar to her. One of the gardeners saw her pass and called a friendly greeting. She waved her hand to him and went on climbing up the path she had taken that first afternoon when she and Teresa had daringly stolen the horses. She went past the bull pastures. Torbellino was peaceably grazing and she thought of the day she had watched the *Rejoneadores* fighting the bull and seen the agony on Lorenzo's face when he was forced to shoot the horse. Was it then that she had fallen in love with him? The *Fiesta de Toros* had never taken place in Madrid, instead the young men were fighting not the bull but their fellow countrymen. Sybilla had come and gone disastrously. But for her Clive might never have been tempted into such madness and would be alive today. It still troubled her deeply to remember her own part in the escape that had led him to his death.

As she climbed higher the wind blew much colder but she

welcomed it, feeling she had been stifled in heat for too long. She pulled up after a while to give Zelda a rest and to look around her. Bare brown mountains rose one behind the other leading up to the highest peaks veiled now in heavy mist. Between them lay deep gorges where she could see the green of trees and strips of cultivation. Far below was the *noria*, the patient blindfolded mule plodding round and round, turning the wheel that brought the brown water bubbling up and irrigating the dry furrows. She drew long breaths of the pine-soaked air. Something in her responded to these lonely places, an affinity that she felt strongly within her and she was overwhelmed with sadness that she was seeing them for the last time.

She had brought a little food with her, some bread, sausage and fruit, and she dismounted by the side of a tiny mountain stream to eat. A lizard scuttled away as she cupped her hands to drink of the ice-cold water. The wind was keener than she had expected and she was thinking it was time to move when a man appeared out of the wilderness leading a donkey and staring curiously at the sight of a well dressed young woman alone in these mountains. He pointed behind him.

"*Hombres, Señorita,*" he said. "*Soldados.*"

She thought he was trying to warn her and for the first time felt a stir of alarm. It would not be pleasant to fall in with a company of soldiers whoever they were. She was English and so she had no real fear, but men were men and she was alone. Above all she had no wish to appear foolhardy in Lorenzo's critical eyes. She finished eating, gave Zelda an apple and allowed her to drink from the stream. Then she climbed back into the saddle and turned down the way she had come.

The first flash of lightning took her by surprise. Zelda shied nervously, nearly unseating her, and the roll of thunder that followed echoed hollowly from hill to hill.

She knew too late that she should have observed the darkening sky and not come so far, but as yet no rain fell and she was not seriously frightened. It was not until she had taken several more turns of the zigzag path that she looked back and caught a glimpse of those soldiers the man had spoken of and realized that if they continued in the direction they were following, they would certainly come down the same road she was taking.

She quickened Zelda's pace and after a short while a well defined path to the left attracted her attention. That would take her out of the path of the soldiers and she could double back when they had passed. Rashly she turned Zelda's head and went trotting down between the rocks and boulders. But she had not counted on the fury of the storm that was steadily increasing in violence. She had never before experienced lightning and thunder in mountains and it was a terrifying spectacle. The sky split open with great jagged flashes and the crash of the thunder unnerved her as much as it did Zelda. She tried to soothe the terrified horse but the sky grew darker and darker, though it was still only late afternoon, until soon she was groping her way through an uncanny twilight. It was only later when it lightened a little and she looked around her that she realized she was hopelessly lost.

The next two hours were a nightmare. Never before had she realized how small and insignificant man is pitted against the elements. She felt she was fighting against the rage of mighty forces, the wind came in great gusts as she went doggedly on while the relentless mountains all about her offered no shelter or guide.

The first heavy drops of rain had begun to fall when Zelda stumbled and almost fell and she saw that she was at the top of long rows of granite steps crumbling and thick with shrubs. With a gasp of relief she realized she knew where she was. Somehow, though she had no notion how it had come about, she had reached the ruins of the Roman theatre of Italica. With the realization came the first heavy scurry of rain. Well, at least now she could find shelter. She dismounted and carefully led Zelda down the rocky slopes and into the cave-like opening at the bottom of the arena. She gained the shelter just as the rain came down in a blinding sheet of water like a curtain shutting her off from the outside world.

Something slithered under her feet and Zelda whinneyed. A snake glided away into the undergrowth and she stood shivering with cold and fear before she could pull herself together. She moved cautiously forward and saw she was at the opening of a long passage leading to the other side of the theatre. She thought it was the place where Clive had taken refuge. The floor was thick with ancient dust and here and there piles of brushwood showed where vagrants had at some time made it their home. The air smelt dank but it was dry. The darkness was the worst part but it was obvious that she could not ride

215

through the torrential rain beating down outside and though she had come before from Seville to Italica, she had not the faintest idea how to find her way to the Castle of Doves. She led Zelda deep into the passage and petted the trembling mare, sharing her last piece of bread with her. Then she piled the brushwood together and sat down trying to tell herself bravely that the rain could not last forever.

She thought afterwards that those hours of waiting were the worst she had ever lived through. Each minute seemed an age as she sat cold and wretched, huddled into herself, flinching as the bats swooped down from the roof, trembling at every sound lest it should be a snake. Ever since a hateful twelve-year-old Clive had put a grass snake into her bed, the very thought of those long sinuous bodies had filled her with a sick horror.

It was there that later that night Lorenzo found her long after he had given up hope, exploring every path, expecting at every turn to see Zelda wandering loose, the saddle empty, and Charlotte's lifeless body lying stretched on the brown earth, the rain falling on the white face and muddying the bright hair.

It was not until after midday when the lightning first struck that Lucy had come to him alarmed because Charlotte had not returned. Tomás, closely questioned, stammered out that he had saddled Zelda and tried to warn the Señorita not to go too far.

"How could she have been so rash?" exclaimed Lorenzo. "Has she no commonsense at all?"

He sent Roberto in one direction and himself took the most obvious one, tormented with anxiety. What did she know of the storms that come so swiftly and devastatingly at this season, turning streams into raging torrents and bringing boulders crashing down the mountainsides?

He had been searching hopelessly for hours and it was only by the merest chance that he ran into the peasant still trudging beside his donkey and soaked to the skin who thought he had seen the Señorita take the road to the left and had called a warning after her which she did not heed.

"*Gracias*," said Lorenzo and threw him a handful of silver before plunging down the path Charlotte had taken before him, his heart in his mouth as he scanned it from side to side.

It was little wonder that when she stumbled to meet him,

laughing and crying at the same time, his infinite relief turned to a towering rage.

She had been standing beside Zelda trying to find comfort in the warm living body of the horse pushing against her, as if the mare too longed for companionship, when the dark figure appeared in the cave opening dramatically illuminated by a flash of lightning. The enveloping cloak he wore made him look enormous and she cried out in fear before she heard his voice calling her name and ran into his arms.

"Careful! I'm drenched," he said and held her off while he heaved over his head the huge *poncho* of closely woven wool that almost completely covered him and threw it to one side.

"Oh I'm so thankful to see you," she stammered, "so terribly thankful."

"So you should be. What the devil were you thinking of riding out into the Sierra on a day such as this?"

"I didn't know – I never thought –"

"Didn't they warn you?" he stormed at her. "Didn't you stop to think what could happen to you? These paths can turn into raging rivers in a few hours. You could have been swept away and drowned before any of us could do anything to help you."

"I'm sorry," she muttered in a small voice. "I'm sorry – I never realized –"

Abruptly his anger vanished as he saw how pale she was and how she shivered. "No, how could you?" he went on more gently and took both her hands in his. "Take heart now. Thank God you found your way to this place. At least here you have been dry and safe."

It still seemed a miracle that he should be there and a warm feeling of gratitude ran through her. It buoyed her up and restored some of her usual resilience.

"Your horse," she asked, "where have you put him?"

"In the cave further along. He'll do well enough there. Now let's see if we can make things a little more comfortable. We may be marooned here for quite some time."

"Doesn't the rain ever stop?"

"It's been known to continue for a week," he said cheerfully. "If it does even this place could be flooded out."

"Oh no!"

"Don't worry. It's not very likely. I'm afraid we daren't risk riding through it at the moment. It's black as pitch outside and

217

Lord knows what floods we could meet. There are far too many hazards. Here we are and here we must stay at least until it is light. Are you hungry?"

"Starving," she said ruefully, "but I've eaten all the food I brought with me so there's nothing we can do about it."

"You'd be surprised. We are accustomed to our mountain storms and never venture out into them without making provision. Stay here and you will see."

He threw the heavy cloak around his shoulders and bolted through the rain into the next cave, returning a few minutes later with a horse blanket and his saddlebag.

"Now I'm going to make a fire," he said practically. "Help me to gather together some of the brushwood."

He was quick and efficient and before long a small fire was burning merrily, driving back the cold and the shadows. He spread the blanket.

"It smells of horse and is a little damp but I think my *poncho* protected it from the worst."

"It's a wonderful garment."

"A friend of mine who travelled to Mexico brought it back with him. It seems they wear them there in summer as well as winter. It's like a tent and is practically weather proof." He held it up so that she could see it was a large square with a hole cut in the centre. He shook it out before he put it aside to dry.

Then he opened the saddlebag and brought out bread, a handful of olives and a slab of meat pasty.

"It was the best the kitchen could produce at short notice. I can't provide coffee or chocolate but brandy should help to warm you."

He took the flask from his pocket and poured a little into the silver cup. She wrinkled her nose at it distastefully.

"Drink it," he commanded. "It will stop you shivering."

She swallowed it at a gulp and coughed, shuddering at the fiery taste but feeling the warmth explode comfortingly in her stomach.

"That's better," he said. "You're looking more like yourself every minute. Now for some food."

He brought out a clasp knife and cut the pasty, handing one half to her.

"It's too much," she protested but all the same she devoured it hungrily to the last crumb.

218

When they had shared the bread and cheese and given some to the horse, she leaned back watching him dreamily in the glow of the fire. The heat had begun to dry his hair into crisp curls. He looked relaxed, almost boyish, and she thought how strange it was that after that first burst of anger they should now be sitting together so companionably in this cave as if it was the most ordinary thing in the world.

It was a small thing that suddenly made it not ordinary at all.

He had taken out a thin black cigar looking at her questioningly. "May I?"

"Yes, of course."

He leaned forward picking up a twig to light it from the fire. "You realize we will have to spend the night here together," he said half humorously. "We shall need to think of a very good explanation to give Guy when he hears of it."

"Why should Guy need any explanation?"

"As your future husband he is surely entitled to it."

She paused for a moment and then said flatly, "I am not going to marry Guy."

"But I understand from what you said –"

"I didn't say anything. You assumed it was so."

"I see." He flicked the ash from the cigar thoughtfully. "Poor Guy, he had quite made up his mind to it."

She sat up, her hands around her knees, staring into the fire. "I can't help that. I like him very much but that is not enough."

"You don't love him as you loved your cousin Clive, is that it?"

She looked at him defiantly, "Since you ask me, I don't, but that was a long, long time ago," and then feeling that on this strange night she could say anything to him, be completely honest, she said, "Do you still love Gabriella?"

He was silent for a moment and then repeated her phrase, "That was a long, long time ago."

And quite suddenly the tension between them was so alive, so strong, that she felt if she put out a hand and touched him it would crackle and explode like the lightning that still occasionally shot a lurid light across the mouth of the cave, and it frightened her. Somehow she had to break it.

She pushed another branch into the fire and said, "Did you meet the soldiers on your way here?"

"Soldiers?" he was instantly alert. "What soldiers?"

219

"I saw them. They seemed to be marching down from the north. That's why I branched off the road and lost my way."

"So Gabriella was right. She warned me of them. This damnable war is coming too close, Charlotte."

"Will they come to the Castillo?"

"They could and then whether I like it or not I shall be in the thick of it." Suddenly he hauled himself to his feet. "But that's tomorrow's worry. Now I'm going to build up the fire and then you must try to sleep a little." He went further along the passage bringing Zelda's saddle. "Can't do much for the horses, poor beasts, but they will survive." He was piling together some of the dried branches, trying to make a sort of nest, and he spread the blanket over it. "Not exactly a couch for a princess but the best I can do."

"What about you?"

"Oh, I shall doze with one eye open and keep the fire going. Roberto and I have done this more than once when we were out hunting and were trapped by the dark or the weather." He swept her a half mocking bow. "*Buenos noches, Señorita.*"

"I haven't really thanked you," she said trying to speak lightly, "I don't know what I would have done if you had not come – run mad perhaps."

"Never. I'll not believe that – not my intrepid English Miss," he said matching her lightness. He touched her cheek with one finger and knew she trembled. "Sleep well. I am going out to make sure all is well outside but I'll be back. Don't be afraid."

He stood quite still for a moment at the mouth of the cave, grateful for the rain lashing into his face. It had taken all his strength to resist the powerful temptation to sweep her into his arms and make violent love to her here and now on the floor of this vile place. And what would she have done if he had? What did she feel for him? He was not sure. He had never been sure of her or himself. He passed a hand over his face feeling sweat break out on his body. That way madness lay, a sweet madness he had known only once before with Gabriella and he had been a boy then. Now it was different.

After a little he took a deep breath and plunged through the black wet night into the further cave. He did what he could to make the horse comfortable and stayed for a while rubbing him down with some old sacks left by workmen, waiting until the fever in his blood had subsided and he was master of himself once again.

By the time he returned Charlotte had taken off her jacket and lay down on the crude bed he had contrived, the blanket partly over her. Her eyes were closed. One hand was tucked under her cheek and her loosened hair caught now and again a red gleam from the flare of the fire.

He looked down at her for a moment and then crossed to the other side of the cave. Outside the lightning still flashed and the thunder rolled, more distant now but he knew well enough that it could come back, reverberating through the hills. He hoped it wouldn't disturb her too much.

He made himself a kind of niche and leaned back against the rough wall. He closed his eyes trying to empty his mind of the worries that could be banished during the day and came back in the shadows of the night. After a time sheer fatigue overcame him and he dozed fitfully.

A tremendous clap of thunder woke Charlotte with a start. She opened her eyes unable to take in for a moment where she was. The fire had died to a dull red glow and the darkness seemed to have crept closer. She stirred a little and her hand touched something smooth and rounded that moved with a sinuous ripple and then she saw it. Attracted by the warmth a large snake had glided out of the inner cave and curled itself up on her chest, its head only a few inches from her face. For the space of a minute she was too numbed with fright to move or utter a sound, then she began to scream again and again in sheer blind panic. In a second it seemed Lorenzo was beside her and had seized the reptile in both hands flinging it out through the opening.

She was sobbing now in a wild hysteria and he came back to take her in his arms, cradling her against him as if she were Paquita waking in a nightmare.

"Hush, *querida*, hush, it's gone, you're all right, you're safe now."

She clung to him seeking reassurance from his strength. "I'm sorry," she gasped, "I'm sorry – to be so foolish – but it was so horrible, so vile."

"Ssh, it's all over now. I'm here with you."

He held her close against him, his mouth against her hair,

murmuring words of comfort until the shaking slowly subsided.

Presently he tilted up her tear-stained face. "Better now?"

"Yes," she whispered and huddled closer to him as if she could not bear to let him go. "Don't leave me alone. Please don't leave me."

"No, I won't. Don't be afraid."

He bent his head and kissed her and it was like lighting a flame. He tried to draw back and couldn't. He kissed her again and felt her tremble. Her lips were warm. They parted sweetly under his and he knew he was going to lose his battle.

Two passionate people had held back from each other for too long. On this wild night with the storm still raging outside, they were carried away by the fury that swept through them. She had no strength, no wish to resist him. This was a moment out of time, in another world. Depths of feeling that had never been aroused before – terror, love, desire, combined to sweep all before them. His hand slipped through her blouse and touched her breast. She fell back against the blanket and his mouth was exploring hers so that she shivered. All the inhibitions, all the restraints he had put on himself, the prejudices, the jealousy of Clive and Guy on whom she had smiled so freely, all gave way before the flood of overpowering passion.

Above their heads eddies of smoke blew hither and thither in the draughts. Zelda whinneyed and stamped her feet while the rain and wind increased in fury but they took no heed, lost in a world of their own.

A long time afterwards she lay shattered but happy, still within the shelter of his arm, and he put out his hand and gently stroked her cheek.

"*Mi amor*," he murmured, "beloved, why are you weeping?"

"Am I? I didn't know."

There are tears of joy as well as sorrow. It was so unbelievable she wanted to savour every moment of it before it vanished away.

He had propped himself on his elbow looking down at her. "You do not hate me – you have no regret – I did not know –"

"You believed that Clive and I had been lovers."

"Once I did – not now." He felt an enormous tenderness and a surging happiness that she had known no other man but him.

222

She said wonderingly, "I never guessed how wonderful it is to be loved. Is it always like this?"

"I shall spend the rest of my life proving it to you."

He drew her towards him kissing her very gently. "Sleep now. In the morning we shall talk."

She was infinitely weary but dreamily content. If nothing else came out of it, if the dream could never be fulfilled because of who and what he was, at least she would have had this. She would have heard him say again and again, "*Te quiero* – I love you," and at that moment it was enough. As she drifted into sleep, his arm around her, his hand on her breast, she did not once remember the portrait that lay forgotten in her trunk.

13

Light was slanting across the beaten earth floor when she awoke. The fire had burned to grey ash and she felt chilled and stiff. Lorenzo had gone from her side and she knew a moment of panic. Then the light moved. He was standing in the opening and she breathed again.

She sat up. "Has it stopped raining?"

He held out his hand. "Come and see for yourself."

She struggled to her feet with cramped limbs and an ache in every bone but none of it seemed to matter when he came to meet her putting an arm around her shoulders and drawing her outside.

Water streamed everywhere, dripping from bushes and trees, running in rivulets down the stone steps, but it was like a new world, washed clean and brilliant, the air spicy and fragrant. She drew a deep breath, revelling in the freshness after the dank fustiness of the cave.

"What time is it?"

"Nearly seven."

"Are the storms all gone?"

"Not entirely. I don't think this lull will last long. There will be more later. We must make our way back to the Castillo as soon as we can."

"Yes, of course."

Despite fatigue, hunger and the need of a good wash, the magic of the night still lingered and she was reluctant to leave it behind her.

"I suppose we had better make ready."

She turned to go in and he put his hands on her shoulders, turning her to face him.

"There is something I must say to you first. Have you forgiven me?"

She looked up into his face bravely. "For what?"

"What can I say about last night? It should never have

224

happened and yet it did. I find it hard to forgive myself."

His face was so grave, so concerned, he who had always been so arrogant, so much in command of himself, that involuntarily she gave him a tremulous smile.

"Are you apologizing to me? You who are always so sure of yourself . . ."

"Not this time. Don't tease me, Charlotte. This is important. Haven't you realized just what it means – don't you know I am asking you to be my wife?"

She raised her eyes to his with a sudden doubt, unable to believe, to trust what he said. "It's not – just because you feel you owe it to me?"

"No, no, no! Mother of God, what kind of a man do you take me for?"

"A man who loved Gabriella and had a child by her."

"Are you reproaching me? What has she to do with this?"

He had once told himself that Charlotte was everything he most disliked in a woman and knew now how utterly wrong that judgment had been. He had not realized how much he had needed a will that could match with his own, an independent spirit that could prove challenging.

"It has taken me too long to find out about myself and now I am sure."

And perversely it was she who drew back, all the arguments she had so often raised against such a marriage flooding in on her, frightening her.

"I don't know. There is so much against us. Doña Gracia will not approve. I am British, I am not of your faith . . ."

His hands tightened on her shoulders. "All that means nothing. I ask only for your love, your companionship, your friendship."

"You have all that. You have had it for a long time."

For a moment he said nothing, his eyes searching her face. "Is that true?"

"Did you never guess?"

"Never. I was so sure it was your cousin Clive who had your heart."

"What I once felt for him was never anything like this."

"My God, how much time I have wasted!" He drew her to him kissing her gently but firmly. "That is my pledge, yours

225

and mine." Then suddenly he laughed, gaily, boyishly. "If I had my will, I would badger Father Bernardo into marrying us in the chapel tomorrow but I am afraid it will be impossible. Doña Gracia would never forgive me. The Marqués de Merenda will be expected to marry in pomp in Seville Cathedral and that will take time. Will you mind that, my darling?"

"I think I shall probably love it. I shall be so proud."

He kissed her again and feeling her response was tempted to linger but knew regretfully it must not be.

He cupped her face between his two hands. "I never thought this place would one day become a paradise but we must leave it. You see those black clouds to the north. We've no time to lose if we are to outstrip them and not be drowned."

It took them far longer than they had anticipated. In some places the road was blocked by trees blown down by the wind or boulders that the rain had torn from their resting place and brought crashing down the mountainside. They splashed through streams that had become small torrents and were forced to go carefully where the path had been washed away.

By the time they were within sight of the bull pastures it was late afternoon. They were muddy to the waist and it had begun to rain again. It was there that Roberto met them.

"Thank heaven you're safe, both of you," he exclaimed in heartfelt relief. "I was just going to send out another search party. Lucy is nearly out of her mind with anxiety."

"Charlotte had taken refuge in the amphitheatre at Italica and it was there I found her," said Lorenzo calmly. "We dare not risk riding back through the night, it was far too hazardous. How are things here?"

"Bad," said Roberto. "There has been serious flooding in the valley. They are streaming in from the village, poor devils. We are doing our best. I have had the barns opened up and food is being distributed to them." He stopped and gave his brother a quick glance.

"Go on," said Lorenzo, "what else?"

"There are very strong rumours that Roméro's men have battled through the storms and are camped somewhere on the outskirts of Triana. You know what that can mean."

"We must be prepared to defend ourselves."

"I've already sent word to Guy at the vineyard and to the outlying farms. Some of the men have come in already."

"Good. You've done well."

"Does it mean that we shall be attacked?" asked Charlotte.

"Not necessarily, but it is as well to be prepared."

When they reached the garden, Lorenzo sent Roberto ahead of him and dismounted. He lifted Charlotte from her horse and took her hand.

"I must go. You do understand? There is a great deal to be done and I cannot leave Roberto to deal with it alone. I had half expected this to happen but hoped it wouldn't come yet." He drew her closer. "Soon you must tell me to whom I must write and ask for your hand."

She had not thought of the practical side. "There is only my mother and my Uncle Nicholas – they will not be very concerned for me."

"More fools they. Isn't it a damnable fate that we should discover our love at a time such as this? Take care of yourself, *querida*." He peeled off her glove, kissed the palm of her hand and closed the fingers over it. "Our secret till the time comes."

Then he was back in the saddle, had taken Zelda's bridle and was trotting after Roberto.

Lucy in her infinite relief at seeing Charlotte return safe and sound abruptly lost her temper and stormed at her much as Lorenzo had done.

"Didn't you remember me when you rushed off like that without a word? What was I to think? Lorenzo was angry too. I know he thought you were crazy causing so much trouble. I couldn't eat or sleep I was so worried and now you come back and stand there smiling as if nothing had happened," on and on she went until at last Charlotte rebelled.

"I'm sorry, Lucy, but it was not deliberate, believe me, and it wasn't a pleasure trip by any means. It was cold and wretched in that cave. There were snakes and bats and I was sick with fright, and now I'm tired, very hungry and badly need a bath."

"Of course you do," Lucy was instantly repentant. "Oh Charlotte, forgive me, what a beast I am standing here scolding you after such a horrible experience. Was it very terrible? I would have died if I'd seen snakes and how marvellous that Lorenzo found you when he did. You might have perished there and no one would have known till they found your body." She shuddered. "It doesn't bear thinking about. When you're rested, you must tell me all about it, every single thing."

"Of course, I will," except for one thing and that she would never tell anyone.

She ought to feel ashamed, overcome with guilt and remorse – she had committed the ultimate sin as was drummed into every young girl, the fate worse than death, and yet unrepentantly she felt nothing but a glow of pride in the man she loved. Did that make her utterly abandoned, a loose woman? If it did, she didn't care. She stripped off her muddy riding habit while Juanita bustled around preparing her bath, pouring in cans of hot water and chattering away about the unwary travellers who had been caught out in the savage storms in previous years and whose battered bodies had gruesomely turned up at the foot of crags or washed up on some deserted riverbank.

"Shall I stay to help you, Señorita?" she asked spreading the large warm towels over the chair.

"Thank you, Juanita, but I can manage now," she said and dismissed her.

What joy it was to step into the hot water and let it soothe the aches out of her bones. It smelled deliciously fragrant from the bunch of herbs Juanita had tossed into it. She looked down at her body feeling it ought somehow to be different but there were the same long slim legs and gently rounded hips. She pressed her hands against her breasts and shivered remembering his kisses. They had awakened hungers she never knew existed. It was scarcely an hour since she had parted from him and already she longed to see him again, touch him, know that what had passed between them was real and not a dream.

When she was dressed she went downstairs to eat supper with Lucy and give her a guarded account of what had happened.

"You're different somehow," said Lucy with a puzzled frown when the meal was over and they had drawn near to a crackling fire of sweet-smelling wood.

"How do you mean – different?" Charlotte had begun to pour out the tea which Juanita had brought them and put on a small table beside her.

"I don't know. It's just something I feel. Were you really very afraid?"

"In that cave I was – before Lorenzo came. For a little while I was in absolute despair."

"That's it then. You faced death – and came out of it."

"Perhaps." Charlotte smiled. "Death – and life. Oh what nonsense we're talking. We're making far too much of what was really very silly on my part. And here I am drinking tea with you, alive and well, to prove it."

During the next few days Charlotte had to keep a close guard over herself. It was hard sometimes to listen to Lucy talking about the delay caused by the storms, how Mr Robinson's predictions had proved right for once and about the life they could build together back in England. She agreed and felt deceitful because she was holding back the plain fact that now all their plans might have to be changed.

The rain came back in increasing force. It was as if the weather, having taken a deep breath, was now endeavouring to wreak its worst for years. Refugees driven from their homes by the floods were being given temporary shelter. The resources of the Castillo were severely taxed but Doña Gracia, who had dealt with emergencies before, organized the servants to provide food, blankets and medical help for those injured or sick. Charlotte joined Teresa in trying to bring order out of chaos and even Lucy played her part, showing a talent for amusing the many children and soothing distraught mothers with their crying babies.

Charlotte scarcely saw Lorenzo. He was out with Roberto and Jacopo day after day, bringing in half drowned animals and risking his life to rescue stranded old men and women trapped by rising flood water.

Once or twice she ran into him as she hurried between house and barns and it was good to see him smile, feel the pressure of his hand or a quick kiss on her rain-wet cheek.

"Is it like this every year?" she asked him.

"Rarely as bad as this and I am afraid that when the rain stops, it could be worse."

"What do you mean?"

"Never mind. Best not to meet trouble half way. It may never happen."

"Lorenzo, don't hedge. Tell me. I am not afraid."

"Roméro is as hampered by the weather as we are. When it clears –"

"Then he will attack. Is that what you mean?"

"It is what we must be prepared for."

She gave a quick look around and then reached up to kiss him. "I love you."

His arms went around her and for a moment they were lost in one another, then he drew away.

"What in God's name is that child doing?"

All that week, lessons forgotten, Paquita had been here, there and everywhere among the refugees, the big dog at her heels and poor plump Amalia puffing and blowing as she tried to keep up with her.

Lucy had gathered some of the children around her. They seemed to like being with her though she only had a few words of Spanish. One of the shepherd boys had a pipe. He was playing a little lilting tune and Paquita was dancing to it, gravely turning and twisting with a rhythmic grace in her pink frilled dress.

The boy dropped his pipe as he saw Lorenzo frown.

"Where did you learn that, Paquita?" he said sternly.

The child looked suddenly frightened. "Mamma taught me."

"Don't be angry with her," whispered Charlotte urgently.

"I'm not angry," he said in English, "I'm just wondering what I've saddled myself with."

Then Amalia had bustled up, scolding and carrying a protesting child away with her.

"Go on. Give them another tune." Lorenzo waved his hand and uncertainly the boy began to play again as he moved away.

"Amalia should keep the child in the house," he said irritably as Charlotte followed after him.

"Oh Lorenzo, why? It's good for her to meet people and play a small part in helping them."

"A child of the Merendas doesn't dance in public," he said obstinately.

"It's scarcely public and you can't stifle her. Paquita has music and dance in her blood. What is wrong with that?"

"It troubles me. I fear the gypsy in her."

"It will be for us to tame it."

"Will it?" He turned to look at her. "That will be your task."

"I shall do my best."

He touched her cheek with one long finger. "Sometimes I wonder how I've lived all these years without you."

"Very well, I expect," she said and smiled at him before they went about their different tasks.

It was very late that night when Lorenzo sat down at last to a hasty meal served to him on a tray in the library. He ate hungrily and had almost finished when there was a tap at the door and Doña Gracia came in.

"Grandmother!" he exclaimed in surprise and half rose to his feet. "Whatever are you doing here so late?"

"Sit down, Lorenzo, you look exhausted. Finish your meal."

"I have had sufficient." He pushed the tray away and poured himself another glass of wine. He looked across at her. "Will you take a nightcap with me?"

She shook her head. "Thank you, no. It is cold in here. You should have had a fire lit." She pulled a lacy white shawl around her shoulders and sat down.

"I've been too busy to think of it. Isn't it time you were in bed?" he went on affectionately. "You've done wonders already. You mustn't tire yourself."

"There is too much stir in the house to rest easily, besides I wanted to talk to you. What is all this going to mean to us, Lorenzo?"

"I don't know yet," he said seriously. "There have already been lootings and killings but I believe Roméro has his eyes on higher game than the Castillo de Palomas. If he could capture Seville that would be a triumph that ought to satisfy even his ambitions. When the weather clears he may decide to march."

"Will he succeed?"

"If reinforcements don't come from the Cortéz, then he most certainly will. The city is poorly defended and I can muster no more than a hundred and though the men can use a gun, they are none of them trained soldiers. We can hold the Castillo against a rabble but we cannot fight a battle."

"I did not think I should see war again in my lifetime and most bitter of all a conflict between our own people."

"That is what old Pepe said when I saw him last up in the sheep pastures."

"What is your own position in this, Lorenzo?"

"You know that as well as I do. I look for a stable government that will give this country of ours peace and I can't see that ever coming under Carlos and his army of bandits. If I'm

231

driven to take up my gun and fight myself, it will be on the side of the government, but I pray God I can somehow keep myself and mine from being involved."

She sighed. "It is a hard choice and I fear it won't be easy for you but that is not really what I came to talk to you about." She paused a moment and then went on steadily. "You know that I never approved of your bringing the child Paquita here but since you intend to acknowledge her as your daughter I must make the best of it. But surely she should not be allowed to run wild among the peasants as she does."

"You exaggerate," he said calmly. "This is an emergency and as a Merenda she must learn to cope with it as Teresa does and all of us. I will not have her shut up and kept ignorant of what is happening."

"I suppose that is the influence of the Señorita Carlotta. I've noticed how Paquita runs to her continually."

"What harm is there in that? Charlotte teaches her English."

"Is that necessary? Lorenzo, I was only too thankful that you were able to rescue this Englishwoman from the result of her own wilful folly but what are we going to do about her and about her cousin's wife?"

"Lucy, I understand, is planning to return to England as soon as it can be conveniently arranged," he said smoothly. He drained his glass and put it down carefully before he went on. "It is different with Charlotte. You may as well know now as later – I am going to marry her."

She looked up startled. "You can't be serious."

"I am – very serious."

"Is this because of the night you rescued her?" she said incredulously. "Some mistaken sense of honour because you feel you have compromised her in some way?"

"Dear God, no." He got up and walked away from the table, standing for a moment with his back to her. "We were stranded on one of the worst nights even I have known in the mountains – to have attempted the journey home would have been suicidal. We were obliged to spend a few hours together in a cold wet cave – is anyone in their sound senses going to hold that against her?" He swung round to face her. "I am marrying her because I am in love with her."

"You were in love, as you call it, with Gabriella but you did not marry her."

232

"It was not for the want of asking. You didn't know that, did you? She turned me down. At the time I raged against it, afterwards I learned to be grateful. If fate had willed it I would have married Manuela and been loyal to her but it is quite different with Charlotte."

"Oh I am sure she is very pleased with herself. I know that she refused Guy Macalister's proposal. No doubt she feels the Marqués de Merenda is a better proposition."

"That's a vile thing to say and totally untrue." His voice had suddenly become very bleak. "I have made up my mind about this, Grandmother, and nothing that you or anyone else can say will alter it."

She knew when he spoke like that it would be useless to argue. She got to her feet and put her hand on his arm. "I think you know that I want your happiness more than anything else in the world but I would beg you to remember that she is a foreigner, she knows nothing of us or our way of life, she is not a Catholic –"

"Charlotte has already faced me with those very arguments," he said gravely, "I hope I have convinced her that they are unimportant."

"There *is* one further thing. Have you forgotten that it was an Englishman who murdered your father?"

"Should I hold her responsible for that? You have told me often enough that it is time I put the past behind me. Now that I have done so, would you reproach me?" He took the thin old hand in his. "I've waited a long time to find what I wanted and now that at last I have, don't spoil it for me."

"Oh Lorenzo," she put up her other hand to touch his cheek, half smiling, half exasperated. "You always know how to persuade me. I only pray that you're not letting your heart rule your head."

He kissed her gently before he said, "I've told you but no one else yet, so I would be grateful if you would not say anything to Teresa or Roberto. When this wretched business is over there will be time enough."

"Will she be silent too?"

"Charlotte feels as I do."

"Very well. I wish I could be happy about it."

"You can, believe me. Despite the fret of this cruel war, I

233

am at peace with myself and that has not been so for a very long time. You can go to bed and rest content."

"I'll try to do so. Goodnight, Lorenzo."

"Goodnight."

He opened the door for her and then turned back into the room stretching and yawning. He pulled back the long velvet curtains. The break in the heavy weather had come at last. The stars shone in a clear sky. Tomorrow would be fine, the waters would begin to recede and in a day or two the army would be on the move. He felt a stir of anger that at this moment in his life, when happiness beckoned, he should be faced once again with the agony of war and with an ultimate choice that he had hoped never to be forced to make.

14

After the days of endless rain it was wonderful to see blue skies again and Charlotte, walking through the soaked windblown garden, lifted her face gratefully to the pale sunlight. Men were already at work clearing the debris left by the storms, sweeping the paths and tying up plants and shrubs. In the barns some of the refugees were beginning to pack up their belongings and load the donkeys with them.

Lorenzo, mindful of Roméro's army lying dangerously near, urged them to stay longer where at least they could be protected and sure of food and shelter but to the peasant his small plot of land, his animals, the four stone walls that made his home, were infinitely precious and he was anxious to find out what damage had been done and set about repairing it.

Reports came in that the encamped army was only just recovering from its own sorry plight but was well supplied with food and ammunition. An urgent message went off to the Government forces under General Ramirez but they were bogged down beyond the Sierra so that for a few days there was a kind of uneasy truce and everyone at the Castillo breathed a sigh of relief. The kitchen returned to normal, food was served again with its usual ceremony and one evening Lucy and Charlotte joined the family at the evening meal.

Doña Gracia presided with her usual grace but Lorenzo was preoccupied and Charlotte sensed a tension that had not been there before. She wondered if Teresa's sharp eyes had already noticed what lay between her and her brother. Lucy began to talk about returning to England.

"Now that it is possible to get through I would like to send Matthew with a note to Mr Robinson. May he borrow one of your horses?" she asked Lorenzo.

"Certainly. Whenever you wish." He exchanged a look with Charlotte. "Let me know if I can help in any way."

235

"Must you go?" said Roberto. "Surely now it would be better to wait until the spring."

"My dear boy, you are forgetting," said his grandmother reprovingly. "Doña Lucia will naturally wish to be with her own mother when her child is born. Isn't that so, my dear?"

"Yes," whispered Lucy, "yes, indeed I would."

Charlotte knew how many stolen hours she spent with Roberto and how unhappy she was. Once she had tried to remonstrate with her.

"Wouldn't it be better for both of you if you saw less of him?"

And Lucy had flared up. "When I go from here, I shall never see him again. Isn't that enough? Every time you look at Lorenzo you give yourself away and I'm not the only one to notice it. So please leave me alone."

It was only too true so she kept silent, but it still worried her.

It was one morning at the end of that week when the temporary calm was broken. Charlotte had been helping one of the women struggling with a baby, two small children and a pile of household baggage when Paquita, escaping from Amalia, came sauntering into the barn, her hand on the handsome silver collar that Lorenzo had given her for her big dog.

Watching her for a moment Charlotte thought that like so many Spanish girls Paquita was born grown up. Already at nearly twelve she walked with an unconscious provocative grace, her nose in the air as she strolled past a little group of peasant boys lounging at the entrance to the barn. Normally at work from dawn to dusk, they were bored by the unusual idleness and spoiling for mischief. One of them grinned as he picked up a stone and threw it at Tonio. Unluckily it hit the dog full on the nose and surprised a yelp of pain out of him.

Paquita turned on them, eyes flashing, voice shrill and imperious. "If you touch my dog again, Don Lorenzo will have you whipped."

The pride, the conscious air of superiority, riled them. They had heard the gossip like everyone else. Who was she to show off – a bastard, a love child, no better than they were for all her airs and graces? A rain of stones followed, accompanied by a stream of abuse.

Their ringleader was totally unprepared for the small virago who hurled herself at him, eyes blazing, fighting, kicking, biting.

236

Horrified, Charlotte ran to separate them. "Paquita, stop! Help me someone."

It took the combined strength of Charlotte and one of the gardeners who happened to be passing to pull them apart and by then the boy's face was badly scratched and his nose pouring with blood while Paquita's hair hung in ratstails around her torn dress.

"Let me go!" she screamed. "I want to kill him!"

"Fighting like a wild cat!" exclaimed Charlotte, holding on to her with difficulty. "You ought to be ashamed."

"Did you hear what he called me?" The child, white-faced, still trembled with rage. "He called me bastard. He called my mother a whore and my father a coward . . ."

"You shouldn't understand such words."

"And it's a lie, a wicked lie. My father was a soldier. My mother told me. He was a brave man and he is dead . . ."

Her voice broke into choking sobs and it was some time before Charlotte could calm her and then found herself faced with a dilemma. Did she continue the fiction or tell her the truth? She took refuge in reproaches until she had made up her mind.

"Come inside at once and change your dress. You look a disgrace. Whatever would Doña Gracia say about such shocking behaviour!"

She took her upstairs to her bedroom and when she was changed into a clean dress, her face washed and her hair combed, she drew the child to sit beside her on the bed.

"Listen to me, Paquita. Have you never wondered why Don Lorenzo brought you here?"

"Mamma told me once that she was very poor and that was why she could not keep me with her," she said sullenly, "and Don Lorenzo was friend to my father . . ."

"Yes, that is partly true, but supposing I was to tell you that your Papa is not dead?"

The girl's eyes widened and Charlotte guessed that at some time she had heard servants' talk and had never dared to question.

"Then who is he?" she whispered. "Do I know him?"

"Oh yes, you know him very well."

Paquita stared at her. "Do you mean that he is Don Lorenzo?" she breathed almost as if it were too unbelievable to be spoken aloud.

"Yes."

"Is it really true?"

"It is true."

The child frowned. "Then – then what about Mamma?"

How to make her understand a passion that had been real once while it lasted but was now dead?

Charlotte said gently, "She is a dancer. She has a career, a life of her own. When you are older, you will understand, but he loves you. You know that, don't you? And you are happy here."

"Sometimes." Paquita was staring down at her feet. Then suddenly she looked up. "May I go now?"

"Yes, if you promise to behave yourself."

She was a strange child, affectionate but reserved, not given to revealing her secret thoughts. She needed time to assimilate what she had been told, so Charlotte let her go and prayed that she had done right.

It was a day or two later when Lorenzo, meeting her unexpectedly, said, "What the devil is wrong with Paquita? Do *you* know? She runs away from me as if I were the devil himself."

"Oh dear, I never thought of that. It has made her shy."

"Shy of me? Why, for God's sake?"

She told him briefly what had happened and he frowned.

"God damn those young devils. I hope someone knocked their heads together. You were right, as always. I should have told her long ago. Now it is up to me. Somehow I will have to make her understand."

What he said to her Charlotte did not know but it had one unexpected result on the day Gabriella came riding in bringing an urgent warning. In the café society of Triana information had filtered through to her that part of Roméro's army was moving secretly up through the valley in the direction of the Castillo.

She stayed barely an hour with Lorenzo and was ready to leave when she saw Charlotte crossing the courtyard and stopped her.

"My daughter turns on me with reproaches and it seems that it is you whom I have to thank for it," she said.

"If that is true, then no doubt she told you why. Paquita had to know who her father is one day."

238

"Surely that could have been left to me or to Don Lorenzo. You take too much upon yourself, Señorita Carlotta." She took the bridle from the boy waiting with her horse and then turned back, a contemptuous smile on the beautiful mouth. "Are you in love with him?"

"That is a question I do not choose to answer."

Gabriella laughed unpleasantly. "So I am right. More fool you, *Inglesa*. There have been more than one. You think yourself so clever but I would remind you that Lorenzo has never forgiven the British for murdering his father. Believe me, it is in his blood and a Spaniard does not forget such things so easily."

"You did not need to tell me that," said Charlotte steadily. "I knew it already."

"Then be warned."

Gabriella vaulted lightly into the saddle and Charlotte, disturbed, watched her ride away. Back in her own room she took out the portrait she had not looked at since they had come to the Castillo, suddenly frightened. How could it possibly affect her and Lorenzo? It was quite absurd to think it had any significance and yet as she stood there with it in her hand, she felt cold as if a dank chill out of her father's grave had swept across her. She was tempted to run to Lorenzo that very minute. She longed to hear him laugh, say it was nothing of any importance, and then put it away for ever. But it was not a good time. He would be greatly occupied with the news that Gabriella had brought. There would be plenty of opportunity when all this was over.

The attack they had all been expecting came a couple of days later just before dawn. The invaders did not march up the road from the village as had been anticipated but crept down from the mountain led by someone who knew the paths intimately. It was a small party carrying flaming torches coming silently out of the night and bent on destruction.

Charlotte, lying wakeful, heard the distant sounds of gunfire, men shouting and the whinneying of terrified horses. She was out of bed in an instant. From the window she could see a lurid glare that lit up the night sky and seemed to be coming from the stables. She was already scrambling into her clothes when Juanita rushed into the room wild with excitement and fear.

239

"They have come," she cried shrilly, "those murdering fiends! They are here. Hurry, Señorita, hurry or we shall all be burned to death in our beds!"

"Be quiet, Juanita, don't be foolish. I am sure there is no real danger to us. I'm going to find out what is happening."

"I will come with you."

"No. You must stay with Doña Lucia."

But she was too late. Lucy, fully dressed, was already out of her bedroom and pulling a thick shawl around her shoulders.

"We will go together, Charlie. I don't want to stay here alone."

"Lucy, this is crazy. You're not alone in the house. The servants are all here and it is well guarded," said Charlotte impatiently. "I'm quite certain there is no danger."

"How can you be sure? Besides the others – they will all be out there."

Lucy was obstinately determined, so at last Charlotte gave in and had to content herself with ordering Juanita to stay close at her mistress's side and not leave her alone on any account.

"You must take care of her. Don't let her come too near."

"*Si, Señorita, si, si.* I understand well. It is not good," and Juanita rolled her eyes expressively with her hand on her belly.

Then Charlotte was hurrying ahead of them up the path that led to the stables. As she drew near she could see the flames leaping up into the dark sky but it was difficult to distinguish anything clearly in a confusion of eddying smoke where men were still fighting amid the plunging hooves of terrified horses.

She paused, leaning against a tree, breathless with running, and presently, as the smoke drifted blown by the wind, a clearer picture emerged. The raiders must already have been driven back though men were still struggling while others lay dead or wounded. Horses were being led to safety and she thought she glimpsed Lorenzo with them. A chain of men were handing buckets from the well in an attempt to dowse the burning stables. Then out of the chaos came Teresa leading Zelda, her face smudged with smoke, and Charlotte grabbed hold of her.

"What happened?"

"I don't know exactly. Roberto roused me and said some of Roméro's men must have crept up silently during the night. He

240

told me not to come but I could not bear to stay in the house. The stable lads were on guard but there were too many of them and they carried torches and bundles of burning straw."

"Are all the horses saved?"

"I hope so. I don't know for sure. I'm going back to see." Between them they soothed and petted Zelda, tethering her securely to one of the fence posts. "Only savages," went on Teresa fiercely, "would want to burn horses to death."

It was strange, thought Charlotte, this was not war. It had no real purpose. It was like the attack on the vineyard, vicious, wanton destruction of something that had been Lorenzo's particular pride.

By now Lucy and Juanita had reached them. The thick coils of acrid smoke were making them cough, but together they moved nearer.

They heard Lorenzo asking if all the horses were out.

"All but one, Señor," answered Jacopo. "The stallion is not here."

"*Dios*, I forgot. He was moved to the far stable," exclaimed Roberto. "I'll fetch him."

"No. Come back, boy. He's savage. You'll never hold him. Leave him to me."

Lorenzo began to run but Roberto was before him. The four women, huddled together, could see the flames running along the rooftops and there was a sudden crash as a rafter fell in a shower of sparks. Through the haze Roberto could be glimpsed tugging at the bridle of the great stallion. The frightened horse reared up, screaming with fear, as the burning beam fell beside him and one flailing hoof caught Roberto on the side of the head sending him spinning.

Lucy cried out and before anyone could stop her she had run across the yard to where Roberto had fallen. Lorenzo caught her in his arms swinging her away from the trampling hooves as the stallion reared up again. Then two of the men had seized the bridle and dragged him away. The edge of her skirt was smouldering in the flames and Lorenzo was beating them out with his bare hands as Charlotte and Teresa reached him.

"Mother of God, what are you doing here?" he said. "Here, take her from me."

He pushed Lucy into Charlotte's arms and knelt down beside his brother.

241

"Let me go, let me go!" Lucy tried to pull away. "Where is Roberto? Is he hurt? Is – is he dead?"

"He's not dead, only stunned," said Lorenzo. "We'll take care of him. Teresa, for pity's sake, take them away from here and then go to Grandmother. Tell her not to worry too much. We have everything under control."

He called some of the men and they began to carry Roberto between them as Charlotte put an arm around Lucy and urged her away.

She was crying now, choking sobs mingled with paroxysms of coughing as the bitter smoke caught her throat. They stumbled back along the path, half carrying her.

Teresa looked at her anxiously as they neared the house. "Will she be all right? I must go to Grandmother."

"Don't worry. I will take care of her."

In the sitting room Lucy lay back on the sofa, white and exhausted, while Juanita busied herself with making tea.

"Try and drink it," said Charlotte when she brought the tray. "It will do you good. Then I think you should go to bed."

"I'm not doing anything until I know about Roberto," gasped Lucy. "Would you go and find out, please, Charlie, please?"

She looked so distraught as she sought for breath that Charlotte was filled with pity.

"I'll go just as soon as we've drunk this," she said reassuringly, "though I doubt if they will know very much just yet."

She persuaded Lucy to sip the hot reviving tea, then left her lying on the sofa with a rug over her and Juanita hovering close by. She threaded her way through the corridors of the huge house and met Doña Gracia coming down the stairs as she crossed the great hall.

"I came to ask how Roberto is. I hope it is not serious."

"We don't know yet. There are lacerations and Lorenzo fears concussion. The doctor has been sent for but it will be some time before he reaches us. We can only wait."

"I am sorry. If there is anything I can do –?"

"Nothing, thank you. I understand from Teresa that you and Doña Lucia witnessed the accident and if it had not been for Lorenzo she might have suffered with him. Was that wise in her condition?"

"It is not easy to be wise when someone you love is struck down."

242

"Love?" repeated Doña Gracia. "I know of course that Roberto cherishes an absurd devotion to your cousin's wife, but I believed she has had the good sense to discourage him."

"That's perfectly true but however sensibly you may wish to behave, your heart can betray you."

"I see. I had hoped that you at least would not support this foolish affair."

"Is it so foolish?" Charlotte was riled by the contemptuous tone.

"Surely even you must recognize that any marriage between my grandson and a widow who is bearing a child to her late husband is totally unthinkable, to say nothing of her being a foreigner and a heretic."

"Is it so unthinkable?"

"I should have thought your own commonsense would have told you that. Roberto is young and hot-headed. Someone must think for him. And now you must excuse me. There is a great deal to be done. He is not the only one to be injured."

She knows, thought Charlotte, looking after her before she went back to their own rooms. She knows about Lorenzo and me and in this way she is letting me know how much she disapproves.

She comforted Lucy as best she could and then, too disturbed to sit and do nothing, she threw a shawl around her and walked up to the stables. The morning was beautiful, the sky clear and the air fresh and sweet. It made the utter devastation of what had once been a well built and orderly stableyard all the more distressing. The stench of the smoke was chokingly bitter. Some of the buildings still smouldered and everywhere there was water and wreckage.

Already men were at work trying to restore some kind of order but the damage was far too extensive. Lorenzo was there and told her that all the horses had been saved except one so badly burned by the falling debris that he had been forced to have it shot.

His face was dark with bitter anger. "I suppose we should be grateful we have escaped so lightly. Buildings can be restored but not lives. Thanks to Gabriella we were at least partly prepared." He looked away from her to the paths that led up into the Sierra. "There is one thing that puzzles me. There was a wanton waste about this attack. If it had been inspired

243

by Roméro, he would have stolen the horses not tried to destroy them."

"You mean it is something personal against you?"

"Perhaps. Either that or a warning. Oppose me and next time it will be worse."

He passed a hand wearily across his face and she saw that he had wrapped a handkerchief around it.

"You are hurt."

"It is nothing."

"Let me see."

She unwrapped the linen and exclaimed at the blistered fingers. "This must have been when Lucy's skirt caught fire."

"Possibly."

"It should be treated."

"Later. It is not important. Is Lucy hurt?"

"No, but very distressed about Roberto."

"We all are."

"I wish so much I could do something to help."

"Thank God, no one has been killed but there are a number of minor injuries. I believe Amalia and Teresa are doing their best until the doctor comes."

"I'll go to them. There will be something I can do and you must come and let me bandage your hand."

"Presently." He touched her cheek gently. "What a wretched beginning to our life together. Do you want to take back your promise?"

"Never! Don't they say 'for better, for worse'," she whispered, longing to put her arms around him but only too aware of the many eyes watching them.

She found Teresa in the barn where the horses had been stabled temporarily and Amalia was there with her. The stout middle-aged Amalia astonished her by showing a calm good sense and a practical skill in treating the cuts and burns suffered by the men who had fought so bravely. Many of the horses had been badly shocked, their coats singed by burning debris. Teresa, quite unafraid, went in and out amongst them helping the men who were treating them. It made Charlotte realize how wrong she had been in her opinion of the family at the Castillo. They were far from the pleasure-loving aristocrats she had once believed and whether they agreed with Lorenzo or not, they followed his lead.

She began to help Amalia, cutting the soft clean linen into bandages, and standing by with the pots of salve and goose grease. It was there that Juanita found her later that afternoon.

"Señorita, please come," she said breathlessly. "I think – I am sure that the baby will come soon."

"Oh no, it's not possible. It's not time yet. You must be mistaken."

But Juanita who had seen two brothers and three sisters come into the world shook her head.

"The Señora is very distressed. She asks for you."

"I think it's a false alarm. Lucy is very nervous," said Charlotte apologetically, "but I had better go to her."

"We are about finished here. Take Amalia with you," said Teresa. "She has helped a great many babies to be born. Isn't that so?"

"It is so," said Amalia diffidently. "If you wish Señorita, I will come willingly."

The rest of that day and the night that followed were like a nightmare, thought Charlotte, raging at her helplessness. Childbirth was something she had never experienced and she was appalled as she wiped the sweat from Lucy's face and watched the slight body shaken by spasms of pain. She sat by the bed holding her hand trying to tell herself that all was well and only partly reassured by Amalia's good sense.

"She is frightened, the little one," she murmured comfortingly. "It is often so with the firstborn. Stay with her, Señorita, talk to her. The baby will not come yet."

Very late that evening Doña Gracia sent the doctor who had been summoned to Roberto. Charlotte took an instant dislike to him. He was small and dark, with a lofty air of boredom, and to her fastidious taste looked none too clean. His black frockcoat was marked by the snuff he used constantly and by other stains she did not want to think about. Lucy shrank away from him as he bent over the bed and she clutched at Charlotte as he moved away to consult with Amalia at the other end of the room.

"Send him away, Charlotte. I don't want him here. He frightens me."

The doctor shrugged his shoulders, said that it would be many hours before he was needed and in answer to Lucy's agitated question he told her that Roberto had already regained consciousness due to his taking a pint of blood from him.

"He is young, he will recover – a bad headache for a couple of days and then," he snapped his fingers, "lively as a grasshopper."

For the first time since she had come to Spain Charlotte longed for England and the reassuring presence of old Doctor Thomas who had looked after all her childish ailments.

The bedroom had become a battlefield, she felt, in those last few hours before dawn when even Amalia's placid face showed signs of strain and Lucy's slim body arched and writhed in agony.

The sky was lightening when the baby was born at last and she lay back pale and spent against the pillows. Amalia, gravely disturbed at her patient's weakness, gave the child to Juanita and continued with doing all that was needful with Charlotte, considerably distressed, doing her best to help her. It was only afterwards that they turned to Juanita.

A fire had been lit against the chill of the night and the girl was sitting close beside it, the white bundle in her arms and tears running helplessly down her cheeks.

Alarmed, Charlotte knelt beside her. "What is it?"

"He breathed only once," she whispered, "and then was gone. I touched his forehead with the water and made the sign of the cross so that he will go straight back to heaven as a child of God."

Charlotte felt her heart contract. She looked down at the baby. He was tiny but already perfectly formed and she felt she could not bear it.

"It can't be true, it can't be. Amalia, are you sure? Is there nothing we can do?"

"Nothing, Señorita. I have seen others. The little one has come too early into a world not ready for him."

How could they tell Lucy? They looked at one another, overwhelmed with the pity of it but in some strange way she had already sensed it.

When Charlotte came to her side she whispered, "The baby's dead, isn't it? And it's my fault. It was I who killed it."

"Lucy, don't talk like that."

"It is true. When I thought Roberto was killed I wanted only to die with him and so now I am being punished for my wickedness."

"You don't know what you are saying. It is desperately sad

246

but it does sometimes happen when a baby comes too early. It is no fault of yours."

"You don't understand," she said wearily and turned her head away.

She did not weep. It would have been better if she had. She lay in a heavy lassitude, not caring whether she lived or died so that it seemed as if all that day and the next it was they who battled for Lucy's life, their will against hers to persuade her to recover and it was then that surprisingly Doña Gracia showed a true kindness and delicacy of feeling.

It was impossible at this present time of uncertainty for the baby who had lived only for a few minutes to be taken to the English cemetery at Malaga so she suggested that the tiny body should be buried in their own family burial ground.

She came to sit beside Lucy, gently taking her hand in hers. "At a time such as this, it is not creed that matters but only thought for the little spirit that has returned to the God who created it."

How she persuaded Father Bernardo Charlotte didn't know, but there was a simple service in the chapel and as she stood trying to hold back the tears Lorenzo came to stand beside her. She felt his hand take hers, gripping it firmly, and drew comfort from it.

Lucy listened in silence when she told her about it and described the flowers that had been brought from the hothouses to lay on the white coffin.

"I had not thought they would be so kind," she murmured. She was quiet for a little and then roused herself with an effort. "Charlotte, there is something I've been meaning to tell you. It came the day before that dreadful fire and after that so much happened, I could not speak of it. But now you must know."

"Know what, dearest?"

"Clive was not drowned."

"What!" For a moment she thought Lucy must be dreaming or suffering some delusion brought on by weakness. "I can't believe it. How do you know? What have you heard?"

"If you open my writing desk, you will see the letter."

The sheet of paper was stained in places and written in a faltering English as if under dictation but the information it contained was very plain.

Clive had been carried by currents further down the coast

from Tangier and washed up on a lonely beach cruelly battered by the waves but miraculously still breathing. There he was found by a fisherman and taken by him to the house of a wealthy merchant, half Arab, half French. There was no identification on the body, nothing to indicate who he was or where he had come from except that with his fair hair and cast of features he was certainly a foreigner and European. For many weeks sick in mind and body he had been unfit to give any information and it was only now, under the care of his kind rescuer, that he had been able to recall his name and had begged him to write to his wife. The letter had been sent many weeks before and had gone through a great number of hands before finally reaching Mr Robinson in Seville and he had despatched it to the Castillo.

"By now he may have already returned to England," said Lucy dully.

"It's so extraordinary, it's almost unbelievable. Can this letter be genuine?"

"I thought that. At first it seemed so impossible and yet somehow in my heart I knew it was true and that I should be feeling relieved and happy that he had been saved from such a terrible death and instead all I could think of was that now I would never again be free. I knew it was wrong. I fought with myself all that day and then that night when the fire came, when I saw Roberto kicked by the horse and believed him killed, all I wanted was to be with him. How wonderful to end it all. I longed for the horse to strike me down too but Lorenzo stopped that. And so, because of what I did, the baby died and and I'm being punished for it."

"You must not believe that."

"How can I help it? Any day now a letter will come from England and I must return."

"But you had made up your mind to go home in any case," said Charlotte gently.

"Yes, I know, but I would still have been free one day."

"And you believed that Roberto would come to you."

"It was foolish but at least I had hope and now there is nothing. I am Clive's wife, all I have is his, where could I go, what could I do if I left him? I'm not like you, Charlotte. You're so brave and strong. I never realized before how hateful it is to be a woman. It is so unjust. Clive can do as he pleases, take other women to his bed, spend the money I gave him, treat me like a chattel for whom he has neither love nor respect, and if I rebel against it, I am a bad woman, an outcast from society." She beat her small hands on the coverlet in a frenzy of frustration.

"Hush, dearest, if you go on like this you will make yourself ill," said Charlotte. "You did love Clive once. This terrible experience may have changed him."

"I wish I could believe that but I can't. People don't change."

Charlotte was looking down at the letter thoughtfully. "We could write to this address but it would take many weeks to get an answer. Better to wait. We must hear from Clive soon. Lorenzo will be glad to know about this."

"Don't tell him, Charlie, not yet. Let me speak to Roberto first."

"But it concerns Lorenzo as much as it does us."

"No, it doesn't, not really, and we don't know anything for certain yet. Can't we wait a little longer before we tell him?"

She was so agitated that Charlotte agreed against her better judgement. She found it hard to accept that Clive was still alive. After so much distress there was relief in knowing that after all she had not sent him to his death. The old affection for her wayward cousin that she had never entirely lost began to revive and with it an enormous pity for Lucy who had found a true love only to lose it. There was nothing they could do but wait and perhaps it was as well that the war brought distraction, unwelcome though it was.

While Charlotte had been confined to the sick room, so concerned with Lucy that she could think of nothing else, events in the outside world had not stood still. It was Teresa who one morning gave her the grave news.

She had brought a handmade lace shawl so rare and fine it was like a cobweb.

"Grandmother had intended it for the baby, a christening robe perhaps, but now . . . it could be worn as a mantilla or even as an evening shawl," and she draped it around her shoulders to show it off.

"It is kind of Doña Gracia. Lucy will be very touched."

"How is she?"

"She improves every day. Soon she will be able to leave her bed."

249

"Roberto keeps asking now he is up and about again."

"I know. She won't see him yet. Soon perhaps."

Teresa carefully folded the lace and then looked up at Charlotte. "I don't know how much Lorenzo has told you."

"I have only seen him briefly these last two weeks. What do you mean, Teresa? What has he been hiding from me?"

"He said I should not trouble you when Lucy was so sick and the baby lost but now I think you would want to know because it concerns us all. Roméro's army has moved to the very gates of Seville. If the government forces do not come soon and he takes the city, the Carlists could overrun the whole of Andalusia."

"What will that mean?"

"I don't know," she said unhappily, "none of us do for certain, not even Lorenzo. We shall all be involved whether we wish it or not, and not only us at the Castillo. Lorenzo is desperately concerned for the peasants and the hill farmers. Tales of atrocities come in every day and the refugees . . . they are so pitiful, Charlotte, far far worse than after the floods. Oh, if only Enrique would come with his guards. He would put a stop to it!"

Charlotte smiled and then was serious again. "Is there any way in which I can help?"

"Lorenzo says it is not your country nor your battle and you should not be part of it."

"But I am part of it. I am here living in your house. I must repay my debt in whatever way I can."

Teresa gave her a quick look before she said quietly, "You love Lorenzo, don't you?"

"Yes," she said simply. No point in denying it now.

"And he loves you?"

"I believe so."

"I knew it," said Teresa triumphantly, "and I'm glad. I used to think I hated him and now I don't. Isn't that strange?"

"No, you've grown up, that's all."

"That's only part of it," said Teresa thoughtfully. "I think it's because of you. He's been different ever since you came, happier, despite all the dreadful things that are happening."

"Do you really believe that, Teresa?"

"Yes, I do, and so does Grandmother though she'd rather die than admit it." She giggled suddenly and then got to her feet.

250

"I mustn't stay and gossip any longer. All this is a great burden on her, poor darling, and I do try and take some of it on my shoulders."

"Will you let me share it?"

"Why not?" She glanced at Charlotte with her old mischievous grin. "After all we may be sisters very soon."

15

Despite what Teresa had told her it was not until the end of that week that Charlotte began to realize the full horrors of this civil war, the brutality, the ruthless looting of sheep, goats and donkeys, a poor peasant's whole livelihood vanished in a single night. There were men who limped in wounded and bleeding from the hopeless struggle, women whose torn clothes and scratched faces showed how they had fought to save their children from starvation and others who did not come at all but lay savagely murdered in ruined hovels and burned out cottages.

She and Teresa did what they could under Lorenzo's direction, when he was there. Gabriella had returned and reluctantly Charlotte had to admit there was something flamelike, something inspiring about her fierce courage that put heart into the most despairing.

One day when she was helping to serve the bowls of good nourishing soup prepared in the Castillo kitchens, she saw a young woman, a mere slip of a girl, with a great bruise on her forehead and blood on her torn skirts. She had moved away from the patient queue waiting for food and was making her unsteady way to the barn door. Something about the wild desperate look on the girl's face worried her. She handed the ladle to Teresa and went after her.

Outside the girl was walking waveringly towards the road that led through the gardens to the destroyed village. She caught up with her and tried to turn her back but met with an obstinate resistance.

"My baby," she was repeating over and over again, "my baby is still there."

It took a long time and much patience to disentangle the story. The young woman had been in the upper room with her little boy when the soldiers had come, brutally smashing into the shack adjoining their stone-walled cottage, driving out the chickens roosting there and dragging away the sacks of flour

252

and grain that would feed their few beasts and themselves during the winter. Her man was away in the fields. She fled down the stairs, screaming, battering at them with futile fists. One of them struck her so hard that she fell senseless to the ground. When she recovered consciousness, she was on the cart with the other refugees being driven to safety at the Castillo. She tried to go back but the others held on to her believing pityingly that her ravings about her child were the effect of the blow on her head.

Charlotte persuaded her to come back inside the barn. Teresa came to join her with Gabriella and the girl stammered out her story again.

"Is there any chance that the child is still alive?" asked Charlotte.

"What soldier wants to be hampered with a squalling brat?" said Gabriella.

"Could we go and find out?" said Teresa impetuously.

"It might be dangerous –"

"Not if they are gone –"

"They've gone all right, the filthy murdering robbers!" growled one of the men who had crawled in during the night dragging a crippled leg after him. "The cursed soldiers have left us nothing but empty husks."

Charlotte thought of Lucy's dead baby and it suddenly became desperately important that she should save this one. They looked at one another and then turned to Gabriella for guidance.

"If we do go, it will give heart to all these here," she said thoughtfully. "They will know how much we, the Cristinos, care even for a lost child."

"Should we tell Lorenzo?"

"He has other things on his mind."

So they had the horses saddled and rode close together out of the Castillo and along the mountain road to the small village hidden in the valley.

Charlotte thought she had already seen the worst war could do but it had been nothing like this. What had been one of the small contented communities she had so often ridden through, where the women gathered at the well or gossiped beside their cooking fires while the children played in the sunshine, looked as if a hurricane had torn it apart, a hurricane that had brought death and destruction with it. It was like the

253

stableyard all over again but far, far worse. The stench met them before they reached it, the acrid reek of smoke, the sour-sweet smell of death. Some of the cottages had been burned to ashes, others were wrecked, doors swinging crazily, pathetic household treasures smashed and trampled into the black mud.

They dismounted, picking their way through the shambles. Charlotte stumbled over a body, realized with relief that it was a dog, and a moment later saw the spread-eagled figure of an old woman lying face upwards, her skirts dragged up to her waist. She swallowed a rising nausea and hurriedly pulled down the ragged petticoat to cover the pitiful naked legs.

"How can men be such *beasts*?" whispered Teresa at her elbow.

"Ssh!" Charlotte stopped. "What was that?"

They stood still to listen and out of the eerie silence came the sudden feeble wail of a hungry child.

"It's coming from over there."

Charlotte ran across the road. She cautiously pushed the door. Miraculously the shaky ladder that led to the shelf-like upper floor of the one room shack was still intact. She climbed it carefully. In the wooden cradle a sturdy nine-month-old baby cried weakly, beating his arms against the wooden sides. She stooped to pick him up, wrapped the wet sour-smelling blanket around him and climbed down the rickety ladder. Teresa at the bottom took the baby from her.

"Let's hope this is the right one," she whispered.

"The boy's alive anyway. Where is Gabriella?"

"Waiting with the horses."

"Let's go then."

They ran back along the path. Teresa was already in the saddle and Charlotte was handing the baby up to her when she heard it, a long drawn out howl followed by a furious barking.

"Come. It's only a dog," said Gabriella impatiently.

"It must be trapped somewhere."

"Leave it."

"The poor creature will starve. I'll let it out and then come."

"No, Charlotte."

But she had already darted back among the houses. She tracked the sound to a shack that had served as a stable for the owner's donkey. The door had jammed, imprisoning the dog who was hurling himself against it in a violent attempt to escape.

She dragged at it with all her strength. At first it refused to budge, then it gave way with a splintering crash and the big farm dog leaped joyously free knocking her backwards. She picked herself up, turned to follow him and walked into the arms of a couple of soldiers who had unexpectedly appeared from behind the stable.

They each took an arm. They were part of a forage party returned to make sure nothing had been left that could feed a hungry army and this was a prize indeed. No peasant but a well dressed young woman who could be used as a hostage, provide a ransom or even give them a little sport if their Captain was willing. They took no heed of her frantic pleas as they forced her along between them.

Horrified, Teresa watched the men take her and would have gone back if Gabriella had not stopped her.

"There's nothing you can do."

"But we can't *leave* her!"

"She is British. She will come to no harm. It would be different for us. Roméro would be only too pleased to lay hands on one of us."

"But we must *do* something . . ."

"Don't be a fool. Do you want us all to die?"

Gabriella gave Teresa's horse a cut across the rump so that he started forward, then she seized Zelda's bridle and galloped away dragging the mare after her.

With a tremendous effort Charlotte had kicked herself free. Running frantically towards them she saw her hope of escape disappear. Gabriella had taken her horse with them. The shock was so great that she stumbled and fell. In an instant the soldiers had reached her and jerked her roughly to her feet.

After the first futile struggle Charlotte tried hard to reassure herself. She would explain who she was, that she had taken no part in this conflict and then they would release her. They would be forced to. Even Roméro would not wish to provoke trouble with the English.

There was a house set a little apart from the others, larger and better built, that had once belonged to the headman of the village. He had been struck down at the first ruthless attack, his wife and children had fled and the house served as a command post for the lieutenant in charge of the search party.

One of the men took her arm and pushed her through the

door and into what was both kitchen and living room. A man sat at the table, head bent over some lists he was checking.

Charlotte's captor saluted. "A prisoner, *Teniente*. We found her in the village. She says she was looking for a lost baby but that's an unlikely tale. She could be a spy from the Castillo."

"The Castillo?"

The man at the table raised his head and with a shiver Charlotte saw that it was Vicente, Vicente the bullfighter, wearing some kind of sketchy uniform, the handsome face coarsened a little, a sullen droop to the sensual mouth, an air of bravado. Teresa's glamorous hero was already running to seed. He stared at her for a long moment before he spoke.

"That was well done, Pedro. I know this lady. Leave her here and finish your work."

"*Bueno, Señor.*"

The soldier glanced from Charlotte to Vicente, then went out closing the door after him.

Charlotte said nervously, "It's not true what he said. I am not spying, how could I? I only came because one of the refugees was distressed at the loss of her child."

But Vicente was not listening to her. He sat back in the one chair, black eyes scanning her from head to foot.

"So . . . the Señorita Carlotta is living at the Castillo under the protection of the Marqués de Merenda." He leaned forward across the table. "Is he your lover?"

"No!" She exclaimed and to her dismay felt the tell-tale colour flood up into her cheeks.

"No?" he repeated derisively. "A great man like Don Lorenzo does not offer refuge to the cousin of an English spy without very good reason." The hand on the table suddenly clenched. He said violently, "If I had been commanding this campaign I would have destroyed the Castillo de Palomas and everyone in it, razed it to the ground, spat upon its ashes!"

The ferocity in his voice so appalled her that she shrank away from it. So it was he who had planned the attack on the stables that but for Lorenzo's vigilance could have been so much worse.

"Roméro refused," he went on with a brooding anger. "He was afraid. 'If Carlos ever becomes king, then he will need men like Don Lorenzo to be at his side,' that was what he said to me. 'Hit him where it hurts, burn the village and his people, but leave him untouched.'"

256

"Why?" she whispered. "Why such terrible slaughter? These people here – they had done nothing."

But Vicente went on unheeding. "I would have destroyed him as he destroyed me," he muttered. "I was on the crest of the wave. I could have risen to the heights, married to his sister I would have been received in society, fêted everywhere, and he took it away from me. He humiliated me, he made me doubt myself, and in the bullring that must not happen. You are master, you are king with the power of a God or you are lost, you must not fail or the mob will tear you to pieces . . ."

She knew then that he was a man with an obsession, who had to blame someone else for his own failure of nerve, who could not accept himself for what he was, and she trembled. It made him frighteningly unpredictable.

There was only one small window and the room had grown dark though it was still light outside. He went to the door and shouted. Presently one of the soldiers came in with candles. He lit them, dripped grease on the table and stood them in it.

"Are the men finished with their work?"

"*Si, Señor.*"

"We move in an hour."

The man glanced at Charlotte. "Does she go with us?"

"When I have done with her."

The soldier grinned unpleasantly and left them together.

Charlotte was still huddled against the wall uncertain what move to make with Vicente in this strange mood. A pistol lay on the table finely plated with silver. Harry Starr had once possessed a pair of them, a gift from his own father on his coming of age. He had taught her to shoot with them, delighting in her quickness of eye and steadiness of hand.

Vicente sat down again at the table, his black eyes glittering in the candle flame. He said gently, almost conversationally, "Take off your jacket."

"What?" She could not believe her ears.

"Take it off and the blouse with it. I want to see for myself the charms that Don Lorenzo finds so irresistible."

"You're mad."

"Take them off." He leaned forward, picking up the pistol and aiming it almost playfully at her, but the voice was dangerous. "Now, Doña Carlotta, NOW!"

257

Very slowly she pulled off her jacket and with shaking fingers began to unbutton the high collar of her blouse.

"Hurry. We've not much time."

"I won't do it."

"Would you rather I tore it off you?"

Biting her lips she began to unfasten the blouse.

Impatiently he crossed to her still holding the pistol. She backed away from him into the corner of the room and he followed after her. With one hand he ruthlessly tore open the thin blouse and with it the lace and ribbon of her petticoat. The touch of his hand on her breast was like a violation. She shivered, so desperately afraid of what he might do next that she did not heed the shouts outside, the sound of men's voices, but Vicente stiffened. He swung around, his eye on the door as Lorenzo came through it.

"Stop! Don't move!" Vicente was master for the moment and enjoying it. "The Marqués de Merenda in person, just as I hoped. You'd better drop that gun in your hand. The slightest move and I kill her."

Very slowly Lorenzo let the gun fall to the ground. His eyes moved from Vicente to Charlotte and he began to take off his sheepskin jacket.

"Stop that!" but he ignored Vicente, shrugged it off and tossed it to her.

"Cover yourself," he said briefly.

Gratefully she snatched it up and pulled it on. It felt warm and very comforting.

Vicente did not move. They were like two dangerous animals facing one another but for the moment the bullfighter had the advantage.

"I have waited a long time," he said, "to have you at my mercy and your English whore with you."

"What has happened to you, Vicente?" Lorenzo's voice was light, amused, mocking. "You've lost your looks. Are you missing the bullring, all those brave bulls you failed to kill, the jeers of the crowd calling you fool, coward?"

He was being deliberately provocative. Charlotte saw Vicente's mouth tighten and his hand grip the gun more firmly, then Lorenzo launched himself across the room as a tiger leaps on its prey so suddenly that Vicente went over backwards, the pistol flying out of his hand and falling at Charlotte's feet.

She picked it up. It felt heavy and unfamiliar in her hand.

They were fighting now with a savagery that terrified her. At first Lorenzo, taller, in better physical shape, had the advantage. They circled round the room, while she stood trembling. One candle went flying across the floor and died. Lorenzo had Vicente bent backwards across the table, his hands on his throat and the murderous look on his face terrified her. Vicente slid sideways, Lorenzo went after him, stumbled over the chair and fell heavily against the wall, temporarily stunned. Vicente was panting, blood running freely from a split lip. She saw him draw the long thin knife from his belt and almost without conscious thought, steadied the pistol, took aim and fired.

The explosion was frightening in the confined space, the recoil nearly unbalanced her. She saw Lorenzo scramble to his feet as Vicente slowly toppled forwards and fell face down on the dirty floor. What had begun between them months ago in the Café Diablo was finished at last.

"I've killed him," she thought with mingled horror and relief. "Oh my God, I've killed him!"

Then Lorenzo was at her side and had taken the pistol from her nerveless fingers.

"Is he dead?" she whispered. She was shivering uncontrollably.

"Whether he is or not, it's time we went. Come."

There was blood on his face and on the hand that gripped hers.

"You're hurt."

"It's nothing. Come now."

"He has men outside."

"They are taken care of."

He put his arm around her, dropped the pistol on the table, picked up his own gun and hurried her from the house. Outside in the dusk she saw the men he must have brought with him and the soldiers they held prisoner. He gave one or two brief orders and then turned to her.

"Can you ride?"

She felt as if her knees were giving way under her but with an effort she braced herself.

"Yes, I can ride."

He lifted her into the saddle. Then they were trotting swiftly away from horror and death and into the cold starlit night.

"How did you know?" she whispered as they rode.

"Teresa came to me."

"It was not her fault. It was mine, all mine. I went back for the dog."

"So I gathered. When are you going to learn, my love, to think before you act. I could have been too late."

She swayed in the saddle and he moved closer, putting his hand on hers.

"Courage. It is over now."

He was filled with a slow burning anger. If it had not been for Teresa she could have been tortured, raped, murdered, and it was Gabriella who had done it, who had taken the horse and mercilessly left her to her fate. His blood ran cold when he thought how easily it could have happened and she had not cared. She had faced him defiantly.

"Would you rather have seen your sister in their hands? She would have been a prize indeed. The *Inglesa* would have suffered no harm, a few hours of discomfort perhaps."

"You did it deliberately," he had raged at her. "Why? Why, Gabriella? Are you jealous?"

"I? Jealous?" She spat the words at him. "Why should I care whom you take to your bed?"

He had struck her then so hard that she stumbled backwards, something he had never done to any woman. He saw the black anger in her eyes before he gathered his men and rode like a madman to the village.

It was fully dark by the time they reached the Castillo and as they went past the outbuildings where the refugees were housed, they came pouring out into the courtyard. The story had run from one to the other. The girl whose baby had been so miraculously restored to her had not been able to contain her joy. She was there as they rode in reaching up to touch Charlotte's hand.

"May the Holy Mother of God bless you, Señorita," she whispered through her tears.

Then they were all greeting her, swarming around the horses as Lorenzo dismounted and lifted her to the ground. He put his arm around her and pushed his way through them with a good-humoured impatience and reluctantly they parted to let them pass.

Exhausted as she was, it gave her a thrill of pleasure. It was like an accolade. Whatever Doña Gracia liked to say, she was one of them now, accepted as Lorenzo's chosen.

There were servants hovering anxiously in the hall when they went into the house and Teresa came running as if she had been on the watch. The words came tumbling out.

"Thank God, Lorenzo reached you in time."

She would have flung her arms around Charlotte if her brother had not stopped her with a gesture.

"Gently now, she's tired out. Let Grandmother know, will you?"

"Yes," but she still reached out to press Charlotte's hand. "We saved the baby anyway," she said impishly, "and the dog."

"Teresa, will you do as I say?"

"All right, brother dear, I'm going," she flashed them a grin before running away and up the stairs.

"I must go to Lucy," murmured Charlotte.

"In a moment."

He took her with him into the library. A lamp had been lit and the fire had burned to a dull red glow. He closed the door and leaned back against it.

"A baby and a dog – *Madre de Dios* – what am I to do with you, Charlotte?" he said wryly.

Then she was in his arms and he was holding her very close, his mouth against her hair. "I thought I'd lost you," he was murmuring, and a little later, "who taught you to shoot so well, my love?"

"My father. I was the boy he never had."

He drew back a little, tilting up her chin to face him. "Always your father. What else did he teach you?"

"A great many things, you'd be surprised, and thank heaven he did."

"Yes indeed or it could have been I and not Vicente lying there."

She shuddered at the memory of that moment and his arm tightened around her.

"Come to the fire. You're shivering."

"I should not stay –" but she let him lead her towards the welcome warmth.

"There is something I want to give you."

He left her for a moment to open a drawer in his desk. He

261

came back with a small case and flicked up the lid. Inside there was a gold ring with an intaglio cut into a deep red stone.

"It once belonged to my father and then it came to me but it is too small for my finger. I intended to have it altered but now it will serve until I can buy one more fitting for you." He took her left hand and slipped it on to the third finger. "With this ring I thee wed, with my body I thee worship . . ." he said quietly.

He drew her towards him and she closed her eyes and gave herself up to his kisses. They were both still very emotionally shaken by what had happened. The blind rage when he had seen her ripped dress, the wish to kill the man responsible, the near brush of death had left their mark. He had made love to her once and knew by her trembling response that it would be easy to take her now and she would not resist him. The desire flamed through him and then died. Not here, not in his own house, not until she was his wife in the eyes of the whole world.

She said breathlessly, "Lorenzo, I must go."

"Yes."

He released her but still held her hand. Then he kissed the finger on which he had put the ring and let her go.

She went quickly out of the library and through the corridors of the quiet house. In their own room Lucy was waiting for her. She looked up frowning as Charlotte came in.

"So there you are at last. Juanita told me that Lorenzo had brought you back. Whatever were you thinking of to go off like that at such a time?"

Charlotte was still living in the warm glow of Lorenzo's kisses, still hearing him say caressingly, "With this ring I thee wed," and scarcely noticed the sharpness in Lucy's voice.

"I suppose it was reckless," she said dreamily, "but it was a baby lost and we did bring the boy back to his mother."

"At what cost? Just look at you? What will they all think? What is Doña Gracia going to say of us?"

Lucy's acid tone penetrated her happiness. She pulled Lorenzo's coat around her torn blouse and pushed back the disordered hair.

"What does it matter what she says or what anyone else thinks? What is wrong with you, Lucy? Why are you so angry with me?" Impulsively she went across the room and knelt beside her. "I've been longing to tell you but Lorenzo wished

it to be a secret between us for a little. Now it is different."
She sat back on her heels, fatigue forgotten, radiant with joy.
"He has asked me to marry him."

"Marry him?"

"Yes. It seems a long time ago now because so much has
happened in between."

Lucy stared at her. "Was it – on the night of the storm?"

"Yes."

"I knew there was something when you came back. I said
so but you denied it." She looked away from Charlotte. "Did
he make love to you?"

"Yes. Oh, it shouldn't have happened. I know that, but it
did – in a cold wet cave, on a bed of bracken and a blanket
smelling of horse." She laughed a little. "And it was wonderful."

Lucy got up abruptly, pushing her aside and walking away
from her. "Charlotte, how could you be so foolish?"

She looked up, startled out of her dream. "What do you
mean?"

"Surely you must realize – the proud Marqués de Merenda
would never marry a woman he has already made his mistress.
It's ridiculous."

"It wasn't like that at all." Charlotte was on her feet stung
to strong indignation.

"Wasn't it? It seems very obvious to me. You of all people,
Charlie, letting yourself be deceived and saying nothing about
it, hiding it from everyone as if you were ashamed. Of course
he didn't want anyone to know – it's not very honourable, is it,
seducing a guest in his house? It disgusts me and then you
going off today like you did. What did the soldiers do to you?
Tear the clothes from you, rape you? How can he do anything
but despise you after that?"

"You're wrong," said Charlotte furiously, "absolutely wrong,
and this proves it." She held out her hand. "He put this ring
on my finger not half an hour ago, his father's ring, as a pledge
of our love. Look at it."

Lucy gave it one glance and then raised her eyes. "Anyone
can give an old ring like that and an empty promise."

"That's a cruel thing to say and untrue. Are you jealous
because Roberto is not your lover?"

"How dare you say that to me? How dare you?" said Lucy,
her cheeks flaming. "At least I know how to behave."

263

For an instant they glared at one another, appalled at what they were doing to the friendship between them, and it was Lucy who broke first.

With a sudden change of mood she sank down on the sofa and covered her face with her hands.

"Oh God, Charlotte, I'm sorry. I don't mean to be so beastly. Ever since the baby I can't seem to see things straight any longer." She lifted her head, staring drearily in front of her. "In a way you are right. I am jealous. Roberto was here this afternoon."

"Did you tell him about Clive?"

"Yes."

"What did he say?"

"He wants me to leave him and stay here in Spain."

"But Lucy, he is Catholic. He will never be able to marry you."

"Who is talking about marriage? If you can take a lover, then so can I."

"Oh Lucy, dear Lucy, forgive me." She went across to sit beside her full of repentance, because in her own joy she had forgotten Lucy's unhappiness.

But the girl pushed her away. "No, don't touch me. I know it won't be any use. I know what I have to do." She got up wearily and moved towards the door. "You had better make the most of Lorenzo while you have him. The Cristinos are marching south at last. The General is likely to make the Castillo his headquarters."

"Who told you?"

"Roberto. He is on fire to go with them."

"Lorenzo won't fight," said Charlotte confidently. "He believes it is more important to protect his people and his lands. What is the use of victory, he says, if it brings only starvation and sickness with it?"

"He may have to make a choice."

She went out closing the door and Charlotte stood still for a moment, the glowing bubble of joy within her effectively destroyed. She looked down at the ring on her finger and then moved to the light to examine it more closely. Deeply incised into the red stone was a dove in flight, the same crest as on the bloodstained handkerchief upstairs in her trunk. It shook her in spite of herself, but she was not going to let it haunt her.

264

Tomorrow or the next day she would take it to him with the portrait and lay the ghost once and for all.

The moment of ecstasy had passed and now she was aware only of weariness and a longing to strip off the soiled clothes and wash away the violation of Vicente's groping hand. She turned out the lamp and went draggingly up the stairs to her own room.

16

General Benito de Ramirez rode in the next morning ahead of his men and with him came other members of his staff including Enrique de Tajo and Diego Alvaro, who had been appointed Captain since the day Charlotte had met him on the road to Palos. Lorenzo was there to greet the great man with Doña Gracia.

"He is an old friend of the family," Teresa had confided to Charlotte. "When I was little I used to call him Uncle Benito. He wasn't quite so grand then. Doesn't Enrique look simply splendid?" She sighed with relief. "Now they are here at last everything will be all right."

Charlotte, with memories of what her father had told her of the arrogance, touchy tempers and quarrels among the Spanish troops, did not feel so confident.

Guy came riding in later in the morning and the men were closeted together most of the day but in the early evening they were all gathered in the drawing room before dinner. Lorenzo had specifically asked Charlotte and Lucy to join them and she dressed very carefully in the green and gold dress, brushing her hair until it shone with a reddish lustre in the candlelight, unaccountably nervous, her hands trembling as she touched the ring he had put on her finger. Last night already seemed to have a dreamlike quality.

She followed Lucy into the room and Lorenzo came at once to meet them.

"May I present our English guests, General? The Señora Lucia Starr and her cousin, the Señorita Carlotta."

The General was in his late fifties but still a fine figure of a man with a sweeping moustache and thick curling grey hair.

"Charmed," he said with a grave courtesy, bending to kiss the tips of their fingers. Penetrating black eyes under tufted eyebrows rested on Charlotte for a moment.

266

"Starr," he repeated thoughtfully. "That name is familiar from somewhere – a long way back perhaps."

She lifted her head proudly. "My father, Captain Harry Starr, fought all through the Peninsula with the Duke of Wellington, General."

He snapped his fingers. "Ah, that will be it of course. I remember now. It was in Madrid – nearly twenty years ago – that was when we . . ." He broke off and smiled, shrugging his shoulders. "Ah well, we were all a great deal younger then. We thought we had won lasting peace for our country and only found out afterwards how wrong we were."

Lorenzo reached out and took Charlotte's hand, drawing her towards him. "It is not official yet, General, but you are such an old friend – I am happy to tell you that the Señorita Carlotta has consented to become my wife."

For an instant there was a stunned silence and in that flash of time Charlotte heard Lucy's gasp, saw Doña Gracia's frown and regretted the hurt look on Guy's face.

"Your wife?" If the General was taken by surprise, he recovered quickly. "My most sincere felicitations, Señorita, and as for you, my dear boy, I couldn't be more pleased. It is high time you were married. These are difficult days, God knows, but life must go on, isn't that so?" and he turned to Doña Gracia. "I am sure you will agree with me."

The Marquésa's frown smoothed out into a gracious smile. "Anything that makes Lorenzo happy, must please me also, Benito."

Then everyone seemed to be talking at once. Teresa came running to kiss Charlotte and give her brother a hug.

"Lorenzo, you old fraud! Fancy keeping it a secret from all of us!"

Roberto grinned and waved his hand to the butler. "This calls for a toast. Marco, bring some of the French champagne."

And while the servants were filling the glasses, Enrique came to press Charlotte's hand.

"I wish you could persuade Teresa to listen to me," he murmured ruefully, "then we could have a double wedding."

Captain Alvaro was giving her a thin-lipped smile. "Didn't we meet once, Señorita, on your way to La Rábida? Did you deliver your dumb servant safely into the care of the monks?"

And she knew that he had guessed about Clive and was

267

still bitterly resentful of the way in which he had been tricked.

"So you have won him after all. What magic did you use?" whispered Lucy.

The only one that remained aloof was Guy and she felt sorry that he should have had to learn it like this but then they were all raising their glasses, Lorenzo was drawing her close to him and it was impossible to feel anything but pride and a warm glow of happiness that sustained her until they went in to dinner.

Always up to now they had eaten with the family in the small dining room but on this night with a large party and in honour of their distinguished guest, dinner was served in the large state room, only used on special occasions, which neither she nor Lucy had entered before.

It was a sombre room even when lit by the blaze of candles in the wall sconces and the silver candelabra placed along the table. Dark family portraits adorned the walls. One in particular hanging at the far end above the carved chair met her eyes with a shock of surprise. It was undoubtedly the same face as in the portrait locked so long in her father's desk. An icy chill ran through her. Lorenzo felt her hand tighten on his arm and looked down at her, smiling.

"What is it?"

"That picture – who is it?"

"That's my father, Don Luis, painted just a few years before he died. Haven't you seen it before?"

"No. I've never been in this room."

"Some say I'm like him. I can't see it myself."

"Oh but you are – at times," she said, somehow keeping her voice steady. "That is what startled me."

All during the meal while the conversation eddied around her, for this short time at least determinedly keeping away from the subject uppermost in everyone's mind, she was telling herself that it could not be so, it could not have been *her* father who had brutally murdered Don Luis de Merenda – it just wasn't possible because if he had done so, then surely he would never have kept so carefully the portrait and the bloodstained handkerchief.

Enrique, sitting beside her, was giving her and Teresa a humorous account of the difficulties the army encountered on their journey south through hail and tempest. She answered mechanically. Every now and again as the servants refilled the wine glasses and brought fresh plates for the next course, she was disconcertingly aware of the General's keen black eyes fixed on her with a curious speculative gaze.

Lorenzo, a little preoccupied with his important guest, turned to her once with a worried frown.

"You're not eating. There's nothing wrong is there?"

"No." She forced a smile. "It's just – oh I don't know – just everything."

"I shouldn't have sprung it on you, but I acted on the spur of the moment. It was thoughtless of me. You're not angry, are you?"

"No. How could I be?"

His hand closed over hers for a moment before he turned back to the General and she tried to take comfort from it.

The iced pudding had been served and the meal came to an end at last. At a sign from Doña Gracia the ladies rose to their feet and withdrew, leaving the men to their wine and more serious discussion.

A map was spread on the table and they pulled up their chairs around it as General Ramirez once again began to out-line his strategy. One part of his force would circle the city entering from the south to bolster up the weak defences, while the greater part of his army would attack from the rear.

"In this way," he went on, "we will hopefully have Roméro caught in a pincer grip and with God's help settle that band of murderers and brigands once and for all."

"Have you sufficient information as to their exact situation?"

"We have our spies, thanks to you. The woman Gabriella has proved invaluable to us. She dances like an angel and better still listens at keyholes." He grinned and slapped his hand down on the table. "The courage of a tigress and the guile of the serpent, eh Lorenzo? She is known to you, I believe."

"Since childhood," he replied coolly. "Her grandfather is one of my men and still lives up in the high Sierra."

"So . . . it gives her an excellent excuse to come and go here at the Castillo."

The General had heard the rumours of a closer relationship but said nothing. It was a long time ago. Young men had to sow their wild oats and Lorenzo was not one to run away from his responsibilities. There was something else weighing on his mind but it was a delicate matter that must be approached with caution. He would have preferred to say nothing about it at all, but Lorenzo was the son of his old friend and he had always taken a fatherly interest in the boy. They went on talking while the decanter passed from one to the other. The General drained his glass, set it down carefully and turned to his host.

"Do you ride with us, Lorenzo?"

"I made up my mind a long time ago that I would not take part in any war that set Spaniard against Spaniard. Oh, make no mistake. I am for the Cortéz and the little Queen. I see no future with Carlos in power. He would lead us back into tyranny and the Inquisition but what our country needs is stability if we are ever to move forward and if I can hold this part of Andalusia in peace and as a refuge for those persecuted unjustly, I think this of more value than charging the enemy sword in hand. Can you understand that?"

"Oh yes, I understand it very well. And as a newly engaged man –"

Lorenzo flushed. "Are you calling me a coward?"

"Now don't take offence. I know you too well for that. Besides, from what I hear you have already suffered considerable damage here and fought it as best you can. In some ways," went on the General musingly, "I am inclined to agree with you. We are a hot-headed lot, too touchy, too ready to murder one another on a point of honour, too apt to take life lightly and regard death as necessary. Maybe it requires greater courage to stand out against it." He hauled himself to his feet. "In any case there seems little more we can do tonight." He rolled up the map and handed it to Enrique. "The next few days will put us all to the test so shall we join the ladies for an hour? Perhaps they will be kind enough to give us a little music."

In the general movement Guy found himself close to Lorenzo. He said awkwardly, "I have not yet congratulated you on your engagement."

Impulsively Lorenzo put a hand on his shoulder. "I'm sorry. I know you had hoped to marry her."

"And she refused me. Now I know why. I might have guessed. I suppose I should say the best man wins."

"That's not true, for God's sake. The more fortunate man I should say. I hope it doesn't mean you are going to desert me."

Guy smiled wryly. "That would be a very poor spirited thing to do now of all times when even the vineyards are under threat. I must learn to live with it."

"You're a good fellow, Guy."

"It's Charlotte who concerns me. I would not do anything to spoil her happiness."

"There at least we are agreed."

For an instant their eyes met, then Guy turned and went out. Lorenzo would have followed him but was detained by the General.

"I'd be glad to have a private word with you," he said quietly and then, when Lorenzo came back looking at him questioningly, he found himself at a loss for words.

"To tell the truth, my dear boy, the news of your engagement came as a great surprise. I did not think you would have chosen an English bride."

"You mean because of what happened to my father. I too thought that once, General, but the heart does not always obey the head. I am very much in love with Charlotte."

"Despite everything?"

Lorenzo frowned. "I don't understand. What is this? What are you hinting at? Is it something I should know?"

"I hoped you were aware of it already. I forget how young you were at the time and how few of us knew the truth." The General drew a deep breath and took the plunge. "The plain fact is that Captain Harry Starr was the British officer who killed your father."

Lorenzo stared at him. "I don't believe it," he said slowly. "I won't believe it. You must be mistaken."

"I'm afraid there is no doubt of it. It was an ugly business and it was hushed up. Wellington at that time had no wish to antagonise his Spanish allies or cause any scandal and we for our part wanted no trouble when victory was at last within our grasp after years of bloody fighting. She has never spoken to you of this?"

"No." Lorenzo's eyes had gone to the portrait of his father that now some of the candles had been extinguished seemed to brood over the room. "Why should she?" he went on with an effort. "She probably knows nothing of it."

"I doubt that. I doubt it very much."

Lorenzo turned on him fiercely. "Why should you say that?

271

She is honest and loyal. She would never lend herself to deceit."

"She might if she thought she could lose you. Most young women would give a very great deal to be the future Marquésa de Merenda."

"That's a detestable thing to say. Charlotte is not like other young women."

"I wonder how many men in love have said that and been proved sadly wrong."

Lorenzo made an angry gesture. "That's a glib statement that means nothing. Oh my God, why did you have to tell me tonight of all nights?"

"Isn't it better than finding it out afterwards?"

"I don't know. Mother of God, I don't know!"

In the momentary silence Roberto put his head around the door. "Are you coming? They are all waiting for you, General."

"Yes, we're coming. We will be with you immediately."

Roberto disappeared and Ramirez put his hand on Lorenzo's shoulder.

"Come, my boy, it's not the end of everything. There are plenty of other young women in the world."

Lorenzo shook himself free. "None like her."

Charlotte was seated at the piano when Lorenzo came into the drawing room with the General. He did not look towards her but crossed at once to where Teresa was seated on a footstool beside Doña Gracia and again she felt that icy stab of apprehension. The servants had brought coffee and while it was served and carried around, Teresa came to join her.

"Lorenzo says the General would like to hear me sing. I can't think why. Last time he heard me was at one of Aunt Marta's parties in Toledo and he talked all the way through my very best ballad."

"I was there too, don't you remember?" said Enrique coming up beside Teresa. "And you sang like a nightingale."

"You once told me I had a voice like a corncrake," she objected.

The young man grinned. "That was when you were ten and I was fourteen. Go on, Teresa. It is a soldier's privilege to be entertained by his lady on the eve of battle."

"Am I your lady?"

"I would very much like to think so."

272

"Oh, don't be silly," but Teresa blushed and began to turn over the sheets of music. "I'll sing if Charlotte will play for me."

"I'll do my best."

It was a pretty lilting love song and there seemed nothing more charming and peaceful than the candle-lit room, the flash of jewelled fans as the ladies listened, glancing now and then at the men sitting at their ease in their brilliant uniforms. It was impossible to believe that in a few days many of them could be lying dead or grievously wounded.

Charlotte looked up from the music for an instant to see Lorenzo's eyes fixed on her. His face which she had seen in so many different moods was bleak and stern. She stumbled over a bar, noticed the surprise on Enrique's face and recovered herself quickly.

The evening wore on. There were other songs. Captain Alvaro surprised everyone by revealing a remarkably sweet tenor and Roberto rattled off a cheerful song that earned a frown from his grandmother and an approving nod from General Ramirez who led the chorus in a rich bass.

During the applause Lucy took the opportunity to excuse herself pleading fatigue after her recent illness and Charlotte rose at once to go with her.

Lorenzo opened the door for her. "May I come to you later?" he whispered under his breath.

"If you wish."

"Goodnight," he said aloud for everyone's benefit and kissed her hand before letting her go.

Back in their own room Juanita had left candles burning on the table and Lucy dropped the lace shawl from her shoulders.

"Well, Lorenzo certainly surprised everyone this evening. Did you know he was going to announce your engagement?"

"No."

"It must have made you very happy."

"Yes."

"Then why are you looking so worried?"

"Am I?" said Charlotte. "It's just that it was so unexpected and I don't think Doña Gracia approved. It's not the way she would like things to be done."

"It's Lorenzo who matters not his grandmother," retorted Lucy. "And you're very sure of him, aren't you? It's quite a feather in your cap capturing the Marqués de Merenda, isn't it?

Did you see how all the other women stared? I wager you never thought of such a thing happening when Clive asked you to accompany us to Spain. You're fortunate. I envy you." Then abruptly she stopped. "Oh dear, I'm being beastly again, aren't I? I'm sorry, Charlie, I don't mean to be. It's just that I thought we would be going back to England together and now I must face up to Clive alone, somehow pick up our life together, never see Roberto again . . . and I don't know how I'm going to bear it." Her voice cracked and she turned hurriedly away.

"Oh my dear . . ." Charlotte made a move towards her and Lucy waved her back.

"No, don't sympathize with me too much. I'm all right. I'm learning that feeling sorry for yourself won't solve anything." Resolutely she bit back the tears. "I'm tired. I think I'll go to bed. Are you coming?"

"Later. I'm too restless to sleep yet. You go up first."

"Very well. Goodnight." Impulsively she kissed Charlotte's cheek. "Don't stay up too late."

Left alone, Charlotte stood for a moment uncertain what to do. She guessed it would not be long before Lorenzo came. General Ramirez would be leaving early on the following morning to join the rest of the army and so would probably retire early. Something in the General's manner, in the way he had looked at her, had alarmed her. What had he said to Lorenzo to cause the change in him? And yet what could he say – what was she guilty of? She came to a sudden decision. She would show him the portrait and the handkerchief, explain how she had found them, how unimportant she had believed them to be. He would understand, he must understand. Whatever it was that had happened between her father and Don Luis, it had nothing to do with them and their love. Surely he must realize that.

She went up the stairs quietly so as not to disturb Lucy and fetched the bundle she had wrapped in a silk scarf. She laid it on the table and unfolded it. The light of the candles seemed to give the eyes unexpected life. Why, oh why had she not spoken of it before? Now there was nothing to be done but face up to it. With dread in her heart she sat down and waited for him.

It was not long, less than an hour, but it seemed an age before she heard the knock on the door and he came into the room. Some trick of the light revealed the high cheek bones, the

274

strong line of the jaw, emphasizing a resemblance to the portrait not usually obvious. She gripped her hands tightly together to stop their trembling and tried to speak lightly.

"I did not expect you yet. Has the General gone to bed already?"

"Yes. Are you alone? Can we talk here?"

"Yes. Lucy won't come down."

He shut the door and came further into the room. She looked up at him.

"What is it, Lorenzo? What has happened?"

"Do you need to ask me that?" He was standing quite still, his eyes on the portrait. "Where did this come from?"

"I found it with the handkerchief in my father's desk after he died."

"So . . ." He drew a deep breath. "So you *have* known all these months."

"What have I known?"

"Don't pretend ignorance any longer, for God's sake. The General told me this evening. The fact that twenty years ago in Madrid Captain Harry Starr murdered my father."

"But I didn't know, Lorenzo, I didn't know. My father loved Spain and he taught me to love it but he told me nothing of any of this, not one single word. I found these locked away in a secret drawer after his death. And if it *is* true," she went on, frightened by the stony look on his face, "if he did kill your father why should he keep his portrait, the handkerchief stained with his blood, why? Why? It doesn't make sense."

Lorenzo picked up the portrait. His fingers fumbled a little on the stiff catches, then the back slid away from the frame and he put it on the table in front of her. On the reverse side of the ivory was the picture of a woman, dark-haired, dark-eyed, with a strange haunting beauty.

"That's the reason why," he said savagely, "that's why he kept it – to remind him of his conquest. It must have pleased him to gloat over his triumph, trampling my mother's honour in the mud and filth of a soldier's lust!"

"Your mother?" she repeated faintly.

"My mother – your father's mistress – while the British army fought its way to Madrid and there, when it was discovered, he struck down the man whose honourable name he had tarnished for ever." The memory of that time, the agony of a boy

275

who had worshipped his mother and saw her shamed, weeping not for a dead husband but for a lost lover, flooded through him. "And you, his daughter, tell me you knew nothing of all this."

"No." She was deeply distressed by the brutal story but still unable to believe that it could be possible. There had to be some other explanation, there had to be. "No, he never spoke of it, never, never!"

"Your father who loved you so much, who shared everything with you?" He stared at her for a long moment and then turned away. "I don't believe you."

"Lorenzo, you must believe me, you must." She was on her feet now pleading with him. "It is the truth."

He was silent for an instant before he said slowly, "Why did you bring them with you to Spain?"

"I don't know. It just happened like that. There was no reason, no purpose in it. When Clive asked me to accompany him and Lucy, it seemed somehow as if – as if it had been meant."

"And you never thought, not even once, of showing them to me?"

"Yes, I did," she faltered, "but somehow the time never seemed right."

How to tell him that she had been afraid, as if she had sensed somehow that it might affect the growing friendship between them that had become so important to her?

"Perhaps you preferred to wait until we were married, until you had me chained? Did you think it might be a triumph to capture the son as your father had charmed the mother?" he said with icy bitterness. "Did you have it all planned? Even that night together in the cave when you knew you had won such an easy victory – you could not even tell me then."

"Lorenzo, it was not like that, truly it wasn't. I never even thought of it. I loved you too much – I love you now . . ."

"Don't go on lying, it sickens me. Haven't you humbled me enough already? The General was right. Guy wasn't good enough for you, was he? It had to be me and I believed in you, I believed in you utterly. My God, what a fool I've been, what a blind fool!"

"How can you be so cruel?" she said in a choked voice. "If you feel like that, you had better take this back," and she

276

tugged at the gold ring on her finger but in her agitation it refused to budge.

"No," he said, "no, leave it, leave it. I've not forgotten I owe you my life . . . and more . . ."

He made a move towards the door and she went after him catching him by the arm alarmed by his manner.

"Lorenzo, don't leave me like this, please, please. What are you going to do?"

He jerked himself away. "I don't know – God help me, I don't know."

He opened the door and was gone, leaving her standing there, looking after him, black despair in her heart.

It was some little time before she could pull herself together sufficiently to wrap the portrait and handkerchief again in the scarf, to take up one of the candles, blow out the others and go slowly up the stairs.

As she passed Lucy's half-open door, a sleepy voice called to her.

"Was that Lorenzo I heard?"

"Yes. He came to say goodnight."

"Lucky old you."

Lucky! Oh God, the irony of it! She didn't know whether to laugh or cry. It would have been a help to find relief in tears but she had never wept easily not even as a child. Her thoughts scattered all over the place as she slowly undressed, splashed cold water on her face, put on her nightgown and got into the bed only to lie sleepless hour after hour.

Could it be *her* father, her gentle loving father who had behaved so brutally? She could not believe it and yet the stark facts stared her in the face. Of one thing only she felt sure. It had been love and not guilt that had caused him to keep the picture so carefully. Maybe it was that painful memory which had formed a barrier in the end between him and her mother.

What would Lorenzo do? Over and over again she heard Gabriella's taunting words – "He will never forgive the British for murdering his father . . . a Spaniard does not forget such things so easily." Was it true? Or was the love that had sprung between them strong enough to overcome the bitter prejudice that had grown within him from boyhood? For the first time she felt at a loss, aware of the differences in race, in temperament. "To a Spaniard his honour means a great deal," he had said once, "for that he would give up everything, even his life." Would he also sacrifice the woman he loved?

The unanswered question would not let her sleep. She lay watching the square of the window until it began to pale with the coming of the dawn. She heard the first drowsy song of the birds in the Nun's garden and felt she could stand it no longer. She got up and, while she dressed, the shrilling of the trumpet reminded her that the General's escort must be preparing to leave. She threw a thick shawl around her shoulders and ran downstairs to find Lucy already there.

"Juanita asked for permission to watch the soldiers ride out so I thought I would go myself," she said briefly. "Are you coming with me?"

If she wanted to see the last of Roberto, then why shouldn't she? thought Charlotte, and she herself would have to face Lorenzo again so why not now?

"Yes, I'll come," she said.

Together they hurried through the corridors of the great house and came out into the courtyard. The General's troop was drawn up waiting for Roberto, horses groomed to perfection, accoutrements glittering. He himself was on the steps bidding farewell to Doña Gracia. His personal staff was already mounted and the other horses were being brought up. Teresa ran to Enrique and reached up to take his hand. Roberto came swiftly towards them and drew Lucy away. Charlotte saw him take her in his arms and turned her back. Let them make their farewells in private.

General Ramirez was already in the saddle with Enrique and Captain Alvaro when Lorenzo came out of the house. He embraced his grandmother, said a word to Guy who had followed him and then took the bridle of his black stallion from Jacopo and swung himself into the saddle, taking his place beside the General. His eyes swept across them.

"Roberto," he said crisply, "we are waiting."

The young man pulled away from Lucy, took his horse from the waiting groom and trotted after them.

Lorenzo must have seen her even though she had drawn back a little, but he had gone without a look or a word and she felt her heart contract. There was an early morning bite in the air but she still stood looking after them as the troop went clattering

278

down the drive. Doña Gracia went into the house with Teresa and Guy crossed to her.

"They make a fine show, don't they?" he said cheerfully. "Almost tempt me into wishing I was going with them. Let us hope that all goes well."

"Why has Lorenzo gone with them? I know he never intended it, Guy, he told me."

"He changed his mind."

"When?"

"It was late last night. He came to my room, said he had decided to go with the General as he knew the countryside so intimately and asked me to stay here and take charge of the Castillo for the time being since the vineyards would be safe enough with Don Evaristo."

So it was after they had spoken together. He must have made up his mind then. It was she who had driven him away. There was no need for him to act as guide. Enrique and Roberto were as familiar with the land as he was. Because of her, because he never wanted to see her again, he had gone with them. In that reckless mood he would be capable of any folly.

Guy said, "Are you sure you're all right? You are shivering."

"It's just this chilly wind."

"You had better come in. You'll take cold."

Lucy had disappeared so she followed him into the house. There they found Amalia trying to control a wildly excited Paquita who had been allowed to watch from the window.

She hurled herself at Charlotte. "Did you see my Papa? He was with the General. Isn't it wonderful? How I wish I could ride with them!"

"Don't be foolish, child," exclaimed a scandalized Amalia. "Little girls riding off to war! Whoever heard of such a thing! Now go upstairs this minute and make yourself tidy for breakfast."

Paquita grimaced, then with a rebellious flick of her long black hair stalked up the stairs as slowly as she dared.

"Such a one!" sighed Amalia. "Sometimes there's no dealing with her!" She turned to Charlotte. "The Marquésa would like to speak with you, Señorita. Sometime during the morning when you are ready."

"Thank you, Amalia." She felt her heart beat a little faster. Had Lorenzo confided in his grandmother or had it been the General in his capacity as old family friend?

279

Guy stopped her as she moved away. "I've had no opportunity," he said awkwardly, "of wishing you every happiness on your engagement. When I came to you, I never dreamed . . . perhaps I should have guessed."

"How could you? I didn't know myself then."

"It's been Lorenzo all the time, hasn't it?"

"Yes," she said in a low voice, "yes, it has. I'm sorry, Guy."

"I'd like you to know one thing. If anything happens – anything at all – I'll still be there and feeling just the same."

In her desolation the kindness in his voice was almost too much.

"Dear Guy." Impulsively she leaned forward and kissed his cheek then hurried quickly away before she blurted out her misery.

Thank goodness Lucy had been too occupied with Roberto to notice anything amiss so she need make no explanation, nor was there any reason to comment when they both ate little or no breakfast.

Later in the morning with a 'now or never' feeling she braced herself to go to Doña Gracia. At the last moment she took with her the silk scarf with its contents which had assumed such a frightening significance.

When she knocked and opened the door the Marquésa was standing at the window. She turned as Charlotte went in, a formidable figure in her dress of corded silk, the delicate black lace falling over the white hair and framing the fine ivory tinted features.

"Amalia told me you wanted to see me. Is this a convenient time?"

"Certainly. Please sit down. We will speak in Spanish if you don't mind, Carlotta. I am not entirely at ease in English but you, I know, are proficient in our language."

"As you wish."

She felt the constraint between them and waited uneasily for Doña Gracia to settle herself in her high-backed chair before she sat down.

For a moment the Marquésa let her eyes run over the girl in front of her, the lustrous red hair smoothly braided, eyes not modestly lowered but looking fearlessly into hers, the tension in the hands tightly clasped in her lap. Enemy or friend? She was a proud woman but she was also a just one and almost against her will she was aware of liking. This *Inglesa* had courage.

She would fight for her love – perhaps that was what Lorenzo needed.

"My grandson told me some time ago of his intention of making you his wife," she began, "but I must admit that I found the announcement of his engagement last night rather disturbing. That is not the way people of our rank behave." She permitted herself a faint smile. "However I fear that at times he can still act like an impetuous boy."

"Does that mean that you disapprove?" Charlotte was feeling her way.

"Not entirely. I admit that I was not pleased when he first informed me, not that I have anything against you personally, but for reasons that you must be fully aware of yourself."

"Lorenzo and I are deeply in love," she said defensively.

"So he told me and I forced myself to accept and be happy for him until . . ."

"Until this morning when he did what he swore he would never do. He rode out to fight with the army. Did he tell you why?"

"Lorenzo told me nothing. It was General Ramirez who came to me last night. He felt as an old friend that it was his duty to tell me that your father, Captain Harry Starr, had been responsible for the death of my son Luis, Lorenzo's father, in particularly dreadful circumstances."

Charlotte said bravely, "Did it come as a terrible shock?"

"Yes and no." She stirred a little in her chair before she went on. "You must understand that my daughter-in-law Maria had told me the whole story before she died. The only thing she withheld was the name of her lover. The General told me that for reasons of policy that name was known to very few and deliberately kept from us who were most concerned."

"When she told you that, did she also tell you how it happened, Doña Gracia? Lorenzo came to me last night. He told me a hideous story of rape and murder which even now I cannot, I will not believe." She unfolded the scarf and put the portrait still as Lorenzo had opened it on the lap of the Marquésa and with it the stained handkerchief. "I found these in a secret drawer in my father's desk, hidden away like sacred relics. He told no one of them, not me, not my mother. Surely no brutal murderer glorifying in his conquest would have done such a thing."

281

Doña Gracia took the handkerchief in her hands. "I remember embroidering this for him many years ago and now to see it stained with his blood . . ." for a moment her voice shook, then she steadied herself and put it with the portrait on the small table beside her, her mind made up. She could have withheld her knowledge but why cause more pain? Enough had been suffered already in the past.

"No," she said, "you are right. It was not like that."

"Then how was it? Please – please tell me if you can."

"It happened when that terrible struggle with Napoleon and the French was at last nearing its end. Your British Commander, the Duke of Wellington, was besieging Ciudad Rodrigo. They tell me it had been a long and arduous siege. Maria, against everyone's advice, had gone to the city some months before. Luis was with the guerillas and over the years they had had very little time together. There was an opportunity for a few snatched days. Lorenzo was barely fourteen and at school in Madrid, Roberto, still very young, was here with me. She was trapped in the city by the French before she could escape."

The calm unemotional voice went on telling the bare facts but Charlotte, listening, saw it all in vivid colours illuminated by her father's stories – the gallantry, heroism and ragged cheerfulness of the Rifle Brigade – that terrible winter when they tramped through snow, through sleet and driving rain, frozen, starved, stricken with fever and dysentery, but still driving on, and then the horror of the night they broke through the defences and smashed their way into the city, their faces scorched and blackened with powder and blood.

It was then that discipline suddenly snapped, heroes turned momentarily into demons or lunatics. They had seen their comrades blown to pieces in front of their eyes and in the blazing streets of the unfamiliar town they went crazy murdering every enemy they saw, breaking into houses and shops in search of drink. Captain Harry Starr, young and desperate, tried hard to hold back his troop, but drunk with wine and victory they raged on, hunting for plunder and women. In her mind's eye she saw him race up the stairs of the old house, hurl back the men who were battering down the door and then pause, staring at the beautiful woman, her back against the wall, terrified but defying them still with dignity and pride of race.

"He protected her against the savagery of the men," went

on Doña Gracia, "but at that time it was impossible to find an escort to take her out of the city. To venture alone would have been suicidal and so he did the only thing possible, he kept her beside him as many men did and when they moved on he took her with him. They stormed on to victory and in those wild war-torn weeks of the closest companionship, starving, taking shelter together, watching men die around them, the inevitable happened. They fell in love."

Charlotte, listening, her hands pressed against her cheeks, lived with them that moment of painful rapture almost as if it had happened to her.

"You must not think badly of her," Doña Gracia was saying. "She had been married to Luis at fifteen. Theirs had been a marriage of companionship and the bearing of children. Perhaps for the first time in her life she experienced passion and it overwhelmed her. She would never listen to a word against him. 'He was so much younger than I, chivalrous and loving,' she said and wept. 'When we reached Madrid and knew it must end, he was broken-hearted.' It must have been then she gave him the portrait. It was all she had."

"I know how she must have felt," whispered Charlotte.

"Luis, with the guerillas, had battled through and it was there he found her taking refuge in the family home. She told him nothing and how he discovered the truth I don't know, but men talk indiscreetly and the result was tragic. He was a man of high temper and he wanted only to find and kill the soldier who had shamed his wife. How it happened who can now tell? Somewhere in that city they met and he was struck down, maybe in self-defence, and the first she knew of it was when his dead body was brought to her and her young son."

"And that was the end of it," she said slowly.

"Not quite. Not long after, Maria discovered she was pregnant and Teresa was born some months later."

"You mean – Teresa could be my father's child?"

"It was possible, never more than that. Maria was never certain and it distressed her greatly. She never recovered from the birth. Lorenzo, I know, has always had it in his mind and it has made him harsh with Teresa. It is only this year that he has softened towards her and I believe that is due to you, Carlotta, you made him realize that too much strictness only breeds rebellion."

283

"Do you think that she is . . .?"

"Your father's daughter? No. It is Lorenzo who has let himself believe because sometimes she has behaved foolishly, but the Merendas have a wild streak too, she is not the only one. Again and again I have tried to persuade him but he is stubborn." Doña Gracia smiled bleakly. "Teresa knows nothing of this and I would not have her told. Why sow doubt when nothing can be proved."

"Thank you for telling me. I understand my father better now. I think he locked it away in his heart but it haunted him for the rest of his life. He was never completely happy." She got up and walked away towards the window. It was a grey day without the golden light she had grown to love. She said painfully, "The worst of it is that Lorenzo believes I have deceived him deliberately, that I knew all this and yet told him nothing. Believe me, it is not true." She turned to look pleadingly at the Marquésa. "You have shown great understanding and I'm deeply grateful to you. You have known him longer than I have, what will he do? Does he know the true story as you have told it to me?"

"Yes, he knows, but you must remember all this happened to him at a very impressionable age. A boy has high ideals, he loved his mother and admired his father's gallant courage. The knowledge of Maria's infidelity scarred him when he was most sensitive. To discover that you whom he loves are the daughter of the monster his imagination has created has been a shock."

Charlotte came slowly back into the room. "Lucy will be leaving soon when the roads are open again. Do you want me to go with her?"

The Marquésa did not answer for a moment, then she said, "Once I would have been glad to see you leave and you must act as you think fit, of course, but I believe it only just to tell you something Lorenzo said to me when we talked of his love for you. 'I have waited a long time to find what I want and now that I have do not spoil it for me.' It may help you to remember that."

Impulsively Charlotte came and knelt down beside her. "That is kind of you. I know I am not what you want for Lorenzo but I love him, I truly do love him."

"You may have to prove it, my dear." The thin hand touched

284

her cheek gently. "Forgive me for asking, but is it possible that you are bearing his child?"

The colour ran up into Charlotte's face. "No," she whispered. "What made you ask that?"

"Something about the way he spoke of the night you were forced to spend together on the mountain. I know my grandson very well. He will never evade his responsibilities or behave anything but honourably."

"He owes me nothing. I would not hold him to any promise he may have made," said Charlotte fiercely. "I only want his love."

"Then we must wait. In these wretched times there is so little we women *can* do, only wait and perhaps pray."

17

The waiting was the worst, thought Charlotte, and prayer, however fervent, did not help in the very least. Doña Gracia's attitude had surprised her. She had expected anger, even open hostility, had braced herself to meet it and was disarmed by the older woman's understanding and tolerance. She found herself looking at Teresa with new eyes. Was she her father's daughter, her half-sister? Was that why she had felt such an instinctive liking and sympathy for her? There was no answer to that question but whether it was so or not, it did explain Lorenzo's strictness. He had feared in her the same wild spirit that had brought his mother and Harry Starr together.

The days dragged and only vague and contradictory rumours reached them. General Ramirez had not swept to a glorious victory scattering the enemy before him as Teresa had confidently expected. On the contrary, they heard with alarm that Roméro had already invested part of the city and was busily entrenching himself so that when the battle did come it would be a hard fought one.

Some of the peasants who had taken refuge at the Castillo had started to creep back to their ruined village showing a resilience that Charlotte could only admire. Guy had the place well organized with men always on the watch. There were roving bands of bandit soldiers in the hills and he told Charlotte not to walk or ride beyond the park boundaries.

She tried to fill the slow hours by giving Paquita English lessons again, but the child was infected with the general feeling of tension and found it hard to concentrate.

"Amalia says you are going to marry my Papa," she said accusingly, looking up from the book they had been reading together one morning.

Charlotte was startled. "She should not have said that. Nothing is settled yet. Go on, Paquita, you're doing very well."

286

But the girl pushed the book away. "She says that when you are mistress here, you will send me away to the Convent."

"Now why should she say that?"

"Because when you have babies, my Papa won't care about me any longer."

There was a slight tremble in the voice and the dark blue eyes so like Lorenzo's were fixed on her face.

Charlotte frowned. "Who has been saying all these things to you?"

"No one in particular but they're true, aren't they?"

"No, Paquita. It is all nonsense. When your father comes back, there will be plenty of time to think about things like that."

"He will come back, won't he?"

"Of course he will." For a moment fear stabbed at her but she thrust it away. "Now let's go on with our reading."

But servants' idle gossip had effectively poisoned the easy relationship between them. Paquita, always uncertain of herself, was plainly jealous and there was little she could do about it. She had told Lucy nothing of what had passed between her and Lorenzo, knowing instinctively that it must continue to be hidden in the past, but it caused a constraint between them.

One morning later in that week she had Zelda saddled and rode a little way beyond the gates, gazing down the road that led to Seville. It was empty, no carts or donkeys going to market, only a queer brooding silence. She had a great longing to go galloping down there, find out for herself what was happening, implore Lorenzo to be careful and not risk the life that, even if he hated her, was still infinitely precious. But it was ridiculous even to think of such foolishness and after a while she reluctantly turned back, taking a roundabout route to the house.

The day was cold for Spain with a sharp bite in the wind that Guy said could mean snow in the mountains. As she trotted through the avenue of ilex down which she and Teresa had cantered all those months ago, she saw a man come riding slowly down the hill path and she paused in the shadow of the trees to watch. Any stranger was suspect these days. He was riding an indifferent hack and wore a long riding coat of very unfashionable cut, a wide-brimmed hat and green-tinted glasses as if he suffered from weak eyes. A curious figure, not a beggar, nor a soldier, nor a peasant – a tradesman, perhaps, except that he rode his plodding nag with a grace and ease that only comes from years of horsemanship. He was looking about him as if uncertain and, suddenly making up her mind, she urged Zelda forward and caught up with him.

"Can I help you, Señor?" she said in Spanish. "You would appear to have lost your way. Are you looking for the Castillo de Palomas?"

He reined in, stood still for a moment, and then turned to her. "Don't you know me, Charlie?"

It was then, in spite of the unkempt hair that straggled to his shoulders, the sallow look of recent illness that aged him by ten years, the disfiguring glasses, that she was suddenly certain.

"Clive!" she exclaimed. "Oh my God, it can't be!"

"Afraid it is, old girl."

"Oh Clive!" She was torn between pleasure at seeing him, alive and well, and exasperation at the recklessness that had brought him back to Spain at such a time. "Why? Why come back here? It's crazy. If you are recognized . . ."

"I won't be," he interrupted confidently. "I'm no longer Clive Starr, the Englishman, but Mohammed Abib, French-speaking emissary of Raoul Ismanli, wealthy carpet merchant of Tangier, with impressively signed passport and all the necessary documents."

"It sounds absurd," she said impatiently, "like something out of an Eastern fairytale. Who on earth is going to believe all that?"

"Everyone has so far without question. They are far too busy hunting down Carlists or Cristinos to worry about a poor commercial traveller trying to sell rugs and carpets."

"How did you know we were here?"

"I've seen Geoffrey Robinson. He is like a terrified rabbit bolting back into his hole at the slightest alarm," he said contemptuously. "You did have the letter, didn't you?"

"Yes, we did, but we thought you would be certain to return to England. Lucy has been waiting to hear from you before she left Spain."

"That was what I intended to do as soon as I could stand on my feet. Then I changed my mind." His voice hardened, losing the bantering note. "I had scuttled out of Spain and I was damned if I was going to play the coward any longer. I

288

decided to come and fetch Lucy myself *and* settle my account with Don Lorenzo."

"What do you mean – settle your account?"

"I'd like to know for certain how much that attack on Felipe's boat was planned and how much pure accident. After all he never liked me, did he?"

"Clive, how can you say such a thing?" she burst out indignantly. "Lorenzo did it for the best and was as much distressed as we were when we believed you had been drowned."

"I doubt that," he said cynically.

"It is true and he has protected Lucy and me all these months when we were practically hounded out of Seville."

"Very generous of him."

"You don't know how generous. You shouldn't have come here, Clive. You don't realize how bitter the feeling is against anyone who has had any dealings with the Carlists. At present Lorenzo and Roberto are with General Ramirez but if you were recognized and accused . . ."

"It might go badly with him and that would distress you."

"Yes, it would – very much. It would be a poor return for all he has done for us."

"You always were a trifle smitten with him, weren't you, Charlie? Well, don't worry. No one will recognize me, not in this rig," and he spread his arms, grinning at her as if he hadn't a care in the world. "A sorry guise, isn't it? Not exactly the nonpareil of fashion."

"Oh Clive, for heaven's sake, stop playing the fool. This is serious."

"And I am serious, Charlie, very serious. I want to see Lucy. Is that impossible?"

"I suppose not," she said doubtfully, "but we'll have to be careful and I shall have to warn Guy. He is in charge while Lorenzo is away."

"Oh Macalister will be all right. He is British after all."

"Only partly, his loyalty is to Spain. We'll have to concoct some story for the servants."

"A messenger from Doña Lucia's long lost husband come to conduct her to Cadiz and into his loving arms – how about that?"

"Such a one would scarcely be received in our private apartments," she objected.

"Or welcomed into the bed of Doña Lucia, eh?" He laughed. "I'll keep out of the way, never fear. Oh come on, Charlie, anyone would think you were not glad to see me."

"Of course I am in a way, but I still wish you hadn't come here."

They dismounted before they reached the courtyard in front of the house and Charlotte grasped the bridles of the horses.

"I'll take them. The stables were burnt down. They are being housed temporarily in the barns. Wait for me here."

Jacopo had gone with Lorenzo and the boy who took the horses from her stared in surprise at Clive's hired hack.

"It belongs to a visitor," said Charlotte briefly. "Unsaddle them both. He will be staying the night."

The boy nodded, accepting it without question. There had been a number of unusual comings and goings during the past few days.

Charlotte hurried back to join Clive, leading him round the back of the house through the Nun's garden and into their own private wing.

Lucy was in the sitting room. She looked up as Charlotte opened the door.

"I've brought someone to see you," she began warningly, but before she could say anything further Clive had pushed past her, sweeping off his hat and spectacles, and flinging his arms wide in a dramatic gesture.

"Here I am," he said, "your loving husband, large as life and twice as natural."

Lucy had risen to her feet, her embroidery falling to the floor in a scatter of bright silks.

"Clive!" she said in a strangled voice. "Oh no, it can't be – it's not possible."

"It is, you know. 'Born to be hanged, Master Clive,' as my old tutor told me when I fell out of the apple tree on my head." He was trying hard to bridge the gulf between them with a forced gaiety. "Come on, Lucy old girl, aren't you pleased to see me?"

"Yes, yes, of course I am, very pleased. It's just – it's such a surprise – we thought – why have you come here?"

"To see you, believe it or not, couldn't wait another minute – but for all the welcome I'm receiving I needn't have bothered. First Charlie giving me a frozen look and now you . . ."

"I'm sorry," Lucy had recovered from the first shock. "It's only that it's so very unexpected." She held out her hand and Clive took it, pulling her to him and kissing her roughly.

Charlotte moved to the door. "I'll leave you together," she said quickly. "I want to change anyway."

"Don't go, Charlie." Lucy had partly pulled herself away. "There is so much to be talked over and you're in it just as much as we are."

"I really think . . ."

She paused in the doorway and Lucy went on hurriedly.

"There's such a lot you don't know, Clive. To start with, Charlie is engaged to Lorenzo."

"Is that so?" Clive raised his eyebrows. "Fast work, little cousin."

"Lucy shouldn't have said that. Nothing is settled yet."

"But the great man *has* proposed, I take it. Good for you. I thought you were very hot in his defence a few minutes ago. And what about the dashing Don Roberto? Has he been pursuing the pretty widow whose husband was so conveniently lying dead at the bottom of the ocean?"

"That's a hateful thing to say," said Lucy.

"Oh Lord, can't I even make a joke?"

"And what if he has," she went on, flaring up at the implied sneer. "Would there be anything wrong in that?"

"So that's the way the wind is blowing, is it?" Clive walked away to the window. "It seems to me a great pity I didn't drown in that abominable sea then everyone would have been happy."

"Oh Clive, for goodness sake! This is no time to indulge in self-pity," said Charlotte brusquely. "The important thing is to decide what is to be done with you now you are here."

"Like a damned awkward parcel, is that it? I wish you'd stop worrying about me. I can look after myself."

"That is just what you can't be trusted to do," said Charlotte with a spurt of temper.

"Wait a moment." Clive came back into the room. "I'm not crazy, am I? The last few months have not given me brain fever, have they? When I left Spain, wasn't there a baby coming?" He turned towards Lucy. "God knows, I heard enough about it. Well, where is it and what is it? Boy or girl?"

There was an awkward pause. Lucy had turned away her head and it was Charlotte who answered.

"The baby was born – too early as it happens. I told you the stables were burnt down. It was a vicious, callous attack, a great many were injured and Roberto was nearly killed. It was very distressing for all of us. As a result the baby arrived unexpectedly. We did all we could but your son only breathed for a few minutes."

"Oh God! I didn't realize . . ." For a moment he still hesitated, then he crossed swiftly to the sofa and sat beside Lucy, reaching out for her hand. "I'm sorry, truly sorry." She still strained away from him and very gently he turned her round to face him. "Poor little Lucy, you had your hell to go through too and I didn't know." She gave a choked sob and he took out his handkerchief. "Here, take this. Any minute now and you'll have me weeping."

Charlotte saw her lean against him before she went out of the room. Perhaps in a mutual sorrow for their dead child they might be able to reconcile some of their differences.

Guy's reaction when she told him that evening was very nearly blasphemous.

"God Almighty, what the hell does he think he is playing at?" he exclaimed. "I beg your pardon, Charlotte, but honestly – to come here at a time like this – it's lunatic."

"I know," she said worriedly, "but Clive has always been like that. He plunges into things without thinking first. That really is how all this started."

And you're still fond of the wretched fellow, thought Guy to himself, far too fond.

"Did you tell Lorenzo about receiving this letter from him?" he said aloud.

"No. Lucy didn't want it. It was so strange, we didn't believe it at first, then afterwards we thought we should wait until Clive wrote to us himself."

"And instead of doing the sensible thing he turns up where he is least wanted. Lord knows what Lorenzo will say."

"Clive *has* changed his appearance and he does possess forged papers," she said tentatively.

Guy grunted. "Not all Spaniards are as gullible as the British like to think. The point is – what would Lorenzo want me to do?" He looked at Charlotte shrewdly. "He is *your* cousin so he wouldn't hand him over to justice, that's quite certain, but

I've got to think what is best for him." He paused a moment and then came to a decision. "Tell him to lie low. Keep him well hidden until tomorrow, then I'll try and arrange for him to return to Cadiz. There he can wait for his wife to join him. I take it Lucy will be going with him to England."

"That is why he has come here. He means well, Guy, he really does. He wanted to fetch her himself. I'm sorry to burden you with all this. When I saw him this afternoon, it was such a shock, I couldn't think what to do for the best."

"It's not I so much, it's how it may affect Lorenzo. I had some disturbing news today. Roméro has demanded the surrender of the city and the *Alcalde*, backed by Ramirez, has refused pointblank so the balloon will go up at any moment. God knows what the result will be."

"They must win, mustn't they? The government troops couldn't be defeated."

"Nothing is certain in war. I think they will win but who knows at what cost. It could be bloody," he said grimly.

"Oh God, I'm so frightened . . ."

"For Lorenzo?"

"Yes, for him and for Roberto and Enrique – all of them." She tried to take hold of herself. "I'm being foolish, aren't I? It's just as bad for Doña Gracia and Teresa, but it makes me feel so helpless."

"You're not the only one," said Guy wryly, "but someone has to carry on if we are to survive. You make sure that cousin of yours keeps himself out of sight and I'll see what I can do about him."

But as it happened, he had no time to make any arrangements for getting Clive away from the Castillo. Even while he was speaking to Charlotte that evening, the first skirmishes had broken out between the opposing parties in the city. The battle escalated with growing intensity all the next day. Contrary to the General's confident belief, Roméro's peasant army did not turn and run at the first onslaught of seasoned troops. Instead they stood their ground and fought stubbornly. The casualties piled up.

The first news that reached them at the Castillo was so confused that they could not make head nor tail of it. Charlotte's anxiety rose to fever pitch and it was all she could do to prevent Clive riding down there and trying to find out for himself. Confinement had always fretted him and with nerves on edge,

293

ugly little scenes flared between him and Lucy which they were both sorry for afterwards and Charlotte found herself the buffer between them.

"Do you know what she said to me?" he confided to her at breakfast which Juanita still took to Lucy in bed.

"She thinks we should live separately and only put up an outward show of being married. Have you ever heard of such an absurd situation?"

"It might be a very good idea for a time. She hasn't forgotten the way you treated her, Clive, and neither have I."

"But, Good God, that's all over and done with. Can't she forgive and forget?"

"It's easy enough for a woman to forgive but forgetting is quite another matter."

"I suppose she's fallen for this fellow Roberto. He always mooned after her, damn him. What has he got that I haven't?"

"Quite a lot," said Charlotte calmly. "He loves her for one thing and he's kind, generous, chivalrous and makes her feel important to him."

"Here, steady on, old girl, you make him sound like some confounded plaster saint."

"He's better than that. If you want Lucy as your wife, Clive, then you must make her feel needed and cherished, not just a woman who happens to have provided you with money to live as you wish."

"I've never done that."

"Oh yes you have and let others see it more than once. You hurt her badly. She loved you once and you did your best to kill it. Only you can find out if there is still a spark left in the dead ashes."

He stared at her as if she were demented and then stormed indignantly out of the room, so that she wondered if the straight talking had done more harm than good.

It was three days later that coming back from a walk with Paquita she saw a man come galloping furiously up the drive and recognized Captain Alvaro.

He and his horse were liberally splashed with mud and when he dismounted she saw that a bloody bandage was wrapped around his left hand.

"I'll take your bridle," she said, moving forward. "Do you bring us news, Captain?"

"We've got them on the run," he said, grey with fatigue but still exultant. "They are scattering into the hills but we're still picking them off as they go. It will be a long time before Roméro can bring them together again."

Paquita was gazing up at him in admiration. "Is my Papa coming soon?"

"Don Lorenzo is with the General."

"He is not wounded?" asked Charlotte.

"Not as far as I know. The General will be here tomorrow. He has sent me to ask if some of the wounded can be brought to the Castillo. The hospitals in the city are crowded to the doors. Some of the poor devils are lying in the streets without even a blanket to cover them . . ." he broke off suddenly and Charlotte saw his face change. He frowned and stared, his eyes narrowing.

She looked quickly behind her and her heart nearly stopped. Clive had come around the side of the house and then halted at sight of them. In shirt and breeches, without the long loose coat and broad-brimmed hat, he looked far too much like the Englishman he was, only the dark glasses and dyed hair providing an unsatisfactory disguise.

He took in the situation at a glance and vanished at once but not before Alvaro had seen him.

He said, deliberately casual, "Who is that man, Señorita?"

She shrugged her shoulders. "Just one of the peasants who have been helping out after the stables were destroyed."

Then Guy was coming down the steps and Alvaro turned to meet him, but she felt sure that he suspected even though he could not be certain.

She handed the horse over to one of the stable lads, sent Paquita to Amalia and went in search of Clive. She found him waiting for her in the Nun's garden.

"Was that the fellow who stopped us on the way to Palos?"

"Yes, it was, and I think he recognized you."

"Nonsense, how could he? I look completely different."

"You forget. We darkened your face and hair on that occasion and he has always been angry that he was tricked so easily. Clive, I think you ought to go."

"I'm not leaving here until I've seen Lorenzo," he said obstinately. "Did he bring any news?"

"Yes. Roméro is on the run and some of the wounded are to

be brought here. Lorenzo will be coming tomorrow with the General."

"That's all right then."

But it was not all right and his casual disregard of danger infuriated her.

She longed for Lorenzo's return and at the same time dreaded it. He had left her in anger and Clive's return, at such a time, putting not only him but the whole household at risk, could only make it worse. She bitterly regretted not telling him about the letter they had received from Raoul Ismanli, but Lucy had begged her to say nothing until she had herself spoken to Roberto and after that everything had happened so quickly there had been no opportunity.

The rest of the day was spent with Doña Gracia and Teresa helping to organize preparations for the wounded, rolling linen into bandages, finding sheets and blankets and ordering the men to spread straw with the palliasses that had been used by the refugees from the village.

The first carts came plodding up the hill very early on the following morning.

"The worst cases are being treated in Seville," said the army surgeon who had arrived with the first wagon. He was a thin, middle-aged man who looked tired to the very bone but proved capable and intelligent. "The General is grateful for help with those only slightly wounded," he told Guy and Doña Gracia.

They had made what provision they could, but it was not nearly enough. Shaken by the sights and smells, the dirt and the blood, they did their best to help the doctor and his assistant.

"If these are only slight injuries, then God help those in the city hospitals," whispered Teresa as they worked. "I do wish I knew about Roberto and Enrique."

"You will soon," said Charlotte and prayed that Lorenzo was not one of those too sick even to be moved.

It so happened that Enrique came with the last load. He climbed down from the cart with some difficulty, his right arm in an improvised sling and a slash down one cheek which oozed blood.

Teresa, who had just come from the house with an armful of fresh bandages, handed them to Lucy and ran to meet him.

"I'm so very, very glad to see you. I've been thinking such terrible things."

"Then you can stop thinking them here and now," he said cheerfully. "Nothing wrong with me," but his sound arm had gone round her slender waist.

"Your poor face!" she murmured, touching his cheek gently.

"An honourable scar, might even improve my looks." He kissed her lightly and gave her a little push. "Go on with the good work, Teresa. There's plenty far worse than I am."

"Don't bully me, you great brute!" she flashed at him.

But Charlotte saw the happy glow in her eyes when she came back, and envied her.

In the late afternoon Doña Gracia came herself, walking amongst the wounded with a smile and a word to each of them. The men followed her with their eyes, cheered that so great a lady should take a personal interest in their welfare.

She spoke to Dr Fernandez and then looked across at the three girls in their stained aprons. She had not really approved of her granddaughter going about so freely amongst the men.

"I think the young ladies have done as much as can be expected of them, Doctor, I am taking them away. They are badly in need of rest and food."

"Certainly," he bowed in acknowledgement. "We have been most grateful to all of you for the welcome we have received."

"Bother!" grumbled Teresa under her breath. "She treats me as if I were Paquita's age. I wanted to stay with Enrique and make sure his arm is treated properly. He doesn't think enough about himself."

Her grandmother made an imperious gesture and with a resigned shrug she followed after her. "You two had better come too," she whispered and Charlotte meekly brought up the rear with Lucy.

None of them noticed Clive. He had been working in the background with Matthew, helping to spread the straw and bring in the mattresses and had discarded the hampering green spectacles. He followed them at a discreet distance.

They were approaching the house when Charlotte saw that General Ramirez had already arrived and was dismounting from his horse with Captain Alvaro. Two men were carrying a stretcher between them. For a moment she seemed to stop breathing, then they set it down. One of the stretcher bearers straightened up and she saw it was Lorenzo and breathed again.

General Ramirez was coming towards the Marquésa. He took her hand in both his.

"My dear Gracia, I am so very sorry . . ."

"Is it Roberto?" she whispered.

"Yes."

"Dead?"

"Not yet, but I greatly fear . . ."

"You have brought him."

"Yes. Lorenzo thought it best. The hospital in the city . . ." he shrugged his shoulders expressively.

Lucy had halted as if stunned. Then suddenly she cried out, startling them.

"No, no, not Roberto!"

She ran past them, falling on her knees beside the stretcher and turning back the blanket so that she could see his face.

Clive went after her, whether out of pity or jealousy, Charlotte did not know. Before he could reach Lucy, Captain Alvaro had stepped in front of him. For an instant they faced one another, then Clive seemed to realize where he was. He turned his back and walked quickly away but the damage had been done.

It had all happened so quickly that for a few seconds no one moved, then Doña Gracia bent down and drew Lucy to her feet.

"Come, my dear," she said gently, "let them take him into the house. We mustn't give up hope."

The General said something to Lorenzo and followed after them.

Charlotte was still so horrified at what had happened that she could not think what to say or do. Had Lorenzo recognized Clive? He must have done. Should she explain or should she wait? She saw Teresa run to her brother, looking terribly distressed, and he put an arm around her. Marco had appeared at the door. Lorenzo gave a brief order and the butler took one end of the stretcher and they began to carry it carefully up the steps. He was preparing to follow when Alvaro stopped him.

"May I have a word with you, Señor?"

"Not now."

"It is important, believe me, very important."

Lorenzo hesitated for a moment before he said quietly, "Go in, Teresa. Tell Grandmother I will be with her immediately." He turned back, facing Alvaro squarely, and Charlotte guessed that he knew what was coming.

"Well," he said with some impatience, "what is it that is so extremely important?"

"Are you aware, Don Lorenzo, that you are harbouring a traitor here in your house?"

"A traitor? Have you taken leave of your senses?"

"That man who was here just now. You saw him as clearly as I did. He is Clive Starr, the British spy whom you and your so-called fiancée smuggled out of Spain."

"Now I am quite sure you are crazy," said Lorenzo. "I know for a certainty, as do the authorities concerned, that Clive Starr was drowned off the coast of North Africa more than three months ago."

"Oh no. I am aware that was the story which was put about," said Alvaro, stubbornly standing his ground, "but it was a lie, wasn't it? And the living proof of that lie was standing here just a few minutes ago."

"My dear fellow, you have allowed the half light to deceive you. Do you imagine that I don't know the men working in my own household? Francisco is a peasant from the high Sierra and deeply attached to my brother. I am afraid his devotion caused him to forget that he has no right to be here along with the family."

"A pretty tale, and do you permit your brother's groom to consort with your fiancée in her private apartments?"

"What was that you said?" There was a dangerous note in Lorenzo's voice and he took a step nearer to Alvaro.

"You seem to forget that I was here yesterday. I saw what I saw."

"I don't care for your implication."

"It didn't take long, did it, only a week since we were drinking your health . . ."

"God damn you for a filthy liar!"

And Lorenzo struck the back of his hand across Alvaro's mouth.

The force of the blow made him stagger for a moment, then he lifted his head. "You'll pay for that," he said thickly.

"When and how you please."

In another second Charlotte would have flung herself between them, taking all the blame to herself, but she was prevented.

The General had appeared on the steps. "What in the name

299

of God is going on?" he demanded in a voice of thunder. "Brawling in what could be a house of mourning? You should be ashamed, both of you."

"You must let me explain, General, there is something you must know." Alvaro had stepped forward.

"Not now. Have you no sense of decency, man? If you have anything to say, then choose the proper time but remember that we leave here soon after dawn. You will see that the men are bedded down and the horses fed and watered, and you will do it NOW, Alvaro," he went on, silencing the protest he saw on his lips. "I do not care for my orders to be questioned. Lorenzo, you will come with me."

He turned and went back into the house. Alvaro, shaking with anger, looked around him furiously and then strode away. Charlotte took a step towards Lorenzo but he shook his head.

"Not now. Later."

He looked tired and drawn and she could not read the expression on his face. Then he followed the General into the house.

An early evening chill made her shiver but she still stood there, too wretched to move, only certain that whatever she did or said now could only make the situation worse. Presently she pulled herself together and walked around the house towards their own rooms but she did not want to go in yet, didn't want to have to find comfort for Lucy or listen to Clive making inadequate excuses for his own folly. In the Nun's garden she sat on the edge of the stone pool remembering the evening she had talked with Lorenzo and he had kissed her lightly, telling her the old tale of love and tragedy. How much wiser it would have been if she had never yielded to his magic. But it was done and could not now be undone.

It was growing dark already but the peace of the garden did not soothe her jangled nerves as it had so often done before and after a while she sighed deeply and went into the house.

18

Dr Fernandez was frowning down at his patient. The bullet had been buried deep and he had found considerable difficulty in extracting it. He was a skilled and careful surgeon who washed his hands and his instruments meticulously before performing any operation and was proud of the fact that on balance perhaps fifty per cent of his patients had survived, but he shook his head doubtfully over Roberto.

"What are his chances?" asked Lorenzo.

"Poor, I fear, Señor. It has gone dangerously near the lung, also there has been great loss of blood with the consequent weakness. There is no more I can do at present and there are others needing my care but call me if there is the slightest change in his condition. I have administered an opiate which will help the pain for a few hours but there is bound to be fever. You must watch for it."

He bowed gravely to Lorenzo and to Doña Gracia before he went out of the room.

Roberto stirred uneasily and his grandmother bent over him, wiping the sweat from his face.

"Amalia and I will stay with him, Lorenzo. It is for you to make sure the General has everything he needs." She paused and then went on bravely, "I think you had better send one of the men for Father Bernardo."

"Not yet. He is not dying yet," he said angrily.

"I pray it won't be necessary but we should be prepared. Lorenzo, you must not blame yourself. I know you have tried to hold him back all this year but if you had forbidden him to go with the army this time, he would never have forgiven you. Andalusia is his home as it is yours and he feels deeply about it."

"I know, I know. I will send Amalia to you. You're sure there is nothing else I can do?"

She shook her head and he escaped quickly out of the room.

He shut the door behind him and leaned back against it wearily. Despite what Doña Gracia had said, he did blame himself though not for the reason she supposed. If he had not let himself be carried away by the anger, humiliation and sheer misery at what he believed to be Charlotte's deceit, if he could have put aside the horror that had swept through him when he knew who her father was, this might never have happened. He had felt he could not remain in the same house with her for a moment longer.

The turmoil within him had driven him into the thick of the battle, taking unnecessary risks, leading a charge of volunteers into the heart of the city with such fury that the Carlists had broken and run. Roberto had seen the sniper before he did. He had shouted a warning, then thrust him aside and taken the full impact in his own breast leaving him unscathed – Roberto, his young brother, whom all his life he had tried to protect. He found it desperately hard to forgive himself for that.

After a moment he passed a hand over his face pushing away the black thoughts. This was no time to give way to self-pity. There was far too much to be done. He braced himself and went down to the dining room. Food was being served to the General while at the further end of the long table Teresa was seated close beside Enrique, cutting up his meat for him. She looked up as Lorenzo came in.

"How is he?"

"Not too good, I am afraid."

"Should I go to Grandmother?"

"Presently." He smiled faintly. "At the moment Enrique would appear to need you more than Roberto does."

The young man grinned. "I have her tamed at last, Lorenzo. She is eating out of my hand."

"It's you who are eating out of mine," retorted Teresa, prodding him with the fork. "I warn you I can be a tigress when I am crossed."

"You terrify me."

"Beast!"

The general helped himself from the silver dish in front of him. "Come and eat, Lorenzo. You look as if you could do with it."

"I am not hungry."

"Nonsense, man. At times like these you eat when you can."

The servants came in with fresh plates and food that had been kept hot for him and Lorenzo sat down.

"Couple of lovebirds, eh?" muttered Ramirez under his breath, nodding towards the two youngsters.

"It's taken a war to make Teresa realize it," said her brother dryly.

"Ah, but that's how it happens. It sharpens the senses. You never recognize your good fortune till you're on the point of losing it."

Lorenzo said nothing. He poured himself a glass of wine and drank it thirstily before putting food on his plate.

Presently, after Teresa and Enrique had excused themselves and gone out of the room, the General sighed and sat back in his chair. He refused the cheese but accepted the cognac Lorenzo poured for him.

"Now tell me – what was all that nonsense between you and Alvaro? Had it anything to do with that serving man of yours who pushed himself forward so impudently?"

"Yes." Lorenzo pushed his plate away and faced up to the General. "That man is no servant of mine. He is an Englishman and his name happens to be Clive Starr."

Ramirez frowned. "The spy who should have been tried in Madrid and whom those bungling fools from Seville allowed to escape?"

"Yes."

The General looked at him shrewdly. "Was that escape your doing?"

"Yes, if you must know."

"May I ask why?"

"I would have thought it obvious. He is the Señorita Carlotta's cousin."

"And you were already so deep in love that you were willing to risk a very great deal for her sake?"

"If you care to put it like that."

The General drained his glass and put it down carefully. "I understood that the wretched fellow was drowned on his way to North Africa."

"So did I."

"You did not know that he was alive and likely to turn up here?"

"No, I did not. It was in fact as much of a shock to me as it was apparently to Alvaro."

"It seems to me that your bride-to-be has been busily deceiving you in more ways than one," said Ramirez dryly.

"It would seem so. I am in your hands, General, you must deal with me as you think fit." Lorenzo's voice was calm but the hand holding the glass suddenly clenched and the wine spilled on to the white cloth.

"I could have him arrested and you with him."

"Yes."

"Except that the matter is closed and in my opinion not worth reopening. I have other things for you to do." He pushed his glass forward and Lorenzo poured more brandy. He sipped it thoughtfully. "If you'll take my advice, and I sincerely hope you will, you will get him away from here as soon as possible before anyone else puts two and two together and comes up with the right answer."

"And if I do that, what will you do?"

"I? My dear Lorenzo, I never saw the fellow in my life and wouldn't know him if we were to meet face to face. If Alvaro believes he detects some resemblance in the half light and likes to make a fool of himself over it, that's his affair. He will certainly get no backing from me. I've more important matters to deal with. Never cared for him in any case," went on the General with a faint contempt, "not one of us. A pushing young man with his eye always on promotion." He leaned forward, putting a hand on Lorenzo's arm. "For that reason if no other don't trust your luck too far, my boy. Get rid of the *Inglés*, whoever he is, and quickly. Come to see me later. I intend leaving you with certain powers here in the south. Now don't argue about it, that's a great deal more valuable than getting yourself uselessly killed. We've won a victory but for how long? Carlos is not beaten yet. He has suffered a setback with this defeat of Roméro but he won't give up so easily. It's going to be a long struggle." He rose to his feet yawning and stretching. "Not much sleep tonight for either of us, I'm afraid, but that's the way it is. Now I must see Doña Gracia and find out how that poor brother of yours is going on."

He went out of the room and after a little Lorenzo got up. Ramirez, stirred by old family friendship, had been remarkably tolerant but he meant what he said. Clive must be got rid of at all costs and it was up to him to see it done.

In the room that looked out on the Nun's garden the three of them sat waiting silently. The arguments, the reproaches, the angry accusations were all over.

"He knows who you are," Charlotte had said urgently. "The General silenced him but for how long? He could be informing on you this very moment for all we know. You should go now, get away from the Castillo. Leave it to us to make up some story."

"No." Clive was adamant. "I'm not leaving you to suffer on my account. I'm tired of running away. Let them do what they damn well please. Lucy won't worry. All she is concerned with is her lover."

"Roberto is not my lover," she said wearily. "How many more times do I have to repeat it?"

"No one would have guessed it from the way you behaved."

"For goodness sake, stop arguing," said Charlotte impatiently. "What does it matter now? The most important thing is you. If you're arrested, what do you think they will do to Lorenzo?"

"That's all that matters to you, isn't it? Well, he is in the clear. I shall explain. I shall take all blame to myself."

"Very heroic and do you imagine that they will believe you, a discredited spy? Have some sense. The Spanish are not all fools."

Then Juanita brought in the supper. They had been obliged to let her into the secret and swear her to silence. She persisted in thinking it highly romantic and kept giving Clive surreptitious glances from her fine black eyes.

The food stuck in Charlotte's throat. Whatever happened now it was all over between her and Lorenzo. He would never forgive her for what he must believe a double deception.

They made a pretence of eating but afterwards they could settle to nothing. Clive stood at the window staring out at the Nun's garden, drumming his fingers on the glass. Charlotte turned the pages of a book she had picked up and the words meant nothing. Lucy's needlework lay idle in her lap. She got up suddenly, throwing it angrily on the table.

"What is the point of all this? What are we waiting for? I'm going to bed."

305

The knock at the door startled all three of them. She sat down again looking frightened, Clive stiffened and glanced at Charlotte. Then the door opened and Lorenzo came in.

He was still wearing his riding clothes, the short sheepskin jacket, the black breeches, the scarlet sash, so that suddenly he seemed completely alien, someone from another world. Was she mad to think she could bridge the gulf between them? Had there really been a time when they had been so close it had seemed impossible that anything could separate them?

He looked from Charlotte to Clive and then back again before he spoke.

"How long have you known your cousin was still alive?"

"It was just before the attack on the stables. We had a letter from a certain merchant in Tangier telling us that Clive had been taken up half drowned, that he had been very sick and it had been several weeks before he was able to give any details about himself."

"And why wasn't I told? Couldn't you have trusted me?"

"That was my fault," began Lucy.

"It's all right," went on Charlotte, "I'll explain. The letter was so extraordinary, so badly written, that at first we could hardly believe it to be true. We thought we should wait until we heard from Clive himself."

"And then you decided to invite him here to my house without even having the courtesy to inform me."

"No," said Charlotte, "that's not true."

"Leave this to me," Clive came to stand beside her. "This is my affair. The girls knew nothing. I came myself, adequately disguised as I believed. My rescuer is wealthy and trades in carpets. He supplied me with a passport and identification papers."

"And in this – this masquerade you turned up at the Castillo de Palomas at a time when you must have been perfectly well aware that any suspicion of who you really were would endanger not only you, but your wife and your cousin, to say nothing of myself. For what reason may I ask? Was it simply a cheap desire to prove your courage?"

Clive flushed at the openly expressed contempt. "Perhaps. I won't argue about that but there was something else, something between you and me that required an answer. That attack on Felipe's boat – was it an accident or was it engineered to get me killed?"

306

"If I had wished to be rid of you," said Lorenzo levelly, "all I had to do was to leave you in the hands of the police. The firing squad in Madrid would have done it for me. I scarcely needed to go to the trouble and expense of arranging your escape."

"Not even to impress Charlotte? Quite the hero, weren't you?"

If he thought to provoke Lorenzo to anger, he failed.

"Not even for that," he replied coldly.

There was an awkward pause, then Clive shrugged his shoulders. "I must take your word for it, I suppose."

"I'm not in the habit of lying." He made a weary gesture. "Enough of this bickering. It gets us nowhere. I don't wish to appear inhospitable," he went on ironically, "but I must ask you to leave – within the hour if possible. The plain fact is that the General knows very well who you are but for reasons which you probably wouldn't appreciate, he has decided to turn a blind eye to it. You'll need to assume the disguise you are so proud of and one of my men will see you on your way."

Clive bit his lip, knowing he had no choice, but still resenting Lorenzo's air of command. "And what about my wife?"

"She can follow you whenever she wishes. I suggest you wait for her in Cadiz. There are plenty of small *posadas* where no questions are asked. From there it should be easy enough to obtain passage to England."

"I would like to go with Clive now." Lucy, on her feet, her face flushed, had surprised them all.

He said, "Lucy, I don't think . . ." and she interrupted him.

"I married you, didn't I? You are my husband. I have no choice."

"If you will forgive my saying so, to accompany your husband would only make recognition more certain," said Lorenzo. "As soon as I consider it safe I will gladly arrange an escort to take you to Cadiz."

"You will not be travelling alone," said Charlotte quickly. "I shall go with you."

"No," said Lorenzo so emphatically that they all stared at him in surprise. "I think that extremely inadvisable." Then he turned to Clive. "I will make preparations. Please be ready to leave in an hour's time."

"I suppose I should thank you," he began and was abruptly cut short.

"There's no need. I'll go now since time is growing short." He nodded to Charlotte and Lucy and went out.

"Arrogant bastard!" muttered Clive as the door shut behind him.

"What did you mean by saying you would come with me?" said Lucy curiously.

But Charlotte did not reply. She had to speak to Lorenzo now. She could not bear to leave it another minute. She went out quickly but the corridor was empty. She paused uncertainly and then saw that the garden door was ajar. She pulled it open. He had walked down the path and was standing by the stone pool where she herself had sat earlier that evening. It was a fine night but cold and she shivered. He turned as she reached him and the faint light from the window shadowed his face into dark hollows.

"I had to speak to you," she said hurriedly and then hesitated, intimidated by his frown into saying the first thing that came into her head. "I wanted to apologize for Clive."

He brushed it aside as of no importance. "In some ways I understand how he feels. Did you mean what you said about leaving here?"

"Yes, I did. Why pretend any longer? It is all over between us, isn't it?"

"Not as far as I am concerned. I stand by my obligations."

She stared at him. "Do you imagine I want you to marry me just because we once made love together and you gave me a promise? You need not worry. I'm not pregnant. There won't be another illegitimate child." She saw the anger and hurt on his face but drove on relentlessly. "You believe I lied and cheated just to trap you into marriage, you think I deliberately deceived you over Clive, but I didn't and this proves it." She had pulled off the ring he had given her and held it out to him. "Take it back, your father's ring. It's a wonder it didn't scorch my finger when you first put it on."

"Charlotte, don't, for God's sake!" It was a cry of pain that found an echo in her own misery. He pushed her hand away. "How you love to humiliate me."

"I? Humiliate you?"

"It's not much more than a week since they were drinking

308

our health, congratulating us. Can't you hear the laughter when you jilt me? Do you want to set every tongue wagging as they hunt for reasons and find them all too easily? Do you think I want the past raked up? Can't you keep up the pretence for a little longer? If only for the sake of my grandmother, or Teresa? Don't they deserve anything from you?"

She knew it was true. She had grown fond of them and Lorenzo had behaved generously, was still holding out a helping hand despite Clive's folly. How could she refuse him?

"Is that the only reason?" she whispered.

"No, not the only one."

With a sudden movement he stretched out a hand and pulled her to him. His mouth was hard on hers, brutal and demanding. Then as suddenly he released her and walked quickly away through the garden. She sank down on the stone rim of the pond heedless of the spray from the fountain, deeply disturbed, uncertain of herself and of him, only knowing with despair that his slightest touch had the power of arousing feelings she believed she had conquered. She knew then that she would agree to what he asked.

Lorenzo strode back to the house angry at his own lack of control. For one mad moment he had wanted to force her to submit to him there in the garden where Pedro had loved his nun, he had wanted to punish her for what she had done to him.

All the time he made preparations for Clive's departure, instructing the reliable Jacopo to go with him, take food, the best horses and money to cover all contingencies, and even afterwards, sitting in consultation with Ramirez, one part of him was concerned only with Charlotte, a part that wanted to believe, and fought with the unhappy conviction that she had deceived him twice and could be doing so again, putting on an act to pull him back to her. Pride and honour? Could he throw them over for the sake of love – what could well be a lying deceitful love – it was a bitter battle worse than leading a cavalry charge against Roméro's bandits, he thought wearily, while he drank black coffee to keep himself alert and heard with relief from Dr Fernandez that Roberto had at least survived the night.

Clive left that same night. Charlotte never asked what he and Lucy said to one another before he went but she thought he had been shaken by her readiness to go with him and share his fate whatever it was and she guessed that despite his fit of jealousy, the very fact that Roberto passionately desired his wife had increased her value in his eyes.

"Don't do anything reckless this time," she said to him when she kissed him goodbye. "And do take care of Lucy. She has been very unhappy."

"You've a pretty low opinion of me, haven't you, Charlie?"

"And if I have, whose fault is that?" she replied lightly. "You did have the courage to come back."

"And only caused more trouble," he said ruefully. "If anything goes wrong between you and Lorenzo . . ."

"Why should it?" she put in quickly.

"I don't know, but after all he's not really one of us, is he?"

"Oh Clive, you talk as if he were a hottentot!"

"Not quite that, but you know what I mean. I'd just like you to be sure that you will always have a home with Lucy and me – that is if you want it."

Would she be glad of it when the time came? She didn't think so. A stubborn streak of independence would prevent her accepting charity.

"Don't be too rash," she said trying to smile. "I might take you up on it."

She and Lucy stood close together, watching him ride into the darkness with Jacopo close behind him. A few days later and the latter was back reporting to his master that Clive was installed in a *posada* on the outskirts of the city and unlikely to be questioned if he kept quiet and behaved sensibly.

"And I pray to God that he does for once," said Lorenzo. "Carry the information to the Señorita Carlotta with my compliments."

"At once, Señor," said Jacopo and went off on his errand a little puzzled as to why the Marqués did not seize the opportunity to convey the good news himself.

310

19

The Sierra was still infested with Roméro's bandit soldiers, starving and desperate, and it was a fortnight before Lorenzo considered the road safe enough for Lucy to undertake the journey. It had been hard for Charlotte to keep up the pretence of a newly engaged young woman looking forward to what everyone would consider a fabulously happy marriage. She was helped by the fact that she scarcely ever saw Lorenzo. The General had left him the task of reorganizing the defences of Andalusia and he was away from the Castillo for days at a time.

On the morning before Lucy was to leave she ran into him accidentally as she crossed the hall and he stopped her.

"I wanted to see you. Come with me."

She followed him reluctantly into the library, a room she had not entered since the night he had rescued her from Vicente. It was too full of memories and she paused just inside the door.

"What is it?"

"Just this. If we are to keep up this pretence, you must wear my engagement ring. It is only now that I have had the opportunity to do something about it."

She looked down at the ring in his hand, a square-cut emerald surrounded with diamonds, rarely beautiful and probably costing a fortune.

"No," she said and backed away from him. "No, I couldn't possibly wear it. It would be all wrong."

"That's being foolish," he went on brusquely. "I am sorry if it is not your choice but believe me it is necessary. What will they think of me? Doña Gracia, Teresa, our friends who come here, even the servants will be expecting it. Give me your hand."

She still held back so he reached out and took it in his, drawing off the plain gold ring and slipping the expensive jewel on her finger.

"I would rather keep the other," she said in a stifled voice.

"It is not fitting."

"Because you still can't forgive me for what my father did?"

"That has nothing to do with it."

She was looking down at her hand and did not see the expression on his face or the half move towards her abruptly checked. He felt as if a wall of glass had risen up between them and he could not break through it without destroying something within himself.

"I don't think I can go on with it," she whispered.

"Is it so hard? It won't be for long, I promise you."

"No, not for long – please."

She drew a quick breath and ran from the room before she did something ridiculous like bursting into tears or throwing the ring back in his face.

Lucy had spent that last afternoon with Roberto. It was Doña Gracia with a rare kindness who suggested it. She sent Amalia to fetch her.

"Don't stay too long," she said when Lucy came into the room. "He is still very weak but he has been asking for you. He wishes to say goodbye," and she went out leaving them alone together.

Roberto was making a very slow recovery. There had been fever and serious infection. He was still in pain and he could not speak much. Most of the time they simply sat hand in hand.

Once he said, "If you need me at any time, I will come to you. You do know that, Lucy, don't you? I don't care about Lorenzo or anyone here. I'll not let them stop me."

"Like the knight in shining armour riding on a white horse that I used to dream about when I was a child," she said and smiled at him with tears in her eyes.

He hoisted himself up in the bed. "Don't laugh at me. I am serious."

"I know you are."

"It is not too late. Stay here with me, Lucy. Don't go."

"I must. Clive is waiting for me and he is my husband." In these last weeks she felt she had grown so much older and wiser than he. How could she ruin his life with her own and that's what it would mean. She had no illusions about it. "Dear Roberto, it was lovely while it lasted. I've never been so happy but it was not meant for us." She leaned forward kissing him on the mouth. "I think I always knew that."

*

312

It was during their supper together that evening that she noticed the ring on Charlotte's finger.

"Did Lorenzo give it to you? It's magnificent. You know once or twice I have thought that something had come between you, that he was angry because of Clive, but now I know I was wrong and this proves it. It's so good to be sure that someone is happy."

"Oh Lucy! You don't know, you just don't know."

"What don't I know?"

The longing to tell her the truth was almost overwhelming except that it meant revealing a story that did not belong to her alone and in any case it wouldn't be fair, Lucy had problems enough of her own.

"Oh it's nothing. It's only that I'm going to miss you so much and I shall worry about you and Clive."

"Come with us," said Lucy impulsively, "why don't you? After all it would be quite natural for you to want to visit your mother before you are married."

For a moment it was tempting. She would be free of this wretched tangle, free to start a new life, but then she knew it was impossible. She was bound by a promise to Lorenzo, bound by that tragic story of the past that still lay unsettled between them.

"No, I couldn't do that. Maybe later I will come."

"On your wedding journey perhaps."

"Who knows?"

Two of Lorenzo's men went with the carriage to the river and saw Lucy on to the boat which would sail down the Guadalquivir to Cadiz. Matthew was there to look after the baggage and see her settled while Juanita, thrilled and excited at the prospect of seeing England, was only too happy to accompany them. Charlotte rode down beside the carriage and waved for as long as she could still see Lucy on the crowded deck. She turned back to the Castillo and the two men kept close behind her. Lorenzo was taking no chances. She would have preferred to be alone and their presence irked her but she knew that whatever she said they would simply bow and smile. They took their orders from the Marqués and from no one else.

With Lucy gone she felt desperately lonely. The great house seemed empty with Lorenzo so often absent and Roberto still confined to his room. Doña Gracia and Teresa spent a great deal of time with him. Some of the wounded still remained but most of them had now moved on to join their regiment. She never thought she would miss Juanita's lively chatter so much.

She could not settle to anything and one morning made a sudden decision to ride over to the vineyard. Guy had gone back already.

"Don't forget us, will you?" he had said when he came to say goodbye, keeping her hand in his and pressing it warmly. "Doña Catalina would welcome you at any time," and she wondered for a moment if he had sensed that something had gone wrong between her and Lorenzo.

It would be good, she felt as she changed into her riding habit, to escape from her gloomy thoughts for a few hours. She had Tomás saddle Zelda and was trotting down the drive and through the park gates when Lorenzo caught her up.

"Where are you going?" he asked abruptly.

"Only to the vineyard."

"I'm sorry but it is quite impossible."

"Good heavens, why?"

"You must know as well as I do that the roads are still dangerous and I can't spare the men to go with you."

"I am not intending to go up into the mountains."

"I still can't permit it. In any case, as my fiancée, it would be quite improper for you to go alone to visit another man."

"I am not intending to spend the day with Guy if that's what you mean. There is also Doña Catalina."

"It makes no difference," he said stubbornly.

"It makes all the difference." She was suddenly furious with him. "You can't stop me. I'm not your prisoner," and before he could prevent her she urged Zelda forward and was off down the road at a spanking pace.

He came after her and it was a race between them until he caught at her bridle and slowly brought both horses to a halt.

"Mother of God, have you run mad?" he exclaimed breathlessly.

"Perhaps." She stared in front of her. "Are you jealous of Guy, is that it?"

"Such an idea is absurd."

"Is it?"

"You know it is." He paused and then went on more quietly, "Is it so impossible for you to trust me for once and do as I ask?"

She turned to face him, ready with rebellious arguments, and

314

noticed for the first time how taut and strained he looked. The angry words died. "Very well, if I must, I must," she said, "but it is under protest."

"Thank you." He drew back to let her go by and watched as she trotted slowly back towards the house.

"This pretence can't go on," she raged to herself, "I can't bear it and I shall tell him so."

But the days passed and there was no opportunity. The strain began to tell and Paquita innocently made it worse.

The child bounded in one morning, her face radiant. "Amalia says that if Teresa marries Don Enrique, then she will ask me to be her bridesmaid. When you marry Papa can I be *your* bridesmaid too?"

"Paquita, you run on so fast I can scarcely understand what you are saying. Who says that Teresa is going to be married?"

"All the servants are talking about it. Cook says that she fell in love with him when he came back from the battle. He was a wounded hero, you see," she went on as if that explained everything.

"You shouldn't spend so much time in the kitchens," said Charlotte reprovingly. "Your Papa wouldn't like it."

"He won't know. He's never here now." She looked up quickly. "You wouldn't tell him, would you?"

"No, of course I wouldn't. Oh Paquita, you are impossible."

The child giggled. "It's nearly Christmas and Grandmother says –"

"Grandmother?"

"Doña Gracia has told me that I may call her Grandmother. She says that now I am twelve I shall go with the family to midnight mass at the Cathedral and will take communion with her and Teresa and Papa."

Paquita's eyes were alight with wonder and she realized suddenly that despite Lorenzo's kindness, despite the luxury of living at the Castillo, the girl had always felt an outsider, neither servant nor part of the family, and Doña Gracia's acceptance had made her at last one of them.

Charlotte put an arm around the slim shoulders. "And that makes you happy, does it, Paquita?"

"Oh yes, very happy. Will you be there too kneeling beside Papa?"

"Perhaps. I don't know."

Teresa when questioned said airily, "Oh I am not sure. I might marry him and might not. General Ramirez has promised him a few days leave soon and he thinks it would be a marvellous time to be betrothed."

"So he is not so deadly dull after all," said Charlotte teasingly.

"He's not exciting like Vicente was, but I suppose part of that was because it was forbidden," she admitted thoughtfully. "Enrique and I laugh at the same things and, if we quarrel, it never comes to anything because he won't take me seriously. When he kisses me I don't tingle all over but I do enjoy it. Perhaps I'm not capable of *la grande passion* – you know, the kind we used to read about at the Convent," she went on rather gloomily. "What do you think?"

"It seems to me you've found a very good recipe for it," said Charlotte.

Teresa shot her a mischievous look under long lashes. "What happens when Lorenzo kisses *you*?"

"Teresa really! I refuse to answer that."

"I used to think he'd make rather a good lover even if he is my brother, dark, gloomy and tragic, like Byron's Manfred."

"Or his Corsair."

"Did you call him that?"

"Lucy did once." Then suddenly the silly banter became far too painful. "Teresa, you're being ridiculous. If you want my opinion, I think Enrique will make a wonderful husband."

"I suppose I do really." She smiled to herself. "He is rather a pet, isn't he?"

It was a few days before Christmas when breaking point came. Enrique had arrived on leave sooner than expected and Doña Gracia said they had been gloomy long enough. Roberto was up and about again even if he did still look like the ghost of himself and it was time to invite a few friends and indulge in a little celebration.

For Charlotte it was an unbearable ordeal. She was obliged to stand by Lorenzo's side, greet his friends with smiles, accept more congratulations, show off her engagement ring to young women who looked at her with envy. She must dance with him, behave like any girl in love, while all the time she was deeply conscious of the abyss that yawned between them.

316

At one moment during the evening Doña Gracia took the chair beside her and put a hand on hers. "I have not asked Lorenzo but is all well between you?"

"Would you be glad if it were?"

"Very glad if it will bring him peace of mind. I am worried about him. He is driving himself far too hard."

She wanted to scream at her that it was all a stupid pretence and they were further apart than they had ever been but someone came to claim her for the next dance and she could escape without saying anything.

The hours went by in empty meaningless talk and she longed for the evening to end. When much later Lorenzo came to her, she turned away from him.

"I don't want to dance any longer."

"Very well. Can I fetch you something, champagne, an ice?"

"No, no, no! I have had enough."

"Well, don't look so angry with me. We shall have everyone asking questions."

"Does it matter if they do?" She swung round on him. "Lorenzo, when is this farce of ours going to end? When are you going to let me out of prison?"

"Is that how you feel about it?"

"How else do you expect me to feel?"

"I don't want to spoil it for Teresa," he said slowly. "She is so fond of you, it will upset her greatly. God knows I've been concerned about her for long enough. I would like to believe that she will find happiness with Enrique."

"Does that mean I must wait till they are married?" she said ironically.

"No, a few weeks longer – after the New Year."

Some of the guests were leaving. He excused himself and moved away from her and she looked after him, puzzled and unhappy. Why did he want to keep her there? What was in his mind? She sighed and returned to her duties in the ballroom.

It was very late by the time the last carriage had driven away into the cool December night and she could go back to her own rooms. Restless and sick at heart she did not go to bed immediately but threw a thick shawl around her shoulders and went out into the garden. She paused beside the fountain feeling the spray on her hot cheeks and then, shivering a little, walked quickly under the arches through the gate and along the path

317

till she could see the long stretch of the house, white and beautiful in the moonlight. Lights still burned in the ballroom and she watched them go out one by one and then spring to life in the windows above. She was turning to go back when she saw a dark figure cross the lawn and after a second recognized Gabriella. They had seen nothing of her since the day she had gone to the village with them and Lorenzo had been so bitterly angry with her, but Charlotte knew she had been with the army in Seville. According to Enrique she would have fought beside the soldiers if Ramirez had permitted such a thing.

"Roméro offered five thousand pesetas for her capture, alive or dead," he had told her and Gabriella laughed it to scorn.

"Who would sell me for such a paltry price?" she had said, though no one knew better than she that such a sum would be a fortune to the miserable starving men who now roamed the Sierra.

She watched her pause outside the house and then go through the door into the wing where the family slept and suddenly she felt sick. He couldn't be waiting for her, it wasn't possible, not after all that had happened between them. She was choked with anger and disgust. She would not stay here a moment longer. She would pack up now and leave at first light. She would ride down to Seville, find Mr Robinson and if he had already left Spain, then she would make her own way. She was not helpless, for God's sake! She had money and she could speak the language.

She spent the rest of the night packing. She would take only bare necessities, the rest could be sent on. She lay down on her bed for an hour but she could not sleep and by six o'clock was dressed and ready. She was about to leave the house when there was a frenzied knocking at the door and Amalia burst in looking distraught, her plump face smudged with tears.

"Paquita, Señorita – is she here?"

"Paquita? No. Why should she be?"

"Her bed was empty when I went to call her. I have searched everywhere, the house, the gardens, and I can't find her. She is nowhere, nowhere at all."

"She can't have disappeared. It is ridiculous. Have you been to the stables?"

Paquita was allowed to ride in the park every day with Tomás or one of the grooms with her.

318

Amalia shook her head, snatching at a gleam of hope. "No, I haven't but she was wearing her riding clothes and the dog has gone too."

"We'll go there now. Have you told Don Lorenzo?"

"Not yet. Holy Virgin, the Marqués will be so angry."

At the stables they found the white pony had gone and a sleepy stable lad believed he heard something but thought nothing of it.

"We must tell Don Lorenzo at once," said Charlotte, firmly taking Amalia by the arm. "He will know what to do."

Back at the house the servants already alerted by Amalia were gathered in the hall all talking excitedly. They fell silent as Lorenzo came down the stairs. He was already dressed for riding and with the prospect of a heavy day in front of him urging the importance of strong defence on city officials who could not see danger until it came knocking at the door, he found it difficult to restrain his impatience. He paused on the bottom step looking around at the faces turned up to him.

"What is it? What is going on?" he demanded wearily.

They all began to speak at once until he raised his hand. "One at a time please. It seems that Paquita has disappeared. Have you by chance said something to upset her, Amalia?"

"No, Señor, no. Why should I do such a thing?" Amalia's tears began to flow again. "All I did was to tell her about her grandfather and she was very excited about it."

"Grandfather? Who does she mean?" asked Charlotte.

"It is old Pepe. Do you remember meeting him when we went up to the high Sierra? Actually he is Gabriella's grandfather. Why on earth should Paquita have gone there?"

"She wanted to see him. She talked about taking him a Christmas gift," went on Amalia through her tears. "I told her she must wait and ask your permission, Señor, but she has always been so self-willed. I never dreamed she would do such a thing."

"It's a devil of a way for a child to ride alone," he said frowning.

And it was then that Charlotte guessed. She said slowly, "Could she have gone with her mother?"

"With Gabriella? But she is not here."

His surprise was so genuine that all her unworthy suspicions

319

of the night before vanished on the instant and the joy was so great that for a moment she could not speak.

He was staring at her. "What made you say that?"

"Only that I saw her, late last night or I suppose it would be very early this morning. She crossed the lawn and went in through the side door."

"Amalia, did you know about this?" asked Lorenzo sternly.

"No, Señor, no, I swear to God. I saw Paquita into bed after she had watched the guests arrive and then I went back to – to see the dancing."

"You did not look in on her before you went to bed yourself?"

"No, no," she whispered. "God forgive me, but I did not think of it."

He was silent for a moment, then he raised his head. "It's a long chance but we must take it. We had better spread out. There are not many roads they could have taken. Jacopo, you will come with me. Have the horses saddled and check my pistols." These days he never rode unarmed.

He wasted no time in useless reproaches but strode off to the stables giving orders as he went and Charlotte followed after him.

Tomás was there and she said quietly, "Saddle Zelda for me."

"But, Señorita, you must not go with them. It is dangerous."

"Do as I say and don't argue."

She saw Lorenzo ride away with Jacopo and then followed after them. She had known at once that this was something she had to do no matter what happened to her.

The going was rough though Zelda kept up gallantly. Lorenzo was riding fast. He looked over his shoulder once as they went through the park boundaries and waved her back but she still followed stubbornly. Up they went past the bull pastures and where the path began to climb steadily.

It was colder now and the wind blew fiercely. When they passed the fields where the sheep had been brought down for the winter Lorenzo shouted to one of the shepherds and the man came running towards them.

"The little Señorita was not alone, Señor. La Gabriella was with her."

"How long ago?"

"Two hours, three hours," he made a vague gesture. To

320

these men out in the meadows from dawn to dusk time had little meaning.

"*Gracias*."

Lorenzo slapped the neck of his horse and rode on at a furious pace with Jacopo close behind him so that Charlotte had difficulty in keeping up with them.

It was some time later that they saw the dog. Lorenzo pulled up and stared grimly down at the pitiful lolling head of the big rough-coated Tonio, but Charlotte slid from the saddle to kneel beside him. The silver collar had been wrenched off. He had been savagely kicked and then shot. His fur was matted and filthy and she guessed that before he died he had fought bravely for his little mistress.

Lorenzo said brusquely, "If they will do that to a dog, God help us. You should not be here, Charlotte."

"I'm not going back. I love Paquita too."

"You heard what he said. Gabriella is with her. There's going to be trouble."

"I'm still coming with you."

"Then don't hinder us. Keep well away from it."

"I'll be careful."

He gave her a long look, then swung his horse round and rode on.

Up to then she had believed at the back of her mind that they would soon overtake Paquita and she would laugh merrily at their anxiety but now she knew that it was not so. It was going to be worse, far worse. There was snow now. It lay patchily on the path and on the bare brown hillsides. In places it was frozen hard and once when Zelda slipped, she lost a stirrup and had difficulty in keeping in the saddle but she still obstinately went on.

The higher they climbed the thicker lay the snow. It was dry and powdery and every now and again gusts of wind blew it up into their faces, stinging and painful. She looked around her and thought they must be nearing the place where they had stopped to eat on that happy day that now seemed so long ago.

Then suddenly to the left they saw a white pony, the reins hanging loose, standing close to a clump of bushes and peacefully grazing on a patch of sheltered grass. It was Paquita's pony, it had to be. Lorenzo turned aside at once. The pony looked up startled as he galloped past it, a spray of snow springing up under the hooves of his horse. Some way beyond he pulled up with a jerk. She saw him dismount and run forward while Jacopo caught at his bridle.

Charlotte followed more slowly, horribly afraid of what she might see. She slid from the saddle. Gabriella was lying where the snow had been churned up into mud and slush, arms flung out, blood on her face and on the torn and disordered riding dress. It was obvious what had happened to her and Charlotte shuddered. It must have been a desperate struggle and someone must bear the marks of her nails on his face before he revenged himself for their bitter defeat in Seville. She knew she was dead. Lorenzo was kneeling beside her, an expression on his face that she had never seen before, an agony of pity followed by a dark burning rage that frightened her and she did not know how to help or comfort him.

She was standing helplessly when something caught her eye, a dark shape on the snow beyond the clump of brushwood. Forgetting caution she began to run, stumbling over the hidden tussocks of coarse grass. The child was lying face downwards as if she had fallen running from the horror that had overtaken her mother. As Charlotte went on her knees beside her she saw that the long black hair was thick with blood where she had been struck down.

Very gently she turned her over. The chalk white face was warm to her touch. She began to loosen the high collar. Then someone shouted and she looked up. A man, bearded, filthy, was coming towards her. Terrified she flung herself across the unconscious child. He raised his gun, there was a shot and he made a choking sound, clutched at his breast and fell away from her, rolling over and over, hands scrabbling at the stony ground. Lorenzo, pistol in hand, was running towards her when she saw that her attacker had not been alone. Another man half hidden by the bushes had raised his gun. She screamed a warning. Lorenzo checked, fired again and missed. He braced himself as the bandit lurched forward. Then the man seemed to spin in the air and fell like a stone. Jacopo with the aim of a practised hunter had neatly picked him off as he might have done a charging wild beast.

She was so shaken it was a moment before she could pull herself together and by that time Lorenzo had reached her.

"You're not hurt?"

Trembling she shook her head. "No." She looked fearfully around her. "Are there more of them?"

"I don't think so. I believe these two had seen us and were waiting their chance to take Gabriella's body back to the camp and claim Roméro's reward." He paused. "You saw what they did to her."

"Yes."

"Mother of God, they are worse than animals."

The horror of it made her feel sick but she swallowed down the nausea. She slipped a hand inside Paquita's riding coat. She thought she could feel the faintest flutter of a heartbeat.

"She is not dead," she said urgently. "If we could get her to somewhere warm . . ."

"Pepe's hut is not far away. I could carry her there. Jacopo will look after the horses. Stay here. I will speak to him."

She began to chafe Paquita's cold hands and then lifted her head on to her lap. There was a slight intake of breath and a little moan. One thing she felt thankful for. Paquita's clothes were undisturbed. They had not yet violated her. Perhaps that had been a pleasure they had reserved for later.

Then Lorenzo was back. With infinite care he lifted Paquita in his arms and began to walk to the main path. She followed him averting her eyes from the two men whose blood was already staining the snow.

"It's about half a mile," he said when they were once more on the path. "Can you manage it? If I ride I think it will jolt her too much."

"I can walk."

It took them a long time to trudge up the mountain. The air was keen and rarefied at these heights and they were both gasping for breath by the time they reached the cluster of huts.

Pepe was at the door already. The sound of the shots must have carried in the thin air. He came hurrying to meet them.

"Murderers!" he exclaimed. "They infest the mountains scavenging and killing like famished wolves. You are not the first, Señor. Is the child badly hurt?"

"We hope not."

"Bring her in."

Lorenzo carried Paquita through the narrow door and laid her down on the pallet bed while Pepe brought blankets and

323

began to pile them around her. He threw fuel on the fire so that it blazed up, then he filled a bowl with warm water from the iron pot on the hearth and found a bundle of clean rag.

He was an old soldier accustomed to dealing with injuries and here, so far from cities, doctors were rare indeed and men had to learn to care for hurts and sickness as best they could.

Charlotte knelt down to help him. Together they washed away the blood and dirt. Then he looked up.

"Not so bad as it might have been. There is heavy bruising and the skin is broken in places but I don't think it is fatal."

Between them he and Charlotte placed a soft pad over the bleeding places and tied a bandage around the child's head to keep it in position. With her own handkerchief she began to clean the mud from Paquita's face. Pepe gently pushed back the long hair.

"There is something familiar about the child," he said and looked up at Lorenzo.

"She is your great granddaughter, old man."

He nodded. "I had heard something. Gabriella's daughter?"

"Yes." Lorenzo paused and then went on quietly, "And mine." The old man had risen to his feet, a long look passed between them, the aristocrat and the simple peasant with his intrinsic dignity, and there was an unspoken acknowledgement and acceptance between them. Lorenzo went on briskly, "She is with me at the Castillo. It was Gabriella's thought to bring her to visit you."

"That was unwise."

"Very unwise as it has turned out."

"She is dead?"

"Yes."

"The same men who would have murdered a child."

"I believe so."

"There was a time when I said I would rather see her dead at my feet than leading the life she had chosen," said Pepe slowly, "but with old age comes tolerance and understanding." He crossed himself. "Let her rest in peace. Is she here?"

"Jacopo will have brought her. I'd best go out and see to it."

When he had gone the old man put a gnarled hand on Charlotte's arm.

"I know him well," he said simply. "He is blaming himself in some way. Go to him, Señorita. Leave the little one with me.

324

I will watch her and prepare food. In this cold you must eat before you go from here."

Outside she paused, breathing deeply, and the icy air caught at her throat making her cough. She had no idea what time it was but the sky had a faint purplish tinge and the snow-crested peaks were etched against it with a gaunt forbidding beauty.

Jacopo had taken Gabriella into the adjoining hut but Lorenzo was not with him. He had walked a little way down the slope and stood leaning against a stone boulder that looked as if some giant hand had long ago torn it from the mountain-side, flung it down and then forgotten it.

She moved down to him.

"I think Paquita will recover," she said.

"If she does, then it will be due to you." He turned to look at her. "Why did Gabriella do this? Why did she bring the child up here? Was it because she wanted to punish me?"

"I think she had given Paquita to you but she still resented it because the child was so happy, so proud that you were her father. Perhaps in this way Gabriella felt she could still keep some part of her daughter."

He was staring at her, his eyes shadowed with pain. "The last time she was at the Castillo I was brutal with her because of what she had done to you, but I never meant to shut her out completely." He shuddered. "God forgive me, but it was a hideous way to die."

"I know. I'm sorry," she whispered and could find no words that did not sound trite and inadequate.

After a little he passed a hand across his face as if trying to wipe the memory away. She made a move and he stopped her.

"Charlotte, don't go. I want to ask you something. Why did you come with us? You knew, didn't you, that what happened to Gabriella could happen to you and still you came. Why?"

She paused, wanting to answer honestly and not knowing how to put it.

"I think I wanted to prove something to you."

"Prove what?"

"That I was not what you believed. That I did not deliberately set out to deceive you."

"I did not think that for very long."

"You acted as if you did." He looked away from her and

325

suddenly she knew that this was the moment. Here and now she must say what had been in her mind even if it was useless, even if he despised her for it.

"I know what you must feel about me and about what my father did – it shocked me too at first but you see, I knew him and you didn't." He made a gesture as if to stop her but she went on steadily. "I want to say something about it just once and then it need never be said again. When Doña Gracia told me what really happened in those few desperate weeks, I knew how your mother felt, I knew it as if it had been myself. I loved and suffered with her."

"No, not you," he said in a stifled voice. "You could never wantonly betray the man you had married."

"Any woman could, even if grief and regret came afterwards. Lorenzo, may I ask you something? When we were together in that cave – did you think me shamelessly wanton?"

"No, by God, no!"

"I think it must have been like that for them when it happened for the first time, something that was inevitable and irresistible and it swept them together. Do you think if we had been trapped there for a week or longer, I would not have willingly given myself to you over and over again if you had asked it of me?"

"Stop, Charlotte, I don't want to hear, I don't understand . . ."

"No, you don't," she went on relentlessly, "and because you have let yourself be blinded, you have been unjust to your mother, to Teresa, and unjust to . . ."

"To Captain Harry Starr."

"Yes, and most particularly to him. Who knows what happened that night when he and your father met? I think he regretted it all the days of his life. I've wanted to say this for a long time and now I have. Now you can take back your ring and give it to a more suitable wife, one who understands Spanish honour and Spanish prejudices and . . ."

"Charlotte, will you stop?"

She had smashed down the glass wall between them and left him defenceless and curiously uncertain of himself.

She had pulled off the emerald ring and he stared down at it in her hand.

"Does this mean that I have lost your love completely?"

"I wish I could say yes but I can't," and suddenly all her

brave confidence deserted her and she was trembling and helpless. "Oh what a fool I have been and still am. The sooner I go back to England the better. Do you know what happened last night? When I saw Gabriella I was certain she was going to you and I was so angry, I packed everything. I was going away this morning. I was never going to see you again and I can still do that. It is what I ought to have done long ago."

She turned to go and he caught at her arm, swinging her back to him.

"You are not going anywhere."

"Lorenzo, you are not God. You can't command the whole world to obey you," she said breathlessly between laughter and tears.

"Not the whole world, just you. Now *you* listen to me. Ever since that damnable night when Ramirez told me, I've been two people. I know it must sound idiotic, but they have been fighting one another and it was worse than facing Roméro's bandits. That was why I could not let you go. I did not know whether it was love or hate or a desire for revenge but I could not lose you. I had to keep you with me. Then today when I saw that devil threaten you, I knew the truth quite suddenly and blindingly. I know that if I lost you, I would not know how to go on living. Nothing else mattered. Your father could have murdered a battalion and I no longer cared."

"Do you mean that?"

"Must I go on repeating it?"

"I don't know . . ." she was still uncertain, doubtful of him and of herself, but he swept on earnestly, vehemently.

"But first you must realize what it means. I'm not offering you an easy life. What has happened during these last months will happen again. I don't know what the future holds for me or for my country. You do understand that, don't you?"

"Yes, I understand."

"Well then – I'm not commanding you any longer, I am only asking – humbly – if you will share it with me."

She looked at him for a long moment, thinking back to that first meeting on the ship. Byron's Corsair but so much more than that – so many contradictions but all of him so very dear.

"I think that's part of it," she said slowly. "All I know is that I want to be with you, never mind the rest."

"Mother of God," he breathed. "You had me on the rack."

He reached out for her hands and it was as if they had discovered one another all over again.

Then Pepe's voice cut between them.

"The child has opened her eyes. She is asking for you."

"We are coming."

He put his arm around her and they went in together.